JAN BURKE

KIDNAPPED

SIMON & SCHUSTER

New York London Toronto Sydney

SIMON & SCHUSTER
Rockefeller Center
1230 Avenue of the Americas
New York, NY 10020

First Simon & Schuster trade paperback export edition 2007

SIMON & SCHUSTER and colophon are registered trademarks
of Simon & Schuster, Inc.

For information about special discounts for bulk purchases,
 please contact Simon & Schuster Special Sales
at 1-800-456-6798 or business@simonandschuster.com.

Designed by Karolina Harris

Manufactured in the United States of America

10   9   8   7   6   5   4   3   2   1

Library of Congress Cataloging-in-Publication Data
Burke, Jan
kidnapped : an Irene Kelly novel / Jan Burke.
p.   cm.
1. Kidnapping—Fiction. Title I.
PS3552.U72326 K53 2006
813'.54—dc22   2006050483

ISBN-13: 978-1-4165-4277-3
ISBN-10:   1-4165-4277-9

For the Incomparable
Marysue Rucci

ACKNOWLEDGMENTS

MANY individuals deserve thanks for their help with this book and, as always, I ask readers to understand that these experts are not responsible for my errors.

Wayne Bowlby, who worked for many years for San Diego County Child Protective Services, patiently answered my many questions when I first began working on *Kidnapped*. Conversations with Detective (Ret.) Ike Sabean, Los Angeles County Sheriff's Department Homicide Bureau Missing/Abducted Children, regarding a subplot in *Bloodlines* led to the questions that began this book.

Additional help with forensic science and police procedural matters came from other members of the Los Angeles County Sheriff's Department, especially Detective Elizabeth Smith, Homicide Bureau; Barry A. J. Fisher, Director of LASD Scientific Services Bureau; and David Vidal, Senior Criminalist, LASD Scientific Services Bureau.

Carolyn Rollberg kindly spent time talking to me about the experiences of those who visit prisoners in California, and her openness is deeply appreciated. I received additional help from several members of the California Department of Corrections and Rehabilitation, especially Tip Kindel, Training and Regional Public Information Officer.

Forensic anthropologists Paul Sledzik and Marilyn London have once again provided invaluable assistance with those aspects of the book.

Major (Ret.) John F. Mullins took time from his own writing to provide helpful advice and encouragement.

Laura Rathe, Beth Barkley, and other dog handlers on the SAR-DOGS list were generous with their time and expertise.

Dr. Ed Dohring has faithfully provided medical information for every book, and has my thanks for that, for daring to hold conversations that gross out other people in restaurants and, most of all, for his friendship.

S.G., Sandra Cvar, Eileen Dreyer, Jerrilyn Farmer, Tonya Fischer, Julie Herman, Sharan Newman, Timbrely Pearsley, John Pearsley, Jr., Twist Phelan, Christopher Rice, and Gillian Roberts have my thanks for their additional support and help above and beyond the call of friendship and family.

Marysue Rucci, David Rosenthal, and Carolyn Reidy—your patience and support have meant so much, as has the support I've received from Micki Nuding and Louise Burke at Pocket Books. Thank you for that and so much more. Thanks also to the sales reps at Simon & Schuster, especially Laura Webb, who will probably never know how terrific her timing with encouragement has been. Rebecca Davis, Tara Parsons, Alexis Taines, and all the others who have worked with me these past two years have my sincerest gratitude. Many thanks are due to Philip Spitzer.

Timothy Burke, I want to share the return-address label with you for a long, long time to come.

KIDNAPPED

ONE

CHAPTER 1

Tuesday, May 9

8:07 A.M.

FLETCHER GRAPHIC DESIGN

LAS PIERNAS

CLEO SMITH firmly believed that neatness counted, especially if you were going to get away with murder. Which was why she now stood completely naked, save for a pair of plastic booties and a pair of thin rubber gloves, in the office of the man she had just killed.

She calmly gathered the clothing she had worn to do the job and placed it in a plastic bag, along with the trophy used as the weapon. The trophy was a heavy, curving metal shape, about ten inches in height. An award her victim, Richard Fletcher, had won for excellence as a graphic artist.

A second bag contained the hypodermic needle she had used in the first few moments of the proceedings. To this bag she added the gloves.

She placed both bags inside a large canvas duffel. This she took with her as she went back to the studio area, admiring but not touching the works in progress in the large, open room. She walked quickly past the windows (blinds closed at this hour) and into the bathroom off the back of the studio.

Richard had designed everything about this office and studio, including the full bathroom and changing area. He had needed a place where he could clean up and change clothes before meeting clients or heading home for the day. This worked admirably for her purposes as well. Taking her own soap, shampoo, and towels from the duffel, she stepped into the shower. She removed the booties, placing them in the plastic bag that held the gloves and needle. She turned on the water, unfazed by the initial coldness of it, and began to cleanse off the inevitable biological debris that resulted from the chosen method of murder. Soon the water warmed. She leaned into the hard spray.

She did not fear interruption. Richard had been a free spirit in many ways, but his days followed a set, personally defined routine. His first three hours of the workday never included any appointments, and he was known for not answering the phone during those hours. She had placed a portable locking and alarm device on the front door, just in case. She had altered it slightly—if someone should try to get past it, it wouldn't screech the kind of high-decibel alarm that would draw unwanted attention. Instead, a remote, much quieter but audible alarm would sound in her nearby bag.

She scrubbed her long, lean, and muscular body. She prided herself on her peak physical condition. Her light brown hair was no more than half an inch long anywhere on her head; she had completely depilated the rest of her body. Her breasts were small—she would readily agree that she was flat-chested, had anyone had the nerve to say so to her face. Her nails were cut very short.

She was proud of the fact that she could easily imitate a male gait or stance, and with the slightest bit of disguise could fool anyone who was not a trained and attentive observer that she was male. With almost equal ease, she could signal femininity. These were just a few of her gifts.

She contemplated the murder, trying to identify any imperfections. One of the highest priorities had been that the victim feel no pain.

He had certainly not felt the blows that killed him. The last sensation he had known while conscious was most likely bewilderment. Perhaps a little stinging at the time of the injection, but there had been so little time for Richard to react before the drug took effect, he did not register much more than surprise. And maybe a bit of dismay.

Cleo Smith frowned and silently conceded that there were moments of anxiety—he did try so hard to move toward the door and did manage to say, "Jenny." Cleo had tried to calm him, but of course, at that point, he mistrusted her. Belatedly mistrusted her.

Still, he was unable to give more than minor resistance as Cleo steered him back to the desk. A second wave of worry came over Richard just after that, but the drug took full effect—he passed out cold while trying to stand up. It was Richard's final act of courtesy—there would be no need to reposition him.

So. Anxiety, to some degree, but not pain.

Cleo had made sure the blows demolished the point of injection. There was some chance that a toxicology report would be ordered, but even if the tests included the substance she used (highly unlikely), the result would not lead anyone back to her. The clothing she had worn during the murder did not belong to her.

Cleo stepped out of the shower and dried herself, put on a pair of men's socks, then used a new set of towels—never before used by her—to wipe down every surface of the shower and anything she might have touched in here.

She dressed in a new set of male clothes. The towels went into the plastic bag with the needle, gloves, and booties. A few necessary moments were spent examining the scene, ensuring that only the appropriate evidence remained.

She checked the time. Another two hours before discovery would most likely take place. One should never, she knew, rely on everything going smoothly.

She retrieved her portable lock and alarm. One last look back at Richard. She said a silent good-bye and pulled the door shut. She locked it, using a key she had taken from Richard's key ring. The clients would not expect to find the door locked at the time of their appointment. If they became angry rather than worried, and stormed off thinking Richard had forgotten their appointment, she would gain a little more lead time.

Eventually, though, the body would be discovered.

No time to linger. She had a busy day ahead of her.

Besides, she wanted a cigarette. She was not, in general, a smoker, but murder always made her want to light up.

She was perfectly aware of what a psychiatrist might have to say about that.

CHAPTER 2

EXCUSE me, Dad," Giles Fletcher said, and stood to take a cell phone call.

"That's incredibly rude," his sister Edith muttered.

Graydon Fletcher merely sat back in his soft, overstuffed armchair in the sunniest of the many rooms of his mansion, and considered the two adult, middle-aged children who were in his company now.

Through the French doors just opposite the chair, he could see one of the most beautiful gardens on his estate. Giles said, "Just a moment," to his caller and stepped outside. He closed the door behind him, looking tense as he resumed his conversation.

Edith was the designer and keeper of the garden just beyond where Giles paced. Designer, Graydon thought, was not the right word. Originator, perhaps. The garden had been her idea.

A wild hodgepodge of plants, it was the children's garden. Over the years of its existence, any of Graydon's children, grandchildren, or great-grandchildren were free to plant a flower or a vegetable or any other plant they might choose, with very few restrictions to inhibit them: They could not harm another child's plant, nor could they plant anything illegal or anything that might easily prove poisonous to the children and pets of the Fletcher family.

The children's garden flourished in colorful chaos, a chaos that required more work of Edith than the estate's more orderly gardens and greenhouse, and yet she never complained. To Graydon's eye, plants that would have been viewed as rather unattractive on their own somehow added to the beauty of the whole. Edith, who neither had children of her own nor had adopted, gave the same loving care to each plant in this garden.

Graydon found her company restful.

Far more restful than that of his eldest son, Giles. Unusual to see him so agitated. Giles, so bright, so driven, capable of achieving anything to which he set his mind. Graydon knew that the family meant everything to Giles, but watching him now, he worried that Giles's devotion was placing him under a strain.

"If he didn't look so nervous, I'd swear he arranged that call to get out of his argument with you," Edith said, setting aside a gardening magazine she had been pretending to read during that disagreement.

Graydon smiled. "I think Giles knows escape would not be so easy. He doesn't get his way in everything, you know."

She looked as if she might respond, then went back to her magazine.

Neither of them were his biological children. None of the twenty-one children whom he had embraced as his adopted sons and daughters, nor any of the uncountable others who had lived here over the years as foster children or on a less official basis, were his biological children.

Both Graydon and his late wife, Emma, had been the only children of wealthy parents. After Graydon and Emma married, in keeping with ideals they shared on the subjects of education and child welfare, they established an innovative private school—Fletcher Academy. The school was widely held to be the best private school in the area and ranked among the top five in the state. The Fletchers always made room within it for promising students who could not have otherwise afforded such an excellent education.

When Emma and Graydon Fletcher discovered they could not have children of their own, they became foster parents. Those children who stayed with them without the prospect of finding another home, they adopted. Others came to them less formally—children, Emma said, who had houses to live in, but not homes. Graydon and Emma showered them with affection and attention, listened to their worries and calmed their fears, taught

them to care for one another when no one else might care for
them. They challenged each child to discover his or her own talents and kept their lively family busy with projects and activities.

Children abandoned or labeled hopeless became achievers who
learned the benefits of cooperating with others. No one could
blame Graydon and Emma for their pride in them. Given the lost
children of Las Piernas, they had returned successful leaders,
business owners, and professionals. The Fletchers used their
wealth and growing family connections to help these children
find places in the world, to pursue dreams, to be of use.

The Fletchers had been amply repaid for their generosity,
Graydon believed. While a few of his children had chosen to be
independent of the family and settled elsewhere, most were in
close contact with him and lived nearby. Every house on this
street was now owned by one of his children. They took care of
one another, helped one another with problems, invested in one
another's businesses. They generously donated to the academy,
adopted children in addition to their own, took in foster children.
Graydon smiled, thinking of how pleased his late wife would
have been to see their dreams being carried forward.

After Emma died, he found he wanted to spend more time
with his grandchildren and less with paperwork. He handed over
the day-to-day administration of many of his business and chari-
table interests to his children. Which was why Giles was here
now. Giles was in charge of Fletcher Academy.

Giles finished his call and continued to stand outside, looking
at the garden. When he turned to come back in, he was frowning.

"Do sit down, Giles," Graydon said as he reentered the room.
"I hope you haven't received any bad news?"

"No, no . . . just business." He sat on the edge of a nearby chair.
"It's a busy day."

"You've done great things for the academy. I hope you know
how much I appreciate that."

Giles seemed to relax a little. He looked at Graydon earnestly.
"I am going to do so much more. As you know, in the last five
years, the Fletcher Day School has helped us to identify
preschoolers who are especially promising. That means that more

and more students of the academy are going to be the best and brightest in the area, and when others see how well its graduates are doing, we'll get the best students not just in Las Piernas or California, but in the nation."

"Is that your goal?"

"That's one goal. Don't you see, Dad? We already have graduates who have become politicians, architects, CEOs, lawyers, doctors, researchers—"

"Gardeners," Edith said dryly, earning a scowl from him.

Graydon smiled. "Yes, and construction workers, waitresses, plumbers—"

"Yes, yes. But more important—"

"My dear Giles, if you think a plumber is not important, I can only pray the pipes in that old house you've bought are in better shape than I imagine they are. What have I taught you?"

"That everyone is important, all jobs are important. And I *agree*. All I'm saying is that I want to help children whose potential would allow them to flourish if they were given the kind of education they can receive in our school."

"Rich kids," Edith said.

"Not at all!" Giles said, clearly stung. "That's not the issue. The issue is the intelligence of the child, the child's potential." He paused. "And being poor isn't a virtue. Some parents don't deserve to have children. My own didn't. My birth parents, I mean."

Graydon stayed silent. Giles rarely talked about the years before he came to live with Emma and Graydon. Graydon hadn't been sure that Giles remembered his childhood before he was brought to this house, forty years ago—a thin, bruised, frightened six-year-old.

"I think quite often," Giles said, "of what my life would have been like if you hadn't taken me in." He paused, and seemed to shake off his mood. "You gave a fortune to your children, all to help them become better members of this society than they might have been on their own. But instead of going broke, the family is wealthier today than it was when you and Mom began. Because you offered those children a way to make the most of their potential, and they gave back to the family."

"What concerns me, Giles," Graydon said, "is that we are only catering to the best and the brightest these days. The late bloomer, the child of average ability, the child who needs extra help—those children seem no longer to be welcomed at the academy."

"Dad, as great as our resources are, they aren't unlimited. We have to focus." He glanced at his watch.

"I promise I won't keep you much longer," Graydon said. "And since you seem to have the support of other members of the advisory board—Dexter, Nelson, Roy, and the others—I'm not going to interfere with how you run the school. I simply wanted to ensure that you understood my position."

Giles stood. "You know I respect you, Dad. I promise I'll try to work something out that will make you happy."

"Oh, I'm happy with you, son." He also stood, and hugged Giles.

Giles was almost to the door when Graydon said, "Oh, one other thing . . ."

Giles looked back over his shoulder. "Yes?"

"About Caleb, Richard's son."

He saw Giles's back stiffen, and the color drain from his face. "Yes?"

"I understand that one reason Richard stopped having contact with us a few years ago is that he felt pressure to send Caleb to the academy."

Giles shot a quick, angry look at Edith, then said, "I gave up trying to talk Richard into that a long time ago. Caleb is in a public high school now, where I'm sure he's getting an inadequate education, but that was Richard's choice to make."

"Edith," Graydon said, "why would Giles think you told me something about that?"

"I don't know," she said. "I always figured Richard simply got tired of Nelson mooning over his wife."

Giles said, "I don't have time for an old maid's nasty remarks," and left.

Edith smiled and went back to her magazine.

CHAPTER 3

CALEB was in his chemistry class, believing at that moment that his biggest problem was how to keep his friends from guessing that he was getting an A in this subject. And every other class he was taking. Thankfully, his brother Mason let Caleb hang out with him just enough to keep Caleb's friends in awe. Mason was an artist and a musician in a popular local band, and five years older than Caleb. Caleb never let on that Mason was as strict and protective of him as his parents were.

He saw Mrs. Thorndike's gaze fall upon him, and knew she would call on him and that he'd either have to answer or feign ignorance, when a skinny redheaded girl came into the room.

The girl stiffened at the smell the room got from the experiments, then glanced around until she saw Caleb.

"Yes?" Mrs. Thorndike said testily, drawing the girl's attention from him—for which he was grateful, because it had been an unsettling look. A look of pity—but why? The girl handed his teacher a slip of paper, glanced at Caleb again, blushed, and hurried out of the room.

Mrs. Thorndike read the note, then walked over to Caleb and quietly told him that he needed to report to the office.

"Don't stop anywhere along the way," she said.

He was puzzled but grabbed his backpack even as his friends laughed and hooted and made remarks like "Yes, Fletcher!" as if he had achieved something great.

"Shut up, you idiots!" Mrs. Thorndike told them sharply, which wasn't like her at all, and everyone fell silent, probably more out of shock than desire to obey.

I I I

ALL the time he walked across the campus, he argued with
himself. He had done nothing wrong, had nothing to worry
about. It was probably just Mom coming by to give him an
assignment he'd left at home. Or asking him to stay home this afternoon and watch Jenny, his three-year-old sister. Or, to loan her
his car, because hers wouldn't start.

Then he remembered the way that redheaded girl looked at
him.

Just a mistake, he told himself. He didn't get called to the office. It just never happened.

Don't stop anywhere along the way.

Why did Mrs. Thorndike say that?

THE moment he stepped through the door, the people in the
office were giving him pitying looks. He went cold. Mr.
Rogers, the principal—students hummed "Won't You Be My
Neighbor?" behind his back—met him at the front desk and
asked him to come back with him to his office, please.

"What's wrong?"

"You're not in trouble, Caleb."

Caleb didn't feel much relieved by that. When he got to the interior office, the principal opened the door but didn't go into the
room with him. Two men waited there. One was a stranger, who
stood just inside the door. The other was seated, and Caleb recognized him immediately, although his presence only increased
Caleb's puzzlement.

What was Uncle Nelson doing here?

In the next instant, he saw that Uncle Nelson was crying—sobbing, really. That made Caleb feel kind of dizzy. It was like seeing your house on someone else's street—familiar, but out of
place.

"What is it?" he heard himself ask.

"Are you Caleb Fletcher?" the other man said.

Caleb turned to look at him. He was tall. Taller than Caleb, who was five-eleven and still growing. The man had short brown hair and regarded Caleb steadily from gray-green eyes. He was as calm as Uncle Nelson was upset. Something in his calmness quieted the riot of questions and anxieties in Caleb's head.

"Yes, I'm Caleb. Who are you?"

"I'm Detective Frank Harriman. I'm with the Las Piernas Police Department. Why don't you have a seat?"

"No thanks." His palms were sweating, and he felt an urgent desire to escape the room, because he knew that whatever was coming wasn't going to be good. He found himself watching this big cop, waiting, somehow knowing the answers would come from him.

Harriman said quietly, "I'm so sorry, Caleb. There's no easy way to tell you this. Your father died at his studio this morning."

His voice was calm and sincere, but the words made no sense.

"Died?" Caleb said, thinking back to breakfast early this morning, his dad alive and well. No. He wasn't dead.

Mistake. Mistake. Mistake.

"Murdered!" Uncle Nelson choked out.

"What?" Caleb felt the room spin. "No—there's some mistake—"

"Your dad and Jenny, too!" Uncle Nelson said.

"Jenny . . . ?" None of this made sense.

Harriman quickly said, "Your sister is missing, so it is far too early to jump to any conclusions about what has happened to her."

Caleb's mind rapidly issued refusals, denying that any of this could be true. He made himself ask, "What happened to my dad?"

"Some sick fuck beat him to death!" Uncle Nelson shouted.

Caleb got that dizzy feeling again. Beat him to death? No . . . *Think of something else!* Why was Uncle Nelson here, and not his mom? Oh, she must be telling Mason. Or looking for Jenny . . .

Detective Harriman said, "Mr. Fletcher, please."

Uncle Nelson buried his face in his hands.

Harriman put a hand on Caleb's shoulder, watched him for a moment, and said, "Maybe you should sit down. Why don't I get you a glass of water?"

"Thank you," Caleb said, feeling as if he had stumbled into the wrong room after all, that any moment now the red-haired girl would come by to guide him out of this impossible universe.

The chair was close to Uncle Nelson's, and his uncle pulled him into a rough hug. "I'm sorry, I'm sorry, I didn't mean to say . . . Oh, Caleb . . ." But the rest was lost in heaving sobs. As Caleb felt the force of his uncle's distress, something in his own mind started to accept how possible this universe was after all.

When Detective Harriman came back, Caleb still hadn't completely found his way out of disbelief.

"Who did it? Who hurt my dad?" *Hurt.* That sounded better.

"We're working on the answer to that," Harriman said.

"You don't know? You haven't arrested anyone?"

"It's very early on in the investigation."

Caleb took a drink of the water. Somehow he managed to swallow it.

"My dad . . . no one would want to hurt him. He's a graphic artist, for God's sake. He never hurt anyone. He's good to everyone. He's always helping people, he's . . . he's . . . no one would want to hurt him."

"Do you have any idea where your brother is?" the detective asked.

"Half brother," Uncle Nelson murmured.

"Pardon?" Harriman asked.

"Technically, Mason is my half brother," Caleb said, feeling irritated. "But I call him my brother."

"So do you know where he is?"

"Isn't Mom telling Mason? I thought that might be why—" He glanced at Uncle Nelson.

"No," Harriman said. "No, she doesn't know where he is, either. She's working with the detectives who have charge of this case. I'm just helping them out. They're doing all they can to locate your sister and your brother. We want to make sure everyone else in the family is safe. We're hoping Jenny is with him."

"Yes!" Caleb said, latching on to this. "Yes, he might have stopped by the studio and taken her so that Dad could get some work done."

"That's what your mom thought, too. So you don't know where he might have taken her?"

Caleb named some places—the park, an ice-cream place, a beach—and Detective Harriman wrote them down but said, "I think these were on your mom's list, too. Can you think of any other places? Maybe ones your mom wouldn't think of?"

Caleb frowned but shook his head.

"Friends that he might be hanging out with?"

Caleb shook his head again. "He never takes Jenny around to his friends' places. He'd never do that. He's like—you know, protective of her."

Detective Harriman wrote that down, which Caleb thought was a strange thing to write. Uncle Nelson reached over and patted Caleb's hand. Caleb pulled his hand away.

Uncle Nelson wasn't crying so hard now, he noticed.

Caleb wondered why he wasn't crying himself. What was wrong with him?

Because this isn't happening, he told himself. This is *not* happening.

Detective Harriman asked a few more questions and then asked Caleb if he needed to go to his locker for anything.

He felt an urge to lie and say yes, just to flee the room, to get as far away as possible. But he said, "No, not really."

Harriman's pager went off, and the detective silenced it and read the display. He excused himself and stepped out into the hall to make a call on his cell phone. To Caleb's relief, Uncle Nelson didn't try to converse.

When Harriman came back in, he said, "Your mom's back home now, so if you're ready to go, I'll give you and your uncle a ride there."

"But my car—"

"Probably best to come back and pick it up later."

Caleb didn't argue. His resistance was failing him, leaving him hollow and numb. He didn't want to try to drive.

Caleb worried about his uncle Nelson as they walked. When they got to Detective Harriman's sedan, Harriman opened the door on the passenger's side of the front seat. But Uncle Nelson ignored him and got into the back. Feeling awkward, Caleb sat up front.

"Are you okay back there, Uncle Nelson?" Caleb said, but his uncle didn't answer him. He seemed lost in thought.

As they drove away from the school, Caleb turned to the detective. "Are you sure . . ." he started to say, then fell silent.

"That it's your dad?" Harriman asked. "The coroner's office will make absolutely certain, but in the meantime, your mom has identified the victim as your father."

After another silence, Caleb said, "Can I see him?"

"Not just now, but maybe later."

"I need to see him."

Harriman hesitated, then said, "Your mom will have to make that decision. She seems like someone who would understand why it's important to you."

Why can't I cry? Caleb wondered, disturbed by the thought and yet half-relieved that he wasn't losing control in front of this stranger.

Caleb looked back at his uncle, who was still staring out at nothing in particular.

"Why did you bring Uncle Nelson?" he whispered to Harriman.

"You're a minor. Your mom agreed that I could come by to pick you up and talk to you in your uncle's presence."

Something in that confused him, but everything was confusing and out of place. His dad was dead. One moment he felt certain it was true, the next moment that there had been some fuckup on the part of the police. *Let it be a mistake. I won't be mad at anyone. I'll forgive anyone anything. That's okay. Just let my dad be alive . . .*

He wanted the car to stop so that he could get out. He didn't want to go anywhere. *Stop right here,* he wanted to say.

"You okay?" Harriman asked.

He shook his head.

"Feeling sick? You want me to pull over for a minute?"

Now that it had been offered to him, he suddenly didn't want it. He needed to know. He shook his head again.

Harriman asked him questions about school, and Caleb answered knowing the detective was just trying to distract him, but appreciating it even so. The man was just . . . calm. A kind of calm that made Caleb feel a little steadier, too.

"I wish you were in charge of the case," Caleb said.

Harriman smiled a little. "Thanks. But the detectives who have it are good at what they do, and they'll have lots of help. You'll like them."

"But if I need to talk to you?"

Harriman pulled out a business card and handed it to him. "Any time, day or night."

They turned down his street and the whole neighborhood looked incredibly normal, which didn't seem right. Harriman pulled to the curb in front of Caleb's house. Two sedans that looked a lot like the one Detective Harriman drove were parked in front. Uncle Nelson's car was in the driveway, next to his mom's. I have to be strong for Mom, he thought. She'll need me to take care of her.

"No press yet, so at least you don't have to cope with that," Harriman said.

Caleb went into the house. He saw his mom rise to her feet from where she had been sitting with two other detectives, saw her trying so hard to be brave for him, and suddenly, of all the rotten times, he began to weep as if he were two instead of seventeen.

CHAPTER 4

THE call came later than expected. The interior of the car parked on the hill and the silhouette of its lone occupant were dimly illuminated as the cell phone rang.

Dexter Fletcher let the disposable cell phone ring three times.

It never did any good to rush these things. He thought of the three brothers he was closest to in the Fletcher family, pictured them in this same situation. Giles would have waited, perhaps even forced a second call. Nelson would have answered in the middle of the first ring—although he doubted she had ever called Nelson. Roy? One never knew what Roy would do.

"Yes?" Dexter answered. "Remember—"

"The line is not secure. I know." Cleo was always so sure of herself.

"The situation?"

"Just as you wished."

He sighed. "Not exactly . . . wished."

"No, of course not. But . . . taken care of."

"Thank you. Any trouble?"

"I could hardly describe it on a cell phone, now, could I?"

He waited.

"Sorry. Long day," she said.

"Yes, it has been. For all of us. Someday I'll have to tell you where—"

"No names or places," she said sharply.

"Yes. Thanks. Anyway, after I was sure you were on your way, I made my call, and you'll never believe where he was. Apparently, he was summoned this morning. Rather unnerving."

She laughed. He had known it would amuse her.

"So," he said, "your report is all we lack."

"In my opinion, as you know, we took an unnecessary risk here, and I object to not . . . completely settling the issue. But I followed your instructions. It's damned cold, though, so I may get my own way after all. It would be easier on everyone."

"You may be right. But thank you for indulging us."

"No problem. Where would I be without you?"

"Likewise. See you soon."

Dexter sat staring out at the city lights for a good ten minutes after the call ended. He felt a mixture of weariness and exhilaration.

Cleo was so good at her work. Really, he had nothing to worry about.

He started the car and drove home carefully. He couldn't afford an accident. There was much yet to be done.

CHAPTER 5

THREE *months and seventeen days.*

San Bernardino County Deputy Sheriff Tadeo Garcia had been saying this to himself throughout his shift. *Three months and seventeen days* from now, no more putting up with the bullshit. He'd retire and get out of this cruiser. Out of these mountains. He could feel the cold and damp in his bones. At home, down in Redlands, his wife was probably running the A/C. She would have the windows open, at the very least. Up here, it was damp and foggy and he was freezing his *huevos* off.

At this stage of his career, Tadeo had hoped to be sitting behind a desk and not a steering wheel. Which only went to show that you could piss off a supervisor at any point in time. The union rep said they were working on it.

Right. What the hell. If he was careful, he should be okay. And for the most part, his assignment, cruising around these roads in this mountain resort area, wasn't anything he couldn't handle.

He tried to think of warm places he would be spending his time in after he retired. He smiled. Probably at home, fixing up the place—his wife already had a list. Hell, she always had a list. That was okay. She'd put up with a lot over the years.

A strange light in the trees caught his attention. Headlamps, at the wrong angle.

If its headlights hadn't been left on, he might not have noticed the car, down in a ditch just off a private road. At first Tadeo figured this was just another moron who had partied a little too much and gotten himself lost up here. Happened all the time. People came to these mountain resorts, thought they were out on the frontier or something, went crazy. Idiot was lucky his wrong turn had just taken him into a ditch off a private road and not over a cliff. Foggy night like this—had to be nuts. Now, to see if the fool had injured or killed himself.

He lit up the patrol car's spotlight and got a better look. The hair stood up on the back of his neck. He checked the plate number—sure enough, it was the one. He called in to let everybody know that he had just found the car that had been searched for in seven counties. The one that might reveal what had happened to the missing family members. He manipulated the spotlight so that its bright beam shone into the interior of the car. He was disheartened to notice that the driver was slumped over the wheel and not responding to the sudden light. Tadeo quickly became more concerned—Jesus, on a damp night when it was barely forty degrees out and the temperature was dropping, was the kid naked? Tadeo, still in radio contact, let them know there might be need of medical assistance; the dispatcher verified that paramedics were on the way. He hoped the kid wasn't hurt badly—they'd never be able to send a chopper with this fog.

Cautiously but quickly, he approached the vehicle, coming at it from behind the passenger side. It was a little difficult getting to it, since it was resting at an angle in the ditch.

The kid was wearing nothing but white boxers and socks. He didn't move. Tadeo let his flashlight play over the interior of the car. No one else in it. A bottle of expensive scotch lay on the floor on the passenger's side, open and mostly empty.

The doors were unlocked; he moved around to the driver's-side door and opened it. He was immediately struck by the smell of alcohol. The kid reeked of it. Tadeo remembered the names from the bulletin—Mason and Jenny. He called "Mason?" several times, but the young man was unresponsive. Tadeo touched a bare shoulder. Mason's skin was ice cold. Dead? No—he touched the boy's neck and found a pulse, and could see now that he was breathing, but neither sign of life seemed likely to last. Tadeo sent in a second call, confirming the need for an ambulance. The dispatcher connected him with the desk sergeant, who quickly passed him along to a captain, for God's sake, who asked him a few quick questions about where he was and what he was seeing, then told him to get a blanket for the kid and then start looking for the little girl.

Tadeo kept calling, "Jenny?" in a loud voice as he made his way back to the cruiser. He hurried back with a blanket and wrapped it around the kid as best he could. Mason didn't even moan. He thought of starting the car up and turning on the heater, and reached for the keys, but they weren't in the ignition.

He played the flashlight around again but didn't see them. A horrible thought occurred to Tadeo. He felt a renewed sense of urgency now and found a button on the dash that released the trunk.

He rushed back, half afraid he'd find the little girl's body there. Instead, he saw an odd and disturbing set of objects. Bloodstained shoes and clothing, fitting the description of what Mason Fletcher had last been seen wearing. A metal object of some kind—a trophy?—that looked as if it was matted with tissue, blood, and hair. He hadn't seen any blood on the young man when he wrapped him in the blanket.

What he saw confused him. He closed the trunk. He noticed, for the first time, that footprints other than his own were in the soft, damp earth. They were near the trunk and led up from the ditch and on to the dirt drive. He saw a cigarette stub there. He didn't touch it.

He went back and looked at the boy's socks. They were clean, even on the underside.

He shook himself. He wasn't a detective. This was not his job. And when the detectives arrived, they'd be pissed off at him if he started spouting theories. He'd already learned that lesson the hard way. "This is what put you up here in the cold, *zurramato,*" he muttered to himself. He cheered up a little at the thought that even the captain of homicide wouldn't handle this one. The crime began in Las Piernas's jurisdiction, which meant the LPPD would be in charge of the investigation.

So Tadeo tried to keep his mind from forming theories and

began calling the girl's name again, and looking in the nearby brush for any sign of her. The more he thought about what he'd seen so far, the less optimistic he felt about her fate, and the louder he shouted in defiance of his own fears for her. Someone opened a window in a nearby cabin and yelled, "Shut the fuck up, asshole! People are trying to sleep!"

Cabron. He considered going up there and making sure that stupid ass didn't get any sleep, just to vent some of his own frustration, but he was distracted by the sound of approaching vehicles and the red flashing beacon of the ambulance.

I found one of them, he thought fiercely. At least I found one of them. He wondered if anyone would care about that, or if they would feel—just as he did—too worried about the little girl to find it much of a victory.

Three months and seventeen days.

CHAPTER 6

Fourteen Months Later
Tuesday, July 16
3:20 P.M.
LAS PIERNAS

CALEB had learned to stop asking himself if it could get any worse. It could. It did.

In just a moment, it would get worse again.

The jury had reached a verdict, they had been told, and now everyone but the jury had crowded back into the courtroom. His brother—Mason Delacroix Fletcher, the defendant—and the attorneys and the judge had taken their places. The jury would come in soon, and this nightmare would enter its next phase.

Caleb sat to the left of his mother in the hot and stuffy courtroom. She swayed against him, leaned her head against his shoulder. He was easily a head taller than her. He worried that she might feel faint, and put an arm around her shoulders to steady her. She trembled. He felt her quiver, grow still, quiver again, felt the fear course through her in strange, arrhythmic waves. He reached across with his left hand and took her right, as if somehow he could shield her from the watching eyes, the cameras. Her hand was ice cold. She held so tightly to him, he thought she might break his fingers.

She was not a weak woman. Elisa Delacroix Fletcher had surprised those who had seemingly watched her every move over the last year. Maybe they didn't understand what it took for a teenaged mother to raise a child alone, as she had Mason until she met Caleb's dad. No one who was weak could survive what she did before she turned twenty-one.

Maybe the television commentators had expected his mother to be unable to go on after losing a husband and daughter under such horrible circumstances. Perhaps her appearance had fooled them—she was pale and almost waiflike—but anyone in her family could have told them there was determination and courage to be seen on a closer look. Trouble was, there were too few members of her family left. Her parents didn't count, Caleb decided, refusing to acknowledge Grandmother Delacroix's attempt to catch his eye. Unforgivably, they sat on the other side of the courtroom. They had never looked upon Mason as anything but a source of shame, which in turn made Caleb feel ashamed of being related to them.

Nelson Fletcher sat there, too, behind the Delacroixes and next to Caleb's other grandfather, Graydon Fletcher. A dozen of Richard Fletcher's other foster siblings were in attendance as well, "aunts" and "uncles" Caleb barely knew. A few of them had attended throughout the trial.

What a jumbled-up family they all were, anyway, he thought. Caleb's father hadn't been related by blood to Uncle Nelson or any of the others. Richard and Nelson had grown up together in a foster home, two of twenty-one children taken under the wing of the famously selfless Fletchers.

Caleb stole a glance at Grandfather Fletcher. The old man was impeccably dressed, as always. Caleb was not especially close to him, but he still felt admiration for him.

Caleb's family hadn't visited Grandfather Fletcher more than once or twice after his grandmother died, and not at all in recent years. Although he thought he understood the reasons his dad had wanted to be independent of the family's influence—his dad thought they got into one another's business way too much, and were kind of like a cult—Caleb felt bad about that distance now. They didn't know Mason, so why should they doubt his guilt?

As if he had felt Caleb's attention, Grandfather Fletcher turned and looked at him, and gave a little nod in his direction.

Caleb nodded back, wishing that somehow there had been no need for people to feel that they must take sides. If Grandfather Fletcher believed whatever Uncle Nelson told him about Mason, Caleb couldn't blame him for that.

The press loved to talk about the "tragic irony," of course. A man who was an orphan gets a lucky break and grows up in a great foster home. Becomes a successful graphic artist. Marries a woman who is struggling as a young single mother. Adopts her five-year-old boy. Loves and cares for him, and has two other children with her. And the ungrateful boy he adopted, Mason, returns his loving care by allegedly murdering him and his youngest child. Little Jenny.

If there was one word members of the press didn't mean when they said it, that word was *allegedly*. But Caleb didn't believe any of the charges against Mason. Mason might have argued a lot with his dad, but he loved him. And he would never, ever harm Jenny. Mason said that he could not remember anything between a party with some friends the night before the murder and waking up in the hospital almost two days later. His friends vouched for him, and said he had not been drinking, but they had, and admitted their own recollections of the evening weren't all that clear. Caleb believed someone had set his brother up, but who—and why?

At first, Caleb had considered calling Detective Harriman about it. But Caleb didn't really have any ideas to offer the police, and couldn't explain away the evidence in any satisfactory way. DNA evidence. A bottle of scotch taken from his father's office. A trophy his father had won in a design competition—the murder weapon.

Caleb and his mom had a great many other worries by then, too. The relief of Mason being found, the fear that he would die in those first chancy hours after he was discovered, the growing terror over Jenny, the shock of Mason's arrest—all compounded their grief over his father's death. The many arrangements to be made in the wake of his father's death occupied them as well.

His dad's business had become almost immediately worthless, since it depended entirely on his father's talents. Fortunately, there was insurance coverage that allowed outstanding debts to be settled and the return of fees on contracts that would now never be completed. Nothing to speak of was left in assets.

Richard Fletcher's personal life insurance policy and other in-

vestments were intended to pay off the house and studio mort-
gages, and to leave enough for the rest of the family to live on for
a couple of years—or would have, if it had not been necessary to
hire a criminal defense attorney.

Caleb didn't believe that Mason would ever hurt his father or
Jenny, but his reasons for believing Mason was being framed
went beyond brotherly faith. When Caleb mentioned them to
Mason's attorney, though, the man shuddered and asked him to
please not talk to anyone else about his brother's "former" drug
and alcohol problems. When Caleb said that he thought the attorney should talk to Detective Harriman, he got a long lecture
about the police not being their friends, and was strictly forbidden from having any contact with the detective.

Caleb didn't like the attorney his mother had chosen, but there
wasn't anything he could do about that. The man seemed to
make an honest effort at defending Mason, which wasn't easy,
given the prosecution's case.

Two clients, partners in a firm that had hired Richard Fletcher,
testified that the day before Richard's death they had overheard
Mason Fletcher in a violent argument with the victim.

His mom wanted to testify that Richard Fletcher obviously
hadn't thought much of this argument, because he hadn't mentioned it to her that evening, their last together. But the defense
attorney decided it wouldn't be a good idea to put her on the
stand, fearing other questions about Mason the prosecutor might
ask.

She had been strong throughout the ordeal of this trial. Most of
the time, anyway. She had a bad moment when the prosecution
showed the jury the oversized photographs of the fatal damage
done to Richard Fletcher. Another when they showed the photographs of Jenny Fletcher—alive and well in those photos, three
years old then, almost four. A reminder that none of them knew
if she was alive or dead. He refused to believe she was dead, no
matter what the prosecutors said. She was just five now—her
birthdays had been terrible, grief-filled days for Caleb, Mason,
and their mother. Did Jenny miss them?

That was the most innocent question he could ask himself about Jenny.

He thought about the less innocent ones all the same, and knew the prosecutors' insistence that Jenny was dead had undermined his mother's hope. Even when they had shown the photos of Jenny, though, his mother had summoned her courage and managed to regain her composure.

She was falling apart now.

T HE jury came in and was seated. They avoided looking at his brother.

They reached the moment when Mason was asked to stand.

Caleb's mom was looking at the jury, but Caleb was watching Mason. Mason Delacroix Fletcher. Mason Delacroix, the prosecutors insisted on calling him, even though Caleb's father had adopted him.

Mason stood next to his attorney, just beyond Caleb's reach, pale and stone still, and Caleb supposed the reporters would say that as the verdict was read, the defendant showed no emotion. But Caleb could see that he was scared, as scared as he had ever been. Caleb was scared, too.

The judge was talking to the jury foreman, but Caleb already knew what the verdict would be. Caleb thought Mason and his mother knew, too.

Caleb couldn't hear the words, not over the part of his mind that wanted to reach Mason, to tell him he would always believe in his innocence, that he would keep fighting for him.

He knew that even his mother didn't believe in that innocence, not completely. He knew the things the police and prosecutors said made her uneasy. Maybe Uncle Nelson's certainty of Mason's guilt, and the certainty of her parents, had damaged her faith in Mason more than Caleb knew.

Her parents had wanted her to give Mason up for adoption, all those years ago, but she had refused.

She didn't abandon him now, either. She sat here dutifully

every day, and paid for the defense lawyer out of her already strained resources, and never breathed a word of the doubts she felt about Mason's innocence to anyone but Caleb, who steadfastly argued that being a problem child didn't make Mason a murderer.

Caleb could tell that for all the trouble between his mother and Mason, she was hoping for the impossible now, hoping that when the verdict was read, the foreman would say, "Not guilty."

But that wasn't what he said, of course. Caleb's mother made a sound, low and harsh, as if the air was being forced from her lungs by a blow, then half-fainted against him.

Even as he caught her, Caleb looked up at his brother, who turned and gave him a soft smile. Cameras flashed, and the guards pulled Mason away.

CHAPTER 7

NELSON FLETCHER didn't like publicity, but he understood the need to give the jackals of the press a little snack, something to tide them over until some other wounded animal came along and drew their attention. His siblings would make sure their father was able to get away from here, but now, on the courthouse steps, at a bank of microphones, Nelson must take this task on.

He would also try to keep the media away from Caleb and Elisa as long as possible. He was proud of Caleb, who had handled himself well in there. To Nelson's surprise, Detective Harriman had been there, and helped Caleb get his mother away without letting anyone shove a microphone at her. If he hadn't known her so well, Nelson would have suspected that Elisa's fainting was a ploy, but she wasn't the type to do something like that. He worried, but there wasn't anything he could do about it now. Caleb would watch over her.

He carefully unfolded his prepared statement. "I'm sure you can understand that this is an extremely difficult time for the family—" he began, but was interrupted by a shouting reporter.

"Did your brother ever express fears about his adopted son?"

He had told himself that he wouldn't let them distract him from reading the statement, but this question was one he would not let pass. "Richard always referred to Mason as *his son*. And that wasn't a matter of hiding anything—we've never hidden the fact that Richard and I were adopted together and raised as brothers. I do not believe having the same biological parents could have possibly made us any closer, allowed us to love each other more, made me miss him any more than I do now. . . ." He paused, took a shaky breath, and went on. "Richard Fletcher was a genius. A bright and creative and kind man. A good man. My brother."

He paused again, pinched the bridge of his nose, set his thumbs hard into his tear ducts. "I see how loyal Caleb is to his own brother, Mason, and I think that would have made Richard very proud. While I believe that the jury made the right decision, I . . . I am not happy about this. Nothing makes this a happy occasion. I understand completely why Caleb and his mother stood by Mason. Just as I had to stand up for Richard and for Jenny, who could not speak for themselves. . . ."

He drew another breath.

"This family is my family. That's all I have to say."

More shouts followed, but he didn't respond to them.

H E hardly remembered the drive home. He left another pack of reporters at the gates of the exclusive community where he lived. He pulled into his garage, turned the car off, hit the automatic garage-door control, and waited until the automatic light overhead clicked off.

He sat in the darkness and remembered.

R I C H A R D, *the youngest of the boys, was crying. When Graydon Fletcher came into the bedroom, he was pleased to see that Nelson was trying to comfort the four-year-old.*

"He had a bad dream, Daddy," Nelson said.

"You're a good boy to take care of him. I'll sit with him now. You go on back to bed."

"Mommy!" Richard cried. Nelson wished he could help him.

"Mommy's asleep right now, Richard."

"Not her! I want my real mommy."

"She's in heaven, Richard. You know that. But we love you and we'll take care of you and keep you safe."

The sobbing went on for a while, then subsided.

"Can you sleep now?"

Richard shook his head.

"Would you like to play with one of your puzzles for a little while? Would that help you feel sleepy again?"

The boy nodded.

"That's a good boy. Put your slippers and robe on. Come on, let's play the math game."

"Yes, please!" Richard eagerly searched for his slippers and, with a little help, donned his robe. He glanced at Nelson. "Can Nelson play, too?"

"Oh, I suppose he can miss a little sleep tonight. Sure."

While Nelson put on his own robe and slippers, Richard looked up at his adoptive father and raised his arms. The man lifted him and carried him easily. Nelson knew that Richard wouldn't have wanted to be carried if he hadn't still felt frightened.

"Ready?"

"Yes!"

"Such a bright little boy." Their father smiled as he looked back at the sleeping figures in the other beds, then reached down and ruffled Nelson's hair. "All my boys are bright little boys."

N E L S O N rubbed his hands over his face and then opened the car door. The dome light went on, and the motion detector in the garage quickly snapped the overhead on as well.

He thought of Elisa. Should he call her?

No, he decided. Be patient.

TWO

FIVE YEARS
AFTER THE MURDER
OF RICHARD FLETCHER

CHAPTER 8

Sunday, April 23
8:15 A.M.
LAS PIERNAS

THE rain was ruining someone's weekend, no doubt, but I didn't mind it at all. I was pleased to be where I was—in bed next to my husband, warm and cozy. We had been awakened by a thunderclap just after dawn, but apparently our houseguest, Ethan Shire, had slept through it, giving us a couple of unexpected hours of privacy.

I'm a reporter and my husband, Frank Harriman, is a homicide detective, so our plans are often overset by the demands of our work. Lately, our schedules had been further complicated by Ethan Shire's recuperation. Ethan was a coworker of mine who was staying in our guest room. Since he had been shot trying to save my life, giving him a place to stay and a little of our time while he recovered wasn't perceived as a burden, but it had changed how we walked around the house in nothing but our underwear.

At the moment, having read the sports section and comics and now feigning interest in the obituaries, I waited for my husband to finish reading page fifteen of the A section of the *Las Piernas News Express*. I work for the *Express,* and a story I had written on missing children was on pages one, fourteen, and made its final jump to fifteen.

He finished and gave me a wry smile. "The phones in Missing Persons will be ringing off the hook."

I shrugged. "Probably in the newsroom, too."

"Tough subject to write about."

I couldn't argue with that, but it was a story I couldn't ignore. A few weeks earlier, looking up some background for a story on an old kidnapping, I had learned that kidnapping is not one of the crimes included in the FBI's national Uniform Crime Reporting system.

This struck me as odd. Not long after the Lindbergh kidnapping in 1932, kidnapping became a federal offense if the abductor crossed state lines or sent a ransom note by mail. The FBI investigated all such kidnapping cases and was often called in to advise on others.

But kidnapping didn't count in one of the leading reports on crime in the U.S. It was literally easier to get statistics on auto thefts than child abduction.

I got curious.

I found a Department of Justice study on missing children for the year 1999. That study estimated that in the U.S., an astounding number of children had been reported missing—797,500—which meant that on the average, Americans lost track of more than 2,100 children every day—91 kids an hour.

If they had just been numbers, I suppose I would have gone on to something else. But they were children.

The reasons for their disappearances were complex. The largest number were reported to be runaways, a sad commentary in itself, and again not a problem with a single cause or solution. It wasn't always a certainty that children labeled runaways had voluntarily disappeared. In some jurisdictions, it was a fact of life that the police would rather not spend time hunting down a teenager who probably didn't want to be returned home. *Runaway* was an easy thing to write on a report if you didn't want to trouble yourself much.

One woman told me that when she sought the help of police in the disappearance of her seventeen-year-old son, she spoke to a detective who did nothing more than take down her son's name, age, and general description. At the end of which he cruelly remarked, "Lady, he probably just wanted to get away from you." That was just about the sum total of the police investigation thirty years ago, and despite continued effort on her part, she never learned what became of her son.

Police claimed that reporting procedures had changed since then, but they simply did not have the resources to devote much attention to cases other than those that clearly indicated the immediate endangerment of a child. Those presumed to be voluntarily missing were a much lower priority.

I talked the executive news editor of the *Express,* John Walters, into letting me write a story about the children who weren't voluntarily missing. This included the second-largest group after runaways—so-called "family abductions"—and I focused on the more than 203,000 cases that fell into that category. In one year, that was the number of children whose custodial parent reported them as abducted by a former spouse or other family member.

Like any good-sized city—about half a million souls live in Las Piernas—ours had its share of these cases. I interviewed several people who didn't believe their former spouses would harm their children, or cause them to be in the way of harm, but who were both angry and heartbroken that they had been separated from their children. They also felt concern over what the children had been told about them, and anxious about the effect that being "on the run" would have on their kids.

I interviewed other people whose children or grandchildren had been taken from their lives by a noncustodial parent, but who had good reason to fear the children might be in danger—the ex-spouses had histories of substance abuse, mental illness, or violent criminal records.

For an accompanying story, one of my coworkers interviewed a fugitive mother who had taken her children from their father—he was the parent who had legal custody. The mother was now living in Mexico with her two kids and her second husband. We talked to grandparents and aunts and uncles, all of whom were affected when a child was abducted by a noncustodial parent.

Frank predicted we'd get complaints on that one.

"We'll get complaints about all of it. I couldn't write about all of them, so other people whose kids are missing will be upset. Noncustodial parents will complain that we didn't write more about them. Some days I think I'm in the business of making the public unhappy."

"Another thing our jobs have in common."

He was about to say more, but we heard Ethan moving around in the living room. The dogs, who had been sleeping on the bedroom floor, perked up and wanted out to see if they could persuade him to give them treats—our animals were gaining weight due to his lack of resistance.

We stretched and hurriedly dressed. I managed not to look back at the bed, although I couldn't help thinking about how much longer those lazy moments would have lasted on most Sundays. I comforted myself with the thought that we couldn't be the only people on Earth who had to get up early on weekends.

CHAPTER 9

CALEB waited at a table in the inmate visitors' center. He had awakened at four this morning, a little earlier than usual for a Sunday, because of the rain. The trip from Las Piernas to Tehachapi took just over two and a half hours when everything went perfectly. Since Los Angeles lay between Las Piernas and the prison, things never went perfectly. If he missed traffic, he caught construction. Rain caused further delays.

Still, this was by far the most convenient of the three locations where Mason had been kept. The first few weeks, when the CDCR—the California Department of Corrections and Rehabilitation—was deciding where Mason should be incarcerated, Mason had been in one of the euphemistically named "Reception Centers" in the desert east of San Diego. He had then been placed in Susanville, at the High Desert State Prison—a Level IV facility, surrounded by a lethal electrified fence, the kind of facility where someone sentenced to "life without possibility of parole" must be kept.

LWOP—life without possibility. Caleb tried to keep that phrase out of his head.

By car, Susanville was ten hours north of Las Piernas. The CDCR said they tried to place prisoners in facilities close to where family members lived, but with half the prison population coming from the Los Angeles basin and only one prison in L.A. County, something had to give.

For a year, Caleb and his mother made the long drive every weekend. During the second year, Grandmother Delacroix— widowed by then, and having a change of heart toward Mason—

joined Uncle Nelson (who wanted to impress Caleb's mom) in the battle to get Mason moved closer to Las Piernas. Grandmother became a determined advocate for Mason. She was joined by the legions of Fletchers enlisted by Uncle Nelson, which made a difference. Mason was transferred to Tehachapi, formally known as the California Correctional Institution.

Tehachapi was overcrowded, as were all the California prisons. More than five thousand inmates were held in a prison built to hold half that many. At first, since Mason had to adjust again to a new group of inmates, Caleb was worried they might not have done him any favors. But if there were new problems, Mason never mentioned them.

Throughout most of the state's prison system, inmates could only have visitors on Saturdays and Sundays and five holidays: New Year's Day, July Fourth, Labor Day, Thanksgiving Day, and Christmas Day. Here in Tehachapi, the visiting hours on those days were from 7:45 A.M. to 2:45 P.M., and Caleb could usually stay most of that time. Once in a while, if a lot of visitors showed up on one day, the first visitors in had to leave a little earlier so that the next group could come in. Father's Day, Easter Sunday, and similar holidays were usually the only times Caleb's visits had to be shorter for that reason.

He had carefully dressed in conservative clothing, in accordance with inmate visitors' regulations. Clothing that resembled inmate clothing—blue denim or chambray shirts, blue denim pants—was forbidden, as were clothes that resembled law enforcement or military clothing, including rain gear. It had been raining when he woke up before dawn today, but by now Caleb was an old hand at dressing for prison visits and didn't make the mistake of carrying a poncho.

He knew the list of allowable items by heart:

His driver's license, which could not be carried in a wallet, but was necessary for identification for each visit.

One handkerchief—no bandanas.

A package of tissues, unopened.

A clear change purse, holding no more than thirty dollars,

which must be in coins or one-dollar bills only. None of it could be left with the prisoner.

A comb or brush.

Two keys on a key ring with no attachments.

Up to six photographs, to be carried in a clear plastic bag.

No chewing gum, cigarettes, food, cameras, pagers, cell phones.

He never wore a belt or shoes that might have metal in them.

He had parked his car and walked to the first processing area. He was in line early, and completed the necessary paperwork, which was checked against computer records to ensure that Mason had agreed to the visit and was available that day. He got the ultraviolet-ink hand stamp and went through security screening—taking off his shoes, walking through the metal detector, putting his shoes back on. He rode the van that took him to the visitors' area for the facility where Mason was held, checked in through a second security screening and went downstairs, checked in again at the booth on this level, then staked out a table and waited the twenty additional minutes it took for Mason to make it through his part of the process.

He tried to shake off the effects of the nightmare he had every Saturday night—that he drove to the prison and waited there, only to have a guard come to the table and say that Mason was dead. On other nights, the dream would be of a phone call to his home—he would drive and drive and never reach the prison to reclaim Mason's body. Only his fear-filled dreams about Jenny were worse.

As Mason came into the room, Caleb felt the sense of relief he always had at first sight of his brother. Dread that he had been hurt or was ill or worse was dispelled, and he could see relief on Mason's face as well. They gave each other the quick embrace allowed as a greeting.

"You're looking tired," Mason said, studying him.

"Just finished a presentation for a class last week." He studied Mason in return. His brother had changed dramatically over the past five years. He was leaner, more muscular. What had once seemed like toughness to Caleb had been hardened, brought to an edge.

For a time, early on, Mason had been depressed. He had come out of that, but the emptiness Caleb had noted in him then had been replaced by constant wariness. On any visit, Mason knew where every other person was in the room, and tracked any changes—when people left, new ones entered, others moved.

In contrast, he told Caleb that he should never make eye contact with, or even look toward, other prisoners during visits, an edict Caleb followed when he learned that Mason could receive a beating if someone else thought Caleb had dissed them with a look.

Caleb was allowed to get up from the table and use the vending machines, but Mason had to stay at the table at all times.

"How was your week?" Caleb asked.

A shrug. "Same as last week." Later, Caleb would coax a little more out of him, although he knew Mason would never discuss much that happened here. He might say more in a letter. Injuries—cuts, bruises, or worse—were never explained.

They had passed through times of awkwardness, the hard adjustments Mason had to make, while Caleb tried to understand what no one on the outside could, even through a period when Mason had refused the visits. Caleb kept asking to see him anyway, but it was when he wrote a letter to say that with Dad gone, he needed a man to talk to about his problems, that Mason quickly relented. Mason now viewed him as an adult, but even prison could not keep Mason from being protective of his younger brother.

"Seen Mom?" Mason asked. He always asked, even though the answer had been the same for the last three years, from the moment she had become engaged to her second husband.

"No."

"She was up here yesterday. With Uncle Nelson." He paused. "She's looking a little tired of him, you ask me."

"That didn't take long."

"She asks about you."

Caleb didn't reply.

"You enjoy hurting her?"

"No. She made her choices."

"This is some mistaken kind of loyalty to me, I suppose. Or is it to Dad?"

"I don't think loyalty to either of you is a mistake," Caleb answered in a low voice, looking down at his hands on the table, forcing himself not to curl his fingers into fists.

"Who's she supposed to turn to if she needs help? Me?"

Caleb looked up. "Is she in trouble?"

Mason lifted a shoulder. "Hard to say. But I think she's having regrets."

Caleb brooded on this for a moment, then decided he didn't want to pursue it. "Anything more from the attorney?"

Mason smiled a little. "God bless Grandmother Delacroix," he said, glancing heavenward.

Caleb agreed with him. One of the things Grandmother had done for Mason before she died last year was to hire a new attorney, one who had been actively involved in seeking an appeal. Caleb now administered the trust that paid the attorney's fees, and made sure Mason's inmate trust account allowed him to purchase small items from the prison canteen and art tools and supplies. His grandmother had also ensured that Mason would have the funds he needed to get a fresh start in life, if they were able to win his release. When, not if, Caleb told himself.

"The lawyer's cautiously optimistic," Mason said. "He's coming up here next week. I'll let you know what he says." He nodded toward the photos. "What did you bring?"

"You wanted to see the new apartment?"

The next hours passed with Caleb telling tales of moving, describing the new place and his adventures in graduate school. Mason talked about a painting he was working on and some of his fellow inmates—people Caleb had come to know through Mason's stories about them. They played a game of gin. Mason won.

"You're being careful?" Mason asked, but not about his card

play. He always asked this question at some point in a visit, especially if Caleb was pursuing some lead that might help them figure out who set Mason up. None of the leads ever panned out.

"Yes, but I'm not in any danger. I can't understand that, either."

"What do you mean?"

"They killed Dad. They took Jenny. They sent you to prison.
Why did I escape any punishment or harm?"

Mason raised a brow. "I don't think you did."

Caleb fell silent. "No, I guess I didn't, but still . . ."

"You didn't. I know you think you're failing me, failing Jenny.
But you aren't, you're fighting for us. And lately—you must feel
as if you're fighting alone. And there's nothing I can do about
that, much as I wish I could."

"When we talk—when I see you—it helps."

Mason seemed surprised.

"It does," Caleb reassured him.

"Well—that's good." He dealt another game of gin. Caleb won.

At 2:15 P.M., it was time to clear out, to start the checkout
process. All visitors were told it was time to leave. The brothers
stood and exchanged another brief embrace—the earlier greeting
and this quick hug good-bye were all the physical contact allowed
between them.

"Thanks for coming all the way up here," Mason said.

"See you next week."

"You don't have to—"

"I know. But I'll see you next week."

That exchange was always the same, every week, as were their
next words.

"Keep looking for her, Caleb."

"I will."

It was their good-bye, and one of the few mentions either made
of Jenny, having long ago found it too hard to say much more.

CALEB began the drive home, wondering how she might have
changed in five years. Hoping she had lived to change.

CHAPTER 10

THE phone had been ringing all day. I'd inadvertently created a hotline for despair.

On that rainy Monday morning, I got more calls than Circulation—and they had to talk to everyone whose copy of the *Las Piernas News Express* had landed in a puddle.

As the day wore on, the rain let up, but the calls didn't. One of the busiest news days we'd had in weeks, and I was answering the phone.

Most callers were people who were divorced and afraid of what their ex-spouses might do. Although the end of yesterday's column had carried a teaser that said, "Next Sunday: What You Can Do to Prevent Custodial Abduction," fearful divorced parents were not going to wait a week for those tips.

The other calls, though fewer in number, were harder to take: parents who hadn't seen their children in years.

Most were people worn out by their hope. What would they have done with their energy, I wondered, if they hadn't spent it looking for a missing child? The slight chance that I might be able to help them had led them to take time out of whatever else they had planned that day to contact me. They would patiently tell me the details of their misery, and I didn't have the heart to cut them off.

They weren't all pleasant personalities, either. Jane Serre was clearly drunk when she called at ten in the morning. The booze didn't make her story any less awful. On a Friday afternoon two years ago, her ex-husband, Gerry Serre, had stopped by a local day-care center and picked up their three-year-old son, Luke, as planned. They shared custody, and he was going to take the boy to San Diego for a week—to see the zoo, Legoland, and Sea World. They never returned. When she checked the hotel he said he would be staying at, they said no reservations had been made under his name. He had left everything—his house, his car, his job—even his band, apparently the one interest he seemed to have outside of work. Hadn't touched his credit cards or bank accounts. Just disappeared. With Luke.

"He always was a secretive bastard, you know?" she said, although it came out closer to "scheecretive." I had been saying "Hmm" to the constant "you knows?," which was enough to keep her going. I considered cutting the call short, but I knew that if I hung up, the phone would ring again, a call from someone else with another version of the same story.

The picture she gave me of Gerry was that of an uncommunicative loner, estranged from his family. Jane claimed that she got most of the friends in the divorce, friends who had been hers to begin with, but a guy who worked with Gerry said her ex mentioned that he had been dating someone recently. No one in his office had the name of his new girlfriend, nor had any of them seen her, but Jane figured this gal had money and had helped Gerry to steal Luke.

The guys in the band, she said, claimed they didn't know the new girlfriend, either, but they had always hated Jane. The feeling was mutual, and the topic of the band was extensively explored. The name of the band was Snaggletooth, which she claimed he had cruelly named after her, but she had shown him by getting reconstructive dental surgery.

Up to that point, I managed to jot down the details despite Jane Serre's slurred delivery. With the dental surgery, I was at the too-much-information stage and ended the call. I wondered if her marriage had made an alcoholic out of her, or if her alcoholism had led, at least in part, to the end of the marriage.

A FEW more worriers called, and then I got Blake Ives. Mr. Ives was a yeller. He wanted to let me know how unhappy he was that we had "glorified kidnappers," meaning the couple in Mexico. Pointing out that I wasn't the one who wrote that story seemed cowardly, so I just listened to him rant. I didn't enjoy that much, but I suppose I half-admired him for still having the ability to yell about his missing daughter, Carla, eight years after his ex-wife and her new boyfriend had taken her. After eight years, no one with a missing child has forgotten that child for a moment, but most people are beaten down.

So I asked for details. As it turned out, I had known his ex-wife—she had briefly worked at the *Express*. The yelling suddenly became even more understandable. I had never liked Bonnie Creci, as she was known before she married the unfortunate Mr. Ives.

I remembered Bonnie as being both smart and sly, one of those women whose supposed concern is carried like a small poisoned dagger. She would take your colleagues aside, and if your name followed the phrase "I worry about . . . ," what followed your name was not genuine solicitude but something meant to undermine your reputation. Some people thought she was smug, but I didn't believe she had the underlying self-confidence to carry that off.

The main reason I had disliked her, though, was that she went out of her way to make trouble for Lydia Ames, who was then assistant city editor. Most of us figured Bonnie was after Lydia's job. Lydia and I have been friends since grade school, so anyone who tries to mess with her makes two enemies. I wasn't the only one who came to Lydia's defense, though. Bonnie found out just how fast the temperature could drop in the newsroom, and she eventually decided it was a little too chilly at the *Express*.

"She hasn't worked here in a decade," I said to Ives.

"She stopped being a reporter after she left the *Express*," he said.

"Oh, no," I said, "she stopped long before then."

He laughed, and after that, he stopped yelling.

By the end of the conversation, his volume had come down to a whisper, harder to take than the shouts—but I still couldn't help him.

I couldn't really help any of them. I pointed them to resources they'd already used and ended up telling them the same thing they had heard from everyone else they had turned to for help. I took down names and numbers, but I don't think any of them thought I'd ever be in touch with them again.

At around two o'clock, in an extraordinary gesture of mercy, John Walters ambled up to my desk and said, "I might need to send you out on a story."

I tried not to look too eager to escape the building, but I knew he saw through it because he laughed.

"Mark Baker is tied up with the oil island story," he went on. "You know about that one?"

"Yes, some of it." The oil islands were oil-drilling operations set up to look like islands, just off the shore of Las Piernas. Five bodies had washed up on one of them that morning, so Mark, our crime reporter, was out there trying to discover what was going on.

"Kids who were rafting in the storm," John said, "but they're local, so I've already got other people helping out on that, and everyone else has his hands full, too. Lydia just got a hot tip at the City Desk. We need someone to go out to the old Sheffield place. You think you can take down some information for Mark without getting yourself in too deep?"

"It's a crime scene?" Since I'm married to an LPPD homicide detective, the paper doesn't allow me to cover stories that involve the police.

"Looks like it. Unless whoever left a severed hand in the woods up there has some reasonable explanation for it. I'm leaning toward crime scene, myself."

"Not one of Frank's cases?"

"No, I checked. Harriman is out on the oil island case, I'm told. But the hand in the woods is a possible homicide story, which is why it won't be yours. Still, I need someone to get some basics for Mark to work with. I'll need photos, too. A waste of your talents, but imagine what's happening to my own while I work here. You want it?"

"Just get me off the damned phone."

He smiled conspiratorially.

Guilt kicked in. I talked to him about the calls that were bothering me. "Do you think we could run photos of these kids as a kind of follow-up?"

"Those kids are nowhere near here, and you know it. The spouse who took them is not going to hang out in the town he or she took them from."

"I guess not," I said glumly.

He called the switchboard from my phone and told them to take messages for me. "Go on, Kelly," he said. "You need some fresh air."

CHAPTER 11

THE area known to most locals as the "old Sheffield place" is surrounded by a chain-link fence, and has been since the house on the old estate burned down. I pulled up to a gate normally used by construction crews, where I was recognized by a friend of Frank's, an old cop who was close to retirement. He regularly angered his bosses, which is probably why he drew this duty on a cold, wet day. He gave me the usual set of warnings about not wandering onto the crime scene itself, and made me sign in—an old hand, he gave me a fresh sheet.

"Trying to keep me from knowing who else has been here?" I asked.

"You already missed the meat wagon," he said with a wink, and told me my friend Ben Sheridan was the forensic anthropologist on the case. He shook his head. "I don't know how that guy gets up those slopes with one leg."

"He's in better shape than you," I said, "and with the prosthesis he has, he can manage just about anything he could do before the amputation."

"Yeah, that's what Frank says," he said, but he was still shaking his head. He took the sheet back, radioed his coworkers to warn them I was on the way, and told me to go slow because the road down to the site was "slicker than owl shit."

His comment about the meat wagon was not lost on me. The coroner had already removed the body. And there had been a body, not just a hand, or they wouldn't have needed the full-on "wagon."

I passed what had once been the main road into the estate. As I went by, I caught a glimpse of new construction, rising over what had been charred ruins. The lost structure, the grand Sheffield home, had been owned by one of Las Piernas's oldest and richest families, and built above the leg-shaped cliffs that gave Las Piernas its name. The Sheffields had once owned vast amounts of land in Las Piernas, and although most of it had been sold off, about six hundred wooded acres remained around the family home at the time it burned down.

The heir donated half of the property to the city on the condition that it be developed into a park. He had worked with the city to create a specific plan before finalizing the donation. Legal and budgetary problems had led to delays, but the mayor was ensuring that development of the park went forward as quickly as possible now.

The rain wasn't helping.

I eased around a curve in the muddy construction road and thought of something Ben Sheridan once told me: Rain brings the bodies out.

In the forests, in fields, and in vacant lots; in open desert spaces, on mountain slopes, near riverbeds, near creeks. Once in a while, in a backyard. A good rainstorm would reveal the secrets of a shallow grave, wash away whatever hid a body from view, or carry remains to a place where discovery was more likely, if not inevitable.

In the days after a storm, Ben often got calls from sheriff's departments and coroners, police departments and forest rangers. On this April morning, it had been the Las Piernas County Coroner's Office.

I negotiated another turn on the access road and was just heading past a turnout when a huge SUV came roaring toward me. I swerved hard to the side to avoid being hit head-on, sliding into the turnout with less-than-perfect control before I came to a halt. The SUV didn't slow, the driver didn't so much as glance back.

I had only caught a glimpse of her, but I knew who she was. She was a person who always made sure she stood out in a crowd. She was in her late twenties, but there was a hardness in her features that made her look much older. Chain-smoking probably didn't help her skin, either. Her hair was cropped close to her skull and was the kind of orange you sometimes see on tigers. It looks better on tigers.

I wouldn't have minded driving Sheila Dolson off the road, but I would have felt damned bad about harming the other passenger—her search dog, Altair.

I sat in my Jeep Cherokee at the side of the road, a little shaken. I'm sure Sheila, who had been courting my attention from the moment she learned I worked for the newspaper, would have been appalled to realize that she had just missed killing the goose she hoped would lay the golden PR egg—she had been urging me to write about her and her wonder dog.

If I could have written about Altair and not his handler, I might have gone for it.

Sheila had returned to Las Piernas after living in Illinois. In the short time she had been back, she had all but taken over the Las Piernas SAR—search-and-rescue—dog group. Ben and his dogs were in the same group, and Sheila's presence in it was a source of irritation to him. Ben's girlfriend—no, recent ex-girlfriend, I reminded myself—was also in the group, and apparently she thought Sheila could do no wrong. I wouldn't say that Sheila caused their recent breakup, but she definitely hastened it.

I wondered what Sheila was doing here, then remembered that one of the things Ben didn't like about her was that she didn't wait to be invited to search scenes.

I carefully pulled out again and slowly made my way to a gravel parking lot at the end of the road. The lot lay at the bottom of a slope. Another small access road ran along the top of the slope. Ben and a young man who looked vaguely familiar to me were studying an area along the slope itself—steep, uneven, and muddy terrain covered with trees, rocks, wet leaves and vines. A scattered set of little flags formed a spill of artificial color down one of the gullies in the face of the slope. Evidence or possible evidence had been found at each of those points along the spill.

Despite my bragging about him at the gate, I wondered if the

slope had given Ben any trouble. I worry like this even though it
pisses him off.

I noticed that the six men at this site all had some of the land-
scape on their clothing—although Ben and his assistant had been
smart enough to don coveralls. I also noticed that the only person
who didn't have mud stains all over the seat of his pants was Ben.
He was being careful. I let go of my concerns for his safety.

They had all looked up when they heard the Jeep approach.
Vince Adams, one of the homicide detectives who had caught this
case, was standing not far from where I parked, going over some
notes. A couple of guys in uniform were present, one standing at
the very top of the slope, the other down in the lot, having a cup
of coffee from a thermos. Ben glanced up at me, then went back
to work with a look of resignation on his face.

From what I could see, things were winding up. Several of the
flags were near places along the slope that had been dug out—the
remains were already on their way to the coroner's office, and
most of what was happening now had the appearance of the end
of an initial search.

Vince greeted me warmly. I hid my surprise. Vince and my
husband both work in Homicide, and are friends, but Vince is
usually fairly tight-lipped around me. I didn't take his cordiality
to mean I was his new best friend. The police were in need of
help from the public on this one.

"Your partner not around?" I asked him.

He shook his head. "Back at headquarters, getting some of the
paperwork started."

"So you drew the short straw."

He laughed and said I must have, too. I explained that I was
just here to get some notes together for Mark Baker, who would
be writing the story. "He'll probably call you a little later today."
That was fine with Vince, who began to give me a basic idea of
what had gone on before my arrival.

A pair of workers, beginning the task of setting up a jogging
path through the woods, discovered that someone had used this
slope as a dumping ground—seven mud-coated green plastic

trash bags lay scattered down it. As they drew closer, they noticed a strong smell of decay. The nearest bag had torn open, and some of its contents spilled out onto the damp ground—the workers were horrified to see a decaying human hand lying among some leaves not far from it. The hand was not attached to an arm.

"One of them said he almost puked right then and there," Vince told me. "And I'm glad he didn't, 'cause I've fallen in every other damned thing on this slope."

Luckily, the workers had called the police without trying to touch or further examine the bags. Training sessions by the police department's new lab director had paid off as well—the first officer on the scene didn't do any exploring, either. This meant the search for the remains and evidence could take place with little disturbance to the scene.

The coroner was tied up on the case out at the oil island, but Ben probably would have been called in, anyway. All of the bags contained body parts. Ben thought they were from one adult male victim.

"That's not for publication," Ben said, walking up to us. "I haven't verified that yet."

"At least one adult male?" I asked.

He hesitated, but Vince said, "Yes."

"Found his head," Vince went on, earning a frown from Ben. "We're hoping a forensic artist will be able to get a drawing out for us. You think the paper would run it?"

"I don't see why not," I said. Always a safe answer.

"We may not need to do that," Ben said, in a tone that told me his patience was worn thin. "We may be able to match dental records with a missing-persons report."

"Got any other identifying information on him? Age range? Height? Weight?"

"That will all have to wait," Ben said firmly.

"What else have you recovered up here?"

"Nothing I'm telling you about."

"Any clues about the killer?"

"Who says there is a killer?"

"I suppose this guy just chopped himself up, stuffed himself into bags, rolled out here, and buried himself?"

"It could be death from natural causes. People have been known to dispose of remains in worse ways."

Vince, concerned that he was about to lose the paper's cooperation, said, "Ben's just joking with you. There's always a chance it's as he said, of course, but we are treating this as a homicide. Too early to talk about suspects, though. If we can identify the victim, that will likely take us a lot closer to figuring out who put him here."

I wanted to ask him more about that, but his cell phone rang and he moved off.

Ben started telling me that I might as well go back to the office.

I looked up at the slope. The young man working there was focusing on something, digging carefully. He was a little taller than Ben, with dark brown hair. "Is that your new graduate assistant?" I asked.

"Caleb—" He caught himself. "No, I don't think I'll tell you his last name."

"For God's sake, you think I couldn't find out if I wanted to?"

He considered this, then said, "I'd appreciate it if you didn't include his name in any stories about this case."

"Not up to me. Not my story. Like I told Vince, Mark Baker will be writing it." I watched his assistant for a while. Ben wouldn't be acting like this unless his helper was someone who had already been in the news. It took me only a few minutes to connect the name Caleb to a story that had been big news in Las Piernas a few years earlier. "Jesus. Caleb Fletcher. So he's one of the powerful Fletcher clan, eh?"

"He doesn't have anything to do with the Fletchers!"

"Not even his mom?"

"Not even his—" He broke off and made a sound of frustration. "Goddammit, Irene . . ."

But before he could say more, Caleb was calling to him, clearly excited about something he had found.

That wasn't lost on Vince, either, and he followed Ben up the slope. I would have done the same, but the uniformed officer had finished his coffee break and was now dedicated to preventing me from getting any closer to the crime scene.

I pulled out a camera and took a few shots. Nothing very artistic, but the *Express* hadn't spared a staff photographer for this, so they'd have to make do. The uniform called up to Vince before I managed to take more than five or six. The whole group was scowling at me now.

They came down the hill in a pack. Caleb reached me first and surprised me by saying, "You're Ben's friend who's taking care of Ethan Shire, right?"

"Yes, he's living with my husband and me until he gets back on his feet." I extended a hand and introduced myself. "How do you know Ethan?"

"Before he was shot, he used to come out and talk to us while we worked on the municipal cemetery case. How's he doing?"

Ethan had uncovered a scandal involving the reselling of graves, grave robbing, and the mixing of remains at a municipal cemetery. I now recalled that several of Ben's graduate students had worked on the project of restoring the graves.

Ben was bearing down on us now. "Look," I said, just as he reached us, "why don't you and Ben come over for dinner tomorrow? Ethan is recovering, but he's kind of down. I think he's bored, just having Frank and me around."

"That would be great! I mean . . . I can make it. Ben, how about you?"

I managed not to smile. I think Ben would have come just to see how Ethan was doing, but I also knew there was no way on Earth that he would let his graduate student spend time with two reporters without being there to oversee matters.

Ben gave me a hard stare but then sighed and said, "Yes, I'd like to see how Ethan's doing, too."

Vince said, "Caleb found a wallet. As you know, that is not even close to a positive ID. May not even belong to the deceased. But make sure Mark gives me that call, all right?"

"For a guy who just got a big break on a case, you're looking mighty grim," I said.

"Let's just say life is full of surprises."

I tried to get more information out of him, but he said that until he cleared things with his department, he wasn't going to say more. I made sure he meant it, then left.

As I drove off, I glanced in the rearview mirror and caught Caleb Fletcher staring at my car. That was okay. I was curious about him, too.

CHAPTER 12

A HOME IN HUNTINGTON BEACH

CARRIE smiled to herself as she washed the lunch dishes, thinking of being able to spend more time with Grandfather Fletcher as soon as she finished. The visit from her uncle and her grandfather had been a surprise. Uncle Giles was always nice to Carrie, but it was Grandfather she was most happy to see. Everyone loved Grandfather.

Her sister, Genie, and their brothers were upstairs with him now, while Carrie washed the lunch dishes. Mom and Dad were in Dad's office, here at home, talking with her uncle. Family business. Uncle Giles was in charge of Grandfather's private school— Fletcher Academy. Carrie wondered if she would be allowed to go there one day. Home schooling was okay, but she wished sometimes that they got out of the house more, could meet children who weren't her cousins. She always tried to be extra nice to Uncle Giles, thinking he might let her in.

Today her parents and Uncle Giles had gone off to talk almost right away. Grandfather had said the children could all take a little break before they went back to their studies.

Carrie dried her hands and went upstairs to their big playroom. Grandfather turned and winked at her as she slipped in, but went on playing the piano, singing to her little brothers, Aaron and Troy. The boys stood as close to him as they could, eyes bright, joining in on the chorus. It was a song for young children, one Grandfather had written. Her nine-year-old sister, Genie, was quietly drawing. She smiled at Carrie, flashed a quick greeting in sign language, then bent her head over the big pad of drawing paper Grandfather had brought her.

Grandfather had taught all of his grandchildren some sign language so that they could communicate with their two deaf cousins. "And when my hearing goes, you can use it to talk to me," he'd say.

As usual, he had brought a little gift for each of them. The drawing pad for Genie. For Carrie, a disposable camera, which made Mom roll her eyes but delighted Carrie—Grandfather had smiled at her excitement. The boys had been given storybooks, carefully chosen for their reading levels and interests—Troy's was a book about dinosaurs, Aaron's about astronomy. The boys loved books.

Carrie went to sit on the cushions on the window seat of the big bay window. She listened to the lyrics of Grandfather's song, which was about the planets in the solar system. Carrie was old enough now to know that most of the songs Grandfather wrote were teaching songs, because Grandfather loved teaching almost as much as he loved children. The song was just the right thing for the boys. Aaron was five and Troy was six. Both of them could name the planets, because they knew this song so well.

Carrie had been able to name them at the age of four. She had learned them without the song.

Grandfather began to play a different song, a song about raindrops. He said that it came from a movie. Carrie, who was sitting away from the others, listened to Grandfather sing it as she watched raindrops on the windowpane.

Suddenly a strange feeling came over her. Inside her head, she could hear another voice singing the song. A man's voice, soft and gentle. She was remembering that voice.

Someone else has sung this song to me. Another man. He sang it to me so that I wouldn't be afraid of the rainstorm, the thunder.

She could almost see the man. In her memory, she could find the scent of him—it was a good and comforting scent, maybe from his soap or shampoo. Then, in snippets of memory that were nevertheless quite clear, she could see the man. His eyes were blue, like hers, and his hair was the same dark gold. As quickly as the images and memories had come to her, they were gone.

She watched the raindrops more intently. She had come up
with a term for these experiences: *a remembering.* She knew Mom
would scold her if she knew Carrie had tried to make a noun out
of a verb, but Mom didn't need to know all of Carrie's thoughts.
Mom would say they were memories, period. They weren't exactly memories, to Carrie's way of thinking. They were something on the way to being a memory. One day, she would
remember more, and *then* they'd really be memories, not these
vague impressions.

When the rememberings first came to her, she had been frightened and upset, and—for reasons she couldn't immediately explain—sad. She knew she was adopted—they all were—but
Mom and Dad said she had been adopted as a baby, not at three
years old, as Genie and the boys had been. So how could a baby
remember a song?

She was a sensible girl, as Dad was always saying, so she didn't
stay upset for long. She worked out several possibilities. She decided her parents had probably lied to her. She must not have
been a baby when they adopted her. She must have been older.
She looked something like Mom—and was probably chosen on
that basis. After her, they gave up on that—Genie and the boys
didn't look anything like their adoptive parents. They just didn't
want her to be hurt by the knowledge that her real parents had a
chance to get to know her before they decided they didn't want
her any longer.

She had seen how the boys cried when they first came to live
here, each in turn. She had watched how wonderfully patient and
kind Mom and Dad had been. Now, two years after the youngest,
Aaron, had come here, he seemed not to remember being part of
any other family. He didn't cry out for his dead parents, or try to
make up another name for himself.

Mom and Dad said Carrie's parents had died not long after she
was born. But she was sure that was a lie.

It made her feel sad that her adoptive parents had lied, even if
it was a white lie. She was old enough now to realize that everyone lied, but still, you didn't have to like it. She knew she was

kind of a liar, too, because she kept secrets, and if her mother asked, "What's on your mind, Carrie?" she didn't always answer truthfully.

She wished she could ask questions about her birth parents, but she was afraid, she admitted to herself. What if she hurt Mom and Dad by asking? What if they decided she was too much trouble to keep? She was happy here, and loved her family. What good would it do to ask questions, especially if she might not like the answers?

She leaned her forehead against the cold glass and closed her eyes. The voice of the man of her remembering came back to her, and she found that she liked thinking about him. She had a series of private daydreams about this father who had not wanted to give her up, but a mean mother who insisted. The mean mother variously kept her locked in a closet, put her in a trunk, or sold her to strangers.

She never came up with a mental image or even a remembering of her birth mother. Only her father. She had another daydream in which her mother died just after Carrie was born, and then her father was in a terrible accident and hit his head and couldn't remember anything and didn't come home, and Carrie was put up for adoption.

That part of the story was inspired by a paperback book she had found in a box in the attic, called *Emily and the Stranger,* in which an earl falls off his horse and hits his head and loses his memory and is found by a woman who lives alone in the woods and who cares for him and marries him, and then she gets kidnapped and he hits his head again and remembers everything, then they learn that Emily was really not a poor girl after all. It was a book that Mom didn't know she had hidden in her room, a book that had taught her many other surprising things. (She and Genie had been told about sex as an element of biological reproduction, but that was *nothing* like what the book described.)

Emily and the Stranger was now in a mailing envelope she had taken from the recycling pile and taped to the back of one of the sliding doors on her closet, one of several places where she kept small treasures. She never hid things under her mattress, though—Genie had told her that Mom hid things under her own mattress, so Carrie was sure Mom searched the kids' beds every now and then.

In Carrie's daydream, her father would be hit on his golden-haired head a second time, but not enough to hurt, just enough to make him remember his past and look for her.

He was her secret, just like the book. No one needed to know. Not even Grandfather. Especially not Grandfather or Uncle Giles, she decided, then wondered why such a thought should even cross her mind.

CHAPTER 13

Monday, April 24
4:30 P.M.
NEWSROOM OF THE
LAS PIERNAS NEWS EXPRESS

ALTHOUGH the City Desk had put a few more people on the story of the drowning victims out on the oil island, Mark Baker still had his hands full with that one. Mark and I have worked together for a lot of years, though, and he knows just by looking at me when I'm on to something.

"They won't tell me anything," I said. "Probably because of Frank. His friends know that he'll be suspected of being my source if any cop gives me anything for the paper. There are still a couple of those guys who will never forgive him for marrying a reporter."

"Can you blame them?" Mark asked, laughing. "Besides, you know that attitude runs both ways."

"True."

"So what's with the body in the woods?"

I told him what I knew about it, which wasn't much. "But I have a feeling, Mark—something tells me it's going to be big. Maybe not as big as the one you're working on, but . . . I don't know. Maybe it's just the location—the Sheffield place has been abandoned so long. What was this guy doing out there?"

"Hmm . . . I'll give Vince a call."

"I'll download the photos I took," I said. "Let me know what's up, okay?"

He agreed to keep me posted.

FRANK called, and after some discussion of what we each had left to do at work, we figured out that he'd be home first. "Looks like it's going to start raining again," he said, "but if it doesn't, I'll walk the dogs." We talked about Ethan and the roster of our friends who took turns staying with him during the day while he was in this phase of his recovery. Ethan was due to see his doctor soon and would probably insist to him that he was now well enough to be left at home alone.

"He'll say that," Frank agreed, "but he likes the company."

We spoke briefly about the parts of Frank's current case that were already public knowledge. I could tell he was trying not to let on that he was feeling a little down—notification of families is one of his least favorite parts of the job.

"I hope you won't mind," I said, as much by way of distraction as confession, "I invited Ben and his grad student, Caleb Fletcher, to dinner tomorrow night. I would have talked this over with you first, but—"

"No, don't worry about it. That will be great," he said. "I've been concerned about Ben since he broke up with Anna. And I know Caleb—it will be good to see him again, too."

A FTER I talked to Frank, I spent some time on my computer looking up archived stories on the Fletcher family. Caleb's name brought up a lot of matches to stories from the trial.

I spent a few minutes reviewing those. The paper had ferreted out family trouble then—his mother's parents and the Fletchers had lined up against Caleb and his mother, Elisa Delacroix Fletcher. Nelson Fletcher's testimony against Mason had helped the prosecution. He said Richard had confided to him that he was having difficulties with Mason, that Mason argued with Richard and often lost his temper.

Although the prosecutor had asked for the death penalty, Caleb and Elisa had apparently been persuasive at that point. Caleb had said, "I don't believe for a moment that Mason killed my father or my sister. But if the jury believes it, I'll ask you to keep him alive, or we'll never find out what really became of her." Mason was given a life sentence.

Kidnapped 71

So now, five years after the trial, Caleb's sister was still missing, his half brother still in prison.

I kept reading.

I got a lot of hits from the business section on the name Fletcher. I narrowed it down to Nelson and still came up with quite a few.

Nelson Fletcher was generally accounted to be a man who loved his privacy. He was the respected owner of several manufacturing firms. I learned that he was actually Nelson Fletcher, M.D.—he had a medical degree from UC Irvine but had practiced medicine for only three years after his residency, during which time he also took up a study of engineering. He held a number of patents on medical devices used in a wide variety of surgical procedures, a line of work that apparently paid very well.

I tried a search for Elisa Delacroix Fletcher and found only one other hit, but a relatively recent one. It was dated about two years ago.

To my surprise, the story was a small wedding announcement: Elisa had married her late husband's brother Nelson Fletcher. First marriage for Nelson. Elisa had a son, Caleb Fletcher, by a previous marriage.

No mention of Mason. No mention of the drama of just three years earlier. Man, oh man, someone in Features had been asleep at the wheel to let that one go in without a shout. Didn't they even notice that she wasn't going to have to change the last name on her checks and return-address labels?

It seemed likely to me that this marriage had led to Caleb's estrangement from his mom. What the hell had persuaded the woman to marry a man who had testified against her son?

I started to wonder if she knew more about her son's guilt than had been said during the time of the trial, and looked more closely at those stories. The reporting was clumsy, not some of the best to come out of the *Express*. From all I could gather, the defense hadn't put up much of a fight. I was trying to piece events together and thinking about looking up the trial transcripts, when Mark walked over.

"Kelly, you haven't lost your touch. Damn if your instincts weren't right about this one."

"What one?" I said absently, still absorbed in my reading.

"The dead dude out at the Sheffield place. You were right—could go big."

"Who is it?"

"If that's his wallet, it's one Gerald Serre."

My jaw dropped. "Gerald Serre?" I spelled the last name out.

Mark frowned, as if I had spoiled a surprise. "Yes, he—"

"Supposedly kidnapped his own child . . ."

Mark gave me a suspicious look. "You talk to Frank or something?"

"No, no—I mean, I did, but not about this. Serre's ex-wife called me today."

Now the look was really suspicious, but I was worried about something that was far more important than dirty looks.

"Mark, if he's dead, what happened to his little boy?"

He didn't get a chance to answer, because Lydia Ames called out to us from the City Desk.

"Mark—Irene—either of you know a Sheila Dolson? Irene, she says you can vouch for her. She claims she and her dog are out at the Sheffield place. The dog just found more remains."

"Shit," Mark and I said in unison. He turned to me and said, "Kelly, you know her. You've got to come with me."

I caught the urgency in his voice and remembered that Mark, who had been viciously attacked by a dog when he was ten, has a fear of them. He's embarrassed by that fear—no one else in the newsroom knew about it—and he's tried to overcome it. But the look on his face said he didn't want to deal with this situation alone.

"Sure, Mark," I said. "Let's go."

Three minutes later, we were on our way to the Sheffield Estate.

CHAPTER 14

THE gate was open this time, and no police officer was stationed at the top of the road. When we reached the parking lot at the construction site, a familiar Chevy Suburban was already parked near the area where the remains had been found earlier in the day. The big SUV belonged to Anna Stover, a professional dog trainer—and Ben's ex-girlfriend. Sheila Dolson was standing outside the vehicle, smoking. In the back, one of Anna's Labradors was in his crate. Altair was in the crate next to his. The back windows were down.

The crime-scene tape that had been tied around the area earlier in the day was nowhere to be seen. I wondered if it had been removed by the police or by Anna and Sheila. I couldn't believe Anna would dare it.

Anna stepped out of the Suburban. Sheila was a little younger than Anna, and there was that tiger hair of hers, but they were both slender and athletic. Sheila's smoking had yet to take a real toll on her.

One other major difference was immediately apparent: Sheila looked extremely confident, in fact, smug. Anna, who usually exuded an air of self-confidence that was not so much smug as based on real competence, looked decidedly uneasy.

I greeted them and started introductions, but got no further before the flashing lights of a patrol car caught our attention. Right behind the patrol car were two vehicles: an unmarked Crown Victoria and Ben's pickup truck.

It was getting crowded in the parking area by then. I heard Anna say, "Oh Jesus, Sheila. Tell me you didn't call Ben."

"I called the coroner's office," she said. "They must have called him."

"Of course they did," I said. "It's his case. But Sheila, you knew that."

Anna looked back and forth between us, frowning. Sheila shrugged and ground her cigarette out beneath the heel of a muddy boot.

A stiff wind came up, and we all hunched our shoulders in defense against it. It scattered leaves below and clouds above. Only a little more than an hour was left before sunset, but the sun declared its presence rather spectacularly, breaking through the clouds to make one of those inspirational skies.

Nothing could have been in greater contrast to the mood of the people quickly gathering below.

Ben got out of his truck, Caleb following. I noticed they had changed clothes.

Vince Adams and his partner, Reed Collins—the two detectives who had worked the scene earlier in the day—emerged from the Crown Vic. The two of them seem like opposites in many ways—Vince looks as if he took up police work after a career in the boxing ring, while Reed looks as if he could leave police work for a film career at any time. More than one criminal has made the mistake of thinking Vince lacks sophistication or that Reed is too genteel to get his hands dirty. They're both streetwise and smart as hell, and have the kind of dogged persistence that solves cases. At the moment, they both looked extremely unhappy. So did Ben and Caleb. The woman patrol officer getting out of the black-and-white added her scowl to theirs.

"Lady," Vince said to Sheila, "I don't know what your game is, but I have a good mind to arrest you right here and now and let you do your explaining in custody."

"Arrest me?" Sheila's smugness dimmed a bit.

"Let's start with trespassing—"

"The gate was open!"

Vince looked to Anna.

"That's true," she said.

"You changing the way your SAR group operates, Anna?" he asked.

Her cheeks reddened slightly. "No, but—"

"So you think it's okay to search a crime scene in LPPD jurisdiction without mentioning it to us?"

"What's more important," Sheila interrupted, "helping a family find the remains of a missing person, or bolstering Ben Sheridan's fragile male ego?"

There were outbursts from several quarters at that. If I hadn't been there on the job, I would have objected, too, but under the circumstances, I had to keep quiet. Ben didn't speak up in his own defense, but Anna didn't speak up, either. I felt my temper rising.

"All right, all right," Vince was saying, taking control of the conversation again. "Exactly what happened during your *unauthorized* search within a fenced-in area surrounded by signs that say Keep Out, No Public Access, and Authorized Personnel Only?"

"I asked Anna to accompany me. I wanted someone who has credibility with the local group—with Las Piernas SAR Dogs— and with your department to witness the search and confirm any find. Anna is the president of that organization, and she graciously agreed to drive over here with us and to bring one of her own dogs." She nodded toward the dogs in the Suburban.

"Anna watched as Altair and I went to work," Sheila went on. "We weren't searching for very long before Altair alerted. I've placed a marker where Altair found these."

She handed a small plastic bag to the detective.

Caleb groaned. "You removed possible evidence! Didn't any of your other cadaver dog groups teach you not to do that?"

She glowered at him but turned when Mark asked, "What is it you found?"

"Teeth," she said solemnly. "I bagged them because I didn't want to lose them," she added with a significant look at Caleb. "There are bound to be more remains! All I'm asking is that you allow us to search again tomorrow. Anna has asked me to be part of the Las Piernas SAR team." This time, her look was one of pure triumph and was aimed toward Ben. It missed its mark—he was looking down at his feet.

For a moment there was silence.

"Lady," Vince said, "I don't care if you found the pope's kneecaps out here and he agreed to make you a saint out of gratitude. I'm still considering taking you in." He turned to Ben. "Ben, can you bring Bingle and some of the other dogs and people on the local team out here tomorrow?"

Sheila started to squeal a protest, but Vince held up a hand. He turned to the patrol officer. "Officer, if she interrupts me one more time, place her under arrest."

He turned back to Ben.

Ben said, "Sure, I'll search with Bingle, but I'm not going to bring anyone from the local team." He looked up at Anna. "As of now, I'm no longer with Las Piernas SAR Dogs."

"Ben, no!" Anna protested. "Ben, let's talk this over."

He shook his head.

Reed, always the quieter of the two detectives, spoke up. "Anna, did things happen here the way Ms. Dolson said they did?"

"Yes. I'm sorry I didn't call you first. I should have. But—but isn't the most important thing that we found evidence?"

"I don't know that you did," Reed said.

"What do you mean?"

"I mean, Ms. Dolson here is not a forensic odontologist, forensic anthropologist, forensic pathologist, or a dentist, is she?"

"No, but—"

"And while maybe some guy on TV can get DNA out of anything and get results in twenty minutes, that TV show probably gets more funding for an episode than our lab gets for an annual budget for DNA."

"But if DNA can be extracted from the teeth, and it does match a missing person's DNA—"

"Then I'm not sure the district attorney is going to like how it came into our possession. When Ben and Caleb were doing their work here today, it was in a completely controlled and documented manner, by people with credentials and expertise. You and Ben are obviously having some kind of trouble, and I'm sorry for that, but it doesn't have anything to with what I'm saying to you right now."

Although she blushed again, after a moment she lifted her chin and said, "I know Ben is good at what he does. He just doesn't always acknowledge that some other people are good at what they do. He has a blind spot where Sheila's concerned."

"Ms. Dolson is new to the area," Reed said. "Didn't you add her to your search team a little quickly?"

"Not at all," Anna said. "She has established credentials in this work. And I've never seen a better search dog than Altair. They could do so much—"

"Yeah, well, they've done more than enough, as far as I'm concerned," Vince said. "And if you ask me, the problems we have with you folks always seems to come from the two-legged animals, however talented the four-legged ones might be. Sounds as if your group might need a refresher on protocols. I'll let you go tonight, but I'm going to have to let my department know what happened here. In the future, I hope you'll give us a call before you even think about going near a crime scene. I suggest you seriously think about calling us before you call the newspaper. That looks bad, Anna."

"Anna has an excellent record of helping your department," Ben said quietly.

She still looked upset—maybe even more upset that he had defended her.

"Anna," I asked, "did Rascal do any searching here?"

"No," she said, "no, he didn't." Her voice was unsteady, but then she took a deep breath and went on, holding her head up, looking me in the eye for a change. "I had him on a lead, and we stayed here and observed. I walked him around a little, but not up on the slope. It's one hundred percent Altair's find. I'll just keep hoping that people will look past one error in judgment and think about what this might mean to a family somewhere. Let's go, Sheila."

When they reached the Suburban, Sheila Dolson yelled, "Mr. Baker! Please call me!" before slamming the passenger door shut. Vince told the patrol officer to make sure they left the grounds and stayed out. "And while you're at it, find out what the hell happened to the lock on the gate."

He walked over to the Crown Vic and turned on a spotlight, aiming it toward the slope. The sun hadn't set yet, but the clouds were gradually starting to move in again. Without saying a word to each other, Vince and Reed grabbed a couple of flashlights and walked up to where the marker was placed. The detectives conferred briefly, then pulled Mark into the discussion, asking him about when we were notified by Sheila and so on. I was left standing next to Ben and Caleb.

"Are you okay?" I asked Ben. "Being around Anna can't be easy."

He shook his head but said, "I'll get there. I'm not used to the idea yet, although I can't say I didn't see it coming,"

"Leaving you a note—that was just chickenshit," Caleb said.

"She broke up with you with a note? Jesus, Ben . . ."

He shrugged. "Maybe it was the only way she could tell me. I don't know."

"She's moved out?"

"Yes, today. I had to leave to come out here this morning while she was packing up the last of her things." He paused. "What time for dinner tomorrow?" he asked, obviously wanting to change the subject.

"Let's make it around seven. Caleb, are you allergic to anything, on a special diet, or do you just plain hate any foods?"

"No, Ms. Kelly."

"Break yourself of that 'Ms. Kelly' habit by tomorrow night—I'm Irene."

"Caleb," Ben said, "do me a favor and see if Vince and Reed will let us have a look at Sheila's evidence."

As soon as Caleb was out of earshot, he said, "I'm not sure I'd make such a great dinner guest—lately, I'm never sure what kind of shape I'll be in."

"That's why you should spend the time among friends. We will take you in any shape. No game face necessary. Which I expect you already know to be true."

"Thanks."

"I mean it."

That merited a quick smile. "I know."

I looked toward the slope. "It seems pretty amazing to me— almost unbelievable, I'd say—that she found teeth out there."

"Supposedly the dog found them," he said.

"You're as suspicious as I am."

He glanced toward the other group and said, "I'm sure everyone here is as skeptical as you are, if not more so. This is not for publication, but the remains we found today? We recovered all the teeth. That's why we were so confident about the dental records match to Serre."

"Then tell Anna that her new star team member planted evidence!"

"It wouldn't do any good, Irene. First, she would say that it was an unfounded accusation. At this point, she'd be right. She can always claim that the teeth belonged to a second victim, one we've simply failed to find. Or a living victim taken by the killer, who knocked his or her teeth out." He frowned over that for a moment.

I'm sure we were both thinking of Luke Serre, Gerald Serre's missing son.

"As it happens," Ben said, "the one person who could have caught Sheila planting evidence is Anna. Unfortunately, Anna probably saw what she wanted to see, and nothing more."

"Why do you say that?"

He shook his head. "Over the past three months, Sheila has been doing everything she can to make Anna into a true believer."

"True believer? Anna has that much faith in her?"

"It seems so to me. Sheila has worked skillfully and patiently to get a set of followers in our SAR group."

"But something about her obviously bothers you."

"I smell a phony, that's all. All her initial approaches were to praise the other handlers effusively."

"'Good dog' works on you guys, too?"

"Something like that. Not on all of us."

"No, not on you, certainly." Accepting praise was not his forte.

He shrugged. "That wasn't the only weapon in her arsenal. She has numerous sad stories to tell about herself. Maybe they're true. Maybe she really is a cancer survivor whose only child died when she got lost in the woods, and that loss really is what inspired her to be a searcher. Maybe it's true that her abusive ex stalks her and tried to kill her by burning down her house around her, and the reason she moves so often is to avoid him."

"Wow. Quite a history, but all of that could be checked out, you know."

"Hell if I'm going to be the one to do it. Everyone else in the group feels sorry for her. Anna found someone who rented her a small house for less than half the going rate, and someone else who got her a part-time job. So maybe I'm the only cynic left in Las Piernas."

"Maybe your group is especially vulnerable for some reason, or needs to look at how it screens handlers."

"Maybe. I just keep thinking, who could be easier prey for someone who pretends to need help than a group of volunteer rescuers?"

"Hmm. I begin to see the picture."

"And then there is Altair. I'll admit he's good. I've seen him at work on training exercises that Sheila couldn't control."

"Ones you devised?"

Another quick smile. "Yes. So the talent in the dog is there, and he is well trained. She's not a bad handler, although she uses a lot of body language—I think sometimes she cues the dog in training exercises."

"So?"

"She doesn't seem to be as experienced as she should be, given the amount of time she's been at this. And Altair's *too* perfect. No team I know of makes as many finds as Sheila and Altair."

"I take it you've pointed this out to other people in the SAR group?"

"Yes. Supposedly I'm jealous." He sighed. "Remember that I said she's been patient and skillful? I, on the other hand, have been impatient and clumsy at trying to discredit her."

He might have said more, but the others were walking toward us then. Caleb was smiling. I wondered what had changed his mood. Reed held out the small bag with the teeth in it. "Caleb says you're going back to the coroner's office tonight. You want to include these with what you're testing? Or should I have Vince leave them under his pillow and see if the tooth fairy leaves him a buck apiece?"

"A buck?" Vince said. "Jeez, I only got a quarter a tooth when I was a kid."

"I think it's higher in some households now," I said as Ben took the bag and studied its contents for a moment. A look passed between him and Caleb, but I couldn't read it.

"Are they children's teeth?" I asked anxiously.

"At first glance," Ben said, "it looks as if they are. But that's preliminary."

"You know more than you're saying."

"Just the opposite. I'm not saying more than I know. Certainly not guessing aloud so that you can fill a page of newsprint with speculation."

I knew this mood, and so did Mark. We headed back to the paper.

As we drove, Mark asked me about Sheila Dolson.

"She's strange. Something's not quite right about her. Ben suspects she's a phony, at least to some degree. I have to say I agree with him, but I also think she's . . ."

"What?"

"I was going to say calculating, but she's not just calculating, she's cold. That SAR group may have seen her charming side, but my own impression is that there's a real mean streak in her. And

I'm not just saying that because she almost ran me off the road today."

"This whole deal is strange," he said. "You think she planted those teeth there?"

"If she did plant them, it's either a hell of a lucky guess or a real problem, isn't it?"

"What do you mean?"

"Next-of-kin notification just took place. Your story will hit to-morrow's morning paper. The most anyone has heard from the media is that the remains of an unidentified man have been found on the Sheffield Estate. Come to think of it . . ."

"What?"

"How did she learn about the search there in the first place?"

"A scanner?"

I shook my head. "No. I was the only reporter there. John said we learned of it from a tip. Every other reporter in town was cov-ering the story you were on—the boys in the river."

"Yes. If any of the major networks had heard about it, they might have sent a camera crew over, as long they were in the neighborhood."

"Exactly."

"Did Anna know Ben was there?"

I was speechless.

Mark smiled. "As my mama used to say, 'Better close your mouth, or you'll catch flies.'"

So I stopped gaping, but I didn't feel any less dumbfounded.

"Is that silence a yes?" he asked.

"It's a— I can't believe it. It would go against— I mean, he might easily have told her where he'd be, or she could have heard him talking to the coroner when he got the call, and she obviously knew he was going to be tied up there for a few hours, because she used that time to move stuff out of the house. That bitch!"

"Oooh. I can see who's going to get Irene Kelly when the two of them divvy up their friends."

"Never in doubt. Not given what Ben and I have been through together."

He grew suddenly serious. "No, of course not. Sorry."

Ben and I were among the few survivors of an expedition to the mountains that had gone horribly wrong. Unfortunately, one of the other survivors was a serial killer. That man inflicted the wound that caused Ben to lose the lower half of his left leg. I just lost at least half my sanity, but Ben helped me back from that, too. It's not too much to say we've saved each other's lives, but that's not nearly saying enough about our friendship.

"No need to apologize," I said to Mark. "I'll be sorry to lose Anna's friendship, if it comes to that. I hope it doesn't. But to go back to what you were saying earlier, it would be . . . let's say, *unlike* Anna to talk to someone about where Ben was working on a crime scene, but not impossible."

"I'll ask Sheila about it when I talk to her. But that wasn't what was bothering you when you were talking about the next-of-kin notification."

"Sorry, got distracted. Here's the thing. Ben sifts through the soil at a scene where there are remains. Children's bones are small and could be carried off by scavengers, but I find it hard—almost impossible—to believe that Ben found absolutely no trace of a child's remains if they were there."

"Okay, not impossible, but I agree, especially because she went to the same search area. And I'm with you and Ben about Sheila—the bullshit buzzer is going off for me, too."

"So if she planted those teeth and pretended to find them— which would be easy enough with Anna standing so far from her— and the teeth belonged to a child, how did she know about the missing boy? The coroner hasn't even issued a press release about the father. So if Gerald Serre's name isn't out yet, why would you assume the body of an adult would be accompanied by the body of a child?"

His response was gratifying. I didn't even remind him about what his mother said on the subject of catching flies.

"If they can get DNA from them," he said, "they'll prove that."

"If—but it's not always possible to get it from teeth. Besides, the county lab is doing all the DNA work now. And they're backed up. DNA will take weeks if not months."

"This will get high priority, I'm sure, but you're right, even if they rush it, we're looking at a week at least."

"So, Mark—let's find out all we can about Sheila Dolson."

"Better leave it to me, Kelly. John won't like you getting yourself too far into this story."

Knowing he was right, and was perfectly capable of doing the job, did not in any way ease my sense of frustration.

CHAPTER 15

Monday, April 24
6:47 P.M.
A CONDOMINIUM IN LAS PIERNAS

CLEO SMITH slept odd hours, waking and rising as suited her needs. At a time of day when others would be sitting down to family meals, she was asleep in her large, antique feather bed. She awakened the moment the phone rang. By the time it rang a second time, she answered it with typical alertness. The person on the other end of the line heard no drowsiness in her voice as she said in a cool and neutral tone, "Yes?"

"There was a disturbing report on the news this evening."

A man's voice. She knew the voice. Giles. While she had been ready to hang up on a misdialer, nothing about this caller caused her to relax. She turned on a small lamp next to her bed. It gave off a soft, low light.

"Really?" she said. Noncommittal again.

"A man's body was found on the Sheffield Estate."

She felt the tension go out of her. She had the upper hand now. "Why are you telling me about it?"

"Don't take that tone with me—"

"Don't say my name," she interrupted, knowing her name would have been the next word out of his mouth. Studying herself in the mirror over the bed, she tapped a cigarette from the pack on her nightstand and lit it.

"Are you smoking?" he asked.

"Yes." She made a smoke ring, knowing he would be annoyed if he could see it.

"What's bothering you?" he asked, his voice gentle now.

"I'm not the one who called."

He waited.

She sighed. "How big a mess are you in?"

"We."

"Hmm. Okay. We."

"No name released yet, but when I learned— Well, it's only a matter of time, and probably not that much time."

She was silent.

"Are you there?" he asked.

"Two years ago—"

"Not this again!"

"Two years ago," she said firmly, "you-know-who gave *my* job to someone else. And what has come of that?"

"You weren't in the country."

"Thanks to you!"

"Are you saying it would have been better if you were here?"

She hesitated, then said, "No. Only that you should have waited for me to return."

"We couldn't wait! Listen—if you want me to say that this whole business is completely fucked up, and that if you had done it, we'd be all right, then fine, you have that admission from me." He paused but could not keep himself from adding bitterly, "Again."

She smiled. Took a drag. Blew a smoke ring.

"I know the address," she said.

"You know . . ." He was clearly shocked. She found it delightful that she could throw him so off-balance.

"I know the address, the layout, the obstacles. I've been preparing for weeks." Years, she added silently.

"I just— You amaze me, that's all."

Time to relent a little. "Say the word, and I'll deal with it."

There was a long silence, but she could hear his breathing, the change in it made by certain kinds of stress. This was always so hard on him. She wished she could be there with him, to actually see the tension in him.

"Please," he whispered at last.

"Of course," she said, soothingly now. No point—or pleasure—in pushing him too far.

She looked at the clock next to the bed, anticipating his next question. He didn't disappoint her.

"When?" Still whispering.

"Within the next few hours. Call me at ten. Not this number."

"Of course not."

She smoked the cigarette, listening to his breathing steady.

"Thank you," he said.

"You're welcome," she said. She made a kissing sound. "Good-bye for now."

"Be careful," he said, just as she knew he would.

"You, too."

He made a kissing sound, too, just before he hung up.

She stubbed the cigarette out in the ashtray—almost never used—next to the bed. She looked up into the mirror and ran her hands over her skin from shoulders to crotch. Then she stretched like a cat—a very proud cat, pleased with what she saw. Time to get up.

She sang a little song to herself as she made her way to the shower.

She loved her work.

CHAPTER 16

JOHN was still in his office when we got back to the paper. Mark and I spent a few minutes filling him in on recent events, then Mark went to his desk to make a few changes in his story—and to try to contact Jane Serre for comment. I was still talking to John when Mark leaned his head in the doorway.

"She's got a photo of her son she's willing to give me. Want to run it?"

John glanced at the clock on his wall. "Hurry. I'll hold the front page as long as I can. If you can talk her out of one of her ex, even better."

As Mark left, John sighed and said, "There goes the whole front page."

He stood up, ready to go out and start ordering changes.

"I'm headed home, then," I said.

"Kelly, hold up."

I looked back at him.

"I know you and Ben Sheridan are close friends, and that probably prejudices you against this dog woman, so I still want Mark to cover this—"

"I understand. I was glad to be of help today, but it's Mark's story."

"Thing is, he's tied up tonight tracking down the widow. But after listening to you talk about this Sheila Dolson, I find myself being as cynical as Ben. Mind putting in a few minutes on research before you head out this evening?"

"A few minutes?" I laughed.

"Just make a start, anyway. By all rights, we should at least cover what happened out there with the dog tonight. We can be careful about how we phrase things, but . . . I smell a setup here, and let's just say I don't want the paper to be burned if it turns out she's a fake."

The paper had been caught up in a scandal of its own making not many weeks earlier, and I knew John was being extremely cautious these days. "Sure," I said, "I'll look into it."

"Good. And tomorrow morning, let's talk about that follow-up piece about the missing children you pitched to me earlier. With this story on the Serres, maybe we can make a go of it."

T H E name Sheila Dolson didn't produce any likely hits on any search engine. That amazed me. She had the kind of need for attention that surely would have put her name up on the Web if not in a newspaper, and stories of dogs finding people—even dead ones—would usually find space in a paper.

I considered trying a business search. Most search-and-rescue work was done on a volunteer basis, but Sheila claimed she was also a trainer. I was about to enter "obedience training"—although I quickly realized I'd probably have to sort through a lot of hits for bondage sites—when I had a sudden inspiration. I looked up the home phone number for Melna Knox, a friend who started out at the *Express* but had moved to Chicago a few years ago and now worked for the *Tribune*. She's a dog lover, and when she lived here, her dogs had been in dog shows and competitions.

Sheila had told me she moved here from the Chicago area and had once mentioned to me that she did agility training, which implied the possibility that she had dogs in competition. Melna's dogs might be involved in something completely different, but there was a chance Melna might know Sheila from that world of highly trained dogs. If so, Melna might be able to give me some insight even a news file wouldn't provide.

Or tell me she had never heard of Sheila, and remind me that in a city the size of Chicago, they could work in the same building and not know each other—but I wouldn't be any worse off for trying.

I dialed, and she answered on the fourth ring.

The hello was sleepy.

"Melna? It's Irene. Sorry—I didn't think you'd be in bed at"— I glanced at a clock and did the arithmetic—"ten o'clock."

"Irene? Oh . . . usually I'm not. But I've had the flu."

"Sorry you've been ill." I felt guilty. I should have just used the computer to search for information. Maybe Altair had his own Web site.

"What's up? Must be a story if you're calling me at this time of night."

"Just trying to get some background. Dog world stuff."

"Unless it's agility competition, there's probably not much I can help you with."

"That's exactly what I'm looking for. Do you know a dog handler named Sheila Dolson?"

"You've got the name wrong, I think."

"No, I don't think so. Dog is a German shepherd named Altair."

"Now I know you've got it wrong. Her name was Chula— C-H-U-L-A. Not Sheila."

The name difference surprised me, but it wasn't what caught my attention. Amazing how one small verb can make you feel cold. "Was?"

"She died—she was murdered near the beginning of the year. Sad case."

I fell silent, trying to take in all the implications.

"Irene? You there?"

"Yes. Sorry. Wasn't expecting that answer. Did she live in the Chicago area? Did the *Trib* cover the murder?"

"Yes to both. Several articles. I think we ran an obit on her, too. I didn't know her, really—she was involved in SAR, so her agility work was related to that, but people say that she and the dog were a great team."

"You know what happened to the dog?"

"I can't help you much there. I remember hearing that some

relative might take him, and there was gossip that the SAR community wasn't all that happy about that. Felt he should go to someone who knew how to work with him."

She woke up enough at that point to ask me why I wanted to know, and I simply said that I thought I had met the relative with the dog and was trying to get some background. She seemed skeptical but settled for an assurance that I'd call or e-mail her if anything connected with Chicago came up. We spent a little time catching up with each other after that, but between her illness and my deadline, we couldn't talk for long.

The name Chula Dolson brought up forty hits, mostly from Illinois papers and television stations. I used the *Tribune* obit as my starting point.

It was dated January 18. A photo of a woman with her arm around Altair was included with the story. The dog in the photo looked exactly like the one I had met earlier in the day. But the woman next to him was at least twenty-five years older than Sheila Dolson.

Chula Dolson had the face of a prizefighter who hadn't won many rounds. She might have been a handsome woman before her nose had been broken and healed crooked, before someone had given her a rope of scar tissue that ran diagonally across the left side of her face and pulled at one eyelid.

She died at the age of fifty-one. She was the founder of the nonprofit Forensic Search Associates of Illinois, Inc., and according to the article, a beloved trainer who had shared her expertise with hundreds of other dog handlers.

She had established what she referred to as "an interdisciplinary search team," using dogs, forensic anthropologists, a helicopter pilot, and a wildlife specialist, and a variety of other experts. She talked corporations into funding their equipment, travel, and other costs. The organization helped various law enforcement agencies throughout the state and had received honors from a number of civic groups. The article noted that she avoided the spotlight and always made sure the group's sponsors received glory in exchange for their generosity.

I stopped and reread that line. It would have been enough to assure me that I was dealing with a different person, even if the photo and the age of Chula Dolson hadn't run with the obit.

The obit included a number of tributes to her from those in law enforcement, who spoke of the help they had received from her work with Altair.

There were also tributes from groups involved in fighting domestic violence, which she also supported, again in a quiet way—mostly by talking to women in shelters. Chula had been severely abused by her ex-husband, Derek Mansfield. She had seen him successfully prosecuted for his abuse, divorced him while he was in prison, moved from California, changed her name, and started life anew in Chicago.

Derek Mansfield was being sought in her murder.

I found the person I was looking for a few paragraphs down the page.

"She is survived by a daughter, Sheila."

OTHER stories revealed more about the murder. Released from prison after serving time for abusing his ex-wife, Derek Mansfield violated his parole and traveled to Illinois. No one knew how he had learned of her whereabouts, but using false identification, he had checked into a nearby motel and apparently spent several days studying Chula's movements. One evening, as Sheila took Altair for a walk, Mansfield entered Chula's home, shot her, and set fire to the house.

Neighbors were able to give a good description of the man they saw fleeing the house after hearing the shots.

A follow-up story, two weeks later, said that police had received a tip that he was staying in a rural motel. His body was discovered in his room; he had apparently shot himself before he could be captured. The gun he used to kill himself was believed to be the one he used to kill his ex-wife.

I I I

One story about Chula came from the local paper of her small town outside Chicago and had a little more to offer about Sheila. Chula's neighbors were quoted as saying that one source of great joy for Chula was that she had been recently reunited with her daughter.

In California, almost thirty years ago, Chula had complied with her then-husband's demands and made arrangements for a private adoption of Sheila at birth. Her husband had gladly pocketed the fee the couple had paid. Over the years, Chula had mixed feelings. On the one hand, she was relieved that Sheila had not grown up with Derek Mansfield's abuse, and had not witnessed the domestic violence Chula suffered, violence that had disfigured her. She knew that the couple who had adopted Sheila had taken good care of her. But Chula was also haunted by her separation from her only child.

I CALLED John over and showed him what I had found out.

"Kelly, you saved us. I knew this one didn't smell right. Taking credit for her murdered mother's work. Ugh."

"I wonder why she didn't just tell me the truth. . . ."

"Some people have a constitutional dislike of it."

"But it would have been so much easier. Why not just come here legitimately, saying she inherited the dog?"

A shout from the City Desk interrupted us. "Is Mark here? It's that Sheila Dolson again."

John started to answer, looked at me, and shouted back, "Tie her up on hold for a minute, then transfer the call to Kelly."

To me, he said, "Go ahead and find out what you can, but keep anything about Ben out of it. I'll still send Mark by to talk to her, so don't ruin that if you can help it."

"John, how the hell am I going to not ruin it if I tell her what I know?"

He frowned, then said, "Okay." He looked around the newsroom, and with his unerring eye for this sort of misery, spotted the one person I really didn't want to work with: Hailey Freed.

I said, "Oh, no . . ." just as he shouted to her.

"Take Ms. Dolson's call," he said to me. "If she wants to talk to you in person, tell her you're bringing another reporter."

"Just send her, why don't you?"

John looked at me in totally faked amazement. He leaned close to my ear and said in a low voice, "Why, Ms. Kelly, you're Hailey's mentor, and last I heard, you don't think she's ready for anything big." He straightened up and smiled as Hailey approached. "I think the story of a search dog handler faking her credentials—and perhaps her finds—could be big, don't you, Hailey?"

She glanced at me and warily agreed.

If nothing else, maybe she was learning that John's smile is not necessarily a sign of goodwill.

CHAPTER 17

Monday, April 24
8:40 P.M.
717 POPLAR STREET
LAS PIERNAS

THIS neighborhood gives me the creeps," Hailey said.
We were sitting in Hailey's Toyota Camry at the curb in
front of Sheila Dolson's house, neither of us too eager to walk
through the downpour between the car and the house. This was
Hailey's work car, as she had once told me. Her other car was a
BMW.

"Not everyone can live on Rivo Alto," I said. Hailey resided in
a million-plus-dollar house—owned but not occupied by her parents, who just wanted to make sure baby was safe—in one of Las
Piernas's most pricey neighborhoods, a man-made island with
canals and private docks.

She always hates it when I mention this, which means I feel
obligated to bring it up at least three times a week.

Sheila Dolson didn't yet know that we were on to her. Despite
the rain and wind, her front door was open behind the white steel
security screen door, and I wondered if she was watching for our arrival. Lights were on. She was in that house, probably feeling
pleased with herself, and ready to both brag to us about her "record"
as a SAR handler and complain that she was abused by the LPPD.
We might even let her do that for a while, if Hailey didn't get too
antsy about being in a neighborhood that wasn't all white, light, and
uptight. At some point, Hailey would ask her something like,
"How well did you know Derek Mansfield?" or "Do those letters
praising Altair also mention the late Chula Dolson?"

"Deadline's not getting any further away," I said to Hailey
when it seemed as if she wouldn't be able to summon the will to
open her car door.

I opened mine. Over the noise of the storm, I could hear Altair
barking. I pulled up the hood of my raincoat and stepped out into
a rainy blast of wind that flipped the hood right back down again.
By the time I pulled it up again, Hailey had decided to join me,
and together we made a dash to the front porch, zigzagging to
avoid puddles—not entirely successfully.

The porch, at least, was deep enough to provide some shelter.
Altair barked all the more loudly. Hailey rang the doorbell,
which seemed redundant to me.

We waited. Somewhere in the house a television was on, the
volume up fairly high. Between Altair's barks, I could hear the familiar theme of a twenty-four-hour news station.

I heard a door close. Maybe we had arrived while she was in
the bathroom.

We called her name.

Altair's barking increased in ferocity.

We waited.

The next sound I heard was a car starting, and I ran across the
porch and peered out along the side of the house. I heard an engine roar as someone drove off down the alley beyond the backyard. Although I didn't see headlights, it sounded to me as if it
had pulled away from the house.

"What are you doing?" Hailey called to me.

"I have an awful feeling our interviewee just left," I said. "You
keep trying the front door. I'll go around back and see if her car is
still here."

Hailey was more than happy to let me be the one to go back
out into the rain.

Altair's barks changed as I cautiously opened the unlocked
gate and made my way along the side of the house. He sounded
frantic. Not a comforting sound. I hoped to God she wasn't about
to let him loose on me. I almost turned back but decided that if
she wanted publicity, then even she would foresee that having her
dog attack me would not be a good way to end up on the front
page.

The back half of the house was dark. I started to make the trip across the big backyard toward the little garage off the alley, to see if her SUV was gone, but I glanced back at the house and got a surprise: The back door was wide open. I cautiously walked toward it.

"Sheila?" I yelled.

Altair's barking suddenly took on a sharp, distressed sound that made me quicken my steps. I wondered if he was in pain. Probably not any smarter to approach him if he was, but the sound was heartrending, and I wasn't about to leave him without at least trying to find out why he was so distraught.

I climbed the steps to the back door. I couldn't make out much, just that I was on the threshold of the kitchen, and called Sheila's name again. Altair was nearby, judging from the sound. I called his name, and the barks changed to loud whimpering.

"What did you do to him?" Hailey called from the front of the house.

I ignored her and fumbled for the light switch. I managed to turn on the back-porch light, but that was enough to see that Altair was crated. His whimpers grew louder and more varied, as if he would do just about anything to get some point across to me.

Over the general stale-smoke scent of the house, a different, sharp smell came to me. Someone had fired a gun in this house, and not too long ago.

I stood frozen for a moment.

Then I let the dog out.

In retrospect, it was a singularly stupid risk. He could have easily attacked me. Instead, he ran toward a hallway. I found another light switch and followed. He was already at the door of a room, clawing at it as if he would tunnel through it, and then hit it hard enough to make it fly open.

The television was much louder, the gunpowder smell much stronger. Altair was whimpering and shivering, his tail tucked between his legs, his ears flattened. He lay down beside the recliner and looked back at me.

Sheila Dolson lay unmoving. She had been shot through the left eye. The back of her head was a bloody mess. I made myself check for a pulse, but there was none. Her hands were empty. I didn't see a gun anywhere. I hadn't really expected to.

There were muddy marks on the carpet. I avoided stepping near them.

I shakily stepped back out of the room and yelled to Hailey to call 911.

"And tell them what?" she asked petulantly.

"That you're blind and suffocating because your head is stuck up your ass!"

As much as it felt better to be angry than shaky, I forced myself to clearly and calmly add, "Tell them to come to 717 Poplar Street in Las Piernas. Tell them a woman has been shot and killed here."

Her mouth formed a soundless O.

"After you call 911, call the paper. Tell John that Sheila Dolson has been murdered. Ask him if he wants us here, or if he's sending Mark." I waited until I saw her actually pull the phone out and begin dialing.

I found a leash for Altair hanging on a peg near the front door. I took it with me back to the den and coaxed him out of the room. He was still acting skittish.

Hailey called out to me that the police and Mark were on the way, and asked if we could leave. I kept hold of my temper and told her no. I let her into the house by using a pen to move the latch on the dead-bolt lock, and warned her not to touch anything. "Probably would be best if we didn't do a lot of walking around, either, just in case they can get footprints or something."

She looked pointedly at the damp prints I had left all over the hallway but didn't say anything. She seemed suddenly to realize that I had a big German shepherd standing next to me. She eyed Altair a little nervously and said, "Does he bite?"

"I don't know. I don't think so. But he's upset—even if I knew him better, that would make it hard to predict what he'll do."

"I'll just wait here by the door," she said. "To let the police in."

Altair was panting, probably part of his fear reaction, so I thought I'd see if he'd drink some water. Besides, I needed to be where I could get to some air. I went into the kitchen again. I saw the light switch but left it off. If the killer had turned out the light, the crime-scene investigators wouldn't thank me for putting my mitts on the switch.

Altair went halfway into his crate and drank a little water. Most dogs that are used to crates feel safer in them, but when I tried to get him to step farther into it, he backed out in a hurry.

The kitchen was neat and clean, except for the mud that I—and someone else?—had tracked on the floor. An area of one of the counters had a phone, a notepad, and some business cards next to it. I took a notebook out of my purse and copied the numbers I saw on the top few sheets of the notepad, being careful not to touch it with my fingers, and to use only my pencil to lift the pages. Sheila had written initials next to most of the numbers, but even with just the initials, I recognized two newspapers, a radio station, and the local television news. Six or seven numbers were unknown to me. I looked at the business cards, moving them with the end of my pencil. One for a veterinarian, another for a groomer.

I could hear Hailey moving around the house. So much for waiting by the front door. She came into the kitchen and stared at me for a moment, her face pale, her eyes big and dark. She said, "I'm scared."

I felt sorry for her. If she were the huggable type, I would have given her one. She's not.

"Did you look in the den?" I asked.

She shook her head. "I know I should, but . . ."

"Not necessarily," I said. That wasn't exactly true, but it wasn't completely false, either. One or two of our bosses would probably have preferred that we teamed up to look in every nook and cranny of the place before the police arrived. I didn't think Mark would get much out of the police if we did that—in fact, no one on the *Express* would get much cooperation if we ransacked the scene of a homicide.

Hailey seemed relieved, but I could tell doubts lingered.

"This story will be given to Mark, Hailey, and not to either of us."

"Thank God," she said, her voice quivering.

I racked my brains for small talk appropriate for homicide scenes. "Have you ever owned a dog?"

"Little ones," she said. "Two Yorkies. Binky and Boo-Boo. They live with my parents."

The Las Piernas Police Department arrived before she finished telling me the ninth "cutest thing" that Binky did.

I considered it a rescue.

CHAPTER 18

Monday, April 24
9:58 P.M.

A CONDOMINIUM IN LAS PIERNAS

TWO minutes to go.

Cleo didn't want to call him, but she would.

There was no use trying to fool him. Sooner or later he would find out—his connections in this city were too many and too far-reaching. One of the ones in the police department would blab to him. Or the one in the coroner's office.

She lit a cigarette, hoping it would help to steady her nerves. She had never smoked to steady her nerves before in her life.

Then again, she'd never had such a royal fucking disaster on her hands.

Calm down. Not a disaster. You took precautions.

Not one to fold under pressure, she had found some relief in making new decisions, taking action. She had already showered and changed and packed.

Now she made the call, using a disposable cell phone. He answered on the third ring, something Dexter had picked up from him. It was a conceit of Giles's, she knew. A routine. Routines could get a person killed. No one knew that better than she did.

The routine of crating a dog. The routine of watching a certain news program at a certain time each night.

"Yes?" he answered. "What's the situation?"

"Taken care of."

He didn't say anything for a minute or so. That, too, was his typical reaction. She knew what he would ask next. She kept her breathing steady.

"Thank you. Any trouble?"

"Yes," she said.

She heard his sharp intake of breath. Of course. She had said something other than the expected.

"What happened?" he asked.

"She had invited someone over."

"Who?"

"I don't know. Two women."

"Did they see you?"

"Be careful what you say on the phone."

"Did. They. See. You." Every word said with his teeth closed. She knew this mood.

"No." She wasn't entirely sure that was true, but she wasn't about to let him know of her doubts.

"Are you certain?" he asked.

He's not a mind reader. Stay calm. Put him on the defensive. Sound irritated.

"I'm sure. And you are, too, or someone would have talked to you about it by now."

She heard him exhale in relief. "Yes. About these women?"

"I have no idea who they are. I'd say either . . . one of her groups or the press. She hasn't had time to make any other connections."

"Yes. We know she has been trying to get her name in the papers."

"Then we helped her achieve her ambition."

"Don't be flip about this," he said angrily.

Cleo said nothing.

Two long minutes of silence passed, then he said, "Anything else you need to tell me?"

She was angry, too. This whole mess was his fault. She thought it would serve him right if she didn't tell him everything. But that would cause more problems down the road, she knew. Was it smart to say this on the phone, though? She took the chance.

"I lost a shoe."

"What?"

"You heard me."

"What the fuck are you saying?"

"I'm saying one of my shoes got stuck in the mud."

"They'll trace it to you!"

"Now, exactly how would they do that?"

He had no answer to that.

"I'm going away for a few days," she said.

"No—"

"Think!"

"I don't like it."

"It's for the best."

"No. No, don't."

"Why not?"

"Because . . . I'll miss you."

She smiled and lit another cigarette.

"Are you smoking?"

"Yes. And I'm going away for a few days. It will be all right. It will be so good when I return. Remember?"

"Yes," he said slowly. A moment later she heard his breathing change and wondered if he had reached for his zipper.

"I'll only be a couple of hours away from here," she said softly. "You know where to reach me."

"Yes."

"I can be back here if you need me."

"Come by. Come by now, before you go."

"Now, that would be foolish. You're going to be busy tomorrow, anyway. You have to find out who the women were."

"What?"

She might as well have dropped ice water on his crotch. It almost made her laugh.

"You find out who the women were. The two."

"What are you planning?"

"So far? Nothing. But we should know, right?"

"I guess so," he said uneasily.

"Be good while I'm gone," she said, and hung up.

CHAPTER 19

I WAS cold, I was tired, I was hungry. And as I had warned Frank, I was bringing a dog home with me.

I couldn't make myself leave Altair to the tender mercies of Las Piernas Animal Control. Apparently the LPPD couldn't, either. They handed me a form—I guess in their line of work, animals left in the homes of arrestees, suicides, and murder victims weren't a rare occurrence. I filled it out and signed it, thereby agreeing that I understood I had only temporary custody of the animal. Then I had to verbally promise that I realized I wasn't being *given* the dog.

He had to come to the *Express* with me first, and although John raised his eyebrows, he didn't make me leave the poor dog in the car. Altair was quiet—he lay next to me while I wrote my story, and otherwise followed me closely everywhere I went, but didn't cause anyone any trouble.

As I pulled into my own driveway, it started to rain again. I didn't mind so much—the lights in the house were on. The menfolk and the menagerie had waited up for me.

My husband gave me a quick hug, while Ethan called greetings through the door of the guest room and assured me that Cody, our cat, was with him.

I brought Altair in and spent the next few minutes making sure the dogs weren't going to chase one another through the house. They didn't, but this was not because there was a lack of desire on the part of our dogs, Deke and Dunk. Their manners, although improving, couldn't match those of Altair.

Luckily, all three dogs had been well socialized, with plenty of time around other dogs. No one was growling or nipping. Altair wasn't as full of exuberance as our dogs were, and they seemed to quickly pick up on his mood—which, understandably, was quiet, bordering on depressed.

I had wondered if he'd be comfortable around men, since his last two handlers were women, but I needn't have worried. He immediately took to Frank.

"Did you eat dinner?" Frank said, rubbing Altair's ears in a way that made the dog look up at him in adoration.

"No, but . . ."

"Why don't you change into something a little less rain-soaked? I'll let Ethan know that he can come out even if Cody decides to stay in, and I'll heat up some soup for you."

The magic of ear rubs had apparently released Altair from the spell that had forced him to shadow me, and I was able to ditch my damp clothing (the shoes were never going to be the same) and change into a sweater, sweatpants, and warm socks. A glance in the mirror told me I still looked as if I had rolled up on the beach with the last high tide, but I didn't have the energy to make improvements.

Frank had been working on the case out at the oil island. A tough day, I could tell, however much he related most of it as a shaggy-dog story about his partner, Pete Baird, getting seasick during the trip across the harbor. Eventually we heard, in far more concise and sober terms, about the sorrowful return trip.

The question of the boys' identities had been resolved rather quickly, mostly because the boys had been missed and several friends had known of their plans. "A couple of the parents are furious with the friends who didn't join in the fun—mad as hell at those kids for not warning them about what their sons were planning."

"Let me guess," Ethan said. "The parents who spent the least amount of time with their kids when they were breathing."

"Maybe," Frank said, in a way that meant yes.

By then I was finished eating, and I told them about my own

day. I was able to get through it fairly easily until I started talking about the events at Sheila Dolson's house. Frank managed to hold on to his temper when I told him I had entered the house before Hailey called the police, a little detail I had left out when I called him to tell him I'd be really late getting home. He kept petting Altair as I told the next part, and I hurried along to the events that took place after the police had arrived.

Sheila's case had been assigned to Vince Adams and Reed Collins, because it was possibly related to the homicide at the Sheffield place. They weren't happy with me for disturbing the scene to the degree I had, but knew that I could have done far worse.

They were also frustrated that I couldn't describe the car or driver, more frustrated when I said I didn't see the driver leaving the house itself—it could have been anyone who happened to be driving down the alley just at that time.

Vince made me go over the business of the lights, although several switch plates and other surfaces had been wiped clean.

"I can almost tell where he's been by where he cleaned up," Vince said.

There were some footprints—apparently our approach had hurried the killer off before the floors could be mopped. My own shoes were low-heeled and smooth-soled. The bottom of the killer's had a definite pattern and tread of some type—a running shoe, hiking boots, or something of that nature.

The rain had let up by the time the crime-scene investigator started to look at the trail the killer had left on his or her run through the backyard. A short distance from the back steps, the investigator bent close to the ground and said that he thought he was going to be able to get some clear impressions from places where the killer's shoes had sunk a little into the mud in the backyard. I was relieved. I had worried that my own tracks in the house might have made a mess of footwear impressions.

A few minutes later he was calling to Vince and Reed.

Vince went to see what he was so excited about and came back into the house all smiles.

"Cinderfella has dropped a slipper for us."

"You found a shoe?"

"Stepped into an especially soft spot in the mud, and the shoe stuck. Guess you put enough of a scare into him, he didn't take the time to pick it up."

"Sure it's a he?"

He shrugged. "It's a man's running shoe, but not a very big one. A woman could have been wearing it."

WHEN I told Frank this part of the story, he said, "If they can get DNA from the shoe, they'll be able to answer that question."

"How long will that take?" Ethan asked.

"If they hurry and bump it up to the top of the priority list, a few days. Otherwise, your guess is as good as mine—a few months to over a year."

"Even then, that won't necessarily solve the case," I said. "DNA at the scene is just half of the equation. It has to match a sample taken from someone with a record."

"Not even that simple," Frank said. "It has to match a DNA sample taken from someone whose sample has been taken and processed and entered into the state or federal database."

Ethan said, "I guess I always thought if you could get DNA, the case was solved."

"DNA is a great form of evidence," Frank said, "and it is important. But it isn't the only kind of evidence the lab has to process, and it's not always available at every crime scene."

"But when you do have it . . . ?"

"Ethan, the whole system is overloaded. There's a backlog of convicts' DNA, not just crime-scene DNA. There's also a possibility that the killer has no record or isn't in any DNA databases, in which case, the DNA will only be useful if some detective's work finds a suspect."

"And the testing still takes time then, I suppose."

"Right. And if it doesn't match, you're back to square one.

Have I mentioned the part about convincing a jury yet?"

By two-thirty we had all wound down from discussing the problems of the criminal justice system.

Altair chose the floor next to Frank's side of the bed over his crate. I chose next to Frank in the bed over any other choice.

I was pleased to be there. Still, I lay awake.

Now that I wasn't working on a story or coping with the events themselves, I couldn't stop thinking about them. I hadn't liked Sheila Dolson. She was an attention-seeking phony. But that wasn't grounds for murder.

I thought of how close I had come to seeing her killer. I kept wondering if my reluctance to get out of Hailey's car and walk through the rain had cost Sheila Dolson her life. Or saved my own.

My restlessness woke Frank. He seemed to know what the problem was without my saying a word. He didn't try to tell me not to worry, or to get me to talk about it. He pulled me closer to him and slowly stroked my back. Worked on me something like the ear rubs worked on Altair. I felt my whole body relax. Sometime just before dawn, we finally caught a little sleep.

CHAPTER 20

GRANDFATHER called, upset. Carrie and Genie helped take care of the boys while Mom talked to him.

Carrie gathered the recycling and took it out to the garage. She had just come back into the house and had stepped into the bathroom to wash her hands, when she heard Mom hang up the phone in Dad's office, which was across the hall, its door not directly opposite, but six or seven feet farther down. Dad, who had just come downstairs, stepped into the office without seeing Carrie.

"What was that all about?" he asked.

"Sheila's dead."

There was a pause, then Mom said, "That doesn't surprise you, does it, Roy?" Her voice was cold, the way it got when she was really angry.

"What makes you say something like that? Of course it surprises me."

Carrie told herself that she should turn on the bathroom light and fan, flush a toilet, close the bathroom door—announce her presence in some way.

Instead, she kept the light off and closed the door all but a crack, making sure that no one would see her or her reflection in the big mirror over the sink.

"You seem to need to meet clients at some odd hours lately, Roy. You drove out late last night in the rain. What the hell was that about?"

"Don't be ridiculous. Now, tell me about Sheila."

There was a long pause. "It's quite horrible. She was shot to death."

"Shot to death!"

Carrie had no idea who Sheila was. She prayed that Genie was handling everything okay with the boys and wouldn't call for her.

"Did you know her well?" Mom asked.

"No, didn't really know her at all. She was a little younger than me. I think she went looking for her birth parents and found out her dad was in prison for beating her mom. Sad story. Who killed her?"

"No one knows." Mom's voice was tense as she said, "Apparently a reporter showed up right after it happened."

"A reporter? Anyone you know?"

"As a matter of fact, yes. We worked together at the *Express*."

Carrie worked hard at not making any noise, but this revelation almost made her yelp. Mom had worked at a newspaper? That didn't seem possible.

"And?" Dad said, impatient.

"Her name is Irene Kelly. And let me tell you, she's a bitch on wheels."

"What do you mean?"

After a brief hesitation, Mom said, "Why, just that she's tough and sharp. She won't let this go. She'll run down every lead imaginable. Even if the police forget about this, she won't. She's a veteran reporter with lots of connections all over the city."

Dad said, "Well, good. That's good. Is Graydon shaken up? Maybe I should go over there."

"Maybe," Mom said. "By the way, I hear Kelly just did a big piece on missing children."

After a pause, Dad said, "Really? I'll have to take a look at it. Did he say anything about that?"

"Oh, not a word."

Carrie heard her father picking up his keys—he'd walk by here any minute. She shut the door to the bathroom quietly and locked it. She turned on the light and was about to turn on the water when she heard her dad say, "Where are the kids? We should have shut the door."

"They're in the kitchen."

"I'll say good-bye to them, then."

Carrie waited until their voices retreated, then quickly washed her hands and hurried toward the kitchen.

"Oh, there you are," her dad said, and gave her a kiss on the cheek. "I have to go into Las Piernas to see Grandfather."

"Where were you?" her mother asked Carrie.

"I took the recycling out," Carrie said.

"She was gone a loooong time," Aaron said.

Carrie froze, but Genie said, "No she wasn't, silly." She smiled at their parents. "Aaron thinks any minute Carrie isn't here to spoil him is a loooong time." She mimicked him perfectly, making both Aaron and Troy laugh. Carrie smiled gratefully at her.

Her mother was still studying her, but that was interrupted by Troy accidentally knocking over a carton of milk. Carrie and Genie immediately set to work on cleaning up the mess while Mom and Dad soothed Troy.

"Sorry to leave you with all this chaos, honey," Dad said to Mom. He watched her, then said, "Do you want to come with me?"

Mom seemed surprised. "Do you mean it?"

"Yes."

"But the kids . . ."

"We can bring them, too."

"At a time like this?"

"You know Dad loves to see any of his grandkids. They'll cheer him up."

"Why does Grandfather need cheering up?" Genie asked.

"One of the cousins died, Genie," Dad answered. "I don't think you ever met her. Do any of you remember Sheila?"

All four children shook their heads. There had been deaths before this—Dad had twenty brothers and sisters, and a few aunts, uncles, and cousins had been lost in the past few years. Grandfather had children, grandchildren, and great-grandchildren now, and many of his children and grandchildren had adopted children or become foster parents with large families of their own. Carrie loved it when the whole family—well, most of it—had its annual reunion. It almost felt as if there was a whole country of Fletchers, even if not everyone used that last name. But she couldn't remember anyone named Sheila.

"She didn't go to any of the reunions," Dad said.

Carrie waited to see if her dad would say Sheila had been shot, but he didn't.

Her mom said, "Roy, is it safe? You don't think . . . there won't be anyone . . ."

"No, of course not. I'll call just to make sure. How soon can you be ready?"

"Kids?"

"Five minutes!" they shouted in unison, a familiar family joke about how much time they would need. Genie and Carrie took the boys by the hand and hustled them upstairs to get them out of their pajamas and dressed.

Carrie was already dressed, Genie just needed to put on shoes. Carrie followed Genie to her room, where she had just enough time to sign to her sister, *Thank you! I have so much to tell you.*

Genie signed back, *Not in the car. Mom will be watching.*

Mom didn't know sign language, and if she saw the two of them engaged in secret conversation, she would put a stop to it. Dad knew how to sign, so they were only supposed to practice when he could watch what they said.

At Grandfather's, Carrie signed as Genie finished tying her shoes.

Yes, her sister signed back, standing. Genie called out to the boys that it was time to go downstairs, even while she continued signing to Carrie, *Yes, at Grandfather's.*

CHAPTER 21

JOHN decided to go with the additional follow-up story about missing children, which kept me busy all morning. When I called Jane Serre about her son, Luke, I found her not only sober but purposeful. Gerry the murder victim buried on the Sheffield Estate was a different man from Gerry the ex-husband who had once been believed to have robbed her of her child. She was determined to find both her son and Gerry's killer. "That bastard not only took my child from me, he made me hate poor Gerry for no good reason. He killed Luke's father."

Neither of us mentioned our worst fears about what might have become of her son.

I started to call all the numbers I had gotten off Sheila Dolson's notepad. The first seven were numbers of news producers or city rooms. If I reached a friend in the news business when I called them, I asked what they could tell me about her. The answer was the same everywhere: She was viewed as an obvious publicity-seeker whose credentials were out-of-state and therefore suspect. Local law enforcement claimed that she had no relationship with the Las Piernas Police Department or Sheriff's Department. One or two news organizations had planned to check into her background with an eye toward possibly talking to her in the future, but now that there would be no future, those plans were canceled. Now, her murder was another matter, and what could I tell them about that?

Not much. Read the *Express* online and you could find out just about everything I knew about Sheila.

Ben Sheridan had called me before I left for work, angry that he had to learn about Sheila's death when Vince and Reed had come by first thing in the morning—and asked him if he had read the *Express* yet. He calmed down and admitted that it would have been a little awkward for me to have phoned him at one o'clock in the morning. He further admitted that he might be reacting so strongly because while he was talking to the detectives, he had received a call from Anna. "She's upset about the murder, upset about Sheila's lies, and . . . I'm not really the person she wants to turn to for comfort in this particular matter," he said.

After we hung up, I realized I needed to ask him some questions that I knew he wouldn't answer without permission from the authorities he was working for, so I called the coroner's office and asked for the county coroner, Carlos Hernandez. I wanted Carlos to give Ben permission to let me know if the teeth Sheila and Altair had supposedly found had anything to do with either Luke or Gerry Serre.

My husband had told me on more than one occasion that Carlos had a terrific sense of humor, but if Frank had seen that side of Carlos, I hadn't. Carlos, in my experience, treated the press with formality and seriousness. After a few moments of solemn consideration of my request, he said, "If the homicide detectives in charge of the case have no objections, I have no objections." He preferred to talk it over with Vince and Reed, and said that he'd ask Ben to call me, or would call me himself. As he ended the call, he said, "I'm sure you are in a great hurry, and I would hate for this office to appear to be too cautious."

That made me start to believe Frank could be right about him.

Ben called less than thirty minutes later to say—with no small amount of exasperation—that he believed the teeth had belonged to two different children.

"Because?" I asked.

"They are the same tooth."

"What do you mean?"

"Numbering systems probably won't mean anything to you, will they?"

"Give me terms that will mean something to our readers."

"What challenges you set before me!"

"Ben." I said it in a warning tone.

"Both teeth are deciduous upper central incisors which seem to have been lost through exfoliation."

"Ben."

"All right—for a layperson—they are deciduous teeth. That means they are baby teeth or milk teeth. Lost through exfoliation—they fell out in the natural way anyone loses baby teeth, just before the permanent teeth appear. You have four central incisors—these are upper front teeth. A child's upper front teeth."

"Okay, so this is why Vince and Reed were joking around about the tooth fairy."

"Yes. These teeth fall out and then the permanent teeth emerge. Except these two aren't from the same child, because they are from exactly the same position in the mouth—left front teeth. They could not be from the same child, because every child has only one such tooth in his or her mouth."

"Could one of them be from Luke Serre?"

"He disappeared two years ago, at the age of three. If he lost one of his front teeth then, it would most likely have occurred through trauma. That doesn't seem to be the case here. Some children lose their baby teeth by natural means as early as five— so if he is alive, it is possible, yes, that out of all the children on Earth, he is one of the two who once owned these teeth. But it seems unlikely to me that two years after he went missing, five-year-old Luke would take his tooth and another child's tooth, then make a trek some distance behind the fences surrounding the Sheffield Estate, to the place where his father's dismembered remains were buried, and leave those teeth in that place before hiking out again."

"I see what you mean. Until recently, the only person who knew where the remains were buried was Gerry Serre's killer, and the killer really would have no reason to take them there, either."

"I agree. Not impossible, but unlikely."

"Any chance of finding out who those teeth belonged to?"

"I don't know if they'll be able to run DNA on them or not. I strongly suspect Sheila got these teeth from a dentist."

"Why would a dentist give them to her?"

"Training."

"You mean for dogs?"

"Yes. Teeth are among the least objectionable materials to train with. Cadaver dog and search dog trainers often have a network of doctors, dentists, pathologists, and others who understand that the handlers need human biological materials for training purposes. It's completely understandable, but not always done on a strictly legal basis, so most SAR dog owners would prefer not to talk to anyone about what's in their freezers."

"Remind me to be careful about what I defrost out of yours."

He laughed. "You mean dinner at your place isn't potluck tonight?"

"No, strictly our treat."

N O T long after we hung up, the security desk downstairs contacted me. I had a visitor: Ben's now ex-girlfriend, Anna Stover.

CHAPTER 22

GENIE wasn't sure why the thought surprised her, but it did: Grandfather's house was made for children. All the other times she had been here, she had been so happy to see her cousins and to play with them, she never noticed how different his house was from that of most grown-ups.

Now, as she walked with Carrie down a pathway through the children's garden, she thought about all the ways in which Grandfather's house was unlike any other she had ever visited, even big houses. Most of the houses she had visited belonged to other members of their family, and they were houses with big yards and any number of rooms given over to the children of the house—the Fletcher family believed strongly in home schooling, so if you weren't lucky enough to go to Fletcher Academy, your house probably had a playroom and a room that was used as a schoolroom. But none of the homes of her dozens of cousins were as close to being a children's castle as was Grandfather's house.

The big house had multiple playrooms, each filled with toys, games, and puzzles in seemingly endless supply. If there was an emphasis on educational toys, no one minded much. There were dolls and stuffed animals and toy soldiers to play with, too.

In the art room, you could work with clay, Play-Doh, papier-mâché, or finger paints—that was Genie's favorite room. It even had digital cameras and a scanner and a computer that you could use to change the photos into funny pictures.

Carrie liked the music rooms. One music room was for playing music, the other for listening. The listening room was filled with beanbag chairs, and if you wanted to just sit quietly and listen through headphones, you could do so. You didn't have to listen to the same music everyone else was listening to—you could choose your own. It was also a nice place to take a nap.

You could always go into one of the spare bedrooms, of course—some rooms were for girls and some rooms were for boys. Genie didn't like them so much if she was really tired, because the girls were always gossiping and giggling and keeping her awake. Sometimes, though, overnight parties were held here for groups of girl cousins near the same age—she didn't mind staying up all night then! The only bad part was coming home and answering all of Mom's questions. Mom didn't like them to go to slumber parties. Or be away from her much for any reason.

When Mom acted like that, it just made Genie feel restless. She had even thought of running away, someday. But then she thought of not being with Carrie and the boys—as well as practical matters, like who would hire a kid to do work—and she would give up on the idea. At least for the time being.

Still, she thought that if she learned more about computers, she might be able to do it one day. People couldn't tell how old you are on the computer. She knew this because of something her dad had said about weird men who posed as children on the Internet, men who then stole children and did terrible things to them. Genie believed him, but she also figured that if a man could pretend to be a kid, a kid could pretend to be an adult. It might work.

Her dad helped other people in the family with their computer problems, so people expected his kids to know about them, but this was not the case. They weren't allowed to use computers very often. There was a great computer room here. The computers at Grandfather's house weren't hooked up to the Internet, but there were hundreds of games and a huge amount of learning software on them. Most of her cousins were allowed to get on the Internet when they were at their own houses, at least sometimes. The fact that she and her siblings were not allowed on it at all frustrated Genie. She tried to learn what she could about it from her cousins, but one day Mom overheard her talking about it and she got in trouble. Dad said they would learn about it when they were a little older.

It didn't make any sense to her. Dad made some of his money by working on the Internet. Genie once got into a lot of trouble by trying to sneak onto his work computer in his office. She had guessed two of his passwords, but not the one that made the browser work. Somehow Dad was able to figure out that she was the one who had used it. Probably because none of the other kids would have dared to try it.

Maybe she would go up to the computer room while they were here, but she would probably spend most of her time outside. There was a swimming pool and a fully equipped playground at Grandfather's house. No one fussed at you here if you got dirt or grass stains on your clothes, or spilled something on your T-shirt. This house always had spare clothes you could change into while yours were cleaned or mended. And if you were the one who needed mending, you would be all right, too—many of the staff had first-aid training. Besides, Uncle Roger and Aunt Susan were doctors and they lived in the house next door. If they weren't home, you could get help at the office of their pediatrics practice, which was less than a mile away.

The staff members weren't strangers. Some of Grandfather's adopted children still lived with him, helping him with his businesses and the school, or helping him with the house and property itself. Other aunts and uncles lived in nearby houses.

Fletcher children and grandchildren lived in other parts of the country and in Europe, Dad had once told Genie, but he also said that most of them liked to be close to home. The uncles Genie knew best were the ones who were closest to her dad, Roy Fletcher.

One was Uncle Giles, who was Dad's oldest brother—Dad let Uncle Giles boss him around. He seemed very ordinary, but when he told people what to do, they always did it. Genie wasn't immune to this herself. Mom sometimes tried to argue with him, but she never won.

Her dad was also close to Uncle Dexter, who was a lawyer. He was kind of quiet. Everyone in the family talked about how good-looking he was, but Genie couldn't see it. His wife, Aunt Maggie, was very beautiful, but she didn't seem to care about Uncle Dex or what he did. She always seemed bored, and was one of only a small number of the older women who didn't seem interested in him. Genie thought that he was interesting, but not in the way that most of the aunts did.

To Genie, who could admit to herself that she was a little bit of a spy when it came to the adults in her life, Uncle Dex's effect on the older women was fascinating and worthy of study. Whenever he came into a room, some of the aunts blushed. Eventually, most of them found a way to stand near Uncle Dex for at least a few minutes. They touched him—put a hand on his arm or shoulder, things like that—more often than they touched the other men in the family. He would look at whoever was talking to him as if they were telling him a valuable secret. He listened to them and said nice things to them. He had a smile—even Genie liked his smile—that made other people smile back at him. He might joke a little with the women, but he never did anything to make the uncles mad at him. Uncle Dex always seemed able to be cautious without letting other people realize he was being cautious.

Mom dressed up a little more when she knew Uncle Dex was coming over. Genie noticed that Uncle Dex was careful to stay near Dad when Mom was around, never came over when Dad wasn't home, and still managed to compliment Mom and make her smile.

Uncle Nelson was the other uncle who visited them sometimes. He was usually too busy to spend much time with them, and seemed uncomfortable around children, but he always made a point of asking Genie how she was doing and if she was happy. He was married, too, but Genie had never met his wife. Mom said he'd married someone who didn't like being around all the Fletchers, especially at big family gatherings. Genie couldn't understand that.

Naturally, not everyone was close to every other member of the family, but Grandfather had worked hard to make sure that family was the most important thing in his children's lives. Genie always felt loved and safe here. That wasn't just because there was always someone keeping an eye on the children, or lots of adults to embrace you and ask you how you were doing. Here, just like at the academy, there were cameras and security people. Most of the latter were Fletchers, too.

This day was an especially quiet one, even though there were a great many family members present. The grown-ups, especially Grandfather, had required their attention when they first arrived. Grandfather had been so sad. Some of the oldest cousins took Troy and Aaron to play in another room, while Grandfather spent time telling the older children (the ones who were nine and older, which meant Genie just made the cut) about Sheila, one of their cousins. Grandfather told them about Sheila's life, how her birth mother had given her to the Fletchers because she knew that Sheila's father was a man who would never be kind to a baby girl.

A few years ago, Sheila had wanted to find her birth mother, and Grandfather had helped her to do that. He said that he was glad Sheila and her birth mother had time to know each other before Sheila's birth mother died, but he was even happier that Sheila had moved back here to Las Piernas. He went on to tell them that he didn't want to frighten them, but he did want them to know that someone had killed her, and he was telling them that because he wanted everyone to be extra alert and not talk to strangers.

The idea of a murder in the family was shocking, kind of thrilling, and scary to Genie all at once. Grandfather didn't tell them much about the murder. He just said the police were working on it. He ended the way he often ended talks with the whole family, reminding them to love one another, to work as hard as they could to learn, to use what talents they had been given by God, and to help one another.

You couldn't help feeling sad for Grandfather today.

They all knew that other people wanted to try to hurt Grandfather through his children.

Once, Genie told Carrie that she wanted to run away, and Carrie freaked out. She didn't tell their parents, but she pleaded with Genie not to leave, and Genie began to see that Carrie needed her. And Carrie told her that she needed to think about not hurting Grandfather, and Genie could see her point.

Being a Fletcher wasn't so bad, after all. People took care of you. If she wanted to go to a good college, and showed that she meant it by studying hard, the Fletchers would help her get into that college. When she decided what she wanted to be when she grew up, Fletchers would help her then, too. When she had children, and her cousins had children, they would all help those children to be happy and healthy and successful. Fletchers helped one another.

Most people outside the family admired the Fletchers, but some people were jealous, of course. They would say that love, learning, and *money* made a difference. In her lessons at home, Mom and Dad made sure that Genie already knew these facts by heart: If you were wealthy, no matter how much you gave to charities or your community, no matter how much good you did, there would always be a few people who thought you owed them what you had earned. Or they would believe you would not miss what they stole from you. A very few wanted to hurt Fletcher children just because they were Fletchers. That was why you could not talk to strangers. That was why the family had to have security people.

Genie wondered if the person who killed Cousin Sheila had done it because she was a Fletcher. When she asked Mom about it, she got a lecture about not asking prying questions. But then she asked Dad about it, and he said, "Probably." He was upset, but he hugged her and told her not to be afraid, that he would always keep her safe.

Being kept safe was one of the reasons you were home-schooled or schooled at the academy and could not go to a public school. Public school was a place where you didn't learn as much, anyway—something Genie was sure was true from the rare occasions when she encountered other children her age and tried to converse with them. Most ended up calling her names that meant she was smarter than they were, and although she could never understand why that should be considered an insult to *her*, it definitely felt like one. It was so much easier to be around other Fletcher children. They had better manners, too.

Not all of the Fletcher children were supersmart, of course, but they all got the best education possible, and the family always tried to help its children discover what they were good at and make the most of their talents. From what Grandfather had said that morning, Genie got the impression that Sheila wasn't one of the supersmart ones.

Grandfather told them that he didn't expect them to be sad about Sheila if they did not know her, but he hoped they would say a little prayer for her before they went to bed tonight. He believed she was in heaven because she had spent the last two years of her life learning how to find lost children with special dogs, which was a good use of her talents.

After that, the children were told they could have the day off from classes and that they should just spend time with their brothers, sisters, and cousins, and enjoy being a family.

Mom stopped them before they left the room, probably to ask them where they would be, but Uncle Giles saw her do this and quickly came up to her. "Victoria, I believe Roy is looking for you." She looked as if she might say she would be there in a few minutes, but he shepherded the girls along with him, saying over his shoulder, "Go to your husband. We *will* keep an eye on the girls. I promise. Your children are not in any danger here."

When they were outside, Carrie said, "Thank you, Uncle Giles."

"For what? Rescuing you from your mother?" he asked, then laughed when both girls blushed. "It was my pleasure, Carrie. Now, you and Genie enjoy your day."

When he had walked back into the house, Carrie said, "Mom's going to be mad."

"Yes," Genie said. "So we might as well have fun, because she's going to be mad, anyway." Genie thought Carrie worried too much about Mom getting mad. Then again, Genie got into trouble more often than her older sister.

CARRIE and Genie had played with their cousins for a time, then wandered off together toward the children's garden. They said they wanted to see how their little vegetable patches were doing. No one questioned this—the girls did this every time they came here. One of the cousins mentioned that it would be muddy, then smiled and said, "But that will make it easier to pull weeds!"

Genie wondered why she couldn't be like that, what Dad called "good natured." But there was something restless in her, and she decided she just never would be someone other girls called "sweet," not even as sweet as Carrie.

It was muddy, but there were boards and stepping-stones to help them navigate their way. The rain had made the garden very green this year, Genie thought. For a time they pulled weeds, although not many had been allowed to grow up among the carrots and beans and tomatoes. Then they went into the greenhouse, where they could deliver the weeds for composting and wash the worst of the mud off their hands.

Edith, one of their favorite aunts, was there. She greeted the girls cheerily, always pleased to see two of her protégées. Edith had found her talent here. She loved the garden, and loved to teach children about plants and their care, so she happily set them up with jars and pots and young plants that needed to be moved into bigger containers. April was a busy time for Edith, and before long, she wandered away from them to work on projects of her own.

Genie gathered the jars to her side of the table they worked at.

"I wonder why you do that," Carrie said.

"What?"

"Pick the jars. You leave me all the pots."

Genie blushed.

"I don't mind," Carrie said quickly. "I just wondered."

Genie checked to see that Edith was not nearby, then said in a low voice, "I like the name."

"Jar?"

Genie shook her head. "Mason. That name has . . . some connection to me."

Carrie looked puzzled. She signed, *Freemasons? Stonecutters?*

After a moment, Genie signed, *I knew someone named Mason. Last name?*

She shook her head. *No, first name.*

From the past? Carrie signed back. *Before?* No need to explain before what.

Yes. A man. He was nice to me. He made me laugh. But she didn't feel very happy thinking about him now. It made her feel unsettled.

After a brief hesitation, Carrie signed, *Your father?*

"I don't know," Genie said softly, frowning, as she filled a jar with soil. "That doesn't seem right." She signed, *Brother or cousin, maybe.*

Carrie made a motion toward the plants they were supposed to be transplanting. Genie made herself get back to work for a minute or two with her pots. If Edith came back and didn't see much accomplished . . . But Edith would be kind, and merely think they'd been chatting with each other instead of working, and that would be okay with her. Edith was one of the oldest of the Fletcher children, and she had not been able to have kids of her own. She was sometimes a little rebellious, and muttered as she worked. More than once, sitting next to her at a family gathering, Genie had heard her say something about how plants grew best if they weren't crowded, in moments when Genie knew she wasn't talking about plants at all. It occurred to Genie that the relative privacy they enjoyed in the greenhouse was not accidental.

Did Edith like being alone? That was something else to think about.

Gradually, with whispers and signs exchanged between gardening work, Carrie told Genie about the conversation she had overheard between Mom and Dad this morning. Genie was as amazed as Carrie about their mom's career in journalism.

"I have to find a way to get a copy of the newspaper article about missing kids," Carrie said.

"That will be easy," Genie said. "Leave it to me."

"How?"

"Tomorrow is trash day, remember? It's my turn to take the trash and recycling out to the curb."

Carrie frowned. *We don't get the newspaper. How can that help? The neighbors do. I've taken theirs before.*

Carrie's eyes widened.

"Honestly, Carrie. You aren't the only person who has realized that things can come *into* the house from recycling."

The color drained from Carrie's face.

I know about the book, Genie signed. *Don't worry, I won't tell.*

Despite these reassurances, tears were gathering in Carrie's eyes. Genie felt bad, even worse as Carrie looked down at the pot in front of her, obviously trying hard not to cry. Tears began to roll off the end of her nose and into the soil.

"I'm sorry! I'm sorry!" Genie whispered, then looked up and saw a woman crossing the lawn with purposeful strides. "Oh no. Mom."

Carrie looked up, then looked at Genie a little desperately. She was scared.

Genie knew exactly what she feared, of course. "We'll have to say why you've been crying. She'll ask and ask about it."

"I'll say Cousin Sheila," Carrie whispered.

"She'll never believe it," Genie said. "Tell her I was mean to you."

"No way."

An idea came to Genie. She hesitated only a few seconds, then knocked one of the jars against the edge of the table. It broke with what seemed an explosion of sound. She held one of the bigger shards toward her older sister. "Cut yourself. Just a little. Hurry!"

Carrie found the resolve to do this just as Aunt Edith called, "What happened?"

"Oh, Carrie! You're hurt!" Genie said, not needing to fake her remorse. The cut was bleeding more than she had expected, and she had not missed Carrie's wince of pain. Genie grabbed a paper towel and pressed it to Carrie's hand. She looked up into Carrie's face, worried.

"It isn't so bad," Carrie managed to say, and stopped holding back the rest of her tears.

CHAPTER 23

ANNA STOVER didn't look so hot. She was pale, had dark circles under her eyes, and it was easy to see she had been crying. I will own up to feeling a little smug about that. She had moved out of her house and broken it off with Ben with a damned note. This was supposed to be her big Independence Day, but life had just pissed on her sparklers.

She stared off into space, a picture of distraction. She hadn't heard me or seen me come down the stairs, I guess, because I startled the hell out of her by saying, "What can I do for you, Anna?"

She shivered a little. Maybe from the chill I put into the question. She looked up into my face, studying it for a moment before glancing toward Geoff, the ancient security guard. I followed the glance and saw that Geoff was looking at her with tender sympathy. Geoff, who by some calculations is rising 130 (and by others, was Tutankhamen's boyhood friend), enjoys the sight of a pretty face but is not one to be swayed by such. So when I saw that look, I felt a little ashamed of my own reaction to her.

"Have you eaten?" I asked her.

"No, but—"

"Then let's have lunch," I said.

I looked back at Geoff, who was beaming at me. "I'll sign you out," he said. That damned old man has controlled my behavior for years.

I took her outside before anyone else from the paper had an unspoken suggestion to make and came to a halt. There's a burger place not far from the paper, but in just a few minutes it would be crowded with other reporters. I thought we might want a little more privacy. She needed to walk off some of that anxiety, anyway.

"There's a place down the street called Rosie's. Ever eaten there?"

"No. We can go wherever you like."

THE walk was silent but did seem to make her a little less woebegone. The sky was blue, the air was crisp and clean, the whole city had washed its face. When we stepped into Rosie's and found a booth, she revived enough to notice the decor of the bar and grill, which had been designed as a tribute to Rosie the Riveter. The proud daughter of a war worker had established the business, then willed it to an old coot named Johnny Smith, who gave me grief for not coming around more often. By the time Johnny and I were finished exchanging news of mutual friends and family, Anna said maybe she'd order something after all.

After we ordered, she said, "About Altair . . . ," but I held up a hand, giving her the palm-out stop sign.

"Until we've eaten lunch, I forbid discussion on three topics: Ben, Sheila, and Altair. After we've eaten, fine."

She looked completely stymied.

"Tell me about your new place. Do your dogs like it?"

She left the description of the new place at "renting a small two-bedroom with a big yard," and named an address very near the one where I had found Sheila Dolson's body the night before. She didn't seem to want to talk about the house, but it has never been hard to get Anna to talk about her dogs.

I wasn't just trying to get Anna to relax, although it seemed she did. I needed to shake off some of my own initial hostility. Working on a story, I would have guarded against softening my attitude over anecdotes about pets, but this was not an interview. Talking about Rascal and Devil enlivened her; hearing her stories reminded me of all the reasons I liked her. She was strong and bright and dedicated to doing good work. She was an animal lover. And someone who could look beyond the superficial when dealing with other people.

We finished eating in a more companionable mood. Johnny Smith came by and cleared the plates and asked us if we wanted coffee; she did, I didn't. Noticing that he was getting a crowd for lunch, when he came back with the coffee I asked if we were tying up his table, but he told us not to worry, a couple of other parties were leaving. He went off to help other customers.

Anna fiddled with the cream and sugar and stirring, then set the spoon aside. It was the starter's gun, I guess, because the next words out of her mouth were, "You must think I'm the worst judge of character on earth."

"Are you talking about Sheila or Ben or both?"

"I . . . I'd rather not talk about Ben. I've always hated spending time with a woman who whines about her lover or husband or ex—whatever the case may be. It's private. It's like, 'Hey, come over here and watch me wash my underwear!' No thanks."

I smiled. "I understand the sentiment, especially if you're talking about the people Frank calls 'town criers,' because they're crying about a breakup all over town."

"Exactly."

"Still, Anna—it can be tough to go through a breakup alone, whether you're the one leaving or the one left. Blabbing to strangers is one thing, confiding in one or two trusted friends is another." I paused. "That said, I guess I'd rather not be your confidante when it comes to Ben."

"Agreed." She traced the rim of the saucer again. "If you and Frank are angry with me, or don't want to have anything more to do with me, I'll understand."

"No need to draw a treaty up over it, is there?"

"No," she said softly. "No, it's not a war."

She gave a little shake of her head, took a sip of coffee, and said, "I misjudged Sheila. Ben suspected her of being a liar, and he was right. I admit that in some ways she was . . ."

"A fake?"

She flinched. "I don't know. I guess so. When I saw the newspaper this morning, I called Ben, and he told me that Sheila probably planted the teeth she supposedly found yesterday."

I didn't say anything—I was distracted by the fact that she had called Ben. Maybe this breakup was only temporary.

"It was a horrible shock, reading the story," she said absently, apparently caught up in her memories of seeing the front page. "It was a bad way to find out what had happened."

"I found out in a bad way myself."

She looked up at me, eyes widening. "I'm sorry—of course it was. I didn't mean that as a criticism. I mean, I know Ben thought you owed us—him—a call, but that's nonsense. You were probably exhausted by the time you got home."

"Yes. It was a long night."

"The article said it didn't look like a robbery?"

I hesitated. Something in her manner struck me as being a little sly. Or maybe I simply trusted her less because she had dumped Ben. Still, I was uneasy. Not knowing where the conversation was headed, I answered cautiously. "No. At first I thought we might have interrupted one in progress, but the police seem to have ruled that out. She didn't own much of value, and the dog would have deterred most prowlers."

"Altair was crated, though."

"I wanted to ask you about that—was he usually crated at night? There were a couple of dog beds in the house."

"She told me she crated him in the evenings. Most of the time, whenever I was at the house, it was during the day and he was loose. She told me she also used the crate during the day when she had to leave him alone, which wasn't often."

"Why crate him, then?"

"Well . . . like a lot of energetic, smart dogs who begin to feel bored if they're left alone too long, Altair can entertain himself in ways that are not appreciated by most humans." She smiled. "Sheila told me he has a real knack when it comes to opening kitchen cabinets and refrigerator doors."

I began to wonder if I should call home.

"She also used the crate for transport," Anna went on. "Or for search situations when there were a lot of other dogs around."

"In any case," I said, "a robber wouldn't know that Altair was in a crate until after he was in the house, right? Most wouldn't take that chance."

"No . . ."

"Look, Anna, do you know if Sheila had any enemies here in town?"

"Other than Ben?"

"Not being her blind follower doesn't make him her enemy," I said tightly.

"No, of course not. For God's sake, I'm not suggesting he would have harmed her. That's not even in Ben's nature. She saw him as an enemy, though, I think."

"Maybe so. Anyone else?"

"No, and even though I spent quite a bit of time around her, she never complained to me that anyone was mad at her."

I found myself wondering if Sheila was capable of perceiving that someone was angry with her. She had always seemed self-absorbed. Even Altair was a way to get attention for herself.

"You said you spent a lot of time around her?"

"Well . . . not blaming him for it, but Ben has been gone a lot lately. Sheila was good company."

I couldn't imagine it. "What *did* you talk about?"

She hesitated. "I guess a lot of it was made up. Based in truth to some degree. Your story has made me face that today. She hadn't been married, so it was her mom who was the battered woman, not her. And what she told me about losing her house in a fire—that was about her mom's death, too. I don't think she ever had a child who got lost—although maybe she felt as if she was the lost child." She paused. "I guess the autopsy will show whether or not she had cancer."

"Let me guess. She told stories, and you listened in amazement."

"It's true—she misled all of us."

It occurred to me that I might not have been the first person to figure out that Sheila was a liar. Maybe Sheila had cheated some-one out of money, or scammed someone in a more serious way. "Okay, let's look at this another way—who were her friends?"

"She didn't have that many. I think all her friends were in the SAR group. I never heard her talk about anyone else." She frowned. "In retrospect, we kind of adopted her, and she seemed to have been very dependent on us, if you know what I mean. She wasn't someone who liked to be alone. She got people in the group to help her with things all the time. One of our team mem-bers all but gave her that place to live. People invited her over for supper."

"People became her neighbors."

She dropped her gaze, but said, "Yes. And even knowing what I know now, I'll miss her." She took a shaky breath. "I . . . I don't think it's really hit me yet. I can't really believe this has happened to her, that she's gone."

I didn't say anything.

"She wasn't a totally lost cause, you know. I think she was ex-perimenting, trying to find her way. Maybe if she had been al-lowed to live out her life, she would have changed, become a better person."

"Maybe," I said, sincerely doubting it. On the other hand, I was certain nobody had the right to use a gun to end Sheila Dolson's great experiment.

"It's confusing to me," Anna went on, "because she *did* have abilities, and she loved Altair, and I'll never believe that someone who was that good to a dog was a total write-off!"

I declined to bring up historical examples. What the hell could I say? "She was lucky to have a friend like you." There, that was honest.

She brooded in silence for a time. I was just about to make noises about getting back to the office when she said, "I under-stand you have Altair."

"Yes," I said warily.

"I'd be happy to take him."

"You and any number of other handlers, from all I can tell."

"You've been contacted?"

"No, just heard rumors from Illinois."

She ran a finger along the edge of her saucer. "Did Ben ask?"

"Not that it's any of your business, but—no."

She nodded once, as if she had just won a bet with herself. "So I'm offering to care for him until things are settled. Work with him."

"Bond with him?"

"He knows me. I've already worked with him."

"Sorry, Anna. No can do."

"Why not?" I could hear a little anger, just held back.

"It's not up to me."

She made a face.

"I promised to take care of him until her family or heirs are located. Do you know if Sheila had a will or an attorney?"

"No. No, I don't."

We parted company not long after that. I knew she had parked near the Wrigley Building, but she didn't walk back toward the paper with me. She said she wanted to do a little window-shopping while she was downtown.

I wasn't sorry that I made the walk back alone.

Not sorry that Altair wasn't going to be walking with her anytime soon, either. It wasn't unreasonable for a top trainer to want a dog that had performed so well, a dog she knew. Yet her petulance when I refused had surprised me, shown me a side of her personality I hadn't noticed before.

The truth was, I probably didn't know her as well as she knew Altair. All my previous contact with her had been in situations when Ben was with us, and often their dogs joined us as well. I had always found her easy to get along with, but I couldn't say that she had revealed a lot about herself. And her friendship with Sheila truly puzzled me.

I sighed and told myself to let it go. In all likelihood, I'd never see her again.

CHAPTER 24

BACK in the office, I continued calling phone numbers from Sheila's notepad. I got lucky on the second call.

"Thank you for calling Big Smile Dental," the voice on the other end of the line said. "This is Bobby."

"Uh, hi, Bobby . . . I'm sorry, I've misplaced the name of the dentist I was supposed to ask for."

"We have four dentists in our office," he said.

Before he could name them, I said, "This is the one who specializes in children's dentistry."

"Well, that would probably be Dr. Arnold Fletcher."

There are Fletchers all over Las Piernas, but I suppose my reading of so many stories on Caleb's history the day before made me dumbly repeat, "Dr. Fletcher?"

"Dr. *Arnold* Fletcher. We have two other Dr. Fletchers here."

"Oh, are they related to—" I stopped myself from saying Caleb's name.

"To one another? Yes. Dr. Arnold Fletcher is the father of Dr. Diane Fletcher and Dr. Kent Fletcher. Would you like to make an appointment for your child?"

"Is Dr. Arnold Fletcher in?"

"Not at the moment. Is this an emergency?"

"No. When do you expect him back?"

"Tomorrow," he said. "But I can't give you an appointment then—he's booked up through June. What is the child's name and age?"

"I don't think I'll make an appointment just now. Thanks."

I ended the call, perhaps a little abruptly. I spent a little time doing Internet searches on Dr. Arnold Fletcher, came up with a rather blah Web site for his practice and the kind of information just about any dentist might have on any site, but clearly he was devoted to children's dentistry.

Why would Sheila, new in town, without children of her own, call a children's dentist? If this dentist was the source of those teeth Altair "discovered," why had Sheila chosen him as her supplier?

I had a lot of work to do on my missing children story, which wouldn't run until later in the week, but it was a major project.

My curiosity about the dentist would have to wait.

CHAPTER 25

LONG before the end of dinner, I was glad Caleb had agreed to come over. Ethan had never complained to us, but I could see that he was enjoying spending time with someone else who was under thirty.

Ben was quieter than usual, but everyone had expected that, and we liked him too much to force him to pretend we were cheering him up. The dogs made more of an effort at changing his mood than we did, and succeeded better, too.

We were sitting at the table, dishes cleared, drinking coffee, when I asked Caleb if the Fletcher dentists were relatives of his.

"I don't know. There are a zillion Fletchers in Las Piernas. My dad kind of pulled away from the family, so I don't really know more than one or two of them."

"A zillion?" Ethan raised his brows. "I think I'm very close to zero in my own family. There's an aunt and a couple of cousins somewhere, but that's it."

"You may be luckier than you think. I have over twenty uncles and aunts, but I was just a little kid the last time I was around most of them." He smiled. "My dad called them the F.C. and used to tell my uncle Nelson that it stood for Fletcher Clan, but he told me and Mason that the *F* stood for . . . uh, something else."

"Do you know why he thought that?" I asked.

"Yeah, he talked about it with Mason and me, 'cause he didn't want us to get trapped into their whole deal."

"What whole deal?"

"Dad thought that after my grandmother Fletcher died, it almost became more like a cult than a family. You were supposed to send your kids to their school, you were supposed to go to the doctors and lawyers and accountants who were members of the family. Dad thought it was weird."

Ben shot me a look that I read perfectly: I had better not be working my way toward talking about the family murders.

To my surprise—and Ben's—Frank was the one who brought up the topic.

"Is Mason's new lawyer still trying to get the conviction overturned?"

"Yes," Caleb answered. "There are a lot of steps to go through, though."

I glanced at Ethan. He obviously knew this much of Caleb's history.

"Fill me in," I said.

"It's kind of a long story," Caleb said. "You know the basics?"

"Yes."

"Okay, so my mom's dad died about a year after Mason went to prison. And my Grandmother Delacroix . . . well, I guess you'd say she started thinking differently when he wasn't around."

"In what way?"

"She was never as hard-nosed about Mason as Grandfather Delacroix had been, and I think after Grandfather died, she started to regret the way she acted during the trial. With Jenny missing and Mason in prison, I was the only available grandchild, and I had stopped speaking to my grandparents after Mason got arrested. I was so angry with them for believing he could hurt Dad or Jenny." He paused. "I still hope to find out what happened to Jenny. I still think it's possible that she's alive. But at this point . . . I understand why other people don't share that belief. I think one reason my grandmother and I started to get along again was that she started to believe that Mason is innocent and Jenny might be alive."

"What about your mom?" Ethan asked. "Did she get along better with your grandmother after your grandfather died?"

Caleb smiled. "She did until Uncle Nelson became her new husband. Grandmother Delacroix couldn't stand Uncle Nelson.

He kept trying to get her to let him 'take care' of her finances, and I think he must have been a little too pushy about it. When she made out her will, she made sure my mom and Uncle Nelson couldn't touch any of her money. Not that they needed it, but I know it chapped Uncle Nelson when he found out about it after she died."

"So did she leave it all to you?" Ethan asked.

"Before she died, I convinced her that Mason had been framed. It was . . . I guess if I end up failing at everything else, at least I did that for Mason. She got Mason to fire his attorney and hire a new one. She set up a trust to help with his legal fees, and so he'd have something to live on after he got out."

"And you?"

"She left me enough to pay off my undergraduate loans, made it possible for me to stay in graduate school, and gave me a couple of my dad's paintings. She had bought them a long time ago, kind of helping my folks when they were first starting out, I think. It was the coolest thing she could have done for me, because after my dad died, we had to sell all of his other works."

"The new attorney shouldn't have any trouble getting the conviction overturned," Frank said. "Mason's case is on the LPPD crime lab's potential dry-labbing list."

"What's dry-labbing?" Ethan asked.

"One of the worst things a forensic scientist can be accused of. Basically, faking results—claiming you tested material you didn't really test. You know there was a scandal in our department's lab?"

"Yes. I just didn't know that term."

"We fired a few people over it. And it's costing the city a fortune to deal with all the problems it has caused. An independent team investigating the lab has looked at all the cases those people worked on, and come up with a list of cases that will need review."

"They've already had to let some people out of prison, right?" Ethan asked.

"A few. There will undoubtedly be more, especially in those cases where there are no eyewitnesses or clear motives. I'd think

Mason's would have a good chance of being overturned if the forensic evidence wasn't really there."

"It isn't easy to get someone out of prison once they're in," Caleb said. "Even if they're truly innocent. No one could place Mason at the scene, but the murder weapon was with him."

"I've always thought that scene with the car was a little too perfect," Frank said.

Caleb gave him a grateful look. "I don't hear that too often from the Las Piernas Police Department."

"I don't imagine the department would be as pleased as you are if they knew that one of their detectives said it," Ben said dryly. "So let's keep this discussion confidential."

"Sure," Caleb said, "but still—thanks, Frank."

I mentally reviewed what I had read in newspaper accounts about the evidence in the case.

"The evidence was processed by our lab, not San Bernardino Sheriff's?" I asked.

"Crime started in Las Piernas," Frank said. "The case was ours."

"The headache, the paperwork, and the costs, you mean," Ben said.

Frank smiled. "Yes, those, too."

"I have copies of most of the reports," Caleb said to me. "Are you interested in seeing them?"

"If she's not, I am," Ethan said.

Ah. A cure for Ethan's boredom. "Let's both take a look at them. Frank, don't you know some of the guys in San Bernardino's department?"

"Sure."

"Do you think you could get the name of the officer who found the car?"

"Tadeo Garcia," Caleb said. "He's retired. He's not too friendly. At least he wasn't to me."

"Is he married?" I asked.

"Yes. His wife is nice. She was mad at him for not talking to me."

"How long ago did you try talking to him?"

"Oh, it wasn't long after Mason was charged. Maybe four and a half years ago, something like that. He wouldn't talk to Mason's new attorney, either."

"Well, maybe it's time for someone else to have another try. I may make a trip out to San Bernardino."

"Take me along?" Ethan pleaded.

"If your doctor says okay, sure."

W E made it an early evening—Ethan was wearing down, and I could tell he was determined to get enough rest to get the doctor's permission for the trek to San Bernardino. Not a grand outing, but he was excited about the idea of any change of scenery.

As Ben and Caleb were leaving, Ben let Ethan, Frank, and Caleb walk ahead of us a little bit. When they were out of earshot, Ben said to me, "Thanks for offering to help Caleb with his brother's case."

"I thought you were opposed to my getting involved."

"Irene, there was never a chance in hell of your keeping your nose out of it."

"Speaking of nosing in, I should probably tell you that Anna came by for lunch today."

"No need to report contact with her," he said, seeming faintly amused.

"If it's any comfort, she didn't want to gossip about you."

"I'm not surprised," he said, then gave me a crooked grin. "I'd be lying if I didn't tell you that I'm also relieved. Talk to you soon—I want to know why you are interested in dentists."

I swore under my breath and he laughed, causing Frank and Caleb to look back at us.

It's so damned hard to get anything past Ben. And judging from the looks on the three other faces, he wasn't the only one I had to worry about.

A reporter, a homicide detective, and two forensic scientists. I was going to have to watch my step.

CHAPTER 26

Wednesday, April 26
9:15 A.M.
HUNTINGTON BEACH

CARRIE allowed her mother to fuss over the cut on her hand. The cut wasn't deep, and there was no chance that it was infected—it had been treated immediately, of course. Mom was worried, though, and had been hovering over her ever since it happened.

This was both a good thing and a bad thing. It was good because right now Mom wasn't paying any attention to Genie, who was outside the house, going through the next-door neighbor's recycling bin. Dad was gone, away at a meeting of some kind, and the boys were here, watching Mom change the bandage. They were staring with fascination at the cut, which looked much worse than it felt.

The bad part was not the pain of the cut but the guilt now weighing on Carrie. Why should she question anything about her parents? She had a good life. She knew other children were unhappy and uncared for, were lonely and ignored. Her mother loved her and was so protective of her. Sure, sometimes she felt a little hemmed in by that, a little smothered, but what was really wrong with being loved so much? Dad loved her, too. Her parents never hurt their children, they really rarely lost their tempers.

Why ask herself about *before*? It just might turn out to be something bad. Wouldn't that be the only reason it was a secret? And if it was bad, then it might bring an end to this life she had now. Maybe she would be taken away from these loving people who had adopted her. Maybe she would never see Genie or Aaron or Troy again. She felt a tear roll down her cheek at the thought of how bad she had been, sneaking around, eavesdropping, wanting to know things that were none of her business.

Her mother saw the tear and gently wiped it away, saying, "Oh, honey. I'm sorry, did I hurt you?"

"No—" she choked out.

She could hear Genie coming upstairs, going into her room briefly, then heard her washing up in a nearby bathroom.

"Is Carrie going to die?" Aaron asked, his face puckering up in sympathetic reaction to her distress.

"No, silly," Carrie said with a watery laugh, hugging him to her side with her free hand. "I'm just being a baby."

"It could get infected," said Troy, almost hopefully.

"We won't let it, will we?" said Mom.

"We Fletchers take care of one another," Aaron said, already knowing the family gospel.

Genie came into the room just then and said, "Of course we do." She came closer and frowned in concern, though Carrie wasn't sure if the frown was at the sight of the cut. "Everything okay?" Genie asked, studying Carrie's face.

Suddenly Carrie thought about Genie risking getting into big trouble, just to help her. Genie, who also had a *before*.

"Everything's fine," she said.

We Fletchers take care of each other.

"Do you think you'll feel up to our shopping trip?" Mom asked, her head bent in concentration as she lightly wrapped the injured hand in gauze. This was their day to go to the grocery store. Dad would watch the boys while Genie and Carrie accompanied Mom to the supermarket. Carrie always loved this outing.

"Sure, I'm fine, really."

I T was just before they went to the store that Genie managed to whisper to her, "I couldn't find one."

"No newspapers?" Carrie whispered back in disbelief.

"I tried five houses."

"Five! Oh my gosh—you could have been caught!"

Genie waved a dismissive hand at this danger. "Everyone around here gets the *Orange County Register*. We need the Las Piernas paper. I should have looked for it at Grandfather's house. Maybe we can get it at the store."

But when they went to the store, they didn't go in through the entrance they usually used. Carrie and Genie exchanged a glance. They didn't need to say what they both knew at that moment— Mom used this other door because the newspaper vending machines were next to the usual one.

Genie quickly signed, *Don't worry. I'll get one.*

Carrie didn't know whether to fear or admire the look of determination on her sister's face.

CHAPTER 27

THE four men sat in silence. Giles, Nelson, and Dexter had listened to their brother Roy without interrupting him. Giles, the oldest of the four, was pleased that the silence stretched.

Graydon Fletcher had often said that if someone laid his or her problems before you, you were to think of it as a privilege, and not respond without taking time to carefully consider what had been said to you. One of Dad's many lessons.

Nelson would be the first to speak, of course. Nelson didn't really have a tremendous amount of impulse control.

Roy was better at keeping his head, but he was also better at keeping secrets. That was useful unless those secrets were kept from his brothers. Giles wondered if Nelson and Dexter suspected that Roy was not being completely truthful just now.

Dexter probably did. Dexter would have made an excellent spy, Giles thought. He could ferret out information from anyone, with the possible exception of Giles. Dexter wouldn't dare to question Giles—he held his eldest brother in a kind of awe. It pleased Giles that this should be so.

Dexter wasn't the only one who looked to Giles for guidance— Nelson and Roy thought of Giles as their problem solver, a role he had taken on from an early time in each of their lives.

Giles knew things about each of them that none of the others knew. He knew, for example, that Nelson still felt guilty for lusting after their late brother Richard's wife. Although Elisa was Nelson's wife now, Nelson had wanted her for years before Richard's death. It was as if Nelson carried Richard's ghost with him, even into bed. If Nelson didn't learn to get over that, he would ultimately ruin his marriage.

Nelson had also badly mishandled matters with Caleb. Giles frowned, thinking of it. He must make additional efforts to bring Caleb closer to the family.

Nelson was doing better with Mason. He had used the family's considerable influence and resources to ensure that his stepson was placed in a facility closer to Las Piernas. The boy was initially ungrateful, but Giles thought that perfectly understandable, given Nelson's testimony at the trial. Elisa had known how much effort Nelson had made, though, and her gratitude had helped Nelson's courtship.

Eventually, Mason came to appreciate Nelson's regular visits. Giles thought of Mason as one of the Fletchers, and hoped to one day help the boy win his release, if it wasn't going to cause the family too many problems. Mason was bright and talented, after all. Giles was keeping an eye on the situation. At the moment he was far more concerned that Nelson's fear of losing Elisa would ultimately drive her away.

Dexter, whose birth parents must have been extraordinarily good-looking to produce such a handsome child, suffered no similar worries about his wife, Maggie. He was as emotionally detached from her as she was from him. She enjoyed being connected to the Fletchers. She enjoyed Dex's wealth. She also enjoyed the envy her marriage to a handsome man brought out in other women. She would do nothing to jeopardize any of that. On the whole, Giles was glad Dex and Maggie had no children, adopted or of their own. She worked at the school, where she was the sort of teacher who inspired the children's attachment simply because she was hard to win over.

He thought that might have been the case with Dex—he was attracted to the aloof. Now that he had captured Maggie, she was no longer of interest to him. That led him to hunt on other, more dangerous ground at times. But Maggie would not cause problems for the Fletchers. Giles had no concerns about Maggie— which did not mean he relaxed his vigilance. His vigilance was exactly why he had no concerns.

Roy. Roy's wife, Victoria—formerly Bonnie Creci Ives—had

been difficult from the beginning. Roy had been crazy about her when he first met her, insistent on bringing her into the family. He was her rescuer, in those days. So the family had taken extraordinary measures to include her and her child in their number, rather than risk losing Roy.

Alas, Roy was finding Victoria to be a difficult wife. Roy was not one who would abandon his children, and imperfect though it might be, Giles didn't believe for a moment that Roy would give up on the marriage. Now Roy had brought his problems to his brothers, seeking advice. Victoria was the topic at hand. As Giles had expected, it was Nelson who spoke first.

"Maybe Victoria is right. Maybe Huntington Beach is too close," Nelson said. "I mean, I don't want you to move away, Roy, but if your wife thinks she'll be recognized by a reporter . . ."

"I can't move much farther away," Roy said. "Not unless I give up a large part of my business. Most of my client base is here in Las Piernas. And I don't want to be any farther away from the family."

"What exactly is it that Victoria is afraid of?" Dex asked.

"The article that you showed me. The one in the *Express* about missing children. Understandably, seeing that her former coworker—this Irene Kelly—is looking into cases of missing children disturbs her. She knows her ex-husband is still looking for the child who used to be known as Carla Ives. Victoria thinks Irene Kelly has a grudge against her or something, and will be fired up to try to find the woman she knew as Bonnie."

"The woman she knew as Bonnie *Creci,*" Giles said. "A woman who was long gone from the paper before she became Bonnie Ives. Her name has changed a second time now. There is no reason to believe Irene Kelly has any reason to know of Victoria Fletcher's existence, let alone that Bonnie and Victoria are the same person. The child's name has been changed as well, and she's not in the public school system. How is it that this reporter will find her?"

"None of these stories have mentioned Blake Ives," Nelson added. "And now that it has published one set of stories on the topic, it probably won't do so again, at least not for a year or two."

"Besides," Dex said, "Huntington Beach isn't really in the news coverage area of the *Las Piernas News Express*."

"I've told her all of this a million times," Roy said, shaking his head.

"Do you think she's losing her nerve?" Dex asked, getting right to the heart of the matter.

Roy hesitated, then said, "I worry about that, given her history of running away from problems."

"What would she do? Try to go back to her first husband?"

"No. She knows I'd find her. She also knows Blake Ives won't forgive her for taking the child. He undoubtedly still thinks of her as the alcoholic he last knew her to be."

"She can't divorce you." Nelson stated this as fact.

"We are married, so technically, I suppose she could," said Roy. "Our marriage was in another state, but under her real name. Her ex-husband believes she was with another man when the child went missing, so her ex has never known about me. If she starts proceedings to divorce me, though, she risks calling attention to herself from a system that's been looking for her in connection with a missing child. And she knows that would lead to other discoveries, would mean our entire family would split up. Our children would be taken from us. She and I might go to prison."

"You could leave her," Nelson said.

Roy shook his head. "Even if I disappeared with the children, she would be able to cause a lot of problems. She disappeared with one child. A man disappearing with four children is another matter. She wouldn't take any of that silently, either. Nothing would keep her in check—she wouldn't have anything to lose. She would cause as much trouble for me as she could."

"Ultimately not just for you and your four children, but for many others," Dex said, in his cool, unruffled way.

"Yes. For many others in the Fletcher family. That's why I've come to you. I want you to be aware of the situation."

"Does she know of your infidelity?" Dex asked.

Roy and Nelson looked shocked, then Roy blushed.

Giles smiled a little. Dex glanced at him, and Giles saw the faintest hint of shared amusement in Dex's eyes.

Roy said, "No."

"No *what*?" Nelson asked. "No, you aren't cheating on her? Or no, she doesn't know?"

Roy took a deep breath and said, "No, she doesn't know that I have cheated on her."

"You don't think she knows," Dex said.

"Does she?" Roy asked anxiously, as if Dex might know his own wife better than he did.

Well, Giles reflected, that was entirely possible.

"She suspects, at the very least." Dex smiled, a look of apology on his face. "At the gathering yesterday? After Sheila's death?"

Roy nodded.

"Victoria approached me and said she was worried about Maggie, because Maggie's looked a little tired lately. I said I thought Maggie looked quite well, as beautiful as ever. She said she thought most men thought Maggie was beautiful. She then wondered how Maggie coped with all the late-night business meetings we've been having, and said perhaps that might account for her lack of sleep."

Roy looked stricken.

Nelson glanced between them, then asked Dex, "What did you say?"

"I didn't deny the meetings, of course. I said that Maggie understood that it was easier for the men with small children if we occasionally met after the children had gone to bed. It gave those men more time with their children." He paused. "She smiled and said Maggie was generous to put her own needs as a wife aside for the needs of the Fletcher brothers. She added that Maggie seemed to get out and about more than the other Fletcher women did, so perhaps she didn't mind my neglecting her in the evening."

Giles said, "Oh, my. Usually Victoria is more subtle with her barbs."

"Yes," Roy said, his voice a dry whisper.

"Let's review," Giles said. "You cannot relocate as a couple, you cannot leave her, she cannot leave you—at least, anyone who left the marriage would lose the children."

"Right."

"She believes this Irene Kelly is a threat. Do you?"

"I won't say that it's impossible for Ms. Kelly to track us down. The *Express* might publish photos of a woman who looked something like Victoria does now, and that might lead someone to identify her, but I think all of these possibilities are highly unlikely. The only place Victoria visits in Las Piernas is Dad's house. I don't believe anyone in the family would try to harm us, do you?"

"No," said Nelson. Giles wasn't so sure, but he kept this to himself.

"What about the possibility of someone in your neighborhood recognizing her?" Dex asked.

"Some people in Huntington Beach subscribe to the *Express,* but they're a minority. Most people subscribe to the *Register* or the *Times.* I've looked around, checking driveways in the morning when I go for a run—I don't think anyone on my street gets the *Express.*"

"Not at home, perhaps, but what if they see it elsewhere?"

"Our neighbors aren't nosy types. We keep the house painted, the garage clean, and the lawn cared for. The children do nothing to annoy them. It's suburban Orange County. All of that adds up to invisibility."

"So far," Dex said.

"Whom would Victoria go to for help?" Giles asked.

Roy thought for a moment, then answered, "The family—our family. She cut herself off from her own family a long time ago. She has a sister who lives in Pennsylvania, but they hate each other. I keep an eye on our phone records. No long-distance calls are showing up."

"What about your . . . your other women?" Nelson asked.

"What do you mean?"

"If you're sleeping around—"

"I'm not! I mean . . . Look, it's one woman, whom I see very rarely and . . . and with complete discretion."

"Not complete," Dex said. "Victoria knows."

"Victoria *suspects,*" Roy said.

Dex didn't reply.

"What does your . . . your mistress know about you, about your family?" Nelson asked. "What if she tries to break up your marriage?"

"Not possible. There won't be any problems there."

"Who is she?" Nelson asked.

Clumsy! Giles thought, and frowned. "Really, Nelson. It's not our business. I'm sure Roy knows what he's doing. He won't take unnecessary risks. When and if he feels comfortable talking to us about her, he may. If he never wants to, fine."

"It's not—" Roy broke off, frustrated. "It's not about my trust for you. It's that I don't want to cause problems for her. It's not my secret—not mine alone—to tell."

"Of course not," Giles said, and turned to Nelson. "Now. Let's talk about Caleb. What progress are you making?"

As a strategy to distract Nelson, it worked perfectly. It also had the desired effect of getting him to leave at the earliest possible moment. Nelson could only admit failure where Caleb was concerned. He didn't want to hear his brothers' suggestions on the matter.

When he had gone, Giles said, "Roy, if necessary, do you think the children can be convinced that Victoria abandoned them?"

Roy sat in silence, then said quietly, "That will be difficult."

"Dex, can you help out there?"

"I never assume that any individual will succumb to my charms," he said dryly.

"It would not be distasteful to you?"

"No," he said, not looking at Roy.

"So you will try?"

"Certainly, if Roy consents." Now he looked Roy straight in the eye.

Roy looked away. He brooded, and Giles thought perhaps Roy was going to be the dog in the manger.

Roy said, "Even if she is . . . happier with Dex, I don't see how it solves the problem in the long run."

"No, I'll work on that. This is just a first step. I think Cleo needs to know about this problem of yours."

Roy blushed again.

Giles appreciated that Dex did not say aloud what they both knew—that Roy had already "talked" to Cleo and more.

But Giles was surprised when Roy said, "I hope it doesn't come to that."

Giles could have sworn that Roy had been working himself up to making private arrangements with Cleo, who—if things had reached that point—would have refused. Oh dear. If he was sincerely attached to his wife, that would be troublesome.

Now was not the time to worry over such things. They had four children to think about. Four very precious and special children.

Plans must be made carefully. But quickly as well.

When Roy left, Giles turned to Dex and said, "So, did you see him leaving Cleo's place as you walked in?"

But Dex, much more discreet than Nelson or Roy, wouldn't answer. He didn't even smile. That, in and of itself, confirmed the information, thought Giles, who perhaps knew Dex better than Dex knew himself.

He would not press the point now. His cell phone was ringing, and as he looked at the display, he saw that the call was from the school psychologist, Jill Lowry.

He answered, saying, "One moment, Jill," and muted the phone.

"New test scores in?" Dex asked.

"Yes. Will you please excuse me? I'll call you in an hour about arrangements regarding Roy's problems."

"Of course."

As the door shut quietly behind Dex, Giles found himself feeling unsettled, although he wasn't exactly sure why. He nearly called Dex back, then glanced down at the phone in his hand. No, he had to take this call now. He unmuted the phone.

"Sorry to keep you waiting, Jill," he said. "Is there something I can help you with?"

Giles had a unique ability to completely and quickly change focus as needed. By the time he finished the call, any worries he had about Dex were forgotten.

CHAPTER 28

FRANK HARRIMAN had spent the morning going over autopsy results with a forensic pathologist, talking about a suicide case that the coroner had now declared a possible homicide. Frank's partner, Pete, had just started a vacation—by now he was probably on a Hawaiian beach with his wife, Rachel—so Frank would be handling this one on his own.

He had a hunch that Pete would be back before they had anyone in custody. They were getting a late start, the scene had been released, so if it was a murder, they were going to have to be lucky to prove it, and in all likelihood the suspected killer was in the wind by now.

He was caught up in these thoughts, signing out at the receptionist's desk, when he saw a blond man in a suit approaching the glass doors at the front of the building, a man who looked familiar to him. Everything about him said he was law enforcement, but he wasn't in uniform, and Frank didn't think he was armed. Young to be in detectives, but maybe undercover?

The automatic glass door slid back and the man walked in, then checked at the threshold when he saw Frank, but after this slight hesitation, he continued forward. Frank tried to place him. A member of the department, not a detective, but not in uniform now. He was carrying a large envelope.

"Can I help you?" the receptionist asked.

"Fletcher, isn't it?" Frank asked, the name coming to him. Fletcher had been first on the scene at a couple of the calls Frank had caught on the west side of town.

The other man gave him a nervous smile and didn't quite

look into his eyes. "Yes, Detective Harriman. Dennis Fletcher."

Frank wondered at the unease. He couldn't think of anything he had ever said to the patrolman to make him react this way. Frank remembered him being bright and quick to catch on, and thought he'd be promoted before long. "I thought you were with the Westside Division—"

"I am, sir. My day off."

Harriman raised a brow.

"I—I'm here about my cousin, sir. I—I think your wife found her?"

Did that explain the nervousness? "Sheila Dolson was your cousin? I'm sorry for your loss, Fletcher."

"Thank you, sir."

Frank thought over all Irene had told him about the woman. "Which side of her family are you related to?"

"Oh, we aren't— We weren't blood relatives. She was adopted by one of my grandfather's foster children. My grandfather is Graydon Fletcher.

"Oh . . ."

"To be honest, sir, she's sort of been estranged from the family. But of course we want to see that, you know, the burial and all are taken care of."

"Your grandfather is certainly a generous man. I guess you've got a lot of aunts and uncles and cousins."

Dennis Fletcher smiled, more relaxed now. "Yes, sir. 'Cousins by the dozens,' as we say."

"One of the cousins had dinner with us last night," Frank said. "Came by with Ben Sheridan."

"Anna?" Dennis guessed.

Frank hid his surprise with a show of embarrassment. "No, I take it they've recently split up."

"Oh, that's too bad."

"Yes," said Frank. "A real shame." Christ, he thought, what will I say next, *These things happen*? But the receptionist was asking Fletcher to sign in, so he seemed not to notice Frank's discomfort. "Well," Frank said quickly, "I've got to get going. Take care, Dennis."

He hurried to the doorway.

He pretended not to hear Officer Dennis Fletcher call out, just as the automatic door closed between them, "If it wasn't Anna—"

H E drove away from the parking lot, found a side street, and pulled over. He took out his cell phone.

After two rings, she answered. "Kelly." Clearly distracted. Her keyboard clicked rapid-fire in the background.

"Don't you look at the caller ID display before you answer?"

The clicking stopped before he finished the question.

"Frank!"

He smiled, hearing the sudden pleasure in her voice.

"Have lunch plans?"

"Not exactly, but . . ."

He knew that tone of voice, too. "You're on a deadline and can't get away. You've ordered takeout."

"Sorry. I would have preferred eating with you."

"Another time. Look, I want to ask you something, but between us, not for the paper, all right?"

"Sure."

"And watch what you say within earshot of anyone in the newsroom."

"Okay, but it's pretty empty right now. People are either out on a story or getting lunch. What's up?"

"You know Anna better than I do. She ever mention to you that she's related to the Fletchers?"

"What?!"

"Surprised me, too. Some sort of a cousin. But in a family that size . . ."

"I know. I'm starting to feel like I'm running into something out of *Invasion of the Body Snatchers*. They've taken over the city. I saw some of them this morning, too. But Anna . . ."

"Not just Anna," Frank said. "Sheila Dolson was part of the family, too."

"I just learned that Sheila was a Fletcher this morning—how did you find out?"

He told her about running into Dennis Fletcher. "Makes me wonder what was going on with the dog group and all of that," Frank said. "I haven't even called Vince and Reed about this yet, just thought I'd find out if Anna had ever mentioned the family connection to you."

"No, she didn't. Not even yesterday, when she might have tried to use it to get Altair." She paused, then said, "I see what you mean. This explains why she trusted Sheila so much, I suppose. I wonder if she mentioned it to Ben?"

"Ben, who works with their long-lost cousin, Caleb?"

There was a long silence.

Frank said, "The dog group Ben is in—I guess I should say was in—was started by his closest friend, David Niles."

He heard her intake of breath. Irene had been on the expedition with David when he lost his life.

"David taught forensic anthropology," Frank said.

"A subject her cousin Caleb was studying," she said. "Caleb, who had severed ties with the family."

Irene never took long to see where he was heading with something. And she reached the next point immediately.

"Oh, shit. If she got into the group to keep tabs on Caleb, and then David died and Ben took over handling David's dogs . . . Oh, no . . . Damn her!"

"We shouldn't jump to conclusions."

"Like hell. The conclusions are jumping at us."

"No. That's not true. Irene, we've seen them together. Do you think she faked her affection for him? Over all that time?"

There was another small silence. She was, he knew, trying to get a handle on her temper. Almost reluctantly, she said, "No. No, I—I can't."

"Me neither. I just hope she told Ben about the family connection."

"How does a guy in your line of work come up with that kind of optimism?"

"That wasn't really optimism. I just don't want to be the one to tell him."

She fell silent again, and he heard the sound of someone talking in the background. Irene said, "Let me call you right back.
You're on the cell?"

A FEW minutes later, his phone rang.
He answered and heard her say, "Sorry, newsroom
crowded up again. Listen, I spent the morning at the dentist."

"You did? I didn't know you were having—"

"No, I mean, about the teeth Sheila supposedly found." She
told him about the number on Sheila Dolson's message pad and
the Fletcher dentists.

"Okay, now I remember you mentioned this to Caleb at dinner."

"Right. So I went over to this dental office today. When I got
there, I ended up talking to a receptionist. Young guy. I told him
that I had heard that one of the dentists, Dr. Arnold Fletcher,
helped search groups train dogs for finding missing children by
letting them use teeth that would otherwise just go to waste."

"Hmm. Did you read his name tag?"

"Yes. Not Fletcher, but so what? Our good friend Anna
Stover—would that have told you *she* was a Fletcher?"

"Good point."

"This guy's name was Bobby Smith, but he's in the family, all
right. Pod people. Seriously. What Caleb's dad said about the eff-
ing clan? Not far off. Anyway, at first Bobby is telling me that I
must be mistaken, but everything in his body language tells me he
knows something. So I say, 'Oh no, Sheila Dolson said she
couldn't have done such wonderful work without help from this
office,' and I'd love to start by interviewing him about that.
Thank God I used that wording."

"Why?"

"Because instead of reacting the way I thought he would—you
know, sort of excited that something complimentary about the
place might be in the paper, and that I'd be helping him get his

own first few minutes of fame—he got really flustered and upset, then asked me to wait outside for a few minutes."

"Did he lock the door and close up for the day?"

"I half-worried about that. But he came back out, sweating and wringing his hands, and said, 'My cousin *promised* she'd never tell where she got those teeth!' And babbles for a minute about how Uncle Arnold, the dentist, will fire him if he finds out. None of this was what I expected to hear, and learning that Sheila was one of the Fletchers left me speechless. Raised more questions than it answered. So I just waited. He said, 'I took the teeth from a box of old ones that Dr. Arnold keeps in his office. He never does anything with them. I didn't think he'd miss a few. I felt sorry for her. I wanted to help her out. But she swore that if anyone asked, she'd say that *she* was the one who took them.'"

"Hmm," Frank said. "Did he say 'my cousin' or 'Sheila' when he told you about it?"

"My cousin."

"I wonder if he thought you meant Anna?"

She considered that for a moment, then said, "No, I only mentioned Sheila to him. Besides, Anna wouldn't have used the 'feel sorry for me' approach to get the teeth. That was Sheila's M.O."

"True. Mind if I tell Reed what you've told me?"

"I'd hate to get poor Bobby at the dentist's office in trouble. And—Mark might be able to trade some information for his story. I'll urge him to call Reed with it."

"And if he won't make the call?"

"He will," she said with conviction.

Knowing Mark Baker, he had to agree. "You left the pad of paper in Sheila's kitchen?"

"I haven't started stealing things from crime scenes," she said indignantly.

He suppressed a laugh. If he told her to calm down now, she'd completely blow her top. "Sorry," he managed. "I didn't mean to imply that."

"You are trying not to laugh," she said, which made him lose it. But she laughed with him.

"All right," she said, "I see what you mean. Reed and Vince would get there on their own. Eventually."

"You and Mark could save them some time," he agreed.

She was quiet for a long time. "I'm starting to wonder about this family. I started out believing Sheila Dolson didn't know a hell of a lot of people in Las Piernas. Now I think I was as wrong as I could be about that."

"It's something we'll be looking at," Frank said.

"I didn't take all of Altair's equipment with me the other night—they only let me walk away with the dog and his collar and leash. It might be worthwhile searching those SAR equipment bags and Sheila's other belongings. If they find a little collection of teeth, it will be easier to prove that Sheila planted the ones she found out at the Sheffield Estate."

"I'll mention it to them," Frank said. "What are you doing the rest of the day?"

"Taking Ethan to see Dr. Robinson at one. Then after that, I'm meeting a photographer at Blake Ives's house. I'm starting on that follow-up story about families with missing children." She sighed.

"Not an easy assignment."

"The best ones never are. Besides, I volunteered for it."

"Let me know how things go with Ethan. And say hi to Doug Robinson for me." She promised she would, then added, "Let me know how things go with Ben."

Which made him realize that he had volunteered, too.

"Maybe it's none of our business," he said, knowing even as he did that he was looking for a way out.

Silence.

"I guess Ben has a right to know," he said. "I wouldn't want him to hear it from someone else."

"You want me to tell him?"

He did, but for all the wrong reasons. "No, I'll talk to him."

"Thanks," she said, clearly relieved.

They made dinner plans and hung up.

"I must be slipping," he said to himself, and drove off, wondering how the hell he was going to break this news to Ben.

CHAPTER 29

Wednesday, April 26
3:40 P.M.
LAS PIERNAS

WHAT else do you want?" the photographer asked me. He had just taken photos of a stuffed animal—a lion that'd had most of his mane, whiskers, and one eye loved off of him. It was one of many stuffed animals he had photographed, some in groups, some alone. But mostly he'd taken pictures of the lion, whose name was Squeegee, for reasons known only to a former three-year-old who wasn't around to be asked about it.

The photographer was being extraordinarily patient this afternoon. He had young children, a daughter and a son, and although his own marriage was in good shape, I think Blake Ives's story horrified him.

While he had been on toy safari, I had taken possession of three CDs of photographs from Blake Ives. Ives had big blue eyes and dark gold hair; the many framed photos of his daughter on his walls showed that she had inherited those traits from him. "I did what you said," he told me as he handed over the digital versions of the photos. "There are ones of all of us—me, Bonnie, and Carla. Mostly Carla, though. Bonnie said I took too many pictures of Carla."

The words were spoken calmly, all the bite well beneath them. The temperamental man who had called me a few days ago was nowhere in evidence. Far from raging, he seemed painfully in control of himself. All three of us were unnaturally subdued, given the reason for meeting—to photograph the Museum of Carla.

The phenomenon wasn't a new one to me. Over the years, I've covered any number of missing-persons stories, and so I had seen these little museums before. Shrines, some would say. Some parents of missing kids had them, others didn't. A few couldn't stand reminders, and boxed them up within weeks, as an act of anger or grief or surrender, or all three. Others came to the first anniversary of loss and put everything into the attic or gave it away on that day, as if the motions of closure would bring it about. They undoubtedly knew closure was not to be so easily acquired, although perhaps these actions brought some form of relief.

Still other parents preserved the child's room, thinking of it as a magnet that would draw their loved one back. A child's bedroom furnishings and toys became something tangible to hold on to when the child himself or herself had unthinkably slipped from their grasp. For some, these rooms were a physical demonstration of remembrance, a defiant refusal to let go. A sign of enduring hope. Sometimes I find myself wondering if there is anything more cruel than enduring hope.

Ives was a curator. Carla's room was just as it had been the last time she was home. Cleaned and dusted. Favorite toys on the bed, the lion among them.

He moved to a closet and opened it. "I gave away most of her clothes," he said, "except for her favorite pj's. I know she won't fit in them now, but . . ."

He went over the story he had told me on the phone, this time in greater detail. In the years after she left the newspaper, Bonnie had apparently gone on something of a downhill slide. Ives had met her about halfway down the slope—when she was already picking up speed, hurtling toward hitting bottom. That came when she grew restless with caring for an infant, and ran off with Reggie Faroe, a man with a criminal record and a drug problem. Blake and Bonnie Ives were divorced by the time Carla was two. The courts, considering Bonnie's history and reports on Faroe, agreed with Blake that he should have full custody. Bonnie moved around a lot but stayed in touch and visited her daughter. As Carla went from infant to toddler, Bonnie's desire to be a mother seemed to be renewed. "She was cleaning up her act—or so I thought," Ives said. "She claimed Faroe was no longer in the picture, but I didn't trust her. I never let Carla spend the night with her. Bonnie seemed content to spend hours with her here. Hinted about maybe getting back together." He paused. "I'd love to say I didn't fall for that, and if I had been by myself, I probably wouldn't have listened to it. But I kept seeing how good she was with Carla, and thinking about Carla growing up without a mother. And Bonnie seemed more stable than she had been in years. So I was tempted."

He walked around the room, picked up Squeegee, and held him.

"She came over one afternoon and asked if the three of us could have lunch together in a restaurant. While we were there, I went to use the gents and came back to an empty table. By the time I figured out that she wasn't just in the ladies' room with Carla, she was gone. I think someone, probably Faroe, must have been waiting outside to pick them up and drive off with them, because I was the one who drove us to the restaurant. A private detective found out that Faroe was living in Nevada around then, but he disappeared not long after Carla was taken, so I think he's taken them to another country, probably Mexico."

He looked down at Squeegee, said, "This guy was her favorite," and gently repositioned the lion on the bed. "She used to get scared when there was a thunderstorm. Lots of kids do, I know, but . . . Anyway, I'd sing that song from *Butch Cassidy and the Sundance Kid,* 'Raindrops Keep Falling on My Head.' She loved that song. Whenever it rains, like it did the other day? I think about that, and then I wonder if she's scared."

He stood up and exhaled hard, like someone who had been sucker-punched in the gut.

The pain, the loss—easy to see. Likewise, his fears for his daughter's safety. What took a little longer to observe was that he had been brought to a halt on a journey that was designed to go on to another end, the one parent and child were meant to share. It took a little longer to see how incomplete this had left him.

He gestured toward a stack of brightly wrapped packages that filled one corner of the closet. "Birthdays," he said. "Christmas."

The photographer wanted Ives to pose with them. Blake hesitated, then did. "She'll be too old for most of them now," he said, and pinched the bridge of his nose, hard. The tears didn't fall, but he looked like hell while he held them back.

The photographer was too well trained to miss the moment. Our bosses would love it. Neither of us took joy in that, despite whatever rep those in our professions may have. I don't expect anyone who wasn't there to understand this, but shying away from Blake Ives's misery would have, essentially, dishonored it.

I looked around the room. "A map of the United States? Books? Flashcards? Wasn't she a little young?"

"She walked before she was nine months old. She started talking before she was a year old. She could name all the states and point them out on the map by the time she was two. She knew how to read simple sentences before her third birthday and was working her way through Dr. Seuss. She could add and subtract." He paused. "I'm sure that just sounds like bragging, but we had her tested. I should say, I gave in and let her be tested. I regret it now."

"What do you mean?"

"I wanted to know, so that we could make informed choices about her education. But once your child is identified as a gifted preschooler . . . let's just say there are people who won't let that kid just be a kid."

"Bonnie one of them?"

"I don't know." He sighed. "Bonnie loves Carla. I know she does. It's the only thing that keeps me from going completely crazy. But sometimes— Yes, I think she pushed her academically and didn't balance it with play and all the other things that a child needs. From Bonnie's point of view, I was holding Carla back."

"What preschool was she in?"

"Barrington Hills."

The photographer whistled.

I looked over at him.

"Not cheap, but kids get into the best prep schools if they go there or Sheffield Gardens. Or to Fletcher Day School, of course."

"That's part of Fletcher Academy?" I asked.

"Not really, even though the family owns both. A lot of kids at the day school do go on to the academy."

"And the academy is the best private school in Las Piernas," I said. I turned back to Ives. "So you paid high preschool tuition?"

"I would have paid twice that," he said, "even if it meant taking a second job. I wanted her to be a kid, but it's not that simple—I also wasn't going to deny her any options for her future. The kids who go to Barrington end up in prep schools that lead to Ivy League schools. I wanted her to have the best opportunities."

I just barely kept my jaw from dropping. "She wasn't even five years old yet. She hadn't started kindergarten."

"The competition is unbelievable."

"Is it even possible to know how smart a child that young is? Or if he or she will like school?"

"Sure—I mean, not always, of course. But in cases like Carla's, you could tell even without the tests."

"Who tested her?" I asked, hoping to get the name of someone who wasn't going to be quite so biased.

"I made copies of her school papers for you. Hang on."

Ives left the room. I turned to the photographer, ready to make a crack about parents who push too hard. The look on his face was wistful, not cynical, though, and he sighed dreamily. "Barrington Hills," he said. "God, I hope I can get my kids in there."

"How old are they?" I choked out.

"My daughter is six months old. My son is two."

I V E S brought back a thick stack of paperwork, including reports from a private eye he had briefly hired, information from the National Center for Missing and Exploited Children, and his notes from a meeting with a psychic he had paid. "I was desperate," he said when I came across that one. I saw flyers with his daughter's picture on them and copies of pages from a notebook he kept on his conversations with police, the notes getting briefer as time went on, the last series at three-month intervals, with the dates, the names of various LPPD detectives who happened to have the misfortune to be working in the low-status realm of missing persons, and the word *nothing* written next to their names.

"When will the story run?" he asked.

"Up to my editor," I answered absently as I looked through his notes. "Next week maybe, but no guarantees. A breaking story could change everything. And I can't guarantee how much of what I write will get in." I glanced up and saw that his shoulders were slumping. I had disappointed him—or dealt another blow. I thought back over what I had just said and wanted to kick myself. "I can call you and let you know once my editor makes his decisions."

"Yes, thanks." He straightened his back. "I've waited this long, I guess another few days won't matter."

I tried to distract him by going over his notebook with him.

As we left, he teared up again. "Thanks for all you're doing to help out," he said.

I made a polite reply, but wondered if six months from now I'd be a name on a ledger, next to which he would write, *Nothing*.

CHAPTER 30

Wednesday, April 26
6:30 P.M.
LAS PIERNAS

WE had just put dinner on the table when the dogs started barking. The doorbell rang a moment later. Sometimes I wonder why we bother keeping it hooked up. No one has managed to ring it before the dogs have warned us of their presence. I suppose it keeps us from opening the door every time someone walks another dog on the sidewalk in front of the house, though.

Frank answered it, and Ethan and I exchanged a look of surprise when we heard him say, "Caleb!"

He invited him in.

"Sorry to bother you," Caleb said, and as he came within sight of the table, he began apologizing again.

"Have you eaten?" I asked. "Why don't you join us? This is my semifamous linguini with asparagus. I'll be insulted if you don't at least try it."

He protested that we shouldn't have to feed him every night, that he'd just stopped by to drop off some notes for me and to ask if I had talked to Tadeo Garcia.

"I haven't talked to him directly," I said carefully. "I talked to his wife. She invited us to come out there on Monday. We'll see if that actually leads to an interview with Tadeo Garcia himself. He may pull a disappearing act if he figures out that she's invited us there."

By then, Ethan had set a place for Caleb at the table, and it didn't take much coaxing to get him to join us.

"You said 'us,'" Caleb said. "Does that mean that Ethan can go with you?"

"Dr. Robinson said it would be okay," Ethan said.

"Under certain conditions," I added.

"Believe me," Ethan said, "'Take it easy' isn't an order I could disobey if I wanted to."

"I think the good doctor is on to the fact that you'll keep testing your own limits." I turned back to Caleb.

This led to twenty minutes of the kind of dinner conversation you can have only with people who work in certain professions, because anyone with more sensitivity or better table manners would put his fork down and turn an unpleasant shade of green. We, on the other hand, demolished platefuls of noodles as we discussed in some detail the damage a bullet could do to one's anatomy, one of us having discovered the facts the hard way.

Eventually talk turned to the case of Gerry Serre and his missing son.

"Not to speak ill of the dead," Caleb said, "but we've dug up most of that slope because of the big ego of the late Sheila Dolson. Didn't find the remains of a child there."

"I talked to Mark Baker," I said. "He told Reed about the family dentist who unwittingly supplied those teeth she planted, and got a little information in exchange. Reed mentioned—off the record for the time being—that some cigarette butts were found up there. So the killer was a smoker?"

"Seems likely to me," Caleb said, "because of where they were found—but I shouldn't be talking about it. We're hoping they'll result in a DNA hit at some point."

By the end of dinner, Ethan was drowsy, and while the rest of us sat at the table after it was cleared, he settled into a corner of the couch and listened in as Caleb went over some of his notes about his brother.

"The prosecutor said that Mason went over to my dad's studio, had an argument with him, killed him, and then killed Jenny. I don't believe any of that happened. I think someone framed him."

"What makes you think so?" I asked.

"Start with Jenny. He never would have harmed her—never.

The prosecutor said that she must have surprised him killing my dad. That's impossible."

"Why?"

"We didn't— We weren't like these people who have nannies, you know? We took care of Jenny ourselves. My mom had two built-in baby-sitters. Mason and I watched her a lot, but mostly it was Mason. He loved spending time with her. He'd take her places even when he wasn't baby-sitting her. I—I wasn't as patient as he was."

He fell silent.

"Preschoolers can try anyone's patience," I said. "She lived under the same roof with you, so you probably had your patience tried. You were studying hard, still in high school, right?"

"Yes," he said, not forgiving himself anything.

"What did Mason do?"

"He was— He's an artist."

"He worked with your dad?"

Caleb shook his head. "No, they didn't get along about that. My dad wanted Mason to work with him. He wanted to teach him things about art. But Mason wanted to be on his own. He had already sold a couple of pieces."

"He was able to support himself with his own art?" Frank asked.

"No, he had a band, too. Played keyboards. He wasn't making a lot of money, but they had a steady gig at one of the clubs downtown."

"You were saying that he watched Jenny," I said. "Is that another way he earned money?"

"No—I mean yes, he watched Jenny, but no, he didn't take money for that. My mom wanted to pay him for it, but he wouldn't let her." He took a deep breath, let it out in a rush. "My mom never would have let him take care of Jenny if she thought Mason would hurt her. If you had ever seen Mason and Jenny together . . . Anyway, he would have known that if Jenny wasn't with me or my mom, she would be with my dad. He knew my mom's work hours. He knew I was at school."

"So he knew Jenny would be with your dad."

"Exactly—no way would that be a surprise."

"Okay," Frank said. "But he was found drunk—"

"That's another thing that's all wrong," he said.

"Drunk and full of barbiturates, as I recall."

"That's how he was found, but he didn't put himself in that condition. He didn't drink or use drugs."

Ethan, who had almost nodded off, sat up at that. "What?"

Caleb laced his fingers together and rested his hands on the papers. His shoulders tensed. "No one ever believes this," he said, "unless they knew Mason. The minute they hear he was an artist, or learn that he was in a band, they assume he must have been high all the time. He wasn't."

Ethan said, "I know what you mean about the stereotypes, but speaking from experience, some people get pretty good at hiding their habits."

Caleb looked up at him.

"Another time," Ethan said. "Keep telling us about Mason."

Caleb's shoulders relaxed. "Okay. When Mason was in high school, he dated this girl named Jadia. She was kind of wild, a little bit of a loner, and so was Mason. You talk about people who could hide their habits—that girl drank and did who-knows-what else, but until it got kind of late in the day, you'd hardly know it."

"And Mason was with her a lot?"

"Not really. Typical high-school romance—didn't last more than a few weeks. That was long enough for Mason to figure out that she had a drinking problem." He paused. "I know that a couple of years before he met her, he was running with a different . . . well, I won't make excuses for him. He tried all kinds of things and he had done some drinking, but he was never big-time into that stuff. By the time he got together with Jadia, he had already done all his experimenting . . . it was no real thrill for him."

"He's six years older than you?" I asked.

"Yes. I was this total pain in the ass—uh, I mean nuisance—"

Ethan laughed. "Dude, she's not your mom. You can say *ass* and all kinds of other stuff. They're cool with it."

Caleb's face reddened.

I could see the amusement in Frank's eyes, which undoubtedly had more to do with the "mom" business than anything else, but I decided to ignore him. "So," I said to Caleb, "you looked up to your big brother?"

He shook his head. "It's not that simple. My brother isn't a saint. I'd never say that about him. He wasn't always easy to get along with. He liked being the rebel."

"Hard on the rest of the family sometimes," Frank said, none of the amusement of the previous moment anywhere in his voice. "My older sister was a rebel. Diana was always making it hellish for my parents, and I didn't like that, but at the same time I also admired her. She was more daring than I was, but she was also always getting into trouble."

I tried not to let my shock show. Frank was twelve when his sister Diana died, and his family had developed a code of silence about her that had lasted decades. That ban had been lifted awhile back, but old habits lingered—this was the first time I had heard him mention her to anyone other than his closest friends.

Caleb, unconscious of this honor, said, "Yes! That's what it was like for me, too. Did she outgrow it?"

"No, she was killed in an accident, so we didn't get a chance to see if they would have been getting along later."

"Sorry." He paused. "I guess that's what I hate most about all of this—losing all the chances. I'll never know my dad any better than I did when I was in high school. I don't know what he'd say to me now, or if we'd even get along. I've already missed knowing what kind of bratty kid Jenny might have been over the past few years. I haven't been able to be a brother to her. At first I thought it would only be a few days before someone would find her." He paused again, and this time the silence stretched out before he went on.

After a while, he said, "Another thing—Mason and Dad never got the chance to be adults with each other. Our family was close, and I didn't like to hear him giving my mom and dad shit all the time, but I think they were seeing that he was growing out of it.

Mason was always braver than I was—still is. He can be funny,
too." He grinned. "I think I was ten before I realized that his biological father was probably not a guy named Mr. Jar. He replaced
that story with half a dozen others, including one about my mom
naming him after a jar because of the way she got pregnant with
him—I was completely freaked out, of course, and he knew I'd
never ask my mom if it was true."

"That's disgusting," Ethan said, but he was laughing.

"Does he know who his biological father is?" I asked.

"No. Mom didn't want the guy's name on anything, because
she didn't want him to try to get custody of Mason. She'd never
tell anyone the guy's name—claimed she didn't know, but none
of us believed that. I asked Mason once if he wanted to know, and
he said, 'Only as a matter of idle curiosity.' He also used to say
that we had different fathers but the same dad."

"Which doesn't exactly fit the picture the prosecution painted
of their relationship."

"No."

"You were saying that you know he didn't drink because of
this girl he dated," Ethan said, demonstrating one of the reasons I
think he'll be a great reporter one day—he never loses track of
any thread in a conversation.

"Right," Caleb said. "Jadia. The way that happened was that one
day Jadia showed up at our house, and she was drunk and wanted
Mason to go somewhere with her. She was going to drive. Mason
didn't have a car of his own yet. My dad wouldn't let Mason go
with her. Mason acted all pissed off about it, but to be honest, I
think he was relieved to have an excuse not to go with her."

"So did they just hang out at your house?" Ethan asked.

"No," Caleb said. "My dad tried to stop her from leaving, but
when he went to the phone to call her parents, she took off. She
made it home safely before anyone could do anything about it,
but she was mad, and said some things about my dad that Mason
didn't like much, and so they split up."

"So that's why he stopped drinking?" I asked.

"No. Two weeks later, she hit a kid on a bicycle—killed him.

He was eleven. I didn't know him, because he went to a different school, but he was my age. Eleven. That's how old I was when it happened. Mason kept saying, 'It could have been you,' to me. So I finally said, 'It could have been you,' right back at him. Kind of shut him up, you know? Anyway, he never did any drugs or booze after that."

"He was lucky to have someone confront him," Ethan murmured.

"I don't know that it was what I said to him. I think he saw how many lives got totally screwed up because of that accident. The parents of the kid, the kid's sister, Jadia's parents—but it was really hard on Jadia, too. And I don't mean because of the drunk-driving charges and all that. Mason told me that she never forgave herself for it. I think he knew that he was the type of person who never would have forgiven himself, either, if he ever did something that hurt somebody while he was drunk."

Caleb glanced at his watch and said, "I'd better get going. I'm working on some things with Ben tomorrow morning." He paused. "He's always good about giving me Sundays off—that's when I see Mason."

"Is Ben doing okay?" I asked.

He shrugged.

When I saw he wasn't going to say more, I said, "Thanks for bringing these notes over. I'll look through them before I talk to the Garcias."

"Thanks. There's not much there. I never was able to be of much help to Mason."

Our protests that he was wrong about that seemed not to make an impression on him. Ethan walked with him to the front door. As Caleb was leaving, I overheard Ethan say, "You believe in him. Don't underestimate how much that means to someone."

ETHAN asked Frank for a painkiller—something he almost always waits too long to do. When he first got out of the hospital, Ethan worried about the possibility of dependency problems with them, and talked things over with his AA sponsor. The decision was made to put Frank in possession of the pills, to dole them out on request, but he was supposed to call the doctor if the requests were too frequent.

So far, there had been no need for a call. If anything, Frank and I worried that Ethan was trying too hard to do without them, and losing sleep to pain.

"Tired of me yet?" he asked us as he headed toward his room.

"No," we answered in unison, and wished him good night.

CHAPTER 31

Monday, May 1
9:30 A.M.
A CONDOMINIUM IN LAS PIERNAS

CLEO sat on her balcony wearing nothing but a fluffy white bathrobe. She sipped fresh-squeezed orange juice and watched the ocean. The morning was overcast, the gray clouds reflected in a gray sea. Her mood matched the grayness.

She stretched her legs out and rested her heels on a nearby chair. The onshore breeze made it a little nippy out here, but quieter than usual—the air was cool enough to keep all but a few joggers away from the beach.

Her own workout had gone well this morning. A little later today she might put some time in at the firing range. She reflected on the fact that much of her life was spent preparing for incidents that rarely occurred. Hours and hours spent training and planning for an action that might take place once a year. The most exciting part would be all over in a few moments. Adrenaline-loaded moments, to be sure, but few of them.

This didn't bother her. She knew that many people worked for years in jobs that never produced one second of excitement.

For her own safety, it was best that she did not work too often. She knew her success depended on controlling certain factors, and one of those factors was the frequency of abductions and kills. If she were to work too often, inevitably a pattern would be seen, small mistakes (a shoe lost!) would be connected to one another, and then to her. She was confident of her abilities, but luck could go lousy on anybody. There were things no one could plan for—like those reporters being at Sheila's house, just at that time. A shoe coming loose, sticking in the mud.

Long ago she had been questioned in connection with a criminal investigation, and she remembered how unnerving that had been. This had taken place in her childhood, when she was known by a different name, and she had never come close to facing charges of any kind. Her memories of her earliest years she kept locked away in a distant corner of her mind, but she clearly remembered the fire and all that had followed.

Investigators believed a set of tragedies had befallen her. Her parents, known by everyone in the neighborhood to be heavy drinkers and smokers, died in a fire. Smoking in bed, arson investigators said. The ten-year-old girl had barely escaped with her life. That's the way it looked to all the adults.

She had been sent to the home of her only living grandparent. Her father's mother, as wicked as he was and as much a drinker. Grandmother had drowned in her swimming pool. There were questions then. A rail-thin detective, with eyes like black buttons, had asked them, while his partner, who looked to Cleo to be yet another drinker, looked on unhappily. Did she know, the thin one asked, why her grandmother had decided to go swimming at night? No, she didn't. Why she went swimming with her clothes on? Cleo shrugged.

The questions had stopped when Vera, her mother's younger sister, arrived from California to take care of the twelve-year-old girl. Vera had two attorneys in tow, both by the last name of Fletcher. She was married to one of them. Within a few days, they were on their way to California, where Cleo would live with her aunt.

Aunt Vera had run away from home at the age of sixteen, pregnant and unmarried. She had the good fortune to be taken in by a family that had a habit of caring for stray kids, and when she decided she was too young to raise the baby, they adopted her infant out to a good home. By the time Cleo arrived on the scene, Vera was married to one of the Fletchers. Cleo quickly learned that Vera was an entirely different kind of person than the other family members she had known, and not just because she didn't smoke or drink. She had not lived under her aunt's roof for twenty-four hours when Vera looked her in the eye and said,

"You thinking of trying to bump me off, Cleo? I hope not, because if I die in any kind of accident, the world is going to know exactly what you are."

Cleo didn't say anything. She tried not to let her nervousness show.

Vera's smile got bigger, then she said, "And besides, it would be a waste of your talents. I've been talking to one of my cousins. The family could use someone like you."

Cleo had never felt warmth toward anyone, and she didn't develop an attachment to her aunt. But Vera and her husband, Uncle Greg, provided a kind of consistency and reliability that had not been part of her life up to that time, and that steadied her. They were strict, but that helped Cleo to develop discipline. And Uncle Greg turned out to have skills in self-defense and weaponry that Cleo had only dreamed of possessing, skills he enjoyed teaching her. She decided they would live.

To Cleo's dismay, her decision was not enough. Vera became the first of Cleo's relatives to die in a true accident, a car wreck. Cleo was fifteen then. For a time, remembering Vera's threat on that first day, Cleo was certain that all her training would go to waste, that a twist of fate was going to cause her to be known as a murderer before she really had a chance to practice it as an art form.

But months went by, Cleo continued to train, and no information was released. Uncle Greg continued to teach her all he could, expanding her lessons to include a wide variety of methods of deception. Whatever grief he felt for his loss of Vera was channeled into making Cleo a perfect "agent," as he referred to her, on behalf of the family.

On her twenty-first birthday, her uncle revealed that upon Vera's death, certain information had been given to him, but he knew that Cleo had not caused Vera's death.

She never learned where Uncle Greg had received his own training. Five years ago, he died of injuries suffered in a rock-climbing accident. At his funeral, Roy had hinted that Greg had once been in the CIA, but she had a feeling this wasn't true.

Cleo rarely spent time around the rest of the family. She never liked being in a crowd, and didn't like the idea of more than a few people being able to recognize her. She moved often, did not encourage neighbors who tried to become friendly. She focused her energies on training for the next situation in which she would be needed. That kept her away from home, for the most part.

Her exercise and training routines provided some release for her energy. A carefully orchestrated series of affairs with men in her "family" provided a release for her sexual tensions. She believed herself to be their superior in every way, and one day she would demonstrate this in a manner they wouldn't like. Well, she might keep one around for fun.

She smiled to herself, picturing how that might work out. As for the rest, someday she'd be running everything. That was going to take planning and patience.

And the removal of a few obstacles along the way.

She stood and stretched and went back into the condo. She had come back from her place in the mountains after only two days. She had meant to stay away longer, but this fit of restlessness had come upon her and she'd returned.

She looked around her living room and sighed. She'd have to move again. She wondered if she should do that before the next job came along.

Uncle Greg's voice sounded in her ear, warning her about staying anonymous.

She would be out of here before tomorrow night.

THE phone rang. She answered it and listened with a growing sense of anticipation.

"Can you handle another job so soon?" Giles asked.

"Of course," she said.

"Keep your shoes on this time," he said.

She nearly hung up in his ear. Instead, she remained silent.

"I'm sorry," he said. "I shouldn't have said that."

"No," she said. She let another long silence stretch, then said, "I'm moving."

"When?"

She moved her schedule up a bit. "Today."

"Today!"

"Yes."

"I suppose that's wise. Do you have the new address?"

"Not yet."

"Call me when you have it."

He was certainly full of demands today. "I have to go now," she said. She disconnected the call. That would be good for him.

She immediately dialed Fletcher Moving and Storage. She asked for Andy. While she waited for him to come on the line, she glanced at the clock near her bed. She hadn't unpacked her gear from her trip out of town, so it would take only a few minutes to gather what clothing she needed from the condo.

Andy answered, excitement plain in his young voice. He knew that any request from her was to be dealt with immediately, and by a handpicked crew.

Andy required a softer approach than the older men. She used what worked.

"Where are we taking things? Not too far, I hope," he said.

"Just store everything for now. It may be a while before I can pay everything I owe you," she said, her voice soft and low. "But if you come over now, I'll give you a special down payment." She paused. "I haven't dressed yet."

He said he'd be right over.

She said that would be delightful, her mind already on what outfit she would wear when she was able to get dressed again.

CHAPTER 32

NTIL we were about fifteen minutes away from the Garcia household, Ethan slept stretched out on the backseat, using three pillows, only one of which was beneath his head. The others were placed so that all the tender places on his back and shoulder were somewhat protected from the jouncing of the car. Dr. Doug Robinson had pleased him by saying he should be able to manage without the need for someone to stay with him during the day—and made him happier still when he said that Ethan could come along for the ride to Redlands—provided he continued to get lots of rest. This was not really something Ethan could avoid, much to his own frustration.

He made a sound as he came awake, one I don't think he knew he made, since he usually tries to hide any sign of his discomfort. He slowly sat up and rubbed his face and hair with his right hand.

"Need something for the pain?" I asked. Frank had entrusted me with a couple of the pills in case the long ride—about seventy-five miles in each direction—proved too much.

"I'll wait until after we talk to the Garcias," Ethan said. "I don't want to be too out of it."

The *we* was not lost on me. "Ethan—"

"Your story."

"Not really a story, but—"

"I won't interfere. Promise." He smiled and said, "But I have to ask, did you mention to Mrs. Garcia that you're married to a cop?"

"Ben tells me that when you first met him, you told him you had considered a minor in anthropology."

"Hmm. That doesn't seem like an answer to my question, but— Did I say that to Ben? Imagine that."

"Imagine is right, since I'd lay money you never took so much as a course in it."

The smile became a grin. "Key word is *considered.* You don't have to take a course to consider a minor. But I get your point— you actually are married to a cop. So you did tell her."

"I went very easy on that. It could have backfired."

"Yes, I see what you mean." He paused. "Frank told me about Anna. That maybe she had other motives for being with Ben. That sucks."

"It bothers me, too. I can't convince myself the whole relationship was a ploy, but it bothers me all the same."

"I've been thinking . . . if you'd let me help you out, maybe that's something I could help with. I could track down Fletchers. You know, do what I can to find out how far the branches of that family tree stretch."

My impulse was to tell him that he should just rest and recover, but I knew how bored he was. Other than doctors' appointments and an AA meeting, he hadn't been out of the house until today.

"If you think you're up to it, sure."

T H E Garcias lived in a two-story house on a quiet block. Like all the other houses on the street, it was neatly landscaped and appeared to be well cared for.

Dora Garcia was a short, slender woman with dark hair that she wore in a chignon. Her big brown eyes had a hint of amusement in them, as if she had just remembered a good joke that she dared not tell in present company.

She welcomed us warmly and fussed over Ethan in a way that I suspect he would not have tolerated from anyone else. He could be a master manipulator, so I wasn't sure about the sincerity of his appreciation, but she lapped it up.

Tadeo Garcia stood aside and watched us make our entrance, then took a seat in what looked like a favorite armchair. He was wide-shouldered and tall, one of those men whose sinewy strength does not desert them in maturity. His arms looked as if he tied knots in railroad tracks for a workout.

He wore a neatly trimmed mustache. His hair was silver and long, tied back in a short ponytail. This surprised me—I don't meet many ex-cops who have given up the burr. His eyes were as brown as Dora's but held no amusement whatsoever. In fact, he looked as if he was more than a little pissed off.

He let his wife do all the talking. This is one of the many ways an interview can go south whenever more than one person is present. One-on-one is almost always best, but given the state of Ethan's health, I could hardly ask him to take Dora out for a walk in the garden while Tadeo and I talked.

I didn't jump right in with the third degree, of course. I've been at this long enough to know that a little patience up front, taking the time to build rapport, pays off later. But every attempt I made to draw Tadeo into general conversation was a bust. Tadeo grunted, nodded, shook his head, or managed a monosyllable. Dora frowned at him and responded at length. I couldn't blame her—if this was the level of interaction the guy offered on a regular basis, she was undoubtedly starved for attention.

I asked him if the group of kids in a picture near his elbow were his children. All he said was, "Grandchildren." His wife was expanding on that answer when Tadeo interrupted her and asked Ethan, "How'd you get shot?"

"The usual way," he said. "Being a fool."

That won the slightest smile from the man.

"Saving my life," I said.

"Not the same thing at all," Ethan said. "And as I recall, you started out trying to save mine. Fool rescue is a dangerous occupation." He looked across the room. "As anybody in law enforcement can tell you."

Tadeo's smile widened a little, and he said to Ethan, "Tell me what happened."

So Ethan gave him the condensed version of the whole tale, minimizing his own role. Somewhere in there, he worked in the

fact that he knew Caleb Fletcher. And as his brief account ended
with his talking about staying with us, he also said, "Caleb has
been over to visit me twice now. He's not the kind of person who
forgets people, you know? He's good that way."

"Does he visit his brother?"

"Every week. That's as often as he can see him."

Tadeo sighed. "I wasn't happy with Dora when she told me
you were coming over here today."

"We picked up on that," Ethan said.

That won a laugh. "Sorry. Nothing personal."

"Like hell," Dora said. "Not personal against the two of you,
but personal to him. Those bastards in his department—"

"Dora . . ."

"It's the truth. It's eating you up, old man, and you know it.
Tadeo's union had to fight the department to get his detective
rank back."

Ethan and I looked at Tadeo. Thank God Ethan knows when
to keep his mouth shut. He was probably thinking the same thing
about me.

The silence drew out. Finally Tadeo said, "Dora told me you
were just working on background. You won't quote me?"

"I want to be completely honest with you about this," I said,
"so let me tell you what I told your wife. I'm not working on a
story. I'm married to a homicide detective who works in the Las
Piernas Police Department, so I rarely cover anything directly related to a crime. I know Caleb, though, and I know what was
happening in our crime lab in the years when his brother was
convicted."

"Yeah, we've heard about your problems."

"So I'm not doing this for a story, I'm trying to see what I can
learn for a friend. If you tell me something that can be corrobo-
rated in other ways, I may try to convince you to go on the record
with one of my colleagues. But it will be your choice."

After another long silence, Tadeo said, "I made a suggestion at
a crime scene, about how a murder might have gone down. It
wasn't . . . in agreement with the way the lieutenant saw it." He

rubbed a hand over his chin. "It's a good department, no matter what Dora says. My problems were with this one guy. Anybody else I've ever worked with would have at least thought about what a more experienced detective had to say. Not this guy. We got into a big argument. He was newly promoted, and kind of insecure."

"And he was a racist," Dora said.

Tadeo shrugged. "Not the first I've met, undoubtedly not the last."

"Your family has been in this country longer than his! Your cousin fought in Vietnam. Your dad fought in World War II. He sees brown skin and right away he assumes you were born in Mexico."

"Nothing wrong with being born in Mexico, Dora . . ."

"That's not what I meant and you know it."

"And as for his attitude—I don't know. You ask me, that wasn't what bothered him most that night. It was his pride, after what happened." He turned to me. "I knew we had press there. He showed up at the scene because of that. What I didn't know at the time—there was a reporter with a parabolic microphone pointed at us. So my theory about the crime got reported in the paper."

"Let me guess," I said. "You turned out to be right."

"Well, yeah. But by the time anyone figured that out, I was already in trouble. I had embarrassed him, so he had me written up for being insubordinate, and eventually he managed to get me reassigned and demoted."

"Tadeo is not a politician," Dora said. "That lieutenant, he was more politician than anything."

"The union helped me out," Tadeo said. "But I was miserable for quite a few weeks before it all got straightened out."

"And it was during that miserable time that you were on patrol in the mountains?"

"Yes." He paused. "It was the most exciting thing that happened the whole time I worked up there. But . . . that's not why I remember it so clearly. I remember it because it has been eating at me for five years."

"Why?" I asked softly.

He looked over to his wife. "Because I should have spoken up and I didn't."

"You're speaking up now," she said.

"About what?" I asked.

He took a big breath, as if he were about to dive into deep, cold water. "I think someone staged that scene."

CHAPTER 33

THERE were all kinds of things at that scene that just didn't make sense, and yet no one from Las Piernas seemed to notice them."

"Give me some examples," I said.

"First of all, the place he was found—makes no sense. He doesn't have a cabin up there—I checked that out. He's supposed to be smart enough to carry out a double homicide in broad daylight and manage to dump his sister's body in some woods somewhere without anyone seeing him, but then he decides to drink and pop pills and get naked in the mountains? You know what the roads are like up there?"

"Curving, with cliffs and steep embankments."

"Right. He's supposed to be blasted—nearly died of the booze and barbiturates alone, but he doesn't drive off a cliff. He doesn't scrape a guardrail. He doesn't even hit a tree. He makes it into a shallow little drainage ditch off a driveway. Hardly any damage, either—doesn't even knock out a headlight. If I didn't know better, I'd think he carefully backed into that ditch."

"Backed into it?"

"The headlights were shining up into the trees, pointed away from neighboring cabins. I looked around—the shape of the ditch, the way the road and trees were lined up along there—the only way I could see the car ending up at that angle was if it had been backed in."

He hunted up a piece of paper and drew a little diagram.

"This isn't exact, just something to give you a rough idea. Okay. He supposedly drives into that ditch, and the sound isn't loud enough to wake the neighbors—I woke them, shouting the little girl's name."

"Jenny."

"Yes. But that's not all that's off about this scene. He isn't bruised or cut—not even a scratch. Although he had two victims to kill, neither of them harmed him in any way. Okay, maybe he held them at gunpoint or knifepoint—but no. No weapons other than that metal sculpture. Some kind of award. Not many people get held up at award-point."

"There was more than one room at the studio, though," I said, thinking about this. "He could have killed his stepfather with the trophy and then attacked his sister by strangling her . . . but . . . yes, I see. If he killed her at the studio, then why not leave her body there?"

"Lots of stuff about this doesn't make sense."

"On that we agree. Tell me more about what you noticed that night, the things that bothered you."

"Okay—no keys."

"What?" Ethan said.

"No car keys. Not in the ignition, not anywhere on the ground that I could see them."

"Wasn't he supposed to have put stuff in the trunk? Maybe he dropped them when he was doing that."

"Yeah, when did that happen? After he hit the ditch? So he wrecks a car on a cold, damp night, he gets out and strips everything off but his socks and underwear, then passes out in the front seat. Does that make sense, even for a drunk? Oh, and there's a laundry miracle while we're at it—the bottoms of his socks stayed clean, even when he walked around in the mud, leaving shoe prints. And the shoe prints he leaves don't look like the bottoms of his shoes, which are in the trunk."

"Wait a minute," I said. "You could see the bottoms of his socks while he was passed out in the driver's seat?"

"Yes."

"Without moving him?"

"Yes," he said, frowning.

"But then the seat must have been back too far."

"What do you mean?" Ethan said.

"When you drive," I said, "you drive with the seat close enough to reach the brake and accelerator, and to reach the clutch if it's not an automatic. If his seat is so far back that the bottoms of his socks can be seen, how did he operate that vehicle?"

"If you ask me, he never did," Tadeo said. "Not that day, anyway."

"But if someone had to move his unresisting but heavy form behind the steering wheel . . ."

"Yes, it would have made it easier if the seat was back as far as it can go."

"You said you didn't see any scratches or bruises on him. What about blood? I mean, spatter or smears from his victims?"

"Nothing. Not on his hands, not on his arms, nothing in his hair."

"Maybe he cleaned up," Ethan said. "Took a shower or something."

"There was a shower in the studio," I said slowly, "but why would he shower and then put bloody clothes on? Unless you believe he drove in his boxers and put clean socks on later . . ."

Tadeo smiled. "That's the funny part, isn't it? A guy's clothing is spattered, but he's clean. He doesn't have any other clothing with him."

"And he's supposedly driving around the mountains on a cold night wearing not much more than his birthday suit."

"Right."

"How long was the car in the ditch?" Ethan asked.

"The last person to drive down that private road before him got home at about ten-thirty. That guy would have noticed the car if it had been there then, because as he came down the main road he would have seen its headlights shining up at an angle through the trees. I found Mason Fletcher at a little after one in the morning."

"Richard Fletcher was last seen alive—by anyone other than his daughter and his killer, anyway—at about six-thirty in the morning on May ninth," I said. "And you found Mason almost eighteen hours later?"

"Yes."

"So to believe he's guilty, you must believe he had Jenny alive with him in his car while he drove around for almost eighteen hours, and that the whole time he was either wearing blood-stained clothes or drove around all but naked with her in the car."

"Or that he had killed her already," Ethan said.

"Why not leave her at the studio, then? He's already left one body there."

"That's it," Tadeo said. "And if he's kept her alive so that he can kill her less than twenty-four hours later, you are hinting that he was up to worse things, that he's really one very sick individual."

"The prosecution didn't suggest that he molested her."

"They made him a child killer," Ethan said. "He's lucky to still be alive in prison."

For all it might be true, it was the wrong thing to say. Tadeo sat brooding silently.

Dora caught my eye and made a little motion indicating that I should keep talking.

"I'm trying to figure out the timing. Let me imagine it two ways—innocent and guilty. If he's innocent, someone gets control of him early that morning or late the previous night, before his stepfather is murdered—otherwise, Mason might have been able to come up with an alibi. A friend might have met him for breakfast, someone might have seen him go to the store. Anything. If the real killer or killers wanted to frame him, I don't think they would have wanted to take chances on his whereabouts during the killing."

"Right," said Dora, encouraging me.

"He's supposed to have gone up to the mountains to bury his little sister, and for several hours—during which law enforcement was actively looking for him—driven around. As we've said, he was either wearing blood-spattered clothing or nearly naked."

"He was in a car, so most people would only be able to tell he was shirtless," Ethan pointed out. "And with a two-hour head start, he could have stayed hidden in the mountains before the crimes in Las Piernas were discovered. Lots of private roads, even empty houses."

"Okay, let's say that's the case. On a cold night in the mountains, he's still hanging around for a long time. Many hours."

"Spent the time getting drunk," Ethan suggested.

"No," Tadeo said. "The bottle supposedly came from his dad's office, and it wasn't empty."

"If he had been drinking it slowly for more than twelve hours," I said, "he wouldn't have been close to dead from the amount of alcohol in his system."

"He could have waited, drank most of it late in the day," Ethan said.

"He wasn't that drunk—it wasn't the alcohol that almost killed him," Tadeo said. "I think a lot of it was spilled on him and in the car. That wasn't what was highest in his bloodstream."

"How do you know?" I asked.

"I stopped by the hospital a few days later, talked to some of the ER folks."

"He mixed it with pills, right?"

"Barbiturates," Tadeo said. "A load of them. And that's another funny thing. The barbiturates were mixed into the booze itself. But no one ever found the empty capsules."

"So if he was opening the capsules and dumping the powder inside them into the booze, you should have seen them on the floor of the car."

"If the scotch bottle hadn't come from his dad's place, I'd say not necessarily. And I suppose he could have buried his sister and then played chemist up in the woods. But that doesn't seem likely to me. Makes more sense to be hidden in the car, I think."

"Maybe he wasn't being sensible," Ethan argued.

"At his trial," I said, "the prosecution said up front that he hadn't arrived at the studio with a plan to kill his stepfather. They said he came there to argue with Richard Fletcher, but it was obvious that he didn't bring a weapon, and they claimed he didn't know his sister was there."

"But it was first-degree murder?" Ethan asked.

"Yes. It's complicated, but legally you don't need to have the thought of killing someone in mind for a long time for it to be premeditated. If he had been in a fistfight with Richard and blindly grabbed the trophy and swung it, they might have brought a lesser charge. But Richard Fletcher was at his desk and struck repeatedly from behind, so he wasn't able to defend himself, and he couldn't have been threatening Mason." I paused. "That's if you believe Mason was there that day in the first place."

"So the prosecution said he discovered his little sister there, took her, drove around with her for a while, then killed her to keep her from talking?"

"Yes. Then, in remorse, later tried to kill himself with a lethal mixture of booze and pills."

"I think he was set up," Tadeo said angrily. "I knew it from the moment I opened that car door, and I'm never going to be able to live with myself if—"

He broke off and looked at his wife, a strange expression on his face.

"It's true," she said softly. "You're a good man, Tadeo. And you won't be able to live with yourself until you make this right."

He frowned, then shook his head. "It's probably not going to make a difference."

"Who says that you only do the right thing if you're going to win? Not the Tadeo I know. And if you were where that young man is now, it would make a difference to you."

She kept talking to him in this vein, and eventually he agreed to talk to Frank. He also told me he would talk to Mark Baker at the *Express* before he spoke to any other member of the press. "And the brother, Caleb—can you ask him to call me again?" he said.

We told him we would.

As we left, Dora refused our thanks, saying we were the ones who had helped her. I didn't think that was the case.

WE started the trip back.
"Are you sorry it won't be your story?" Ethan asked, re-arranging his pillows.

I thought about it for a moment and said, "A little, I suppose. Mostly not."

But he had already fallen asleep, wasting my honesty.

He slept through the brief calls I made to Frank and Mark Baker, and the stop I made at the police department, where Frank met me in the parking garage. Memories of seeing Ethan in an ICU were far too new—neither of us wanted to wake him or leave him alone asleep, so we stood outside the car and spoke softly. I gave Frank a quick summary of what I had learned and told him how to contact Tadeo. He told me Reed had found a little tin container hidden in Sheila's house. It held several small, individually wrapped teeth.

"He nearly didn't find them. She put them in a Yahtzee game. He only figured it out because the game was in her bedroom, and after imagining a few wild variations on Yahtzee, he decided she probably wasn't the type to be playing any of them in bed."

"Thank you for that image."

We promised to catch up on other events of the day when we saw each other that evening.

I stopped to refill the Jeep's nearly empty gas tank, then headed home.

I don't know when Ethan woke up, but about three miles from the house I heard him say, "Did you know we're being followed?"

Honesty made me admit I didn't, but he was right.

CHAPTER 34

Monday, May 1
3:15 P.M.
LAS PIERNAS

So you don't know how long you've been tailed?"

"I don't think it's been for very long. I think I would have noticed someone following me all the way from Redlands. I stopped off at the police department, and again to get gas."

"You did?"

His disbelief over that gave me a moment to glance again in the mirror.

"Don't let him see you checking the mirror," he said, making me want to tell him that I wasn't born yesterday, but why emphasize the obvious? And it's hard to sound wise if you're the one who didn't notice the tail.

"He's staying far enough back that I haven't been able to get a good look at his plates—or at him," he added. "He's wearing a cap and shades. Driving a dark blue SUV. Not one of the giant ones, but high enough off the ground to see you from a few cars back."

"I did figure out which car it is," I said. He didn't laugh, which made me think he was more worried than he was letting on.

I made a turn, traveling away from the house. "Don't sit up," I said to Ethan. "He may not know you're in the car, and that might be helpful."

"No problem. But the seat belt might be giving me away."

I made another turn and glanced at Ethan. His face was pale and drawn. "Are you in pain? Don't lie to me."

"Let's call it discomfort. I can handle it."

The blue SUV appeared in traffic a few cars back. I thought over my options.

If I turned on to a more deserted street, I would either make him shy away or become more aggressive. If he was only trying to figure out where I lived, he might hang back a bit, but if he intended harm, it would be a bad choice. This was no time to give him the benefit of the doubt.

So I stayed with bigger roads. The SUV stayed with me. I had a full tank of gas but couldn't keep this up much longer, or I'd end up driving Ethan to the ER.

Same with pulling any fancy moves through intersections—if I had been the only one in the car, I would have taken turns faster and blown a red light. I would have to try to lose the SUV with subtler moves, or lead him somewhere he definitely didn't want to go.

I thought of going back to the police department, but that might only be a temporary solution, since I could have been followed from there. And I was afraid the issue might be forced before then.

I grabbed my purse and pushed it toward Ethan. "Take out my cell phone—it's clipped to the side. Hold down the number two and it will dial Frank's cell phone. Tell him what's happening, and ask him if a patrol car could pull one of us over."

"Pull one of us over! Why not him?"

"My first choice, of course, but I'll take scaring him off any way we can."

Frank had just answered when the SUV turned down a side street, disappearing from view.

"He's gone," I said.

Ethan still told Frank what was going on. He spoke to him while I made a few more unnecessary turns, making sure I hadn't been handed off to a second tail.

"Frank says stay on the phone with him until we get home."

So they talked, mostly about the visit to Tadeo, with occasional interruptions when Ethan relayed a question from Frank, mostly to ask if I was sure I didn't have another shadow.

When we reached the house, a patrol car was parked out front.

"Don't worry," Ethan said. "Frank made sure it wasn't Officer Fletcher."

"I don't want to become paranoid about *everyone* in that family," I said, not entirely sure that it wasn't too late to prevent that from happening.

I recognized the officer as Mike Sorenson, a longtime friend of Frank's, and felt the last of my fear easing.

"Dude," Ethan said into the phone, "he's so old."

I heard Frank laughing.

"Ethan," I said, "he'll be able to protect us from anything short of an act of God."

We said good-bye to Frank and hello to Mike. Ethan was perfectly polite to him, perhaps because when Mike helped him into the house, he got a better chance to see that the man is built like a steel vault. Ethan took a painkiller and headed for bed.

Mike told me he was going to stick around for a while, if I didn't mind.

I didn't, because even knowing that sooner or later he would have to return to regular duties, it was a relief to have him there. The dogs, friendly as they were, were also protective, and would undoubtedly hear anyone trying to approach the house.

I kept trying to figure out why anyone would want to follow me. Who could it be? Sheila's killer? But if the killer was worried that I had told the Las Piernas police something about him, reading the *Express* would have let him know I hadn't seen the person who ran off. And the person who ran off might not, after all, have been the killer. It would be too late to come after me now to shut me up, anyway—I had already talked to the police that night, and the public knew it.

To prevent me from testifying later? Testifying to what? The risk of being caught while coming after me would be greater than any threat I could pose in a courtroom.

It didn't seem likely to me that whoever followed me was the killer. I thought about the other stories I had been working on lately and couldn't come up with anything that would merit that sort of effort, unless it was the story about missing children and custodial kidnappings. I thought about what had appeared in the paper so far, but couldn't see how anything in that story would result in my being followed. What had I done that would make anyone that nervous?

If I had been followed from the police department today, how could the person in the SUV know I would be there or at the gas station?

No matter how hard I thought about it, I couldn't see what threat I represented to anyone at this point. The only person I had upset lately was the kid at the dentist's office, Bobby Smith, and he wasn't the type to stalk with intent to harm.

This could easily be in connection with something less recent than Sheila Dolson's murder, I decided. I had made enemies over the years.

I looked in on Ethan, who was already asleep again. Altair had taken up his post next to him but watched me with his big brown eyes. The dog's closeness to Ethan would last until Frank came home. Cody, ensconced at the foot of the bed, allowed this much sharing of Ethan. The big cat was jealous of any affection given to Deke and Dunk, but even Cody had been won over by Altair.

It suddenly occurred to me that someone who wanted Altair might have been in that SUV. It would fit perfectly—a vehicle for carrying search dogs. Did the SUV driver know I was married to a cop? If so, maybe he had simply waited until I came by police headquarters.

I don't show up at the department very often, but it wouldn't be hard to learn that I was married to Frank. Suppose the driver was planning to follow him home? A stupid move, because Frank was unlikely to miss seeing a tail. I hoped. Although I have encountered some major-league meanies over the years, he has more violent enemies than I do.

If Frank was the person the driver of the SUV intended to follow home, my stopping by the department must have seemed to be a great stroke of luck.

Altair sighed and lowered his head to his forepaws. I knelt next to him and scratched his ears, winning another sigh, this one of satisfaction.

I worried that even with the company of Cody and the other dogs, he might be bored—SAR dogs are often trained several times a week, in what are extended play sessions as far as the dogs are concerned. I didn't know what Sheila's routine had been, but Altair didn't get to his level of proficiency without work on the part of his handlers.

At least we knew another skilled handler, someone I could trust completely—Ben had promised to come by to work with him tomorrow. I suspected that would cheer the dog up a little.

Ben had been surprised that Altair had so quickly and strongly attached himself to Frank and Ethan. "Usually a dog will attach himself more quickly to a human of the same sex as his previous handler. He's worked with me and other men on the team, but he's been living in female-only households. Makes me wonder what was going on with Sheila and the dog."

"She seemed to me to have a mean streak, but you sound as if you think she might have abused him."

He hesitated. "I certainly won't make a horrible accusation like that without more facts. He's not shying away from you, right?"

"Right."

I thought back over that conversation now, and about Anna's attempt to get me to hand him over to her. I wondered if the Fletchers would lay claim to him somehow, produce a will saying Sheila had left him to them. Or say that he now belonged to the family even if she hadn't left a will.

How badly might someone want him? Enough to steal him?

We might not be Altair's final home, but damned if I was going to let him be stolen. I'd have to talk to Ben about who drove what on the Las Piernas SAR team.

CHAPTER 35

Monday, May 1
10:15 P.M.
HOME OF GILES FLETCHER
LAS PIERNAS

So soon?" Roy asked.

"I'm afraid so," Giles said sympathetically. Roy had been agitated for the last hour or so. Giles congratulated himself again for excluding Nelson from this meeting. The two of them would have worked each other into a ridiculous state of anxiety.

"Couldn't it wait a few days? Perhaps on Saturday?"

"Many more of your neighbors will be home on Saturday, Roy. If something goes wrong, we really don't want to attract attention."

Roy looked toward Dex in appeal.

"Will it help your resolve to know that she asked me to help her leave you?" Dex asked.

Roy dropped his gaze.

"She confided that she wasn't made to live shut up in the house all the time," Dex went on. "She assured me she wouldn't try to take the children away from you, but it seemed to me that was just another way of saying she was eager to be free of her responsibilities. She hopes the children will be allowed to go to our school, to socialize. She thought it would be safe to let them do so if she wasn't in the picture." He paused. "She feels certain the Fletcher family will help her reestablish herself in her new life. She wants us to offer . . . how did she put it? Oh yes, 'money to ensure that she stays silent.'"

"One must give her credit," Giles said, "for not pussyfooting around."

Roy covered his face with his hands. No one said anything else for long moments. When he looked up again, he said, "Maybe that wouldn't be such a bad idea. I mean, just let her divorce me. She's Carrie's mother, for God's sake—"

"Roy," Giles said gently, "none of us were raised by our birth mothers. This family, more than any other, knows that good parents are more important to a child than biological relationships. Have you forgotten why we dared to take matters into our own hands to create your family? It was for the sake of those children. They needed us. Needed our intervention."

"Yes, but they were so young then! They accepted change more easily. This will be so hard on them. I was against the idea of divorce before, but compared to the other alternatives . . . And even if Victoria says she doesn't want responsibilities, I know she loves the children. She wouldn't do anything to cause them problems. We could wait a while to make it official, until no one was watching for her. Or even help her establish a new identity."

"And you think this plan of yours would be easier on your children? To know she's intentionally abandoned them? To see her once in a while and let her influence their thinking? To abandon them again and again, each time a visit ends? Alienate them from this family?"

"It might not happen that way," Roy said, dropping his gaze to the floor.

Dex said, "You've spent years trying to rescue her, haven't you, Roy?"

Roy looked up at him.

"You saved her from the low-life scum she was living with when you met her," Dex said. "You helped her to become free of alcohol and drugs. You wanted children, but she had become infertile. You were ready to adopt, but she must first have her own child. You changed your whole life so that she could be reunited with Carrie."

"Yes," said Roy. After a moment he added, "I do see her faults. She can be . . . difficult. I suppose that's why I've . . . why I've strayed. But I never meant that to lead to something like this."

"It's not your fault, Roy," Dex said. "It's hers. She was as ready to *stray* as you were, but you don't want to abandon the children and blackmail the family in the bargain."

"No. But there has to be some other way to deal with this."

Giles exchanged a quick glance with Dex, then said, "This should be your decision, Roy. No matter what you decide to do about Victoria, though, you must take the children away for a while."

"Because of the newspaper reporter."

"Yes." Giles looked again to Dex. "Tell him about Ms. Kelly."

Dex said, "I was . . . busy for part of the day, as you know. As I was over the weekend."

Roy winced.

"Later," Dex went on, "Giles asked me to try to learn what Ms. Kelly was working on, but that's not as easy as it seems. Newspapers are always concerned that someone is trying to publish a news item before they do, or steal a story from them, so no one discusses what they are working on. I called Ms. Kelly's office, just to see if she was in, thinking I might follow her from the *Express* when she left. But her outgoing voice mail said she would be out of the office all day."

"So?"

"As you know, she recently wrote a story on missing children. She worked with your wife—when your wife was known as Bonnie Creci—and may be able to recognize that Victoria Fletcher and Bonnie Creci are the same person. Ms. Kelly was at the scene where police were digging up the remains of your son Aaron's birth father—the man who supposedly abducted Aaron in a custody dispute two years ago. She arrived at Sheila's house just after Sheila died. Within hours, she had uncovered a great deal of Sheila's history. Caleb, who apparently didn't know her until last week, dined at her home two nights in a row. Her husband has alerted Ben Sheridan to the fact that Anna Stover is our cousin. Do I need to go on listing reasons why we may want to know what she's up to these days, and why she may be a threat to your family?"

"No," Roy said. "No." He put his head back in his hands. As if asking the floor, he murmured, "So where was she today?"

"We don't know," Giles said. "Dex followed her for a brief time this afternoon, from police headquarters, but he was spotted almost immediately. Her husband is a homicide detective, as you know."

"Yes."

"Did you notify your clients?" Dex asked.

"Yes," Roy said, his voice flat. Beaten, Giles thought. He's giving in.

"And?" Dex prodded.

"No one expects me back for at least three weeks."

"Good," Giles said. "And now, you remember what you're to do tomorrow?"

He sat up straight. "You agree with me, right?"

"What do you mean?"

"About the divorce. Separation. Whatever it ends up being."

"Yes, as I said, it's your decision."

"In that case, plans will change a little." He held up the prepaid cell phone Giles had supplied. "You'll call me at home on this phone at about ten o'clock and tell me to come over to Dad's house. I'll bring Victoria and the kids there in our SUV and leave my work van behind at the house. You'll have a new SUV in Dad's driveway, packed with everything we'll need for the trip to the mountains ready and waiting. Once we're in the mountains, you'll call me to let me know what to do from there."

"Hmm. That's not quite what we said, and I think it would be best if we didn't change that aspect of the plans," Giles said. "It would be much better if you left with the children, but not Victoria. She can follow you a little later."

"But—"

"Think this through, Roy. We need to work out details of the divorce with Victoria before she knows where you and the children are, or she really has us in a terrible bargaining position. When it comes down to making sure she won't take advantage of the family, I think it would be best for you to leave that to us, don't you agree?"

He stared at them. Giles wondered if he would object, but in the end he said, "I'll trust you to do what's best, Giles."

"I'm honored by that," Giles said. "Now, let's send you home. Do you need anything to help you sleep?"

"No. I don't think so."

"Dex, why don't you give him something just in case he changes his mind?"

Dex moved to a cabinet in a nearby bathroom and came back with a bottle of sedatives.

Roy looked at the label. "This says these are for Victoria," he said in surprise. "And they're dated six months ago."

"She called Susan—" Dex began.

"Our Susan? Dr. Susan?"

"Yes."

"Why?"

"Victoria asked her to prescribe something to help her sleep," Giles said. "Around the time you were . . . working so late."

"Oh." He pocketed them. He stood and lurched toward the door. The staggering walk of a drunk, although Giles knew his brother was completely sober. Roy was caught between his long-cherished hopes for Victoria—his dreams of helping her to become the perfect wife and mother—and the facts that continued to present themselves to him. That Dex and Giles continued to present to him. Dexter's astute observation this evening that Roy loved to play the rescuer was undoubtedly correct. Roy's tendency to view himself in that way probably also accounted at least in part for his infatuation with Cleo, although Giles nearly laughed aloud thinking of anyone trying to rescue Cleo. The poor boy was in terrible shape, but Giles had no doubt that he would pull himself together eventually.

Roy stopped at the door and turned to look at Dex. He held up the bottle of pills. "They *are* just sleeping pills?"

"Oh, yes. She could safely take a dozen of them."

"A dozen . . ."

"Yes."

When they heard his van pull away, Giles said, "I think that went rather well, don't you?"

Dex shrugged and said, "We'll know soon. I'm heading home. Maggie will wonder where I am."

Giles sincerely doubted that but wished him a good night.

CHAPTER 36

Tuesday, May 2
4:35 A.M.
HUNTINGTON BEACH

THE two girls silently watched the street from their bedroom window. The pickup truck for the delivery of the *Orange County Register* had gone by some time ago, and Carrie began to wonder if they were now waiting in vain.

She was so sleepy, but at the same time too worried and excited to fall asleep. Genie was drawing on the window with her fingertip, breathing out to make the glass fog, then making faces in the moisture. Carrie couldn't turn on a light to read or do much of anything to keep herself occupied while they waited.

She had never realized how quiet it was at this time of day. After a while, she gave in and made faces on the window just as Genie did. Genie smiled, and a few minutes later they began playing tic-tac-toe.

They both gave up this pursuit and sat up with a start when lights came on at Mrs. Pherson's house across the street. Carrie remembered something and whispered it to Genie. "Mrs. Pherson works in a bank in Los Angeles. She has to leave early to drive there."

Mom didn't like Mrs. Pherson, they knew. Genie had once heard Mom and Dad talking about her. Mom didn't like Mrs. Pherson because she flirted with Dad, but Dad said she was just trying to be neighborly.

Carrie had long ago noticed that women paid a different kind of attention to Dad than they did to other men. They didn't become as silly around him as they did around Uncle Dex, but they smiled at him a lot.

That made her think about Uncle Dex's visit yesterday while

Dad was gone. Uncle Dex had been over here several days in a row, but Carrie hadn't been here when he showed up on Saturday and Sunday. Dad had taken the kids to the zoo and over to Grandfather's house again this weekend, and Mom had stayed home. That was strange, because usually Mom came with them everywhere they went. Dad had seemed unhappy, and it kind of spoiled the fun. When they got back, Mom had mentioned that Uncle Dexter had stopped by, and Carrie hadn't thought anything of it. But yesterday's visit made her uneasy, because Uncle Dexter had never stayed for more than a few minutes when Dad wasn't home. This time, he was here for a long time, and Mom had asked Carrie and Genie to watch the boys while she talked privately with him.

Carrie was glad for it, in a way, because it gave Genie time to carry out the first part of her plan—calling the *Express* and subscribing to the paper. Carrie still couldn't get over how bold Genie was.

Still, it might not have worked. Maybe the person in Circulation at the *Express* had not been fooled by Genie, had recognized that this was a child's voice. The phone had rung a few times later in the day—maybe the paper had called to confirm something, and Mom had said that there was a mistake.

No, if that had happened, the paper would have asked about the address and the credit card, and she would have pressured both girls into telling her what they had done. The thought of this happening at some later point made her feel scared.

Last night the boys blurted out the news to Dad that Uncle Dex had visited, of course. Dad was cheerful with the boys about it, but he looked at Mom, and she gave him a smug kind of smile. After that, Mom and Dad didn't look at each other all night. They didn't talk to each other. Dad went out for a while and didn't get back home until late. Thinking about this made Carrie's stomach hurt.

"Listen!" Genie whispered.

They both heard the noise before they saw the headlights, a low motor sound punctuated by drawn-out, high-pitched squeals.

A pickup truck with bad brakes was coming up the street. It was going slowly, as if the driver wasn't sure of his destination. He stopped the truck in front of their house.

Hurry up and get out of here! Carrie screamed inside her head. At long last the paper was tossed and landed at the foot of the driveway with a soft thump. The truck drove off. The girls hurried silently to the stairs. Carrie followed Genie's method of going down them, stepping at the outer edges, avoiding the one that sometimes creaked.

Genie was at the front door in a flash and waited there for Carrie to reach the security system controls.

Ignoring the shaking in her fingers, Carrie entered the code on the keypad exactly as Genie had told her to. This did not set off the howling alarm, as she had feared it might, but the three quick beeps acknowledging that it was disarmed seemed loud enough to wake the whole household. Genie smiled at her, but Carrie cringed, expecting their father to come running down the stairs. He didn't—the house slept on, even through the soft swooshing of the opening of the door. Carrie hurriedly grabbed the door before it could swing shut. Genie was already on her way to the end of the drive.

It would be easy! It would be easy after all!

Then, as Carrie watched in dismay, Mrs. Pherson came out of her house. She halted and stared at Genie. Her attention moved to Carrie, standing in the doorway.

"Good morning," she called to the girls. "You two are up early!"

Carrie felt her shoulders hunching up, as if she could become a turtle. But Genie smiled and nodded, then hurried back inside.

Carrie softly shut the door as Genie rushed upstairs, then Carrie reset the alarm.

Carrie was halfway up the stairs when her parents' bedroom door opened.

Her father stepped into the hallway and shut the bedroom door behind him. He was fully dressed and seemed distracted. He did not see her, frozen in place, until he reached the top of the stairs. "Carrie?" he asked in a low voice, freezing in place as well.

"Good morning, Dad," she said softly back.

"What are you doing up?"

She shrugged. "I couldn't sleep."

His brows drew together in worry. "Your hand bothering you?"

She nearly lied, but foresaw that this might lead to further worry on his part, or a trip to see Dr. Susan, where her fakery would be exposed. "Not really."

He moved down to where she stood, sat on the stairs, and patted the place next to him. Obediently, she sat.

"You're cold," he said. "You should have put slippers and a robe on. Or . . ." He frowned, seeming to notice she was dressed. "Shoes and a sweatshirt."

She found herself wondering, as she looked more closely at his own attire, why he was fully dressed so early in the day. He saw her notice, and seemed to try to head off any questions about his own early rising. "Not feeling sick, are you?" he asked.

"No, I'm fine."

He studied her face.

"Carrie, is anything troubling you?"

Suddenly it seemed as if the truth had become a big fish inside of her, swimming hard, wanting to break to the surface. He asked this question so sincerely, so lovingly, she felt the certainty of his love for her, and of her own love for him in return. But she had Genie to think of.

And then, looking at him, she saw the trouble in his own eyes. The big fish changed into a question of her own.

"Daddy, what's wrong with you and Mommy?"

She hadn't used these younger child's terms for them for so long, but she felt small now. Afraid.

He tensed, then looked away. "We'll be okay," he said.

"I don't like Uncle Dex," she blurted out.

He put an arm around her and hugged her to him. "It's okay," he said. "It's okay." His voice sounded funny, almost as if he might cry or something, which made her very afraid. She took his hand in hers and held it. He smiled and took a deep breath and said, "Don't be mad at Uncle Dex, honey. He's not a very happy man. Right now . . . well, your mother's not very happy, either."

"Why?"

"Hard to explain. But no one would want to worry you, not me, not Mom, not Uncle Dex. Soon things will work out. I promise you. Everything will be all right, and you and I won't let anybody worry us or make us get up early in the morning." His voice had lightened by the end of that, as if they shared a little joke. He squeezed her shoulders again and said, "Think you can get back to sleep?"

"I think so," she lied.

"Good. Now, I'm going for a little drive, just to clear my head."

"You aren't leaving us?" she asked anxiously.

"Never, Carrie. Never. You remember that, okay?"

"Yes." She hugged him hard, smelled his aftershave, and felt comforted by the familiar scent. He ruffled her hair, then helped her to her feet as he came to his own. She promised she would go back to bed, and he kissed her cheek before he left.

He was gone from the house for several minutes before she climbed the stairs to her bedroom. Everybody was acting so weird. Where was he going so early in the morning? What was bothering him?

Genie was waiting for her, her eyes wide and her face pale. She seemed scared, but at the same time wore an expression that Carrie immediately recognized as her most determined look.

"Don't worry," Carrie said. "I'm not in trouble. And he doesn't even know you're awake."

It was as if she hadn't spoken.

"What kind of animal is Squeegee?" Genie asked.

"A lion," Carrie said.

Genie burst into tears and handed her the A section of the *Las Piernas News Express*.

CHAPTER 37

Tuesday, May 2

6:25 A.M.

HUNTINGTON BEACH

WHAT are you doing?" Carrie asked.

In the time since Carrie had read the article, they had whispered questions that could not be answered and reassured each other a dozen times that they were "sisters no matter what." They had cried softly while hugging each other, then sat quietly together. They had made and discarded half a dozen plans. Now Genie had taken her by the hand and was leading her downstairs again.

"We have to call her now, before Mom wakes up," Genie whispered back.

"Who?"

"Irene Kelly."

Irene Kelly was the reporter who had written the story about Carrie. Or a story about a girl named Carla, whose picture looked like pictures Mom had of Carrie as a baby, but who seemed to Carrie to be a different girl. The room—the room that belonged to that little girl named Carla—looked familiar.

And a lot of the story was about Mom, whose picture was in the paper, too, even though the color and length of her hair had changed since those photos were taken. The strange thing was, Carrie could remember Mom looking like that, although Genie couldn't. In the story, Mom's name was Bonnie, not Victoria.

Carrie wasn't so sure about the man named Blake Ives. One minute he seemed familiar to her. The next minute he seemed to be a complete unknown.

The man Bonnie Creci Ives ran away with when she divorced Blake Ives looked mean. Reggie Faroe. Apparently he was one of the reasons Bonnie Ives didn't get custody of her daughter. Reggie Faroe was one of the reasons Blake Ives was scared about what had happened to his daughter. Carrie didn't blame him.

"I don't remember Reggie Faroe at all," Carrie had told Genie.

"You were only two when your parents divorced," Genie had said. "You were too little. She didn't take you from your dad until a year later."

That was the way Genie was talking now, as if it were all about Carrie and not Carla. As if you could believe everything you read in the paper.

But Carrie was finding it impossible to convince herself that the story was about a different girl.

IRENE KELLY'S e-mail address and phone number had appeared at the end of the article. On almost all the local stories in the paper, reporters' e-mail addresses and phone numbers appeared, with an invitation to readers:

Care to comment on this story?

On this story, the ending part was a little different. In addition to the comment line, it said that if you had information on the whereabouts of Carla Ives or Bonnie Creci Ives, to e-mail or call Irene Kelly.

"I don't think we should call her," Carrie said.

"Why not?"

"Maybe I should just ask Mom and Dad about it."

Genie just looked at her. This was not the first time the proposal had been made. Mom and Dad were angry with each other right now. Bringing this up would only make them turn that anger toward whoever was stupid enough to mention it to them.

"If Mom didn't make life awful for you," Genie said, "she would lie about it. And so would Dad. Because they have been lying about you every single day."

Carrie was silent.

"Doesn't that make you angry?" Genie asked.

"Yes," Carrie admitted. And hurt. And confused. But she had

already told Genie about those feelings, and didn't repeat that now. Besides, they had all pretty much turned into one feeling at this point: numbness. Genie pulled her into the downstairs office and closed the door softly behind them. Carrie stood still as Genie made her way through the darkness toward the desk.

Carrie almost hoped the moment in the dark would last forever. She could hide in its nothingness without having to make choices that might hurt people or cause problems.

Genie turned on the desk lamp. As if she could read Carrie's mind, she said, "We both know that something is going wrong around here. It isn't just you. And you aren't causing problems. You didn't make Mom have sex with Uncle Dex."

"Genie!"

"Well, she did." She picked up the phone and started to dial.

"Wait! I don't think we should call now!"

"Why not?"

"We might wake her up," Carrie said, knowing that the real reason was that she was so scared, she felt as if she needed to go to the bathroom.

"It's a number at the newspaper," Genie said. "See? The reporters' phone numbers all begin the same way."

It was the kind of thing Genie was always quick to figure out—relationships of numbers, codes, and visual groupings. Maybe, Carrie thought, I could have figured it out if the story was about Genie. She found that since reading the article, she wasn't able to think right.

"You're scared to do it?" Genie asked.

Carrie nodded.

"I'll do it for you."

She finished dialing. She motioned Carrie closer and held the phone so that Carrie could hear the outgoing message.

"You've reached the voice mail of Irene Kelly at the *Las Piernas News Express*. I'll be out of the office on Monday, May first, but I'll return on Tuesday. Please leave a message after the tone, including a callback number with your area code. If this is urgent, press three to reach our news department or zero to reach an operator."

Genie took a breath and said in a soft voice, "Hello, Ms. Kelly. I'm calling about the girl you wrote about in today's paper. She would like to meet you—"

Carrie reached over and hung up the phone.

"What did you do that for?" Genie said, forgetting to keep her voice low.

Carrie cringed and looked up at the ceiling.

Genie scrunched up her shoulders. "Sorry!" she whispered.

They listened for long moments but didn't hear any footsteps or other sounds coming from upstairs.

Carrie looked at Genie in exasperation. "Why did you tell that reporter I wanted to meet her?"

"Because you need to get more information. What if your real dad isn't nice? She'll know. She's met him."

"So has Mom."

"Mom won't tell you the truth about him."

Carrie had to acknowledge that this was likely. But what might happen if she met this reporter? "Maybe I could just call her and talk to her about him."

"Carrie," Genie said, rolling her eyes. "We are calling her at six-thirty in the morning because we can't make phone calls at a normal time without Mom knowing. If we didn't call Grandfather and our aunts and uncles on their birthdays, we wouldn't know how to use a phone!"

"We call our cousins. . . ."

That got another roll of the eyes.

"How am I going to meet her?" Carrie asked. "It's harder to get out of the house than it is to make a phone call."

"Oh, no it's not."

"Yes, it—"

"Carrie! Listen to me. Dad is already out of the house. We have Mom outnumbered four to one. When it's time for you to meet Ms. Kelly, I'll start a game of hide-and-seek. You'll just take a little longer to be found than the rest of us. You'll go down to the corner, let her see that you are the girl in the photo, and come back here. Then hide behind the shower curtain in the downstairs bathroom. The boys will never look there."

Temporarily distracted from her worries, Carrie said, "They won't? Why not?"

"Troy and Aaron think there's a bogeyman who lives in the shower."

"Why?"

"I told them there was one, of course. It means there's at least one bathroom I can use without little boys bugging me. Although I think Troy is starting to have doubts."

"You wonder why you get in trouble more often than I do? What if they tell Mom?"

"They won't tell Mom because I said that right now the bogeyman was trapped in there by a hex, but that he always knew what little boys said to their parents, and if they mentioned him to Mom or Dad, he'd go live under their beds."

"Oh, poor Troy and Aaron!" Carrie tried to make it sound the way Mom would, but she ruined it by smiling.

"To answer the first question, I've never wondered why I get in more trouble."

Carrie sighed. "I'm not as brave as you, Genie."

"You are. You just don't know it yet."

"What if I get caught?"

"I'll take the blame. I'm the troublemaker, remember? They'll believe it was totally my idea."

"It *is* your idea!"

Genie smiled. "See, even you believe it."

Carrie had to clap her hand over her mouth to stifle a laugh.

Genie dialed the phone again. "Ms. Kelly sounds nice," she said as she listened to the outgoing message again.

"Hi, Ms. Kelly, it's me again. I'm sorry about the last time. Please meet me today in Huntington Beach. Please come to the corner of Playa Azul and Vista del Mar Streets at ten-fifteen this morning. Please do not tell anyone else you are meeting me, especially not Mr. Ives. I don't want to hurt his feelings if I'm wrong. Thank you, and please don't try to call me. If you aren't at the corner at ten-fifteen, we'll just try another day, but it might be a long time before I can do that, so please, please, pretty please try to make it today. Alone. Thank you. Good-bye."

Genie hung up and looked at Carrie with triumph.

"I think I'm going to be sick," Carrie said.

"No, you aren't."

"What do I tell her?"

"Okay, first, you don't get in the car with her."

"Even I know better than *that*."

"She'll see that you're Carla just from the photo."

"You think so?"

"Well, she might. Anyway, tell her that you want to know about Blake Ives."

"And that I'm happy and have a good family and I don't want to hurt them."

Genie seemed not to hear this. "Tell her about your rememberings. Ask her if a family by the name of Mason is missing a girl my age."

"Do you remember them?"

She shrugged. "It's like it is for you. I get these pictures in my head, or remember smells—I remember the smell of paint." She began snooping around the desk. Genie was always getting into things.

"Paint?"

"Like oil paint." She looked up from a stack of outgoing mail she had been studying. "Isn't that funny? Voices." She shrugged again. "People, but I can't really see their faces. I wish I knew more about them." She was studying the big Priority Mail envelopes now.

"I'm not so sure I want to find out more about my father," Carrie said.

Genie smiled. "You just called him your father. You want to find out. You read that article—he's sad without you."

"But Dad would be sad without me."

"True. So would I. But I think that we're going to be sad and upset if we keep wondering about this. We aren't going to be able to hide what we know from Mom and Dad forever."

This thought didn't help settle Carrie's stomach.

Genie put an arm around her shoulders. "Ask Ms. Kelly to

help you. She might know how you can live with us but still see your father."

"Or she might call the police on Mom and Dad."

"I don't think so. Don't worry. I didn't give Ms. Kelly our address or phone number. Make her drive off before you come back to the house."

"And if she won't?"

"Run to another house and hide in the yard."

"And meanwhile? What will you be doing?"

"Lying like crazy," she said, and they started to laugh, having a really hard time not being noisy.

But their laughter was cut short as they heard the automatic garage door opener kick into gear.

"Oh no, Dad's home!"

"Shhh," Genie said, snapping off the light.

This time, the darkness didn't seem so friendly.

CHAPTER 38

GENIE took Carrie by the hand again, leading her through the dark room with an unerring ability to avoid furniture, making Carrie wonder how many times Genie had been snooping around in the office.

They stopped at the closed door and pressed their ears to it. They heard the sound of the garage door closing again, the motor of the van shutting off. The van door closing. Dad opening the door into the house, his footsteps passing by. They held their breath.

He didn't hesitate near the office. He walked quickly toward the kitchen. They exhaled.

Genie carefully opened the door, transferred her hold on it to the knob on the outside. She let Carrie step into the hallway and then shut the door silently, slowly rotating the knob until the door latched again with a small snick.

They waited for some reaction to that sound, but in the kitchen, Dad was making quite a bit of noise. If he was fixing his own breakfast, they might be able to pretend they had just come downstairs. They usually got up at around this time to make breakfast for the family.

They had crept halfway down the hallway and were about to turn the corner leading to the kitchen when they heard the boys coming downstairs. Their voices carried to where the girls stood hidden from view.

"Daddy!" That was Aaron.

"Hi, Dad," Troy said. "What are you doing?"

"Good morning, boys! You're just in time to help me out. Will you go upstairs and tell Mom we're going to serve her breakfast in bed?"

"Is it Mother's Day?" Troy asked, confused.

"No, just a special treat for Mom."

"Why are you making it?" Aaron asked. "That's a girl's job."

Carrie and Genie exchanged a look. Genie signed, *Aaron gets oatmeal for a week*. Carrie smiled and signed agreement. Aaron hated oatmeal. Mom said the boy-girl thing he was into was just a phase, but it seemed like a long phase.

"No, no, it's not a girl's job," Dad said. "When you and Troy are a little older, you'll learn to cook, too. Boys have to be able to take care of themselves. You might not always have a girl in the house to cook for you." He paused, then said, "Go on, go upstairs before Mom gets up. Hurry. Stay up there with her—it's your job to make sure she doesn't get up before we bring breakfast to her."

The girls waited for the boys to go upstairs before they entered the kitchen. Dad was washing a small bowl at the sink. When he saw them he wished them a good morning and told them his breakfast-in-bed plan. Although he was trying to act cheerful, Carrie could see that he was still just as upset as he had been earlier this morning, when they sat on the stairs together.

Carrie suddenly thought of Uncle Dex, and wondered if Dad was doing this to make Mom like him again.

"How can we help?" Carrie asked.

"Would you please make some eggs and bacon? You know how Mom likes them."

"Sure. Over medium."

"I'll make some toast," Genie said.

"Thank you, girls."

"What's this for?" Genie asked, holding up a stalk of celery.

"Oh, for the special drink I'm making her."

"Celery juice?" Genie said with disgust.

He laughed. "No, no. A Bloody Mary—a type of one, anyway. One without alcohol in it."

"Bloody Mary? Like the queen?" Carrie asked.

"Yes, although I don't think she actually had anything to do with the drink."

"What queen?" Genie asked.

History was one of Carrie's strongest subjects. "She was the queen of England. Mary Tudor, daughter of Henry the Eighth and Catherine of Aragon. Queen Mary I." She began to tell the tale of how the queen got her nickname. It was a good and comfortable thing to do, to talk about history, even sad history. She noticed that Genie and Dad seemed to relax, hearing her little kitchen lesson. Genie asked questions, and Dad did, too. They could forget about any problems or worries they had right now and concentrate on the troubles of people who lived centuries ago. History was something she knew, something certain—or so it seemed, even though Grandfather told her that history changed depending on who told it. She could understand that.

She fell silent, thinking that maybe her father—Mr. Ives, if he was her father—might have one version of history to tell and her mom another. More than what was in the newspaper. She would have to listen to both versions. And to Dad's, too.

Genie glanced at Carrie in concern, then asked Dad about the Bloody Mary drink. When he told her the ingredients, she said, "That sounds weird."

"Mom will think of it as a special treat."

Something about that upset him again. Even Genie noticed that. She looked at Carrie and quickly signed, *What's wrong with Dad?*

Carrie made the sign for *mother* and left it at that.

Carrie was making up the tray, which usually only got used if someone was sick and couldn't get out of bed, or on Mother's Day or Father's Day.

Genie said, "Dad, is Mom sick?"

Carrie wondered if she had been reading her thoughts, but turned to see her holding a prescription bottle.

"No, no," he said, taking the bottle of pills from her. "This is an old prescription, see?"

They saw that he was right.

"Go on, take breakfast up to Mom before it gets cold. And Genie, thank you for finding these. It was dangerous to have them down where the boys might get to them. Mom probably meant to throw them away. I'll go do that now and be right up with you." He started toward the bathroom, then turned back to them and said, "Don't mention this to Mom, okay? She'd probably get upset if she realized she left them down here. I don't want to ruin her breakfast."

As they went up the stairs, Genie whispered, "Does he know about Uncle Dex and Mom?"

"I don't know. I—I think so."

"That stinks."

"Yes."

D A D joined them upstairs. Dad was supernice to Mom. The way he looked at her made Carrie want to cry. Mom was enjoying all the attention, but she gave Dad a kind of look that Carrie spent a long time trying to name. She finally decided that the right word was *cynical*. As she looked between them, she felt sure that Mom didn't love Dad anymore.

If she had realized that yesterday, Carrie thought, it would have caused her to be really upset. Added on to everything that was hanging over her head right now, she just felt sad about it in a distant way, the way she felt sad about the reign of Mary Tudor.

"Well, this has certainly been a nice surprise," Mom said, as if no one had done more than said "Happy Birthday" on her birthday.

"I have another one for you," Dad said. His voice trembled a little.

Mom smiled and raised an eyebrow. "Oh? I can hardly wait. Then again, there are good surprises and bad surprises."

"Kids, I think Mom needs another break from all of us, so today we'll spend the day in Las Piernas, and Mom can just relax here in peace and quiet. Or go for a drive, or whatever she wants to do."

Mom studied him, then covered a big yawn. "I am tired. Where will you be?"

"Oh, I thought I'd take them to see some of their aunts and uncles."

"Are we going to Grandfather's again?" Troy asked happily.

"We might. Get your own breakfasts, then let's clean up the house for Mom before we go, so she can just relax all day. We'll leave here at about ten. Will that give everyone enough time?"

The boys shouted gleeful agreement. Carrie and Genie looked at each other. Carrie said, "Maybe I should stay here with Mom, in case . . . in case she needs anything."

"Don't be silly, Carrie," Mom said. "You go along with the others. I'll be fine." She gave Carrie a little kiss and a hug, and then gave hugs and kisses to the others, too.

Dad stayed behind as they cleared the tray and herded the boys out. Carrie glanced back and saw him giving Mom a long kiss, and Mom seemed to be kissing him back. Any other time, such a display of passion would have embarrassed her. Instead, she found it gave her a little bit of hope. Maybe Mom just didn't know what she wanted.

Maybe they would be all right after all.

A F T E R breakfast, as the boys raced to their room, Genie whispered, "I'll call Ms. Kelly back and tell her not to come by today."

"Thanks," Carrie said.

S H E started cleaning up the kitchen. She noticed that the little bowl Dad had used was a mortar. The pestle had been set alongside it to dry. Poor Dad. He must have gone so far as to crush fresh spices for the Bloody Mary. Thinking of this made her feel another wave of hopelessness. One kiss wasn't going to change things between Mom and Dad.

Genie came running into the kitchen. "Shit!"

Carrie's eyes widened.

"When I called back," Genie said, as if she hadn't just spoken a totally forbidden word, "it wouldn't let me leave a message."

"What do you mean?"

"It says her voice mail is full."

"Don't feel so bad. She'll drive here, I won't be around, and she'll drive away. I mean, I'm sorry that she'll waste her time, but we can't help it."

"I guess not," Genie said. "But it might be hard to get her to come here again." After a moment she said, "Let's bring the camera Grandfather gave you to his house today and take pictures of you, and then ask him to get them developed for you. When they come back, we can mail them to Ms. Kelly."

Carrie could think of a number of ways this could go wrong, but agreed enthusiastically, because she could tell Genie was trying so hard to be helpful. She didn't think she fooled her sister, but maybe Genie was just disappointed about having to change plans.

THE house was never messy, but there were a few chores to be done. Dishes, laundry, dusting—there was never an end to them. Genie supervised the boys while Carrie did the sort of work she'd never entrust the boys to do.

As she put the mortar and pestle away, she saw a jar of strawberry preserves one of their aunts had given them. A Mason jar.

She thought of Genie, of her plea to ask Ms. Kelly about someone named Mason.

THEY were finished with the chores before ten. Genie had even managed to get the boys dressed and ready.

Mom and Dad hadn't come out of their bedroom.

"Now what do we do?" Aaron asked.

"I know," Carrie said, wondering if her mother had given her the ability to be an actress. "Let's play hide-and-seek."

Genie stared at her. "Are you sure?"

"Of course. I'm braver than you think."

"I don't think that's possible," Genie said, then turned to the boys and said, "I'll be 'it' first."

She covered her eyes and began counting. "One-alligator, two-alligator, three-alligator . . ."

CHAPTER 39

NOTHING like a day away from the office to ensure that your next morning will be delivered hot and fresh from hell.

I heard my phone ringing from across the room as I made my way to my desk. John was motioning me into his office, Mark Baker was calling my name, and Lydia Ames was waving a thick fan of pink message slips at me in an imperative way.

I raised my index finger in the waitress-style "be right with you" sign to John, Mark, and Lydia, and answered the phone as I dropped my purse onto my desk.

"Irene? It's Caleb. I'm sorry to bother you at work, but I was just wondering . . ."

I sat down under the pressure of a load of guilt. "Oh, hi, Caleb. Of course you want to know what happened yesterday. Sorry, I should have called you as soon as I got back from talking to the Garcias." I quickly gave him a synopsis of what we had learned. He was excited and full of questions. I answered a few, then said, "I can't go into much detail right now—I just got into the office. I can tell you more after I get off work, or you could call Ethan. He was awake when I left the house this morning."

He thanked me and said he'd call Ethan.

Lydia walked over with the stack of message slips before I finished talking to him. "Your voice mail is full," she said the moment I hung up the phone. "Here's hoping one of these people can help you find her."

"Help her father find her," I said.

That seemed to amuse her, but she only said, "Better talk to John."

The talk with John didn't take all that long. He was pleased with the story. Mark had done his usual fine work, following up on the aspects of the story that concerned the police work in the case of Carla Ives. His review of their efforts ran as a companion piece to mine.

I told John about my visit with the Garcias, and he called Mark in to talk that over. He decided, as I had thought he would, that I should keep my mitts off the story, since it so closely involved the Las Piernas Police Department. If it had gone to certain other reporters on our staff, I might not have been so complacent about it.

I got back to my desk and started picking up messages from my voice mail. I had another set of calls from parents of children who were missing, all of whom wanted me to put a story in the paper about their own child. I could understand their desperation. I doubted they would understand that I was already pushing the limit on the number of stories I'd be able to write on the subject, and that I wasn't the one who decided what would be in the paper each day. I spent a brief moment contemplating what the paper would be like if I did, another contemplating the headaches that went along with that power, and went back to listening to calls. Several were about children allegedly taken by noncustodial parents.

A few were from people who thought they'd seen a girl who looked something like Carla Ives. Two of these I recognized as people who called the paper about twice a week, claiming some connection to various stories. I made a list of the others, although most sounded vague—like the man who said he had seen her in a grocery store with another little girl in Huntington Beach, but had no idea where she lived or who she was with. When he added that he thought she might be deaf now, because the two girls were using sign language, I was almost positive he had seen someone else.

I got a real surprise about halfway through the playback process. A woman's voice said, "My daughter Jenny has been missing for five years, and my son was wrongfully convicted of killing her and my husband. My name is Elisa Fletcher. . . .”

She went on to leave a callback number and a request that I contact her as soon as possible. I hesitated over it, then copied her name and phone number on a second slip of paper and gave it to Mark. “Curiosity is killing me,” I admitted. “I’ll want to talk to her at some point, but I don’t want to step on your story.”

When I got back to my desk, I got a call from Reed. He had some questions about the Fletcher dentists, most of which I couldn’t answer.

“I’ve been thinking a lot about Sheila’s presence at the scene of Gerry Serre’s burial, though,” I said.

“Oh?”

“Are they rushing the DNA on the cigarette butts found at the scene?”

“That’s not something for publication,” he said. “How did you find out about it?”

“I’d rather not say. And I couldn’t write about it, anyway. You know that.”

“You could talk to Mark.”

“This sounds like a roundabout way to try to get me to tell you who talked to me.”

He laughed. “The DNA in the cigarettes was tested. No hits in any of our databases.”

“Did you check it against the shoe DNA?”

“That hasn’t come back yet. We’re hoping they’ll finish it this afternoon.”

“How about comparing the cigarettes to Sheila’s DNA?”

There was a pause. “Now, what makes you ask something like that?”

“I can’t help but think that she had some reason to be at the scene out at the Sheffield Estate. Some reason other than searching with Altair. She wasn’t really trying to find anything, and if it was supposedly for attention, why did she arrive there before the press was on hand? She didn’t know I was going to be there—she damned near ran me off the road when I got there, and kept going, so if it was publicity she was after, what was up with that?”

"She made sure the *Express* was there that evening, for the show with the teeth."

"Yes. A show."

"If she knew something about the death of Gerald Serre, that little show probably got her killed by his murderer."

"Hmm. Maybe."

"What's on your mind, Irene?"

"What if she knew something about his murder or burial because she was there when it happened? Or killed him herself?"

"Revisiting the site in full view of the newspaper and investigators?"

"Offering to be of help in the investigation. Don't tell me she'd be the first killer to do that."

"No, of course not."

"Reed, what if she *wanted* the press to be able to say there was a reason for her DNA to be found there? That we had seen her smoking there, and so on?"

Another pause. "Ben documented every step of that recovery process."

"Did she know that?"

He thought about this for a moment. "Maybe not. She got there after the coroner left. Anyway, we'll be running her DNA as part of the investigation of her murder. I'll ask the lab to do a comparison."

I went back to listening to messages and making notes. About three messages after the one Caleb's mom left, I heard another one that piqued my interest.

"This is Martha Hayes. I used to be Martha Faroe. Reggie Faroe was my son. I'm very sorry about that man's little girl, but Reggie had nothing to do with her being taken, and I can prove that. Please call me." She left a number, so I gave her a call.

She thanked me for returning her call, then said, "Reggie was no angel, and nobody knows that better'n me. His daddy was trouble, too—got killed in a bar fight. He passed his drinking along to Reggie, I guess. And his ability to charm the ladies. That boy was in trouble one way or another most of his life."

"You speak of him using the past tense. . . ."

"That's exactly my point. Reggie was dead a week before that little girl went missing."

"I'm sorry. . . ."

"Absolutely no need to be. I loved him, I was his mama, and I wished he'd straightened out. But I would be a liar if I didn't tell you that he made life miserable for me and Mr. Hayes and my children from my second marriage."

"How did he die?"

"No certain answer to that. His body was found in Arizona."

I was silent, thumbing through the photocopies I had from Blake Ives. When I found what I was looking for, I said, "Mr. Ives hired a private investigator, who was able to trace Reggie to a Nevada trailer park around the time Mr. Ives's daughter disappeared. And your son and a female companion disappeared from the trailer park around that same time."

"I know all about that PI—he come by here asking about Reggie, told me he thought Reggie and Bonnie had that little girl." She laughed. "I told him that I could no more picture Reggie wantin' to live with a little kid than I could picture him flyin' to the moon, and that's the truth." She paused. "I even told him that Reggie and Bonnie wasn't together, but I seen he didn't believe me. I don't know who that—what'd you call her?"

"The PI called her a 'female companion.'"

"Yeah, well, I know some cops who'd like to know who she was. Anyway, back then I didn't know Reggie was dead."

"I don't understand."

"Reggie was left for dead out in the desert. He might have been murdered, but it wasn't a sure thing—he was at the bottom of some cliff out there, and it was a question whether he fell or was pushed. Nobody saw him fall, or even ever saw him out there or knew why he was there. Didn't have no wallet or anything on him to say who he was."

"And you say he was found before Carla Ives went missing?"

"The date they give me for the body being brought in was a week before that little girl went missing, if she went missing when you said she did."

"What's your theory about what happened to him?"

"I tend to think he pissed somebody off and got himself killed, because he wasn't exactly the type to go hikin' in the desert. Anyway, I don't think whoever it was left him there expected he'd ever be found, but as it happened, some rock hunter out looking for gems come across the body and called the sheriff. Well, they didn't have nothin' to go by, because Reggie wasn't missed by no one."

"There was no missing-persons report."

"No. You see, Reggie disappearin' for long periods of time wasn't exactly anything new to me. And then I have this PI come along and tell me he's run off with this Bonnie, that I know left him some time back, and her little girl. But back then I thought maybe they got back together. And when I didn't hear nothin' from Reggie, I just thought maybe he'd decided to become a family man, and well, leave it to him to do it such a lousy way."

She paused, then said, "I did him wrong, thinking of him like that."

"You say you were contacted by an Arizona medical examiner's office?"

"Yes. Just about two years ago, I got a call from Arizona. Somebody down there was goin' through cold cases, John Does in the morgue. A trainee or something, and they give him this job to do. Decided to run the fingerprints. That's the one time I guess I was lucky Reggie had a prison record. He was in the FBI system, and so they matched him up that way. And my husband, Mr. Hayes, he paid so I could go down there and bring Reggie's ashes home."

By that time, she said, she had forgotten about the PI who had been asking about Reggie. My story had reminded her of him.

"I'm not mad at you or Mr. Ives for what's in the story," she assured me, "but I started to think about it and figured Reggie got blamed enough for things he *did* do, maybe I'd set the record straight for him. I mean, I know you don't come out and say he took that girl, but people will suppose it, just like Mr. Ives does. And maybe if Mr. Ives stops looking in the wrong place, he'll have an easier time finding her."

She gave me the names of her contacts in Arizona. I thanked her, made some notes, and went back to retrieving messages.

I logged onto my computer and found my e-mail in-box nearly as overloaded as my voice mail, although a few of the subject lines told me I had the usual amount of déjà poo in there, too—jokes and links that had been sent to me a dozen times before. Nothing dies on the Internet.

I was deleting spam while half-listening to messages, which is why I had to replay one of them—a young girl. I wondered why she had hung up before finishing her first message, and felt relief that she had left the second one.

A scared young girl, whispering two messages. Messages left before seven in the morning. Not the usual hour for crank calls by kids.

Huntington Beach—where a man had seen a girl who matched Carla Ives's description.

For a few seconds, I told myself that I shouldn't jump to conclusions. But I hadn't reached this point in my career by ignoring gut feelings. I jumped: If this wasn't Carla Ives, I wouldn't lose much time following one false trail.

Playa Azul and Vista del Mar. I looked up the location, printed it out, and hurried over to the City Desk. "I have to follow up on a lead," I told Lydia. "You can reach me on my cell phone."

I heard her surprised "What—?" and not much more as I left the newsroom.

I glanced at my watch again when I reached the car.

If I didn't run into traffic, I could just make it on time.

CHAPTER 40

CLEO posed before the mirrors on the sliding closet doors. She felt pleased. She had done a really excellent job this time. The man's suit looked good on her. She liked the shoes. They made her look like someone who was about to take care of serious business.

Well, what could be more serious than murder?

The thought made her laugh.

She had a hat to go with this one. When she put the hat on and adopted certain mannerisms and a way of walking, she knew for a fact that no one watching from a neighboring window would be likely to identify the person they saw as a woman.

In the trunk of the BMW 325xi parked in the garage, she had carefully stored coveralls and work boots, as well as her second complete outfit. Now, that one really looked great on her.

She looked around her. She liked this little house. Only two of her neighbors on this quiet suburban street had met her, and neither knew her real name. She told them she was an international sales representative who traveled a great deal. Nothing of real value was kept in the house, but she used a security system she controlled from her laptop to monitor alarms, as well as the small cameras mounted outside the house and in the various rooms to turn lights and radios off and on. The system would page her if anyone set off an alarm. No one had done so yet, which was something of a disappointment—she planned to deal with the problem personally if it ever happened.

A lawn service came by twice a week to ensure that the yard was clean and green, and that leaflets and flyers were removed from the porch. Her mail was forwarded to a private mail drop.

She had Roy to thank for the inspiration of living invisibly in suburbia. His example taught her to be the perfect, quiet home-owner who never annoyed her neighbors and was never annoyed by them. She never held parties, and did not cause concern by bringing unsavory strangers as visitors to the neighborhood. She never brought any kind of visitor to this house.

She couldn't stand the place for more than a few days at a time, but it provided excellent quarters when she was in the process of relocating her main residence.

She spent a few moments going over her preparations for her work. She was already wearing a well-concealed knife—she was seldom out of reach of at least one knife. She had already checked and rechecked her Beretta. She smiled, thinking of it. She liked a weapon small enough to be concealed in the palm of her hand. The Beretta had served her well. Loaded with .22 shots, thrust up against the back of a skull—it hardly made more than a popping sound.

She didn't like the kind of shot she had made on Sheila—she forced her thoughts away from that job. Not everyone would have been able to escape in that situation.

A small duffel bag held gloves, clean-up supplies, and Plans B, C, D, E, and F: the garrote, the restraints, the plastic bag, the syringes, and the drugs.

Roy had called her this morning. She had already given him advice. She wondered if he'd followed it. He was a nervous wreck.

Something in Roy appealed to her, made her like him a little more than the others. Giles was full of himself. She had been drawn to him because of his arrogance and power, but lately that had grown old. Dexter—Dexter was a fabulous lover, and more like her than any of the others. They understood each other. But Roy—Roy was kind of sweet, she decided. Protective of her. It was really funny if you stopped to think about it, but none of the other men even thought of treating her that way. And he would do anything for his children. That had made her like him for more than the sex. An image from her own childhood rose to mind unbidden, and she quickly suppressed it.

She checked her watch. Almost time to go. She began a series of meditations she used to hone her concentration.

A soft alarm sounded, distracting her. Someone was walking up her driveway. Probably a salesperson or one of the seemingly endless number of tree trimmers who littered her porch with business cards and flyers. She hid the bag and silently moved toward a monitor.

A slightly built brown-haired man in his fifties, wearing jeans, a light windbreaker, and running shoes, neared the porch steps. She recognized him immediately and swore. She quickly strode to the door.

What the hell was Giles doing here? He wasn't even supposed to know this place existed. The son of a bitch thought he owned her.

She felt her hand go to the Beretta.

She was going to shoot him. She was going to shoot him now. No, not here.

She managed to rein in her fury enough to take her index finger away from the trigger of the gun.

She watched him look toward the street as he raised his fist to knock on the door.

She quickly opened the door before his hand made contact with it. She caught his wrist in a crushing grip and yanked him through the doorway, pulling him off-balance. She kicked the door shut, then slammed him up against it, knocking the wind out of him and pinning him. She used her other hand to take hold of his collar and twist it.

"What the fuck are you doing here?"

She was pleased to see that his smile was a little wobbly. He was also getting an erection. That was no surprise to her, nor was it gratifying. Giles's sexual response to her was beginning to bore her.

"Let go of me," he croaked, "and I'll tell you."

She released him. He stumbled forward, then awkwardly regained his balance.

She smoothed out the suit. "I'd better not have any wrinkles in this."

"I'm going with you," he said, looking at her clothing with fascination.

"Like hell you are. And you aren't going to sidetrack me now. How did you find out about this place?"

He smiled again. "Cleo. You know I am always interested in the whereabouts of the members of my family."

She considered threatening him, then rejected the idea. Giles knew far too much about her activities.

Besides, there was no reason to threaten him—she could take action instead. For now, though, she would need to seem to give in.

"If you're changing the plan," she said, "I need to know now. We're running out of time."

"I merely wish to observe."

"Then why are you carrying a weapon?"

His smile faltered. Did he think she wouldn't notice the gun?

"Cleo, aren't you the one who always likes to have a backup plan?"

"What's really going on, Giles? Tell me now."

"It's Roy, I'm afraid. At some point I think we'll need to intercept him."

"Are you crazy? He'll have the kids with him. You know my rules," she said fiercely. "No hurting kids."

He cowered a little, caught himself doing so, and straightened his back. "Of course not. What has this been all about? It has always been about the children."

She eyed him skeptically.

"These are precious children, indeed," he went on smoothly. "That's why you need me. When we've made sure that Victoria is no longer a problem, I'll go with you to take the children under my care, and you can deal with Roy."

"You'll make them lose both parents in one day? Don't you think that will be a bit traumatic?"

"Are you so fond of Roy that you won't be able to carry this out?"

She laughed. "Is that what this is really about, Giles?" She moved closer to him, stroked a hand along his cheek. "You aren't jealous of your little brother, are you?"

He moved away from her hand. "Certainly not."

She wasn't convinced, but she stayed silent.

"Have you seen this morning's newspaper?" he asked.

"No."

"There are photos and stories in it concerning some people who may be familiar to you. Bonnie Creci Ives, known to you as Victoria Fletcher, wife of the man with whom you've been having an affair. Fortunately, between the plastic surgery on her nose and eyes and the changes in her hair color, length, and style, she looks quite different."

"Yeah. I'm sure a few birthdays and a lot more sobriety may have made a difference, too."

"Perhaps," he conceded. "There is speculation in the stories that she stole her daughter, Carla—you know her as Carrie. The photos do show some resemblance, but the computer-aided attempt to show what she might look like now may throw people off. I am a bit concerned that some of the family members may remember what she looked like as a child."

Cleo swore. "I told you not to bring her around them!"

"We took your advice for a few years, but eventually we had to develop her sense of devotion to the family."

"Really? How many Fletchers have seen me?"

"Very few, and you've done more for the family than just about anyone other than my father. But you've always been extraordinary, Cleo."

"Whatever. It doesn't matter."

"Oh, I should also mention that the reporter who wrote the story is Irene Kelly."

Cleo didn't like hearing that name. She wasn't going to give Giles the satisfaction of seeing her squirm, though. "So what? She writes lots of stories for that rag."

"In this one she mentions that Bonnie Creci probably took Carla away from her ex-husband with the help of one Reggie Faroe. Name ring a bell?"

"Sure. You asked me to take him hiking."

"Cleo, how long do you think it's going to take her to learn that Reggie Faroe is no longer living?"

"I don't care. It will be a dead end. That's what you always have me working on, right? Dead ends. You knew that if Blake Ives ever went looking for Faroe in other states, he'd find a heap of bones. And then he'd have nowhere to go."

"Provided you didn't leave anything like—oh, say a shoe—at the bottom of a cliff."

"Very funny. I'll tell you what I think, Giles. I think it's stupid to carry out this plan today. You should call Roy and cancel the whole thing."

"I'm afraid I don't understand."

"It never has been one of your best plans, but carrying it out now would be a huge mistake. Think about it. You want it to look as if the family just moved out."

"The cover story will be a little more complex than that, Cleo."

"Okay. But you think no one is going to notice that they took off the day after the story ran in the *Las Piernas News Express*?"

"Circulation is down in Las Piernas itself, Cleo. I doubt anyone on that street in Huntington Beach reads the *Express*."

She shrugged.

"Another reason for me to be there with you today," he said, "is that it will reduce suspicion if I let you in. I've been seen entering that house on any number of occasions."

"Getting into places has never been a problem for me," she said.

"It will take less time to load the body in the van if I help you," he persisted.

He had a point. "You might not like it much. Have you ever touched a dead body, Giles?"

"No," he said.

She glanced at his crotch. "Christ. And now the very thought of that gives you a damned hard-on. Next thing, you'll be fucking corpses."

"No, I like my women warm. In fact—"

"Forget about it. Where did you park?"

"Two streets away from this one."

"Anybody see you and your big pokey Johnson come saunter-ing down the street to my house?"

"No."

"So you hope. You brought gloves?"

He showed them to her.

"Okay, get in the Beemer—"

"You borrowed Dexter's car?"

"Dexter's? Hell, no. I bought one of my own."

His look of surprise cheered her.

"Why?"

"Do you think anyone in Roy's neighborhood will think twice about seeing a BMW pull into Roy's garage? Dex's has been over there fairly often, especially lately, right?"

He was wary now, she could see. Time to reassure him. She ruffled his hair. "As I was saying, get in the Beemer. It's in the garage. I'll be there in a minute. I've got to make sure I've got coveralls and booties for you, too."

He kissed her and walked toward the garage.

The kiss was a tolerable annoyance. She didn't like that he knew where the entrance to the garage was without being told.

What mattered to her most, though, was something that made her smile to herself: He obeyed her.

CHAPTER 41

Tuesday, May 2
9:56 A.M.
HUNTINGTON BEACH

IT was dark in the bathroom, even though the bathroom door was open, because the hall light was off. Genie had thoughtfully turned it off as she supposedly looked for Carrie. The darkness would make it less likely that the boys would come this way. Carrie stood behind the shower curtain, glancing at the glowing dial on her watch. Dad was usually fussy about being on time.

She heard Genie moving around the house, calling out to the boys that she was going to get them. Genie went up and down the stairs, in and out of the garage.

Carrie knew Genie was up to something, but it took her a while to realize that she was stalling until it was time to leave. Carrie mentally reviewed her own plans again, looking for possible problems.

She'd wait until Dad left with all the other kids to go to Grandfather's house. She'd sneak out. She'd meet Ms. Kelly and talk to her for a few minutes. Then she'd hurry back home. With luck, Mom wouldn't be out of bed yet. Mom could take her over to Grandfather's later.

She heard Dad calling from upstairs. "Kids! Get in the car!"

"Which one?" Genie called back from somewhere in the kitchen. Obviously, she wasn't looking very hard for the boys.

"The SUV," Dad called back. "Hurry up. We're leaving now."

Carrie thought his voice sounded strange, as if he was upset.

"Olly, olly, oxen free!" Genie called.

The boys squealed with delight as they came out of their hiding places. "We won! We won!"

"Yes, you won."

"Get in the car *now*!" Dad yelled, and they fell silent.

Carrie heard Genie hurrying the boys down the hall, and caught a glimpse of them as they passed the darkened bathroom. If Dad was so angry, maybe she should come out of hiding and join them. Maybe she should try this on some other day.

She heard Genie say in a low voice, "Boys, will you help Carrie and me?" and their quick assurance that they would.

"Good! Now, it's just a game of pretend. . . ."

Carrie didn't hear the rest—the door to the garage had closed behind them.

Dad came down the hall, although his footsteps sounded strange, almost as if he was stumbling. Carrie had to suppress a gasp of surprise as he turned the bathroom light on. She thought he must have seen her. He went out of her narrow range of vision, and she cowered, waiting for the curtain to be pulled back.

Instead, to her shock, she heard him throwing up.

Long moments passed. The toilet flushed and water ran in the sink. She heard him sobbing as he washed up.

She nearly stepped out then, to comfort him. But she worried that he would be embarrassed about throwing up and crying, and angry that she had not made her presence known before now.

He turned out the light and left the house. She heard the SUV's engine start up as the garage door was raised. The car drove off quickly.

She stood in the shower in the dark for a few minutes more. She was shaking. She tried to calm down, to make sense of what was going on.

She suddenly decided that she needed to get out of the house no matter what. Even if her dad came roaring back down the street and saw her walking down the sidewalk, and got really, really mad at her for not being in the car, that was better than staying in this crazy place.

For a moment she considered going upstairs, but if her mom was awake, she might be mad to find Carrie still here, or insist that she stay home. No, Genie had worked so hard and risked so much for this chance, Carrie had to do her part.

She went to the alarm keypad, thinking she would need to disarm the alarm, then reset it. Dad always set it when he left the house so that they would be safe. But when she reached the keypad, it showed the alarm wasn't activated. Thinking of how distracted he had been, she wasn't surprised. She set it now, then quickly went out the door within the time frame it allowed.

She looked at her watch. Ten-twelve A.M. She should hurry.

Once she reached the sidewalk, she had to force herself to walk slowly so that she didn't attract attention. She found she could not do this for long. Out in the air and light, away from the house, she was a creature freed from its cage. This was the farthest she had been away from home on her own. She was terrified and thrilled all at once. She walked faster and faster, and before long she was running to the corner. It seemed to her that at any moment an adult in one of these silent houses would stop her, would order her to go back.

She glanced at her watch again. Ten-fifteen. What if Irene Kelly never heard the message? Wasn't coming here today?

Then she would just go back home.

She was looking for a good waiting place when a Jeep Cherokee turned onto Playa Azul. She felt a spike of panic. She should find a hiding place, a place where she could observe without being seen. There were bushes along the side of the house on the corner, but there was also a dog in the yard. How could you hide if a dog was telling everyone right where you were?

The Jeep slowed, and Carrie saw that it was being driven by a woman with dark hair. When the car stopped and the passenger window was rolled down, Carrie could see that this was the reporter. She looked a little different from the small photo that was next to her story in the newspaper, but not that much.

"Hi," she said. "I'm Irene Kelly."

"Hi." It came out more like a croak than a greeting.

"Are you the one who called me?"

Carrie hesitated. "I'm the one you're supposed to meet."

"Oh. Okay . . ."

She waited. Carrie liked that, that she gave her time.

"I don't want anything bad to happen to my family," Carrie said in a rush.

"I can understand that," she said. "I wish I could promise you a lot of things, but I don't want to get to know you by telling you a lot of lies. What happens to your family won't be up to me, though."

"No. Of course not."

There was another silence, then she shut off the car's engine. Carrie felt a little afraid, but Ms. Kelly didn't get out of the car.

"Do you think you might be Carla?" she asked.

Carrie nodded.

"So do I. You can call me Irene. Do you want me to call you Carla or another name?"

"Carrie, please."

"Okay, Carrie. Do you want to talk here or is there somewhere else you'd like to go?"

As silly as she felt standing outside the car, Carrie could think of no other alternatives.

"Here, please. I'm not going to get in your car."

"That's okay. You shouldn't get in the cars of people you don't know. Do you want me to stand outside with you? I'll keep my distance if you'd like."

"Okay."

She rolled up the windows, slowly got out, and locked the doors. She came around the car, then stood several feet away from Carrie, leaning on the car, not moving nearer.

"Okay?" she asked.

Carrie nodded.

"Good. Tell me about yourself, Carrie."

Chapter 42

No one had said a word. Genie had never known the boys to be so quiet for so long. Dad wasn't looking at anyone. Genie was relieved that the boys hadn't been forced to join her in the lie she originally planned—to say that Carrie was asleep beside her in the far back of the SUV—because she could see now that wouldn't have worked well. It just would have made Dad really mad later.

The pressure to do something like that was off now. It would take them too long to get back to the house. By now Carrie would be talking to Ms. Kelly. Even if they turned around right this minute, it would be too late to stop Carrie from finding out more about her other dad.

Genie was happy for her, but she was also pretty sure that Carrie would have to leave their family. Her hope was that Mr. Ives would see that it would make Carrie miserable if her mom went to jail. Maybe everything could be worked out so that Carrie could visit them.

She felt tears welling up and quickly rubbed her eyes. She would not cry. She would *not*.

The boys looked back at her anxiously from time to time. She would smile at them and sign, *It's okay*. They wouldn't look convinced. They were too smart to think everything was okay. Any minute now . . .

"Excuse me, Daddy," Troy said, as if he had read her thoughts.

Dad made no response.

"Excuse me, Daddy!" Troy shouted.

Dad looked up in the rearview mirror, as if surprised to see them in the back of the SUV. "Yes, Troy?"

"You should turn the GPS on."

"What?"

"You're going the wrong way."

Dad didn't answer.

"You're going the wrong way, Daddy. This isn't the way to Grandfather's house."

Genie had known they weren't going to Grandfather's from the moment they got in the car. The SUV had an ice chest and groceries and a lot of sleeping bags in it. There were also duffel bags, although she didn't get a chance to look inside them. In a way it was good, because when she piled the blankets and the big doll in the back, hoping she could say it was Carrie, asleep, she realized that the back of the SUV would look cluttered if Dad glanced in the mirror.

"You're right, Troy," Dad said. "I changed my mind."

"But how will Mommy and Carrie find us?"

Genie thought of a lot of words she would have been punished for saying aloud.

"They'll— Wait!" Dad looked in the mirror, almost as if he was just now noticing them. He cussed and then pulled to the side of the freeway, in the lane you were only supposed to use if you had a flat tire.

"You'll get a ticket!" Genie said.

He frowned but kept driving. He took the next off-ramp and parked the car at the first curb where he could safely do so. He turned around and looked right at Genie. He was furious. As angry as she had ever seen him. It frightened her.

"Where's your sister?"

Genie swallowed hard. "She's at home. She was worried about Mom."

He turned white and made a horrible sound, like a growl, but almost like he was hurt. "Goddammit!" he shouted.

The boys started crying.

"I'm sorry. I'm sorry," he said.

His hands were shaking as he took out a cell phone and made a call. Genie, sure that he was calling home, knew that she had just gotten Carrie in big trouble.

"Hi," he said. "God, I'm so glad I reached you. Listen, call it off. The whole thing. Carrie's at the house."

He listened for a while, then said, "Giles?"

He glanced back at the children, then got out of the car. Genie saw him grab his forehead. He looked really, really upset.

He held the phone between his ear and his shoulder as he hurriedly pulled a little notebook and a pen out of his jacket pocket. He wrote something down. He read whatever he had written, hung up, then leaned against the side of the SUV and put his head in his hands. Genie said, "Stay here, boys," and unfastened her seat belt. She opened the door nearest her and climbed down to the curb just as a car pulled alongside the other side of the SUV.

The woman driving the car rolled down her window and said, "Are you all right? Do you need me to call nine-one-one?"

"Oh, I'm fine, thanks," Dad said, looking up. "I'm afraid I allowed myself to get too frustrated over getting lost."

The woman smiled in understanding. "Do you need directions?"

He held up his cell phone and the notebook. "Just got them from my cousin. Thanks. Very kind of you to offer to help."

The woman said it was no problem and drove on.

Genie put her arms around him. "I'm sorry, Dad. I didn't mean to make you so upset. I know you're mad at me. . . ."

He hugged her back. "It's okay. Everything will be okay. I'm not mad. I'm sorry I yelled. Let's get back in the car before some other Good Samaritan stops to help us."

They got back in the car and he apologized to the boys, who stopped crying. He asked the boys to sing a song, and they picked "Bingo."

He started the car, turned the GPS on, and entered an address. He made a U-turn, getting back on the freeway going north. Genie looked out the window as she listened to the boys sing and clap, their voices sweet and high.

Something was wrong with Dad. Whom had he called? What did he want to call off? He'd never tell her. When she got a chance, she'd have to do some snooping.

She watched the scenery without really seeing it, all the while repeating to herself, "Be safe, Carrie. Be safe."

CHAPTER 43

I KNEW even as I pulled up that this was Blake Ives's missing daughter. Until that moment, I had only focused on getting to the intersection of Playa Azul and Vista del Mar. Now, seeing her, I realized that I was with a frightened child who was probably about as confused as a person could be. My own thinking wasn't exactly clear, either. Now what?

When she allowed me to stand near her, I decided that it would be a good idea to get some idea of her history as she knew it.

She told me about her family. It didn't take long to realize that she felt loved, was attached to her mother and the man she called Dad, was both bright and articulate. She didn't look undernourished. Her clothes were of good quality and clean. I saw no bruises or easily discernible signs of physical abuse.

Her story was also one of isolation, though. She was homeschooled, and the only other children she interacted with were members of her family.

"It's a big family," she said, "but I don't even see my cousins more than a few times a year. Really, the only people I see a lot of are Uncle Giles, Uncle Dexter . . ." I wasn't sure what the pause after his name meant, except that something about him upset her. But it was the next statement that made the hair on the back of my neck stand up.

" . . . and, of course, Grandfather Fletcher."

"Fletcher?" I took a guess. "Graydon Fletcher?"

"Oh yes, do you know him?"

"I know of him," I said. "I haven't met him yet, but I hope to do so soon."

"He's the best grandfather in the world. I mean, I don't know a lot of other grandfathers, but he's kind and good to us. That's where the rest of my family is today. Everyone except my mom."

"And you."

"Yes. I was supposed to be with them, but I wanted to talk to you, so Genie and I played a trick on everyone, you might say."

THE garage door is open," Giles said in disgust. "That idiot didn't close it."

Cleo had planned to look things over, to check out the level of activity on the street and then circle the block and park some distance away. Seeing the open garage door and the utter absence of life along the street, she changed her mind.

"What the hell are you doing?"

She pulled into the garage, quickly got out of the vehicle, and hit the control that shut the door. She found the light switch as the door closed.

Giles got out of the car, angry.

She was already taking off the suit jacket, putting on the coveralls. Seeing the look on his face, she held up a halting hand. "Don't you dare shout in here."

He drew a hard breath but said nothing. She straightened, hands casually at her sides.

"Do you plan to draw on me? Go ahead, let's see who's faster."

He shook his head. "No, of course not."

"Good. Now you listen to me, Giles, and listen well. This is what I do. It's what I'm best at. You, on the other hand, aren't even an amateur. You're a tourist. So you are going to do what I tell you to, and you are not going to question shit. When this is all over, you can go back to calling the shots. But not until then. Do I make myself clear?"

"Yes."

"Good. Now go into the house and call Victoria."

"What?"

"Giles, you're doing it again."

He swallowed hard. "She'll be asleep. Roy drugged her."

"You also told him to close the damned garage door, didn't you?"

"Yes," he said, with a meekness that made her feel a little shiver of excitement.

"So, if she happens to still be awake, she knows you and won't react the same way she would to a stranger, right? Coax her downstairs, and bring her out here to meet me. That way there will be a little less evidence inside the house, right?"

"Yes, of course."

He reached for his weapon, and she stopped him by quickly grabbing his wrist.

"For God's sake, don't do that. What's gotten into you?" She smiled. "Don't be afraid of her, Giles. She's drugged, and she has no reason to suspect why you're here."

"Right."

As he reached the door into the house, her cell phone rang. Giles jumped, and it was all she could do not to laugh at him.

The ring tone let her know that the caller was Roy. Good. She had been meaning to call him. But she didn't want to talk to him in front of Giles. Still, she'd better find out what he wanted. She made a shooing motion at Giles as she answered.

"Hello?"

"Hi," Roy said. "God, I'm so glad I reached you. Listen, call it off. The whole thing. Carrie's at the house."

"I'm afraid that's not possible. Hang on."

She said to Giles, "Giles, hurry up!"

"Who is it?" Giles asked.

"The movers. I have to settle this now. I'll be right here if you need me." She gave him a hard stare.

He went into the house.

G I L E S was tempted to go right back into the garage and demand that she hang up and—

His attention was caught by a high-pitched whistling sound. What the hell was that?

"Victoria?" he called. Then more loudly: "Victoria!"

The whistling continued as he moved toward the sound. Some kind of— Oh, Jesus Christ, it was an alarm.

"Victoria!" he shouted desperately.

THE moment the door closed, Cleo said in a low voice, "Yes, Giles is with me! Listen to me, Roy, and get out a piece of paper and a pen while I'm talking, because we have maybe one minute to save your life and that of the kids. Remember what I told you this morning, about not taking that SUV because he'd have some kind of locator on it? Well, sure as shit, Giles is setting all of you up. Do not—*repeat, do not*—go to the meeting place he arranged. Go to this address." She gave him the address of one of her cabins. "That's my place—you'll be safe there. The door opens with a keypad combination." She gave it to him. "There's also a booby trap that's not on the alarm system." She told him how to disarm it. "Now, I'll do all I can to bring Carrie with me, but I have more to tell you about that when I see you. Don't contact *anyone* from the family. You understand?"

"Yes," he said weakly.

"Read the address, combination, and disarm instructions back to me."

He had just finished when the alarm sounded piercingly from inside the house. "Christ! Giles has set off the fucking alarm. What's the code?"

GILES cringed as the alarm howled at a painful level of decibels. He reached the keypad and madly entered Roy's birthday, to no effect. Apparently that wasn't the code.

He saw movement out of the corner of his eye and looked up the stairway. Victoria stood on the upper landing. "Victoria!"

She frowned, said something he couldn't hear over the noise, and took a lurching step forward. She missed the first step entirely and tumbled down the stairs, her body pitchforked against stairs, railings, wall, and finally the marble of the foyer, coming to rest at his feet.

He stared in shock.

O H , " Carrie said, "before I talk any more about myself, I have a really important question to ask you."

I was trying to absorb all the implications of a connection to the Fletchers, so maybe I wasn't concentrating as much as I should have been when Carrie took a deep breath and said, "Do you know someone named Mason who is missing a little girl?"

"Mason?"

"Yes."

"My God . . ."

But I didn't get to say more than that before we heard a loud alarm going off somewhere down the street.

"My house! That's my house!" she cried, and began running away from me.

C LEO was inside, pressing buttons on the keypad almost before he was aware of her presence. There was an instant silencing of the alarm, although he was sure some echo of it was still ringing in his ears. She looked down at Victoria, felt for a pulse, and said, "That was quick if noisy work, Giles."

"I didn't—"

"Yes, I'm sure. Now grab her ankles and carry her out to my car. Now!"

He obeyed, too numb to do otherwise. Victoria was surprisingly heavy. When they reached the Beemer, Cleo opened the trunk, then said, "Wait a minute."

She lifted a set of clothing on hangers covered in a dry cleaner's plastic bag and hung it in the back of the car.

"That's a Las Piernas Police Department uniform!" Giles said.

"Put her into the trunk. We have *no time* to waste."

As they lifted the body, the phone on the wall of the garage began to ring.

They unceremoniously dumped her on top of a thick piece of plastic inside the trunk. Cleo closed the trunk lid.

"Answer the phone. It will be Fletcher Security. Tell them who you are and that the code word is *Graydon,* and that there is no need to send a police unit here. Tell them you agreed to look in on the house while Roy was on vacation and accidentally set off the alarm."

He did as she said.

He watched her clean up drops of blood on the outside of the car.

When he hung up, she said, "I talked to Roy when the alarm went off. He told me Carrie isn't with him."

"What?"

"Yes. So you are going to wait here and intercept her."

"What if she's already in the house?"

"With that alarm going off? Now listen to me, will you? You keep her from going into that entryway by any means necessary. You get her into that van and meet me at the rendezvous point. We'll hand her off to Roy there."

"You're leaving me alone here?"

"For now, yes. You can handle one little girl, can't you?"

"Perhaps you—"

"I'm a stranger," she reminded him.

"Yes, of course."

"And Giles? If you harm one hair on that kid's head, I'll saw your balls off with a dull knife. For starters."

"I'd never hurt Carrie!" he said indignantly, but she didn't miss seeing his hand flinch protectively toward his crotch.

"Follow instructions. That's all I ask." She reached into her jacket and tossed him a set of keys. "I'm getting out of here. Hit the garage-door opener."

He did, looking forlorn as she pulled out of the garage and sped down the street.

CHAPTER 44

I CAUGHT up to her in a few strides, grabbing hold of her arm.

"Let go of me! Let go of me!" she screeched, pulling hard against me.

"Carrie, wait! If someone has broken into your house, it could be dangerous for you to go back there!"

"My mom's in there! He might hurt her!"

"You can't help her by getting hurt, too," I said.

She relented a bit.

"I've got a cell phone," I said. "Let me—"

Before I could finish the sentence, the noise of the alarm abruptly cut off. Carrie looked up at me.

"Maybe my mom set it off by accident," she said. "Don't call the police."

"I won't, not if you don't want me to. Did I hurt your arm?"

She shook her head. Her face creased with worry as she looked back at the house. "If my mom comes out of the house and she sees me out here talking to you, I'm going to be in so much trouble."

"I know your mom. I think I might be able to talk to her about all this," I said, hoping that wasn't a huge lie.

"Is it true she used to be a newspaper reporter?"

"Yes. We worked together on the *Express*."

"That seems . . . impossible. I mean, that she was a reporter. She's a good teacher. I could see her being a teacher in a school."

"Earlier you mentioned a couple of things I'd like to know more about. You mentioned someone named Mason?"

"I told you my brothers and sister are adopted, right?"

"Yes. Genie is nine, right?"

"Yes."

Jenny Fletcher would be nine, if she still lived. Could it be the same girl? I realized that deep down I had believed she was dead. Maybe that was a result of having just read a lot of material on child abductions. Or reading about the violent circumstances under which she disappeared. No matter what Caleb's faith in his brother might have been, I hadn't thought it was likely that his sister survived.

Until now. What the hell was going on? I silently lectured myself about not jumping to conclusions based on next to no evidence, even as I felt hope begin to soar. "Could Mason be a much older brother?"

She shrugged. "I don't know. Maybe. I just know that my sister, Genie, has rememberings of someone by that name."

"Rememberings?"

She blushed. "I know that's not a real word. But I couldn't find a real word that worked. Do you know what I mean?"

"Boy, do I."

"You've made up words?"

She was starting to relax some, to not look as if she might run off again. "I can't use them in the newspaper," I said, "but sometimes one made-up word seems better than two or three real ones."

"Name one."

A term Lydia and I used for the publisher of the *Express* came to mind. "Pagusting. That's when something or someone is both pathetic and disgusting."

She smiled. "It's a good one, if you mean pathetic in a sardonic way."

"Uh, yes. So tell me about rememberings."

"They aren't quite memories. They're just . . . little pieces of memories. Feelings. Impressions. Sometimes . . . I think mine have been about my . . . about the man you wrote about."

"Blake Ives? Like what?"

"He used to sing this song to me, when I was scared." She hummed a few notes of a familiar tune.

I sang a line of the lyrics to go with it—"Raindrops Keep Fallin' on My Head."

"Yes! That's the one!" She frowned. "Was that in the article?"

"No, that's a detail that didn't appear in the story. But he told me about singing it to you when thunderstorms scared you."

She gave a big sigh of relief. "Sometimes I thought I was crazy."

"Do you want to meet him?"

"I think so. . . ."

"Do you want me to go to your house with you and talk to your mom about it?" I had a great many things I wanted to discuss with Bonnie Creci.

She thought it over and said, "I guess it's worth a try."

She stood still, though. We were well down the block from her place.

Her brows drew together. "Maybe instead . . . do you have his phone number?"

"Yes," I said.

We heard a car engine. A moment later the garage door began to rise.

"Wait a minute," she said. "That was open when I left the house."

A black Beemer quickly backed out and immediately headed down the street, away from us. The windows were tinted, and between that and the angle of the sun, I didn't get a look at the driver. We were too far away to read the license plate.

"Know anyone who drives a car like that?" I asked.

"Uncle Dexter," she said quietly.

"Could he be the one who set the alarm off?"

She nodded. Tears started rolling down her face.

The garage door closed again. The tears fell faster.

"Carrie?"

"I hate her. I hate her!" She started running toward the house again.

I followed, not trying to catch her this time. She sped up the front walk and into the house. I wasn't sure exactly what was going on, or even what I could do, let alone what legalities might be involved. Could I legally take a minor back to the custodial parent? Should I just call the Orange County Sheriff's Department or the Department of Child Protective Services and let them handle all the details? Call Blake Ives? Maybe Frank would know.

No matter what else happened, I didn't want to lose track of Carla Ives. Blake Ives would be so happy and relieved to know she was alive and well, but he'd never forgive me if she disappeared again.

I also didn't want her to have to face Bonnie alone.

I moved faster, running up the front walkway and pushing the unlatched door open.

I came to a halt in the entryway and let the door close behind me. There was blood on the beige marble of the foyer, and as I looked up the stairs, I could see blood and bits of scalp and hair marking the wall and railings. Someone had come downstairs the hard way. Who? And where was he or she now?

To my left, I heard a little sound of distress.

"Carrie?"

I turned to see her being held tightly by a man who had a gun lodged against the underside of her chin.

"Lock the door!" he shouted at me.

I did as he said.

"Drop your purse on the floor and kick it away!"

I obeyed again, doing my best to avoid the blood spatter. Praying none of Carrie's blood or my own would be added to it.

"All right." He drew a harsh breath. "You have a choice, Ms. Kelly. You can die knowing that you caused Blake Ives's daughter to be delivered to him in a body bag, or you can do exactly as I say."

CHAPTER 45

SOMETIMES a man with a gun gets to have things his way. When we first got on the San Diego Freeway, I started saying that I thought this was a bad idea, that I would be missed.

"Just shut up and drive," he said.

He had a gun and I didn't, so I stopped talking about what a big mistake he was making. I held tightly to the steering wheel and tried to make myself think clearly, but strategies about survival weren't coming to me as quickly as they might have if I had been given a little time to mull things over.

The man with a gun was in a big hurry.

He wasn't sitting within reach, so even if I had summoned the nerve to try it, I couldn't take the gun away from him. He was in the back of the van I was driving. The van was some sort of working van, although it looked as if it had been adapted so that it could be used for either passengers or cargo. The middle section of seats had been taken out, but a bench seat in the back was in place. That's where he was.

I glanced at him in the rearview mirror.

He wasn't a big man, or a young man. That didn't matter. More important, and not so good for my own chances of a future, were the three A's—he was anxious, angry, and armed. No, there was a fourth. He was an asshole.

The sweat that had stained his shirt at the armpits an hour ago now drenched the front as well, dampened his forehead, and plastered his hair to his head at the temples. The stench of his fear reached me, masking the scent of my own. Knowing he was afraid did not comfort me at all.

I could have taken chances with his aim, tried to escape, or driven the van in a way that would throw him off balance, then jumped out while he stayed in it to crash. After all, his gun wasn't pointed at me.

It was pointed at Carrie.

Although he had bound her wrists and ankles with duct tape, and placed a fat strip of it over her mouth as well, he seemed to think she would yet escape him, and never let her move more than a few inches away. Most of the time, he clutched one of her slender, pale arms in a bruising grip.

Her blue eyes were dilated almost to black with fear. Blue eyes that caught mine in the mirror, pleading.

I looked away, to the off-ramp just ahead. I couldn't think clearly about much at that moment, but I knew that I couldn't sacrifice her life in an attempt to save my own.

So I got off the freeway just like he told me to, driving this van, which would shield anyone's view from what was going on in back. They could only see me, and no one seemed to notice I was terrified.

Terror never stays at the same level over time, though, and the initial adrenaline rush had passed off even before we were ordered into the van. But the cold knot of fear in the pit of my stomach seemed to have amazing staying power in this situation. After over ninety minutes of it, I was having a hard time not driving erratically, or in any manner that would displease him.

I did not want him to be any angrier, any more nervous than he already was.

Sometimes a man with a gun gets to have things his way. I didn't even object when, on one of the slow stretches of Interstate 5, he began going through my purse, which he had picked up off the floor of the foyer. He pulled out my cell phone and pocketed it.

As time passed, I began to wonder what had happened to Bonnie. To wonder where Carrie's "dad," Roy Fletcher, and the other three children were right now, and how long it would be before they missed Carrie. To wonder how long it would be before I was missed by anyone.

I followed his curtly delivered directions, and now we were in the high desert area north of Los Angeles, the Antelope Valley. The valley lies on the north side of the San Gabriel Mountains. He told me to exit the freeway in Palmdale and made a call on my cell phone.

"It's me," he said.

After a pause he said, "Palmdale, but—"

He sighed. "I know, I know. Yes, I know I'm late! Listen to me . . . Yes, there are . . ."

He glanced at me and lowered his voice. "Things are a bit complicated. Carrie wasn't alone when I found her."

I could hear someone cussing him out.

He hung up. He gave me another series of directions, so that we were headed east.

A few minutes later, my cell phone rang. He looked at the caller ID display and pressed the button that answered the call, but didn't speak.

He was getting cussed out again, but this time he said, "Shut up or I'll hang up again and do as I damned well please."

He looked more nervous than he had been five minutes earlier. He glanced constantly between Carrie and me. He still held the gun on her. I had formulated plans to throw his aim off if he actually looked as if he was going to lose it and squeeze the trigger. Unfortunately, almost all of them seemed just as likely to result in my own death, if not also causing her life to be lost in a crash.

"She was with that reporter. Yes, Irene Kelly. I-I-I didn't know what to do. . . . Of course not. Not there . . . no. Oh really? Well, you weren't there, Cleo, so I had to come up with something, right? So she's driving. By the time I got everything arranged, we hit traffic."

There was another silence.

"Well, thank you. Really? Well, I thought it was the smartest thing to do. I mean, under the circumstances . . . yes, yes. Exactly. All right." He made a kissing sound into the phone and hung up.

His anxiousness seemed to evaporate. I wasn't sure I liked him looking so smug, though.

We went through a town called Lake Los Angeles, the existence of which I would have doubted if I hadn't seen it myself. We turned south, toward the mountains, without seeing either a lake or angels. I'm sure both were there somewhere.

We crossed the California Aqueduct and kept going south. He started watching ahead more often, calling out directions more quickly. We were soon in desolate territory, turning onto pot-holed roads that seemed to have been laid out for communities that never materialized, some developer's mirage, now abandoned. We left those for an even more isolated dirt road.

We were in the foothills when the angels belatedly made their appearance. We passed a side road, and less than a minute later I saw the red light of a law enforcement vehicle—I couldn't see any markings to make out the agency. I had to fight back tears of relief—we would be rescued! In the next moment I realized that things weren't exactly resolved. How would the gunman react to the news I was about to give him? Not knowing what it might literally trigger, I braced myself and said, "We're getting pulled over."

His reaction seemed odd. He smiled, then quickly frowned and said, "Pull over and act natural. Don't do anything to make him suspect what's going on back here, or the girl dies." He was talking like a TV gangster. He forced Carrie to lie down and covered her completely with a blanket.

"I'll need my wallet," I said.

He smiled again, found it, and tossed it to me.

Something wasn't adding up. I kept the engine running. I had one weapon—the van. I didn't see many possibilities to use it that would lend themselves to happy endings.

A single uniformed officer got out of a vehicle I couldn't see. The officer had almost reached my now-lowered window before I realized she was female. The uniform looked damned familiar. Frank was already in Detectives before I married him, but I knew what a Las Piernas Police Department uniform looked like.

We were way the hell out of Las Piernas's jurisdiction.

The style of this uniform was known as a Blauer, with the officer's name embroidered over the pocket.

D. Fletcher.

The rest of the outfit wasn't a convincing fake job. She was missing most of the fifty pounds of equipment a patrol officer carries. Her sidearm was holstered and she made no move to reach for it.

"License and registration."

I played along, thinking that if I drove off, I might cause the man in the back of the van to shoot Carrie—or me. I needed a better opportunity. Or something that even vaguely resembled even half an opportunity. She moved to the front of the van and then around to the sliding side door. She knocked on it.

Now the gunman was frowning in earnest.

Still holding his gun, he moved awkwardly over to the door and opened it.

She had her own weapon out, a small handgun, and not the larger piece that was still holstered. The woman grabbed the wrist of his gun arm.

This, I thought, was as good a chance as I was likely to get.

The van was moving just as she pulled him out of it. I stepped on the gas, raising a huge cloud of dust. I heard a little popping noise and thought she was shooting at the tires.

In the side mirror, I saw the man drop in a heap.

The woman wasn't looking at him.

She was staring after us.

CHAPTER 46

SHE might have been staring because she knew what I didn't—that the dirt road ended a short distance ahead. I braked and swerved to avoid going into a dry wash, yelled to Carrie to hang on or brace herself any way she could, and turned the van around. As I did, the side door slid on its tracks and shut again. At least Carrie wouldn't roll out.

I had to disable the BMW. If the shooter got into her car, she'd easily outrun the van.

As I drove back toward her, she was smiling. She had unholstered the bigger gun. I think she expected me to simply surrender, because when I aimed the van at her, she looked surprised. Maybe it was wishful thinking on my part, but her hands seemed a little shaky. I crouched as low as I could behind the steering wheel, and I drove right at her. She raised the gun and fired. A spray of glass pebbles came at me as some of her shots blew out the windshield, and I heard the ping and hammer of the bullets hitting metal as they did some damage to the van, but I kept going, hoping to God that nothing was going to ricochet into Carrie or me.

The shooter's surprise turned to a look of white-faced fear. She did an awkward rolling dive away from the front of the BMW.

I couldn't afford to hit the BMW in a way that would risk disabling the van, and I didn't want to injure or kill Carrie by sending her flying around the back of the van in a big collision. So I braked and skidded to a sliding halt, adding to the cloud of debris that was coming into the van. I lined up the back end of the van with the left front side of the Beemer, then threw the van into reverse and gave it some gas.

It made a loud bang, and I pulled forward. The BMW's front wheel tilted at a nasty angle and the tire was flat. I had certainly done more than fuck up the paint job on the rest of the front end. Good enough.

I drove away like a bat out of hell.

As soon as I felt sure that I had put enough distance between the shooter and us that we were out of immediate danger, I pulled over and went back to Carrie. She had managed on her own to free the blanket from her face, and maneuvered herself against the backseat. "I'm so sorry," I said. "Are you hurt?"

She shook her head. Tears rolled down her face, over the tape across her mouth.

I glanced around. The floor of the van was littered with glass and the contents of my purse. My cell phone, alas, was out in the desert in a dead man's pocket.

"I'm going to move you up by me so you don't get cut by this glass, and then I'll work on getting this tape off of you, okay?"

She nodded.

I pulled the blanket off, causing more beads of glass to fall. At least it had protected her from the initial shower of windshield fragments. I picked her up as carefully as I could, an awkward business in the confines of the van, but we made it to the front seats. I set her on her feet, brushed off the passenger seat, and helped her to sit down. I strapped the seat belt on her. "Just in case we have to take off in a hurry," I said.

She nodded her understanding.

I started to worry that somehow the shooter would find some way to catch up with us. The woman was still armed, after all, and dressed as a police officer. Maybe she'd carjack a vehicle from someone, or use some shortcut I didn't know about.

I reached into the glove compartment and found a first-aid kit. It contained a cheap pair of round-end scissors.

"I'm going to cut your hands free first so you can work on the rest," I said to Carrie. "I want to try to get us farther away from that woman."

She nodded enthusiastically.

I cut the tape between her wrists and left the scissors where she could reach them.

Unless you're wearing goggles or a helmet with a face shield, driving without a windshield is not the freeing experience you might expect it to be. All kinds of grit, grime, and insect life came blowing up off the road. I made another stop and searched for my sunglasses.

By then Carrie had shaken the circulation back into her hands, cut the tape from her ankles, and bravely ripped it free from her face.

"Are you okay? Did he hurt you?" I asked, handing her the blanket so that she could use it to shield her face and eyes from debris.

"I'll be okay," she said, cautiously touching the tips of her fingers to the marks left on her face by the tape. "I'm just kind of scared."

"Something would be seriously wrong with you if you weren't. I'm sorry about the rough ride. But I think we've lost them, whoever they were."

"My uncle Giles," she said angrily.

"What?"

"Uncle Giles," she said, pulling her feet up onto the edge of the seat and rubbing her ankles. "He runs the school. Fletcher Academy."

I tried to let that sink in as we turned onto what looked like a promising road.

"On the phone, he was talking to someone named Cleo," I said. "Do you know anyone by that name?"

"No."

"A woman. Tall, athletic, short brown hair. Probably in her late twenties. At first I thought she was a man."

"A woman who looked like a man?" She thought for a while, then said, "I have a lot of cousins, and I haven't met all of them, but I can't think of anyone who looks like that."

If you asked me to retrace the route I took from there, it would require hypnosis to pull the memories out. I really didn't have a clear idea of where the hell I was at any given moment, or where I was going. An aerial view of my progress would have made me look like the mouse voted least likely to find the cheese.

Eventually I ended up on Pearblossom Highway. We attracted a certain amount of attention, which I hoped would lead to some cell phone calls to the L.A. County Sheriff's Department, but I kept driving until I found a minimart gas station that was fairly busy.

We were both dirty and dehydrated, and I suppose our hair made it look as if we had tunneled out of a fright-wig factory. I found my wallet and went inside with Carrie. She took hold of my hand, which was fine with me—I wasn't exactly feeling all that steady myself. I asked the clerk to please call the sheriff's department, because someone had shot at us and blown out our windshield. He peered out at the van, then made the call. He was solicitous after that, allowing us to use the restroom to wash up a bit, not charging us for the bottled water we wanted to buy, and even letting me use the phone. A cynic might say that it was only about five bucks' worth of kindness, but to us, after about three hours of terror, it seemed as if we had found the most generous soul on earth.

Frank, as it turned out, had been looking for me by the time I called.

"We were supposed to have lunch, remember? Then Lydia said you had hurried out, and I couldn't reach you on your cell phone. . . ."

"Sorry, but a dead man's got it now. I was abducted. With Blake Ives's daughter. We're okay now, though. I think."

I should have broken it to him differently, but I wasn't thinking all that clearly by then. Now that I was out of the way of immediate harm, reaction was setting in.

I interrupted his own quite understandable reaction and said, "I'm borrowing someone's phone, so I can't talk long. Can you come out to the sheriff's station in Palmdale—maybe see if you can get Zeke Brennan to come along with you? I'm not in as much trouble as I was in an hour ago, but I think I'll need an attorney. And I . . ." I took a deep breath, struggled to stay calm. I tried to give him a condensed version of my day so far. He interrupted, asked for the phone number I was calling from, and wanted me to tell him exactly where I was and to give him the name of the store. So I handed him over to the clerk, who provided all of that information, then handed the phone back to me. He was looking at Carrie and me in wonder.

"Are you okay?" Frank asked.

"Getting there." I asked him to call Blake Ives, and to try to reach Roy Fletcher, who might still be at Graydon Fletcher's place. "And if he's got a girl named Genie with him, I think that might be Caleb's sister— Oh, here's the sheriff's department," I said, seeing a cruiser pull up. "Oh, and the *Express*."

"The *Express* is there?" he asked with some heat.

"No, but will you call them?"

"Maybe. That may cause some difficulties. Let me talk to the deputy."

Apologizing to the clerk, I waited for the deputies to come inside, then handed the phone to one of them saying, "It's for you."

Before he took it, he asked his partner to wait outside with us.

Carrie, who had stayed huddled next to me, was trembling as we walked out. I put an arm around her shoulders, and her tears began to fall. Part of it was undoubtedly just the scare setting in, as it was for me as well, but it occurred to me that she had probably never been this far from home or around so many strangers at one time.

"You okay?" I asked. "Sure you aren't hurt?"

"What will they do to me?" she whispered.

"Do to you? What do you mean?"

"I mean, who will I live with?"

"I don't know." I thought about it for a moment. "Maybe your father, Mr. Ives. Or they may find someone for you to stay with while they sort things out. They'll probably try to contact your . . . your dad, and I know they'll try to find out where your mom is."

She looked away from me, then started crying hard. She curled back into my shoulder. I tried to think of words that might soothe her, and decided just to let her cry. I don't think she had any more real hope that her mom was alive than I did.

After a time, she quieted.

"Do you have kids?" she asked in a small voice.

"No, I don't."

"Don't you like them?"

"Oh no, I like them a lot. Why do you ask?"

She turned red. "Maybe they'd let me stay with you."

I hugged her shoulders. "I would love to have you stay with us, but I don't get to decide that. Besides, you might not like it—I have a husband, a friend, three dogs, and the fattest cat you ever saw living at my house. Here, I'll show you." I opened my wallet and flipped to the photos of Frank, Deke and Dunk, and Cody. "I don't have pictures of our friend Ethan or of Altair yet. They're just visiting."

She asked questions about the animals and Frank. We only spent a few minutes doing this, but somehow it had a calming effect on both of us.

OVER the next several hours, the Los Angeles County Sheriff's Department, the Huntington Beach Police Department, and the Las Piernas Police Department all wanted to talk to us. So did a tremendous number of members of the media, although they didn't get much more than footage of us leaving the LASD Palmdale Station. They made up for that by talking to neighbors in Huntington Beach ("very quiet," "kept to themselves") and getting aerial shots of an abandoned BMW and the removal of remains from the desert.

The bodies of Giles Fletcher and Bonnie Creci/Victoria Fletcher had been found half a mile from the border of the Angelus National Forest, a half-mile that kept the Park Service and the FBI off the list of our questioners.

Frank arrived with three passengers. I had expected Blake Ives and my attorney, Zeke Brennan, but I was amazed to also see Graydon Fletcher, who was hanging back a bit.

As he hugged me, Frank whispered, "You okay?"

I nodded.

"Don't worry about Graydon."

When Blake Ives was introduced to her, Carrie smiled uncertainly and said hello. When she saw Graydon, she ran to him, shouting, "Grandfather!" and burst into tears as she hugged him.

I had to admire Blake Ives. He was overjoyed to see her, weeping, in fact, but he didn't push or make a scene. He patiently waited while Graydon comforted Carrie.

Graydon soothed her, and when she had calmed down again, he said, "Carrie, do you know who Mr. Ives is?"

She nodded.

"I'm so happy that he's found you," he said. "We all have lots of questions about how you were separated, and I know you've had an upsetting day. But he's a good man who has been hoping to see you for so many years, and I wanted to come to let you know that no matter what else has happened today, this part of your life will be just fine. Meeting your father is a reason to rejoice."

She looked back and forth between them, then said to Blake, "I read Ms. Kelly's story about you in the paper. It's . . . nice to meet you." She held out her hand.

He took it and, although I could see it was killing him, refrained from doing more than gently shaking it for a moment.

He came down to eye level with her. "Carla—I mean, Carrie—do you want me to call you Carrie?"

She thought about it and said, "Does it hurt your feelings?"

"No," he said softly.

"Okay, well, if you don't mind, Carrie's what I'm used to hearing. I like the name Carla, but I might not remember you're talking to me when you say it."

"Carrie it is, then. I look forward to getting to know you again. Mr. Fletcher has been telling me about you on the way here. He's right—we're both so glad you're all right and weren't hurt too badly, and we both want to make sure you're happy and safe— that's what matters most to both of us, okay?"

"Thank you," she said. She looked to Graydon. "Where's Dad?" She blushed and said, "I mean . . ."

"It's okay," Blake said.

"I don't know where he is, Carrie," Graydon said. "I'm worried about him and your brothers and sister. I have a lot of questions to ask him, but mostly I'm worried."

"Mom . . ."

"I'm sorry."

That brought on the tears again. Somehow, in that upset, she let Blake comfort her, too.

A pair of Fletcher's sons who were lawyers arrived, apparently on their own initiative. Graydon refused to follow their advice about not saying anything, and simply told them to be quiet or wait for him in the lobby. I guess he still held some power as the patriarch, because they shut up.

Graydon couldn't explain—for her benefit, or to the various law enforcement officials who wanted to know—why Giles Fletcher had taken his niece and a newspaper reporter hostage. He couldn't imagine any reason for Giles to harm Bonnie—whom he referred to as Victoria—or anyone else. He had been shocked, he said, when reading the morning paper to see the story about Blake Ives. "I didn't see the paper until late this morning, but I immediately recognized Victoria's photo, and while I wasn't quite so sure about Carrie, of course, I could see the resemblance. I—I wanted to talk to Roy. I've been leaving messages for him."

"He didn't go to your house?" Carrie asked.

"No, honey, he didn't. Is that what he said he would be doing?"

"Yes." Her forehead wrinkled in worry.

Carrie told the story of her morning, including some parts I hadn't known. Except for her fear and a quality of innocence, one could easily forget she was a child—her vocabulary was beyond that of a number of adults I know, and so was her intelligence.

"I've been thinking about it," she said. "I think Dad put a sedative or something like that in Mom's drink."

"Tell us more about this," Graydon said, looking grim.

III

So we heard about the Bloody Mary, the mortar and pestle, the pills. Joe Travers, the detective from Huntington Beach, was madly taking notes. Travers either had kids of his own or had questioned children before, because his manner with Carrie quickly won her over. I suppose the fact that no one was trying to stop her from being honest with him helped.

With Zeke Brennan's able advice, I was able to be honest, too—I just didn't tell anyone how much I'd wanted to kill Cleo. I was glad for Zeke's guidance. People who make lawyer jokes should think about how well they'd do with trial by ordeal.

Graydon Fletcher said the name Cleo was familiar to him, although he had not seen her since she was a teenager. "I don't know if it's the same person," he said. Then he pretty much described her exactly, in a younger form.

"Where could we find her?" the detective asked.

"I have no earthly idea. But I will ask my family members to cooperate completely with you."

An urgent bulletin was issued regarding Roy Fletcher and the children who were with him. The Huntington Beach police were searching for photos. None were on the walls of Roy Fletcher's home, but Carrie mentioned a digital camera. "Dad kept a few of our pictures on his computer," she said, although she couldn't provide a password. That frustrated her, but then she said, "Wait! My camera. Remember, Grandfather? You gave it to me the last time you came to see us. I took our pictures." She described where it could be found in their room. "Genie might have taken it with her, though," she cautioned, "when she put my things in the car."

I marveled as she told us about Genie's Plan B, thought up on the spur of the moment when she found my voice mail was full. None of these kids were dull-witted.

"Do your brothers and sister look like you?" Detective Travers asked.

"No, we were all—" She broke off and gave me a questioning look. She was already wondering if anything she knew of her family history was true.

"Mr. Fletcher," I said to Graydon, "Carrie was raised to believe that she was legally adopted at birth. She's since realized that Bonnie—Victoria—was her birth mother. Do you know any of the details of the adoptions? Did you ever see adoption papers?"

"Why, no. So many of my children have gone on to become adoptive or foster parents . . . oh." He looked stricken and fell silent.

Priorities were agreed upon, and the first was to find Roy Fletcher and the children—their legal status was less important than finding them alive.

The next was to locate Cleo Fletcher. When I mentioned that she was dressed as a Las Piernas cop, I was told that Officer Dennis Fletcher's uniform (reported stolen weeks ago from Fletcher's Dry Cleaning) had been left behind in the car, and presumably she was wearing something else now. So far, no one knew where she had gone since I saw her dive away from the BMW.

When we were all talked out, a question arose regarding Carrie. Blake had all the papers to prove he had the right to legal custody, but apparently he had studied up on reunions like these and was taking it slowly. As a result, Carrie had gone from being wary of him to being openly curious. She sat next to him and talked to him while I was being questioned separately.

By the time we were calling it quits for the day, a social worker was on the scene as well. When she asked Carrie what she would like to do, Carrie looked at Graydon, and even at me, then turned to Blake and said, "I'm not three anymore."

"No," he said, "you've grown up."

"It might be fun to see Squeegee again. And there's this song I want to ask you about. . . ."

W H E N she left, Graydon Fletcher seemed to age before my eyes.

"Dad," one of his attorney offspring said, "we'd better get you home."

"Yes," he said, "yes." But before he left, he took hold of my arm

with a gnarled hand and reassured me that he was going to do all
he could to discover what Giles and Cleo and Roy had been up to.
He repeated this reassurance to the Las Piernas detectives.

"Please, please don't judge the rest of us by their actions," he
said, and released my arm.

I wanted to trust him. I wanted to believe him.

If I hadn't met Cleo and Giles earlier in the day, I might have
been more open-minded. Instead, I wondered if Graydon
Fletcher's family was helping Roy and Cleo flee the country while
he distracted us. If they had escaped, they probably had two
young boys and a girl with them. A girl who might be Caleb's sister—living proof of Mason Fletcher's innocence—with them.

CHAPTER 47

CLEO had familiarized herself with the area she had chosen in the desert, so she knew which way she must travel to reach any sort of dwellings. She was in good physical condition, if a little scraped up, and the hike had not been difficult, even carrying her duffel bags. She had stolen a car, a small Honda, from the first home she found. The fuel gauge was nearly registering empty. She didn't want to risk being videotaped by a gas station security camera, so she drove that to the edge of the nearest cluster of homes that passed for a neighborhood out here. She abandoned the vehicle after thoroughly wiping off anything she had touched—and she had been careful not to touch many surfaces. The Honda would keep police busy searching this area.

Stealing the motorcycle had been easy. She would have preferred to steal a car, but the owner of the motorcycle had been the most careless of his neighbors, and she didn't have a lot of time to spare. The coveralls had helped her move from house to house without causing alarm—she moved in a determined way, a meter reader or other workman. Opportunity presented itself on her fifth try.

The motorcycle was kept in a garage, but the garage was unlocked. The bike's key was in the ignition, and the helmet sitting right on it. She mentally called her unknown donor of transportation a fucking idiot.

Putting all her gear on the bike had been problematic, but the owner of the motorcycle had bungee cords on his workbench, and after she changed into her warmest clothes, the bags were less bulky.

The motorcycle owner's head was a little bigger than hers, so she had to stuff one of her shirts into the helmet to serve as a liner. It looked weird, but no one would see it, because she would keep the face shield on.

She carefully closed the garage door and rode back toward the place where she had abandoned the Honda.

She was careful not to go too near it, but one advantage of wide-open spaces was that you could see a fuss being made from a distance, and clearly, law enforcement and media were already on the scene. She called Irene Kelly a fucking idiot, too.

She cut across an empty dirt road, then made her way to Big Pines Highway. The road twisted and climbed into the San Gabriel Mountains. Soon she was riding through Angeles National Forest. Earlier in the week, what had fallen as rain in Las Piernas arrived here as soft spring snow, although the low, plowed heaps along the roadside were already slushy. So far, the road remained clear, but wet with runoff. There was some traffic, but not enough to be irritating.

S H E kept herself going through the earliest part of the process of escaping the desert through sheer will. For a time, the mountain road required all her concentration. Eventually, though, her thoughts turned to that horrible set of moments in the desert, when she thought she might die.

Until today, she had been in control in every situation. Her careful planning, her preparations, her training were all aimed toward minimizing variables that could result in her death or arrest.

If today had gone as she had planned it, Roy would have made sure that Victoria's drink was drugged, turned off the alarm, and taken all four children with him. How hard was it for him to count to four?

Even if Bonnie had refused the drink, Cleo could have taken her out. Having that stupid ass Giles along would have made it a little more difficult, but not impossible.

So what happens? Roy fucks up all but one of his assignments, and even so, things still might have been okay if Giles would have stayed calm and simply gone outside and met Carrie and told that reporter tough shit, he's her uncle, no interviews, and good-bye. Instead, the dipshit packs a goddamned newspaper reporter into the van! Gives her directions to where Cleo is waiting with a dead body!

And worst of all, the idiot says her name in front of the reporter. Cleo had thought quickly then, realizing that he'd just freak out and tell the woman God knows what if Cleo didn't calm him down as fast as possible. So she had lied and said he was great and did all the usual stroking of his ego that he required. And decided, as she hung up, that she'd had just about enough of Giles.

Her mistake had been in not shooting the reporter right off the bat. She saw that now. She had let her anger toward Giles get in the way of accomplishing her goals. At the very least, she should have taken the keys away from that bitch. Instead: amateur hour.

The killing of Giles had been nice and clean, and she had expected that the reporter and Carrie would be grateful for the rescue. Instead, the crazy bitch had driven off. And then, *then*—Cleo still couldn't believe it—then the bitch had turned around and tried to kill her!

No one had ever tried to kill Cleo. It had made her go cold all the way through. It gave her a kind of sick and wobbly feeling that threw her aim off. The thought of someone else feeling that way was one thing, but she was not supposed to be in that situation herself.

And the look on that woman's face! She had to stop thinking about it, she decided. It was too, too upsetting.

SHE didn't dare stop to rest. She didn't want any clerks or waitresses to have a reason to say where they had seen a woman matching her description.

I I I

THE sun was going down by the time she finished hiding the
motorcycle. She hiked up the slope that led to her cabin, carrying her bags.

Roy was sitting at the kitchen table with the kids when she
came in. There was a look of surprise on every face when she
opened the door, then she saw Roy look anxiously beyond her.

"Carrie's not with me," she said. Then, seeing the look on the
faces of the kids, she quickly added, "She decided to stay with
Grandfather Fletcher."

The kids were immediately relieved, but Roy still looked worried. One of the kids, the girl, said, "Can we all go to Grandfather
Fletcher's house?"

"No," Roy said. "No, we're going to stay here for a little
while."

They were all too well-disciplined to question his authority,
but Cleo could see that this decision didn't meet with their ap-
proval.

"Where's Mommy?" the youngest boy asked.

"She decided to stay with your grandfather, too," Cleo said, "so
she asked me to come up here and take care of you and your
dad."

That resulted in puzzlement, but no rebellion.

"Who are you?" asked the older boy.

"She's your cousin Cleo," Roy said, before she could warn him
not to give them her name. Well, what difference did it make,
now that Giles had made a gift of it to that reporter? Now that a
reporter could describe her to the police, to the world? It occurred to her that her whole life would have to change.

Fine, she thought, but she would make that reporter pay for all
the inconvenience she was causing.

CHAPTER 48

DEXTER FLETCHER thanked the first-class-cabin flight attendant as he accepted the glass of wine. The flight attendant lingered for a while, saw that he wasn't in the mood to converse, and withdrew. He made sure she didn't feel slighted, that she believed he was merely tired. He was an expert in the fine art of making a woman feel that, if at all possible, he would give her all his attention.

He often took this nonstop to Paris, and therefore made no effort to travel under an assumed name. That would change once he was on the ground, but for now he answered to Mr. Fletcher, as always.

Once he was sure he would not be disturbed for a while, he picked up his copy of the *Las Piernas News Express* and read the article once again. He closed his eyes and imagined all the ways things could go wrong with Giles's plans. Almost too many to imagine.

He had known there would be trouble once the story was published. Knowing Giles was about to make it worse, he decided it was time to go.

He had managed to get an early copy of the *Express* every morning through an arrangement he made with a nephew who had a job delivering the paper. That was why, at four this morning, Dex had been on his way to LAX. By six, his flight was in the air.

Conceivably, if Giles really screwed up, someone in law enforcement might greet him when he arrived in Paris tomorrow morning at half-past seven. It would be—he looked at his watch and calculated quickly—ten-thirty at night, still Tuesday, in Las Piernas.

Possible, he decided. Unlikely, but possible. Still, smarter to leave now and discover everything was fine at home, that Giles's plan had worked, than to regret staying.

He had called Nelson just before he left. He'd always had a soft spot for poor Nelson.

Rich Nelson, most people would say. Nelson was successful. Nelson was brilliant in his line of work, but he had always relied on Dexter to keep him clued in about other people, to take care of him and protect him from those who wanted to take advantage of him. He paid Dexter handsomely to deal with legal matters, but Dexter believed the most valuable advice he gave his brother had little to do with the law.

He sighed, thinking of Nelson. He had done what he could for him. Now he had to try to save his own neck.

He had been planning for this day for a number of years now. He had always provided a number of safe houses for Cleo, with the understanding that the day might come when he would make use of any he chose.

More than anyone currently in her life, Dex thought, he knew her.

Dex adjusted his seat into a bed so that he could sleep comfortably cocooned for a few hours.

He closed his eyes and smiled to himself. Cleo was a resourceful little devil, and she'd never trust Giles completely. With any luck, he had just wasted the price of a one-way ticket to France.

His eyes opened. Would he return to the family if he could? The idea of leaving it had once been unthinkable. Now . . . now there were all sorts of possibilities.

He closed his eyes again and slept soundly.

THE flight attendant, passing by a little later, removed the empty wineglass. Dex Fletcher was always a pleasure to serve, not fussy or demanding, always remembered not just your name but if you had kids, and asked after them. Took an interest in people, unlike a lot of the jerks you got in first class. What a lucky woman his wife was. Looking down at his handsome face, somehow even more attractive in repose, she turned off the reading light he'd left on. The newspaper, she left—trying to take it from him would probably wake him up. Poor guy. Earlier, when they were talking, she'd had the feeling he was tired.

CHAPTER 49

Tuesday, May 2
12:35 P.M.
LATITUDE 33°10'0''
LONGITUDE 118°11'15''

NELSON FLETCHER stood on the deck of the trawler formerly known as the *Elisa* and gazed out at a beautiful day, which, as it so happened, was also the most miserable of his life.

From here, looking off the stern, he could see Santa Catalina Island behind him. San Clemente Island lay ahead to starboard, the coast of northern San Diego County to port.

Dexter had called him at five this morning. Nelson had pretended it was a business call. Pretended he was being called out of town for a few days. By the time he dressed, his wife, Elisa, had fallen back to sleep. Her skin was soft and warm when he kissed her good-bye, half-waking her.

He nearly screwed it all up then and there, because he almost broke down and held her close, almost made too big a deal out of leaving.

Then he thought about how much she was going to hate him by the end of the day, and held himself in check.

Dexter had warned him almost a week ago that Giles was up to something that was going to cause too much trouble for everyone. He had finally given in then and arranged for the trawler to be surreptitiously renamed and docked elsewhere. It would need to be painted later.

When Nelson first became involved in Giles's plans, almost seven years ago, Dexter had taken him aside and talked to him about the importance of having a plan to leave the country.

No use thinking of going back in time, he told himself. No use thinking of what he would have done differently. Shame, guilt, regret—they were constant companions now. And yet . . .

And yet he had married Elisa. Without Giles's plan, would that have come about? No.

They might have married once, long ago. He met her, and dated her, and was crazy about her from the start. He was awkward around Mason, who was never impressed by anything Nelson tried to do to win him over.

Whatever mistakes he made with Mason were nothing compared to his biggest blunder: He introduced Elisa to his charming brother Richard.

Richard and Elisa had forgotten everyone else from the moment they were introduced. Oh, at some point Richard asked him if he would mind . . . if he would mind! But Nelson had been hurt by what seemed to him a double betrayal, and his pride had been injured. Richard and Elisa had been blissfully unaware of how much it cost him to keep up his act of nonchalance.

Giles had seen it. Dexter and Roy, too. They saw that over the years, the pain of it ate at him.

He worked hard to stay in Richard and Elisa's lives, just so he could be around her, help her. They maintained contact with him and no other member of the family.

Nearly fifteen years passed in this way. He kept waiting for some other woman to draw his eye. For his desire for her to lessen. But no one else could ever appeal to him.

He told people he was married to his work. In some ways, that was true. He was sure that with the exception of Giles, Dex, and Roy, he had succeeded in deceiving everyone.

Then one day Richard put an end to that delusion.

"Of all my brothers," Richard said, "you're the one who has always been the kindest to me. That makes this especially difficult, because I don't want to hurt you, but I can't see any way around it. You'll have to spend less time with my family, Nelson."

"What do you mean?" Nelson asked in disbelief.

"I'm sorry. I know this hurts you. But even Mason has noticed that you're still . . ." He seemed to search for a word. "You're still enamored of Elisa."

"Mason! He doesn't show either of you an ounce of respect. The things you let him say to Elisa! He makes her so unhappy—"

"It won't work, Nelson. This time you won't sidetrack me, especially not by complaining about Mason. Mason's fine. He'll outgrow all this rebellion. He's bright and talented and good-hearted." He sighed. "You see, it almost worked again. Mason's right this time, as it turns out, and he had the guts to confront me about it. I kept hoping, kept wanting to believe you'd accept the fact that Elisa and I are happily married, but I think I've only done you a disservice by not facing this earlier on. It's only a matter of time before the other children become aware of it. Caleb already has, I think, on some level. At his age, it won't be long before he can name the reason he keeps wanting weekends with 'just our own family.'"

Nelson tried to protest, but Richard interrupted him and said, "Look me in the eye and tell me you aren't in love with my wife."

When the silence stretched between them, Richard said, in that gentle way of his, "I think, Nelson, it will be better for all of us if you limit your visits to my home to once or twice a year. You can visit me any time at my office, but—"

"Has Elisa asked you to say this to me?"

"No, right now this is between the two of us," Richard said. "Do you want me to discuss this with her?"

"No," he said quickly. That would have been the final mortification. "I would ask," he added, not quite steadily, "that you never mention this to her. It would make her so . . . uncomfortable."

Richard agreed and thanked him for understanding.

THE banishment. That's how Nelson thought of that awful day. He acknowledged now that long before the banishment, he had been thinking that it would be convenient for Richard to die. He had not brought himself to think of murdering him. He just wanted him to have a fatal car wreck, a drowning accident, or a heart attack. Something quick.

The banishment made it easier to listen to Giles, as he talked of bringing the best and the brightest into the family sphere of influence, of taking children—who would never be allowed to otherwise reach their full potential—away from the parents who hindered them. To think differently of Richard, think of him as hard-hearted and misguided. To believe that Giles's plans could give Nelson what he wanted. He convinced himself that it would give Elisa a better life, too. He could love her better, give her more.

His part, too, was so simple. Take the child, Jenny, with him. Jenny knew him, trusted him. He had already taken her to visit Roy and Victoria, and she adored Victoria's little girl, Carrie. That day he simply did what he had done on three other mornings. Because he wasn't coming to the house, Richard had no objection to his brief visits to the office. He had missed Nelson, he said. Jenny clearly was happy to see him. And it did make it easier for Richard to get work done if Nelson entertained Jenny.

So when Nelson arrived that last morning and asked Jenny if she wanted to come with him, she didn't hesitate.

Two business clients who had been referred to him by Nelson found Richard's body—as Nelson had known they would—so when police arrived, the clients asked the police to contact Nelson, just as Giles had predicted.

The grisly murder scene had nearly made Nelson faint. He had not expected it to be so bloody, for Richard to be so . . . damaged. A single thought repeated itself over and over:

What have I done? What have I done? What have I done?

He had not expected this horror. He discovered that the anger he had felt toward Richard seemed petty and misplaced. He thought of the child Richard, whom he had always protected and cared for as an older brother should, and a sudden upwelling of great and genuine grief overcame him.

IN his rosily imagined versions of how it would go, before it actually happened, he could pursue Elisa by comforting her, and go on from there. Mason, who tormented her, would be in prison, at least for a time. Jenny, adorable as she was, would have made it difficult for them to have the kind of honeymoon-forever lifestyle he envisioned. He knew Elisa would miss her child, but that child would have a wonderful upbringing, with more advantages than Richard could have provided, and other children to play with as she grew up.

Jenny was hardly more than a toddler, and would eventually accept what she had been told—her parents were dead, Roy and Victoria were her new mommy and daddy. To Jenny, Uncle Nelson would still be Uncle Nelson—although Nelson would ensure that Elisa remained aloof from the Fletchers, and if she did have contact, she would never be at Graydon Fletcher's home at the same time Roy's family was there.

Caleb would be in college. Nelson hoped to help him grow closer to the rest of the Fletcher family.

IT hadn't happened that way, of course.

Oh, parts of it had. Elisa never developed any interest in the Fletchers, which was a blessing in some ways, but unsettling to him in others, because the family meant so much to him. Jenny settled in—or so it seemed to him, although guilt kept him from visiting Roy's family very often. Still, he hadn't counted on how long and deeply Elisa would grieve for Jenny, how persistent she would be in her belief that Jenny lived.

Nor had he predicted how much she would miss Mason and worry over his well-being. So he did all he could for Mason after the young man was convicted. That actually helped Nelson's pursuit of Elisa more than he could have dreamed possible.

Caleb had proved as impossible and stubborn as his father. Elisa had been terribly hurt by Caleb and missed him, too, but she was angry with him on Nelson's behalf. She saw Nelson's attempts to befriend him and his rejection of Nelson, and felt disappointed in her son.

Nelson tried to make her life as comfortable as possible. She had needed someone to lean on after Richard's death and all her other losses. Nelson loved helping her to embrace life again. She was an amazing woman, much stronger than some supposed.

He loved her, and he was convinced that she loved him. Or loved the man she believed him to be. That would all change now.

If he committed suicide, she would have his fortune at least. He felt the sea breeze, the warmth of the sun on his face. Not yet, he thought. Not yet.

He'd wait until he was sure Dexter was right. He had waited so long to be with Elisa, he would wait a little longer to let go.

CHAPTER 50

SAN BERNARDINO MOUNTAINS

"GENIE," her dad said, "Cleo and I are going to go outside for a little while. Boys, go upstairs and brush your teeth and get in your pajamas. I'll come back in to tuck you in soon."

The boys glanced at Genie, who gave a small nod, and they went upstairs. She turned to see Cleo watching her. She smiled and said, "Thank you for letting us stay at your cabin, Cousin Cleo."

"You're welcome, Genie." Genie thought she might say more, but Cleo seemed to change her mind, and went to a closet to gather a warm coat, mittens, and a wool cap.

When they were out of the house, Genie felt a sense of relief. She felt sure that Cousin Cleo was a liar. Genie had made a point of mentioning Carrie several times, and could see that Cleo didn't like that. She hoped that meant that Carrie was with Ms. Kelly, or maybe Carrie was already meeting her real father. She found it hard to think about the idea of Carrie maybe not coming back to live with them.

Cleo also didn't like it when Aaron cried and said he wanted Mommy. She gave Aaron a mean look that made him cry harder. Genie had quickly comforted and distracted him, and he stopped. Genie had to admit that Cleo hadn't said or done anything to him, but that look . . . that look was scary.

Dad seemed not to even notice they were there. You had to say his name a bunch of times to get him to pay any attention to you. Two minutes later it seemed as if he hadn't heard anything you said to him, or had forgotten you were there. Since Cleo got here, it was even worse. Dad was willing to do whatever Cleo said.

Even before they got here, Dad didn't seem to be himself. On the way to the mountains, when they stopped to buy gas, Genie asked if she could ride up front with Dad, and he had said yes. He ignored the boys' protests. He told them they could come into the convenience mart with him while Genie watched the SUV.

When he came back, she discovered he had bought each of them a bag of chips. They never ate junk food—Mom did not allow it. The boys had delighted in this new experience, but Genie decided to save her chips for later.

Genie had a feeling that something was going wrong, really wrong, and she didn't think it had to do with Carrie. There was some other trouble, and no one was telling the kids about it. She hated when that happened.

When they got here, Dad made everyone wait in the SUV, even though the boys had to go to the bathroom really bad. It was just past noon, but he took a flashlight with him, putting it in his jacket pocket. He went to the door, which used a keypad instead of a key, but didn't go inside. He then went around to the back of the cabin. When he returned, his clothes were dirty.

The cabin was the only one at the end of a long road. There were trees and boulders all around it at the front. Dad pulled the SUV into a garage, and once the boys had gone to the bathroom, for a time they were busy moving things from the car into the cabin.

Dad called it a cabin, but it was big enough to be called a house. There was a steep slope at the back. A small deck was built out over this, with a telescope on it, and if you held it just right, you could see the glint of a few other windows and roofs, and a stretch of the main road. It was pretty here, but Genie felt too worried to enjoy the view.

Before Cleo showed up, Genie had snooped through the cabin, and in the desk, which had a strange panel of LED lights next to it, she found some things she thought she might be able to use— envelopes and stamps. She took one stamp and an envelope. She had brought paper and pens and a few art supplies, and she planned to use them to mail a letter. She'd noticed that there was a mailbox at the end of the long dirt road that led back to this cabin.

The biggest temptation in the house was a television set. It was hooked up to a satellite dish. But Dad unplugged it as soon as they came in.

While she was snooping, Genie also saw three guns. Dad didn't keep guns at home, but Grandfather had taught all the children rules about them: If you see a gun, don't touch it, get an adult. So she hadn't touched them, and told Dad about the one in the closet and the one in the kitchen, because she was afraid the boys might find them. She had to do a lot of hinting to get him to discover the one in the desk and even pretended that she was looking in it for the first time, because if she had just said, "I was snooping around and found one there," she'd have been in trouble.

He sighed when she showed him the first gun. "Leave it to Cleo not to even have the safety on." She watched how he removed the thing that held the ammunition—he said it was a magazine—in each of the guns. He answered her question about the safety and showed her about keeping guns pointed down and away from anyone. "You might think this gun is safe now, but it isn't—you must always treat every gun as if it is loaded, and never pull the trigger to find out if it has a bullet in it. Watch." He showed her that a round was already chambered, and ejected that one. He did this with each gun, and searched the closet and found several boxes of ammunition.

He locked all the ammunition, including the magazines, away in the rear cargo hold of the SUV. She told him he should probably make sure there weren't others, and even said, "In the bedrooms or something," but he didn't look. Mostly, he just sat around looking sad.

There was a lot of food in the pantry, so that was good, and Dad had brought a lot of food in the ice chest, so they wouldn't have to worry about that. In payment for the stamp and the envelope she had taken, she left the bag of chips in the pantry.

She found Dad's notebook in his jacket and read through the

most recent page. Her eyes widened at the word *booby trap,* and she read those instructions carefully. She had a good memory, so she didn't need to take the page out of the notebook. She replaced it in the jacket pocket.

There was a strange bedroom at the end of the upstairs hall that had a lot of mirrors on the walls and ceiling. It was the biggest of the bedrooms. The bathroom was big, too—it had a fancy shower in it. A look around the bathroom, even under the toilet-tank lid, did not reveal any hidden weapons.

Genie went back out into the mirrored bedroom. She saw the big bed and recalled how her mom hid things between the mattress and the box spring of her bed at home. She tried one side, then the other. On the second side, her hand touched something metal, and she drew out a fourth gun. She removed the magazine by pushing the button she'd seen her dad push on the other guns, which were identical to this one, and pocketed the ammunition. She ejected the chambered round as well.

Near the bed was another panel with some LED lights on it, identical to the one next to the desk downstairs. The green ones were lit now, but there was a row of red ones, too. She thought it might be the alarm system for the house.

She searched the nightstands on either side of the bed, then looked through the closet and the dresser drawers. Mostly it was the usual sort of thing grown-ups kept in such places, although Cleo's clothing wasn't much like Mom's. In one of the nightstands she only found condoms—the same brand Dad kept hidden in his desk at home—and a local phone book.

Genie spent a few minutes making strange faces in the mirrors and looking at reflections of reflections. But after a few minutes, she decided the room was creepy. Later she was relieved when Dad didn't put his things in there.

When they first arrived, they had played outside in the snow. That had been fun. After the long drive the boys needed to expend some energy. They built a snowman, and Genie used Carrie's camera to take a picture of Troy and Aaron standing next to it. She would get it developed and send it to Carrie. She had tried to stop worrying about Carrie, but she couldn't. Maybe Mom had found out and was punishing her. She didn't like to think about that.

After Cleo came to the cabin—Genie still wasn't sure how she got there, since she hadn't arrived in a car—they all had to stay inside. Cleo said some people who wanted to steal them away from Dad might be looking for them. They had heard about people wanting to steal them before, but somehow, when she said it, it made them all believe it could happen at any minute.

Genie could see that all of this was upsetting the boys and that if the boys were upset, Cleo got mad. Mom could be the same way, so Genie found herself in the accustomed role of taking care of her brothers, finding ways to entertain them. Now the task of making sure they brushed their teeth and got into bed fell to her. She tried not to think about the fact that she and Carrie always did this together.

Fortunately, between the stresses of the day and the time they had spent playing in the snow, the boys were tired now, and she didn't have any arguments from them as she tucked them in.

She made up a story for them, about a girl who was a princess looking for her father the king, and although they at first objected to a story about a girl, when she was done they asked her to tell it again. They fell asleep before she got very far the second time around.

She went to the room where Dad had told her she would sleep. Keeping the lights off, she carefully approached the window. Earlier, she had raised the blind, so she had to be careful not to be seen.

Beneath the window, out in the moonlight, she saw Dad and Cleo. They were hugging. It gave her a kind of sick feeling, so she quickly stepped back and lowered the blind. Was Cleo going to be their new mom or something? That didn't seem possible.

She turned a bedside lamp on and sat at the side of the bed. It was a big bed. She was glad she had brought the big soft doll. It made the bed seem less empty.

She felt lonely without Carrie and spent a little time looking through the few things she had brought along for her sister, thinking they were going to spend the day at Grandfather's house. She had packed them both to fool Dad and in case things went wrong and Carrie ended up joining them. She picked up Carrie's camera and thought back to the alternate plan they had made to take pictures of Carrie at Grandfather's house and mail them to Ms. Kelly. Was that just this morning? This had been such a long and crazy day.

She changed into her pajamas. She had realized several hours ago that the duffels were full of new clothes and pajamas and underwear, all in the right sizes. There was even one for Carrie. Any other time, she would have been excited about new clothes, but she couldn't help wishing she had her own comfy pj's instead of these new scratchy ones. She decided to put her sleeping bag on top of the bedspread. At least it was something familiar.

She got her drawing pad and colored pencils, as well as a flashlight she had found downstairs, and climbed into bed. She began writing her letter.

> Dear Ms. Kelly,
> I am Carla Ives's sister. Please tell her we are at 14 Cold Creek Road in the San Bernardino Mountains. I think the nearest city is Big Bear Lake. We are at Cleo Fletcher's house.
> Thank you.
> Yours truly,
> Genie
> P.S. Tell her I miss her a lot.

She heard the front door open and hurriedly turned out the light. She hid the drawing pad and the pencils and flashlight beneath the new clothes in Carrie's duffel bag and quietly got back into bed.

She pretended to be asleep when her dad opened the door to her bedroom. She heard a strange metallic sound.

"Cleo, wait!" Dad whispered from the doorway.

"What the hell is that on the pillow next to her?" Cleo whispered back.

"A doll," he said in a low and shaky voice. "Just a doll." He paused. "I think she misses Carrie. Please, put the knife away."

"I was only going to protect her," Cleo said.

"I know," he said soothingly. "I know. You're taking care of all of us."

Genie heard him close the door and walk toward the mirrored room. Cleo's footsteps were much softer, but they followed his.

Genie pulled the doll closer. She fell asleep whispering the words "Six Hundred Broadway, Las Piernas, California" over and over to the doll, because, according to a little piece of newsprint she had memorized this morning, that was the address for the *Las Piernas News Express*.

CHAPTER 51

QUESTIONS abounded. Whenever one question about the Fletchers seemed resolved, ten more took its place.

We thought we knew who was missing from the house in Huntington Beach, until the Huntington Beach Police Department released photos of Roy Fletcher and his children. They discovered Roy's digital camera, and fortunately, the last few photographs had not yet been deleted from its memory. The police blanketed the media with them.

After seeing the photos, it seemed likely that the only person in the Roy Fletcher family who was using his or her legal name was Roy himself.

A hunch I had based on the story Reggie Faroe's mother had told me led to a check of Arizona records. They showed that Roy's late wife, Bonnie, had legally married Roy there under her real name but apparently she stopped using it from then on. Now the fact that her previous boyfriend, Reggie Faroe, was found dead at the base of a cliff seemed even more suspicious. The man she ran off with died in the desert, her name changed, and she acquired not only her own daughter but also three other children.

Bonnie's body had been left in another desert, and although the circumstances strongly suggested Giles or Cleo had killed her, it was not clear that she had been murdered—even an autopsy might not be conclusive about whether she fell or was pushed down those stairs. Toxicology tests would take six weeks or more, but Carrie's account indicated that Bonnie might have been drugged by Roy, another factor to be considered. Fingerprints,

DNA, and firearms evidence had been collected from the desert scene and the bullet-riddled van—the fingerprints found in the BMW would be sent through IAFIS, the FBI fingerprint system; DNA would be compared to DNA found in the shoe left in Sheila Dolson's backyard; the bullets would be compared to the one that killed her.

Reed told me that Sheila's DNA had matched that on the cigarettes found at the scene of Gerry Serre's burial on the Sheffield Estate. That meant she had at least been present when he was buried.

"Does any of the DNA on the cigarettes you found out there come from anyone else?" I asked.

"No. All Sheila's. Which make us think she could have carried this out alone. We're going to try to figure out if she dated Gerry Serre before he died. We're a long way from being certain she's the one who murdered him."

The news stories about the children hadn't yet aired on television when I talked to him. Once they did, local police departments began to take a different view of Roy Fletcher.

I saw the photos of the children Roy was calling his own while I was in the newsroom working with Mark on the last few details of his story on the ongoing investigation into the Roy Fletcher family. I had already turned in a first-person account—from that point on, I was off the story as a reporter.

Frank was sitting next to me, off duty from all roles other than protective husband. I have accepted the fact that he can't help himself when it comes to that one, and would be lying if I said I didn't appreciate it that evening. John Walters is fond of telling me that he doesn't want me to bring cops into his newsroom, but in truth, he likes Frank and enjoys talking to him. Over time he's learned that I didn't marry "Frank Harriman, Police Spy." Despite the evidence, Frank's employers still suspect he married "Irene Kelly, Newspaper Spy."

John told me he had uploaded the photos and sent them to my terminal. I was exhausted, really ready to go home, but my curiosity overcame all of that. I saw a photo of a boy, captioned as *Troy Fletcher.* Cute kid, but not one I recognized. The next one, labeled *Aaron Fletcher,* made me sit bolt upright.

"My God—it's Luke Serre."

"Luke Serre?" John said, as he crossed the room toward my desk. "The murdered man?"

"No, that was Gerry Serre. This is his son. Didn't you recognize him?" I called up the photos Jane Serre had given me a few days ago, when I interviewed her after her ex-husband's body was found on the Sheffield Estate. I placed the photo of the boy now going by the name of Aaron Fletcher next to the most recent photo she had given me of her son.

Only two years had gone by, and while Luke had gone from toddler to little boy in that time, the likeness was unmistakable.

"Well, I'll be damned," Frank said.

"Better call your friends about it," John said, but Frank already had his cell phone in hand and was calling Reed Collins.

"Two of those four kids were kidnapped from Las Piernas," John said, and barked for Mark not to go home.

My phone rang. It was Caleb, calling from our house. He had stopped by earlier in the evening to visit Ethan. Ben was there, too—he had stopped by to work with Altair, and ended up waiting with Caleb and Ethan for word about my adventures in the high desert. Since I had to go to work before coming home, they ordered pizza and kept Ethan company.

"On the news!" Caleb said. "The younger girl—she's my sister!" He had just seen the photos on television. As he spoke to me, I pulled up the image of Genie Fletcher and agreed I could see a strong resemblance to him. He told me he was certain Genie Fletcher was Jenny.

"I don't want to create false hope," I said. "And you've done enough work in your field to know one photo isn't enough to make anyone certain of an identification."

"You sound like Ben," he complained.

"Ben's right. I don't know if Genie Fletcher is your sister, but you and your mom may want to talk to Detective Joe Travers of the Huntington Beach police. Do you think your mom is still awake? Maybe you should call her."

There was a long silence, then he said, "I'll call when I know for sure it's Jenny."

Despite this, I could tell the bit about false hope had been a useless caveat.

T H E television screens in the newsroom were full of stories about the events of the day and showing photos of the children, Roy, and Bonnie/Victoria. A forensic artist's sketch of Cleo showed up, too—no one seemed to have any photos of her. Speculation was laid on thick by various commentators, but that would be nothing compared to the hours of live guesswork that were bound to come. I was already thoroughly tired of seeing the clips some of them had captured out in Palmdale. My fifteen minutes of fame, and I looked as if I had stepped out of a sandblaster.

I kept hoping that all the coverage would result in solid leads, thinking that surely someone would have seen Roy and the three children. Calls did come in to the police. Frank told me that if all the sightings were accurate, Roy and the kids had been able to manifest themselves in more than six hundred places in the United States and Canada, almost simultaneously.

As the hours from the time of Roy's disappearance lengthened, worries grew.

J U S T before I left work, Edith Fletcher, a daughter of Graydon Fletcher who lived with him, called on his behalf. She said he wanted me to know that the police had been informed that Giles Fletcher had been seen leaving an SUV—registered to a corporation none of them had ever heard of—parked in front of Graydon's house. "And apparently Roy came by very early and unloaded it."

"What did he take out of it?"

"The security cameras didn't catch many details, but apparently it was sports or camping equipment—duffel bags and an ice chest, things like that. The police have the vehicle and the tape. We're hoping this might help them to locate Roy before . . . before anything happens."

"How often was Roy's family over there?"

"Oh, Roy would stop by every few weeks or so, but we rarely saw the children. Still, I'm very fond of them. I know the girls better than the boys. They like to help me in the greenhouse. Such smart girls! They were here just after Sheila died." She paused. "I didn't really know Sheila, but—well, I'm now wondering if I knew Giles or Victoria or Roy! I can't believe all of this is happening. And Carrie's father—to have worried so about her for all those years! Thank goodness you were able to save her. I'm so grateful to you for that, I can't begin to tell you. As for Genie and Aaron and Troy, I do hope nothing bad has happened—" She wasn't able to finish. I found myself trying to reassure her. We talked for a while, and I found myself liking her. I thanked her for calling, and passed word on to Mark about the second SUV.

Just when I wanted to write them all off, I'd meet one of the kinder family members. If Edith Fletcher wasn't genuinely concerned about those kids, and genuinely appalled by what she was learning about certain other family members, she was the best actress I'd encountered since becoming a reporter.

John Walters stopped us on the way out of the newsroom. "Kelly, you look like hell. Take the day off tomorrow."

"Are you sure? I already took—"

"Don't argue with me, Kelly."

"Don't argue with him," Frank chimed in, and steered me out the door.

F R A N K got another call as we headed home that night, from his new lieutenant, Jake Masuda. I caught Frank's attention and said, "I wonder if the woman Gerry Serre dated before he was murdered bore any resemblance to Cleo Fletcher?"

"We do sometimes think of these things," he said to me, and went back to talking to Jake.

Well, if he was going to be like that . . .

When he hung up, he told me there was a lead on the third

child, Troy Fletcher. "A preschool teacher called to say she remembered him as Troy Sherman, one of her brightest, so I'm going to go talk to her tomorrow."

I smiled and wished him luck, and if my tone made him suspicious, he didn't say anything.

At home, we found that Caleb and Ben had left, and Ethan had fallen asleep. I made one more phone call, to a night-owl friend down in San Diego, Tonya Pearsley. She's a school psychologist. Apparently my misadventures had made the news down there, so she was glad I called. I was glad she already had some background on the day's events. I asked her about IQ testing of young children, and she verified that there were intelligence tests for preschoolers.

"Yes, but it's not foolproof. There is some question about the reliability of the results based on socioeconomic factors and the home environment. You can't tell how bright a child is just from a test score, you have to look at the whole child. In general, if you wait until a child is in second or third grade, you'll get more reliable information from testing."

"But it can be done?"

"Yes. Beyond reliability, though, the controversy surrounding the testing of preschoolers is mostly over how the information from the tests is going to be used."

"You mean questions over whether to put kids in accelerated classes early on?"

"Partly, yes. Private testing is becoming more popular with parents who want to push their kids, although the schools are more inclined to try to use the tests to identify kids with learning problems, so that we can help them as soon as possible. Is this associated with a private school in the area?"

"You saw the kids in the newscast. They weren't all at one private school—in fact, they were home-schooled. But they seem to be exceptionally bright—I mean off-the-charts smart. It's the one factor I know they all have in common."

"So you wonder who identified them as being so bright at such a young age? You're probably looking for an educational psychol-

ogist. Not that many people do testing of preschoolers, so that
may help you."

I thanked her and promised we'd try to get down that way
sometime soon.

When I hung up, I realized Frank had been eavesdropping.

"Sorry I was sarcastic earlier," he said, proving he does figure
out some things on his own. He had an impish smile on his face as
he apologized, though, so he hardly presented a portrait of contri-
tion. Alas, I'm a sucker for that smile.

"You want to know what Tonya said, I suppose."

The smile grew. "Yes. But I really am sorry."

"Hmm. If you hadn't driven all the way out to Antelope Valley
and hung around with me in the newsroom, I'd have my doubts.
But you've scored big points." I explained what Tonya had said.
"Roy and Bonnie took Carrie to live with them in Huntington
Beach. She's especially bright. But then, three other especially
bright kids from Las Piernas came to live with them—I find it
too unlikely those are chance adoptions, especially given the clois-
tered lifestyle these kids were leading."

"I agree. We aren't talking about two people who were blithely
unaware that someone was handing off stolen kids to them."

"Caleb's sister was a relative, so even if Richard Fletcher was
estranged from the extended Fletcher family, Giles or someone
else could have observed her intelligence. I keep wondering who
might have flagged these two boys for them—identified them as
especially bright."

"I'll ask the preschool teacher I'm meeting tomorrow about
who did Troy's testing."

"No AMBER Alert on these kids?" I asked.

"That was debated by the task force they've formed on these
cases. You know an AMBER Alert only gets used if the child may
be seriously injured or killed—no one wants the public to become
complacent about those alerts, so they try not to overuse them.
You ask me, Roy Fletcher conspired to kill his wife and repre-
sents a threat to the kids. He could be suicidal at this point. But
given everything Carrie said about the family, the higher-ups in

the task force decided it was parental abduction. I hope that won't come back to bite them."

Not wanting the children to come to harm, I hoped so, too.

We agreed to call it a night. As we got into bed Frank said he'd like it very much if I'd stay away from people with guns for a while, but I reminded him that in that case, I would have to avoid him and most of his friends. So he amended the request: I was to avoid anyone with a gun who was not officially on the list of Frank Harriman Approved Gun Owners, which was a pretty darned short one. I said that was fine with me, really.

CHAPTER 52

GENIE had fed the boys breakfast an hour ago and was now trying to get them to settle down enough to get their jackets and mittens on. Dad and Cleo had come downstairs just as the boys finished eating, and had a not-so-quiet argument about the TV, which had been settled with a compromise. The compromise was that the kids could go outside with Dad while Cleo watched TV. The boys wanted to stay inside and watch TV, too, of course, but Dad snapped at them and they gave up on the idea. They were always full of energy after breakfast, and now they were being little devils. It would be good to get them outside and let them run around a little.

Genie tried not to show how excited she was about going outside. She had addressed and stamped the letter, and now she had it tucked inside her jacket pocket.

The air was cold, but most of the snow was gone. A few patches could be found under the shadiest trees or near the biggest rocks. The little snowman they had built yesterday was already a lump of ice and dirt and sticks. She was glad she had used Carrie's camera to take a picture of him before he melted.

Dad didn't come outside right away, and so she took her chance. "Race you to the road!" she called to the boys.

They took the challenge and headed up the drive.

They had not reached the first bend when she heard Dad yell, "Kids, no!"

The boys stopped immediately, but Genie pretended she didn't hear him. She kept on going.

"You two stay right there!" she heard Dad yell at the boys. "Genie! Genie!"

She kept running, turning up the bend, now out of sight of the cabin.

But Dad's legs were long and it didn't take even a minute for him to catch up to her. He grabbed hold of her arm, clutching it hard. It hurt, and something about that grip made her go crazy. All her worry, all her fears about Carrie and Mom and their family came boiling up inside her, and she did something she had never done before in her life—she tried to hurt Dad.

He was not quite on balance as he took hold of her, or it never would have worked, but she twisted and kicked and thrashed, and the combination of her movements made him stumble and fall. She fell, too, but got up faster and ran.

He quickly caught up with her again, and this time he grabbed her and completely overpowered her, pushing her to the ground, pinning her. His face, looming over hers, was red with anger.

Now she was frightened in an entirely different way.

He stood up and pulled her up by the shoulders. He shook her. "What the hell are you doing?" he shouted. "Are you trying to get us all killed?"

She looked at him, wide-eyed. She nearly began to cry. This man wasn't Dad, not the Dad she loved. At this thought, her anger rose up again and she shouted back at him, "What happened to my father?"

His face went pale.

"You aren't my dad! You act like someone I don't know!"

He set her down but kept his hands on her shoulders. His hands were trembling. He looked awful. Suddenly she felt bad about yelling at him.

He glanced at the ground and frowned, then bent to pick up the envelope, which had fallen out of her pocket. "My God . . . Genie . . ."

She didn't say anything.

"Genie . . . Genie, sit here with me for a minute, okay?"

She nodded, and they moved over to a big rock. He called to the boys, who were standing still in shock. "Genie and I are going to talk for a minute. Why don't you build another little snowman out of the snow over there?"

"We could make a snow*boy*," Troy suggested.

"Yes, that would be good."

Despite the coolness of the air, Dad's face was sweating. Genie tried to catch her breath. Now that she had yelled at him, and all the rest, she felt shaky, too. Although they were sitting close to each other, it seemed to her that Dad was far away, that something important had changed between them. She wasn't sure she wanted it, and even as she wished that it was a week ago and she and Carrie had never talked about rememberings or called Irene Kelly, she could hear one of Grandfather's sayings, "What's done is done, even though we might wish and wish to change it. So when there is no going back, you must go forward." Until now, that had only been something she thought when she broke a plate or a glass while doing dishes. Now she had broken her whole family.

"Did I hurt you?" Dad asked.

He had, but she shook her head.

"Good. I never, ever wanted to hurt you, Genie. Always remember that, okay?" He started crying. Although yesterday she had wondered once or twice if he had been crying, she had never seen him break down in front of her before. He brought his knees up and put his right arm over them, then rested his forehead on his arm, hiding his face.

Genie, on his left, moved closer to him. She took his free hand and held it tight. "I know, Daddy. I know. Please don't cry."

"I've ruined everything," he said.

"We'll be all right," Genie said, patting his arm. She quickly glanced over to where the boys were playing and was relieved to see that they were engrossed in gathering snow for their snowboy.

Dad wiped at his face, took some big breaths, and sat up a little straighter. "I'm sorry," he said again, but in a stronger voice. "It doesn't help for me to fall apart, does it?" He pulled her closer and said, "Whatever happens, I want you to know that I love you and Troy and Aaron and Carrie."

"I know, Dad. We love you, too. Don't be sad."

He took another big breath. "I don't know how long Cleo is going to be inside, so I'm going to tell you some things, just in case—well, just in case.

"Genie, I made a big mistake—a lot of big mistakes. We're here because I—I liked Cleo, and I believed that Cleo would keep us safe. But instead . . . instead, we're all in danger here."

"Why don't we leave?"

"I want to, but we have to be careful. If we're not careful, someone could get hurt. Cleo . . . Cleo has special skills."

"All those guns—"

"She kills people, Genie. I'm being very serious about that."

"She's a murderer? All those guns—Dad—let's get in the car and get away!"

"She has the keys to the car. Besides, I think she has some kind of alarm and God knows what else set up in the garage now, too. She warned me that it would be unhealthy to try to go in there. And one of the first things she did when she got here was to destroy my cell phone."

Genie frowned.

"Even though she's a little . . . out of control, she likes me, Genie. And she wanted to help us. But she's not like other people. She doesn't think like other people do. I don't want her to hurt you or the boys. For now we have to make sure she stays calm and doesn't feel threatened by us, all right? Sooner or later we'll get a chance. Or she'll figure out that she can do better on her own and leave us."

Genie frowned. "Dad, she won't want us to tell people about her. If she kills people . . ."

"That's why we have to be cautious, Genie."

"The guns. The booby trap—"

"You know about the booby trap?" He looked shocked.

"It's under the house."

"It's . . . it's like a bomb, Genie. She can easily go back under the house, hook it up again, and trap all of us inside. If someone comes through the door while that thing's hooked up, it will blow them—and all of us—to kingdom come."

He took another shaky breath. "From this cabin, someone can look out and see down the slope, right?"

"Yes."

"She can see people coming up the road. She even has perimeter alarms set. You know what those are?"

"I know what a perimeter is. . . ."

"Those alarms go off if anyone comes close to the cabin. They won't ring out or anything—they're a set of lights near her bed and by her desk downstairs. She checks them all the time. If you had gone up the driveway, she would be able to tell."

"Mom and Carrie will be worried. They'll look for us."

She saw the stricken look on his face.

"What? What's wrong?"

"Mom has been hurt. Very badly."

Genie tried to take this in. "Did Cleo hurt her?"

"I don't know. I honestly don't know. She says she didn't. She says Mom fell down the stairs before she got there. It's my fault. It's my fault. . . ."

Because you gave Mom pills in her drink, Genie thought, remembering the mortar and pestle. Cleo lies, and you lie, too. She suddenly felt cold inside, and wanted to move away from him, but she stayed still. "Carrie . . ." she whispered.

"Carrie is safe."

She looked up at him.

He held the letter up. "Did you and Carrie write to Ms. Kelly?"

"No," she said.

"Tell me why Ms. Kelly came to our house, Genie. Tell me the truth. It's really important. I mean it."

So she told him everything she knew. When she came to the part about figuring out about the pills in the Bloody Mary, she skipped over that, but thinking of it helped her find some defiance. "And I remember someone named Mason. Who is he?"

He looked away. "Your brother. He's in prison."

Brother, yes! Her mental picture of him came more sharply into focus. Then the next words registered. "In prison!"

"Yes."

"Why?"

He hesitated, then said, "He was wrongly accused of a crime."

He took a deep breath and added, "If anything happens to me, Genie, try to get Aaron and Troy away from here. If you find someone to help you, tell them to call the police. If they won't call the police, don't go near them. A good person will call the police if you ask them to, okay?"

She nodded.

"Ask the police to take you to Grandfather and tell him that he must take you to your aunt Elisa—to her, and only to her."

"Who is she?"

"She's—she's someone who will love you. I promise you that. She will know who you are. She'll . . . she'll help you to get your brother out of prison." He paused. "You have another brother, too. His name is Caleb."

Caleb. A face came to mind with that name, a face not so unlike her own. A dark-haired, teasing teenaged boy, a boy who helped her to learn to read.

She felt confused, unable to take in all he was telling her, to fit these half-remembered people into her own idea of herself. Mason and Caleb were her brothers, but Dad had never mentioned them before. Dad let Mason stay in prison, when he knew it was wrong. Why? An aunt she had never met would love her and take care of her. . . . She knew Dad wasn't telling her everything, but she couldn't even manage to make sense of this much of it.

"Aunt Elisa will be good to you, I promise," Dad said.

Genie decided she could straighten out the past later. She had bigger worries ahead of her. What was going to happen to her family? The boys . . .

"Will she love Aaron and Troy, too?" she asked.

"Absolutely."

"And Carrie?"

"Yes."

Something about the way he said that single word tipped her off. "You know what happened to her!" she accused.

"Yes." He seemed upset, and she feared the worst, but he said, "Carrie is fine, I think. But Uncle Giles tried to hurt her, because she surprised him when she came to the house with Ms. Kelly." He became even more upset as he talked about it. "There was no excuse for it! None! He should have just let her go." He paused, tried to calm down again. "Cleo rescued them—Ms. Kelly and Carrie. Unfortunately, Uncle Giles fought with her, and she killed him."

"Killed him!" *Cleo is a liar.*

"I'm sorry, I'm sorry, this is too much to be laying on you. I shouldn't have told you—"

"No, I want to know the truth. If he was trying to hurt Carrie . . ."

"He was," he said angrily. "And he wanted to hurt us. That's why Cleo brought us here, to protect us."

"But if he's dead now . . ." she began to ask reasonably.

"It's all confusing, I know. I wish I could explain everything to you. But even though Cleo killed Uncle Giles for a very good reason, she . . . she doesn't want to go to the police. She's afraid of them."

"So she told you she saved Carrie and Ms. Kelly from Uncle Giles?" *And you believed her?*

"Yes."

"Carrie is safe?"

"Yes."

He seemed sure. She wanted to be sure, too. "Carrie will tell other people about us. They'll look for us."

"Yes. But . . . but that might not be good, Genie. Not if Cleo gets upset or worried, and right now she is upset and worried. So please forgive me, but . . ." He tore up the letter. "If Cleo thinks you're trying to contact Ms. Kelly, she might kill us all."

"We have to get out of here!" Genie said.

"Daddy!" Aaron called. "Look at what we made!"

"I like it," Dad said, and he stashed the torn pieces of paper into a crevice between the rocks.

"We'll talk more later," Dad promised.

They had just walked over to the little snow figure the boys had made when Cleo burst out of the cabin.

"Everybody inside! Right now!"

CHAPTER 53

LAS PIERNAS

I SPENT the morning with Ben, Ethan, and Caleb—Caleb asked us to come with him to talk to his mom. I had hesitated to be there during what probably should have been a private re-union, but Caleb persuaded me that she'd want my reassurance about how the children were being treated, based on my en-counter with Carrie. "Besides, you've heard Jenny's voice," he said. "On your voice mail."

Elisa Delacroix Fletcher proved to be as smart and resilient as Caleb, although she was understandably having difficulty coping with Nelson's betrayal of her trust. She'd had less than a day to consider his apparent role in Richard's death, Mason's imprison-ment, and Jenny's disappearance. "You knew him for what he was!" she said to Caleb.

"No, Mom. If I had known, I probably would have killed him."

By the time we had finished talking, I had a clearer picture of Giles, Nelson, Dexter, and her late husband, Richard. Police had told her that Dexter was being sought in France, and that Nelson appeared to have taken their trawler and headed to Mexico or places south.

"He'll be back," she predicted. "He travels, but Las Piernas is his comfort zone."

If he had seen the look in her eye when she said this, I doubt he would have thought of Las Piernas in quite that way.

We left Caleb talking with his mom. I invited Ben back to the house for lunch. We had just started eating when Frank called. Ben's pager went off at about the same moment, and he stepped outside to use his cell phone.

"I probably won't be home for dinner," Frank said. "I'm on my way to the San Bernardino Mountains to help out with the search for the Fletcher kids."

"Where in the San Bernardino Mountains?"

"Half of us are going to Forest Falls—that's where I'll be. The others are going to Cedar Glen. The San Bernardino County Sheriff's Department is going to be supplying most of the personnel—we think we've got a couple of leads on where they might be. The GPS on the vehicle left outside of Graydon Fletcher's place had an address in Cedar Glen entered on it, but there was a map and a set of keys to a place in Forest Falls. They've already checked both places and came up empty, but we're going to be doing some door-to-door work in the neighborhood, and we want to see if the dogs can pick up on a trail. The Las Piernas SAR dogs group is on the way, too."

"Does this mean Anna's going up there?"

"Our department specifically asked that she be excluded from this one, but she's got friends in the San Berdu department, so who knows what will happen. She was pretty hot under the collar about being left out."

He told me that more bits and pieces of information had been coming in as more people became aware of the story of Roy Fletcher and the missing children. One of Roy Fletcher's credit cards had been used to buy gas, and videotape had shown the boys entering the gas station's convenience market with him. Genie did not appear on the videotape, but the camera trained on the gas pumps had shown Roy talking to someone in the SUV before he got back into the driver's seat, and the attendant remembered that Roy had asked the boys to choose a bag of chips for their sister.

"Where was the gas station?"

"In Riverside, near the interchange for the San Bernardino and the Riverside freeways."

I tried to picture it. "Before Waterman Avenue?"

"Yes."

"So from there he could have gone up any of the mountain resort highways?"

"Yes—Highway 18 toward Lake Arrowhead, Highway 330 toward Running Springs, Arrowbear, or Big Bear, or out to Highway 38 and Forest Falls. But he had directions to only two of them. So wish me luck."

"Good luck. Any news about Troy Fletcher?"

"None of this goes to the paper, right?"

"Not my story now. And no, I won't pass it along to anyone else—except—can I talk to Ethan, Caleb, and Ben?"

"Caleb and Ben won't be a problem—they know the rules. Swear Ethan to secrecy. There will probably be a press conference later this afternoon, but I'll be in deep shit if the *Express* gets it first."

"I understand."

"Okay. We believe his first name really is Troy, but his last name is Sherman. He was enrolled in a preschool run by a church. They have a program for children whose families wouldn't be able to afford preschool otherwise. Smart kid, bad family situation."

"How bad?"

"His parents each had more than a dozen arrests—mostly for theft, a few for possession. One day Troy didn't show up for school. The school followed up, turned out nobody was home. The Shermans seem to have taken off—left without paying the rent. No one saw them leave, no one was surprised they were gone. Seems they had a habit of moving around."

"So do you think they moved voluntarily?"

"I have a feeling that's a question I'm going to be working on all next week, if not longer."

"So how did the Fletchers learn about him? Is the minister of the church a Fletcher?"

"No. Catholic preschool, as it happens. Turns out Troy was tested by a woman named Jill Lowry, a school psychologist who volunteered to help assess the kids in the program. Guess who tested all three of the other kids?"

"Has she been questioned?"

"Reed and Vince are with her right now, which is why I'm the errand boy sent off to the mountains."

His cell phone signal was breaking up, and we lost the connection at that point.

Ben was back inside, sitting at the table with Ethan. I noticed Ben's sandwich was untouched. I came back to the table in time to hear Ethan say, "Poison. Pure poison."

"Are you talking Ben out of eating the food I've prepared?" I asked. "Because I noticed yours is gone."

"We weren't talking about you. And yeah, my appetite is coming back—good sign, huh? In fact, if there's any more . . ."

I got up to make him another sandwich.

"Trouble?" I asked Ben.

"That was Anna."

"Oh?" I looked down and realized I had smashed the bread a little as I cut it.

"Wanted to know if I could talk Frank into letting her help with the search. Says she knows the kids and is worried about them."

I'm afraid I took it out on the bread. "Really."

"Told her I was sorry, but she knew as well as I did that I couldn't help her out. Reminded her that I wasn't going up with the local SAR team, since I've left it."

"What did she say to that?"

"We argued. What did Frank have to say?"

I received the required oath of secrecy and quickly filled them in on our conversation, then handed Ethan's second sandwich to him. He looked at its squashed edges and said, "Ten-yard penalty for unnecessary roughness."

I ignored him and said, "Excuse me a minute—I need to get something out of Ethan's room."

As I went down the hall, I heard Ethan sigh and say, "My belongings, probably."

I came back with the *Thomas Brothers Guide for San Bernardino County* and a set of USGS topographical maps. I went to the table that held the information Caleb had given me on Mason's case.

"What are you doing?" Ben asked. "Aren't you going to eat?"

I asked him to pass my plate over to me. "I'm going to see

where a hunch leads me. I keep thinking about what Elisa said about comfort zones." He exchanged a look with Ethan, and they both went to work on their meals. They watched as I checked my notes and opened the *Thomas Guide*.

"The problem, I think, is that we've forgotten Mason. Well, we haven't, but I think the police have."

"What do you mean?"

"First of all, he's alive."

For a second or two, they looked at me as if I'd gone simple-minded. Then Ben said, "And we know that Cleo isn't reluctant to kill."

"Exactly. I think she was supposed to keep him alive, frame him for Richard's murder and for Jenny's supposed murder. If he stood trial and the public believed he did it, then no one was going to expect their neighbor kid to be Jenny."

"So what are you thinking?"

"I'm thinking that the last time anyone saw Mason Fletcher before he was found by Tadeo Garcia was the previous evening. Leaving a party—what a perfect time for a woman to ask for his help, or slip something into a drink."

"He didn't drink, remember?" Ethan said.

"Right—okay, his nonalcoholic drink or his food. Or maybe she gets him to help her out to her car and jabs him with a needle filled with Versed. Or any other drug that makes it impossible for the recipient to remember events."

"I vote for something in his nonalcoholic drink," Ben said. "She can't take a chance that he'll remember her too clearly."

"Okay, she slips him some Rohypnol—no odor, no taste, and we're off to the races. He had to be kept somewhere—and his car had to be kept somewhere—out of sight while the murder of Richard Fletcher was taking place."

"Right, otherwise he might end up with an alibi," Ben said.

"Let's say she's drugged and abducted Mason the night before. Gives him the first round of barbiturates to make sure he's going to be knocked out for the duration. She stashes him and the car in a place where discovery is unlikely."

"Okay," Ethan said. "Then what?"

"Then Nelson Fletcher—or Roy, or Giles, or—who was the other one?"

"Dexter."

"Right. Let's say Nelson, because we know he coveted his brother's wife. Besides, Jenny had spent time around him and would probably be more willing to walk away from the studio with him than with the others."

"Makes sense."

"So Nelson and his deadly cousin Cleo stop by Richard's office. Jenny steps outside with Nelson. Cleo stays behind to kill Richard."

"Then she takes the trophy with her," Ethan said.

"Right. She had to have it to frame Mason. I think that was a mistake, though—if Mason had committed the crime, why on earth would he take the weapon with him? Especially such an awkward one. Why not just drop it on the floor? It's not as if he could expect to defend himself from the police with it."

"But she feels compelled to take it," Ben said, "because if Mason's found without it, there's not much to connect him to Richard's murder."

"Exactly. So she kills Richard, takes the trophy. Also takes the bottle of scotch—because she doesn't know that Mason doesn't drink—and the sample of Jenny's blood that Nelson has left for her, and heads up to the mountains—which is where she's left Mason."

"A lot of driving for her."

"True. Worth it to her, because she feels safe up there. After murdering Richard, she can't be seen driving Mason's car any distance. She can't risk being caught with Mason and the bloody trophy in the car. Way too much explaining to do if that happened. And she has to have a place where she can control him without a lot of neighbors watching her move a man who is knocked out cold."

"Is she strong enough to do that?"

"She looked pretty damned strong to me, but I will admit to being scared shitless at the time."

"Being shot at will do that to you," Ben said.

"Anyway, the mountain resorts have another advantage for her. Many of the places up there are second homes, and intentionally isolated from one another to some degree. Half the population or less may be full-time residents."

"So she could take Mason up there after dark," Ben said, "and come back down to Las Piernas in a different vehicle, and perhaps not risk anyone observing her."

"Some cabins are cheek and jowl with each other, but I suspect Cleo chose one off the beaten path, and with a way to see this spot, and within walking distance of it."

I pointed to a road on one of the Big Bear Valley pages of the *Thomas Guide*.

"That's where Mason was found."

"I understand the walking distance part," Ethan said, "but why would she have to see it?"

"That's a guess. I think she likes to be in control, for one thing. If she had to make sure that he stayed alive, she might want to be able to see him."

Ben nodded. "Even if she wanted him to die, she might have a vantage point. Some killers like to observe the activity that follows a kill."

"Add it all up, I think it's likely that Mason was left not far from her mountain hidey-hole." I started studying the topo map. "There are several places along here that would work."

Ben said, with emphasis on every word, "Call Frank. And call the San Bernardino Sheriff's Department. Tell them."

He was a spoilsport, but I obeyed. I even turned on the speakerphone—"So that you won't think I faked these calls," I said. I got Frank's voice mail. From the sheriff's department, I got a polite kiss-off. Understandable. They wanted people with facts or sightings calling in, not theorists.

I hung up, and we sat in silence. Altair came up to Ben and started staring at him.

"Do you have Caleb's cell phone number?" I asked.

He called it but didn't hand his phone over to me. "Caleb," he said, "does your mom have anything of your sister's that I could use with Bool?"

There was a brief silence. At Ethan's questioning look, I whispered, "His bloodhound tracks from a 'prescented' article. Altair and Bingle work in another way."

"Great," Ben said to Caleb. "Can you get her to take you over to my house? See you there."

I saw the wistful look in Ethan's eyes and braced for an argument. A moment later, he looked at me and smiled, then said, "I guess I'd better keep trying to reach Frank so he can be there in time to strangle you. I hope I can stay awake long enough to make that happen."

"Ethan—"

"*Don't* test my willpower," he said.

"I won't. But—thanks."

"Better get some warmer clothes on."

"Okay," I said meekly, and hurried off to change.

Not much more than fifteen minutes later, Ben, Altair, and I were out the door.

CHAPTER 54

SAN BERNARDINO MOUNTAINS

GENIE was in the kitchen, wiping the counters down with bleach the way Cleo wanted them cleaned, when she heard Aaron begin to cry. She hurriedly took off the too-big rubber gloves she was wearing and made her way to the living room.

"I said stop crying!" Cleo shouted.

Cleo grabbed Aaron by both arms, lifted him off the floor, and threw him hard. She threw him toward the sofa, and he landed against it, but Genie knew that even a landing on a sofa could hurt if you're little enough and someone throws you hard enough.

"Stop it!" Genie shouted, and ran to her brother, who was now crying in earnest. Dad, who had gone upstairs with Troy, came running into the living room. He saw Cleo staring at them with her fists clenched, her face tight with fury.

"I didn't hurt him," Cleo said. "I don't hurt kids!"

He looked helplessly between them, then came over to the sofa and took Aaron into his arms. "It's okay," he said, rubbing Aaron's back as the boy clung to his neck. Troy stood at the foot of the stairs, eyes wide with fear.

"Cleo, maybe you should take another look around outside," Dad said. Genie thought he sounded a little desperate.

"I'll decide when I should do that, Roy, not you. Besides, I checked not twenty minutes ago." She made a sound of exasperation as Aaron continued to cry. "Come upstairs when you've shut that brat's yap. And it had better be soon."

ı ı ı

CLEO had been like this ever since she watched TV. She had taken Dad into the mirrored bedroom and yelled at him about Carrie and Irene Kelly, and Uncle Giles and Uncle Nelson. Dad made her lower her voice, but she stayed mad. Most people cooled off over time, but Genie thought Cleo was getting angrier by the hour.

Even going outside didn't help Cleo to calm down. She made everyone stay inside, and the boys didn't understand why she could go out and they couldn't. There weren't enough toys or games or books here to keep the boys occupied for long.

As soon as Cleo had gone upstairs, Genie said, "She picked him up and threw him!"

Dad looked miserable, but he kept speaking softly to Aaron.

"I want Mommy!" Aaron cried.

Genie felt her own eyes fill with tears. She had cried a lot for Mom last night, but her fear of Cleo and her attempts to keep the boys happy and busy forced her to hide her feelings during the day.

"Mommy can't be here right now," Dad said. "She's on a vacation."

Genie looked sharply at him, but he avoided eye contact with her.

"Why did she take Carrie and not us?" Aaron asked between sobs.

"She didn't take Carrie," Dad said quickly. "You'll see Carrie soon. Carrie's waiting for you at Grandfather's. Won't that be nice? Now, try to calm down, pumpkin. It's going to be okay. Everything is going to be okay."

After a moment, Aaron calmed. Dad said, "Troy, take Aaron into the kitchen and get him a drink of water, please. Go on with Troy, Aaron. I need to talk to Genie. Everything is going to be okay."

Reluctantly, the boys obeyed.

He patted the sofa next to him, and Genie sat down by him, although she was angry.

"You keep telling them it's okay," she said in a fierce whisper, "but it's not! Cleo hates us. She keeps hurting the boys."

Dad pulled her closer and said in a low voice, "I'm so sorry, Genie. I didn't think— I didn't know she'd be like this. She was excited about having the three of you with her at first, I think, but she hasn't ever been around small children."

"We've got to get away from here."

"I've been thinking about that, honey." He paused, then said, "Can you find your way to the road?"

She nodded.

"When I go upstairs, I want you to take the boys outside and go down the driveway and out to the road. Then turn left and follow the road downhill toward the lake. No matter what sounds you hear coming from the cabin, just keep going. Next you'll come to a big road—be very careful. Don't get into a car with anyone—just ask anyone you meet to call the police. Don't even get into the car with Uncle Nelson or Uncle Dexter—especially not with either of them. Promise me that you will stay out of reach and make them call the police."

"I promise. What about you?"

He swallowed hard. "I'll be fine. Just tell the police that I'm here and that Cleo probably has guns, and maybe explosive devices. Okay? You have such a good memory, you can remember that, right?"

"Yes, but—why don't you just come with us?"

"I'll be fine. But you and I need to do this to help the boys get away from her safely. I'm depending on you, Genie. Now, give me a hug, and when I go upstairs, wait about five minutes, then leave."

She hugged him hard, and he hugged back and kissed the top of her head. "You're such a good girl."

He stood up quickly and called to the boys. He hugged and kissed Aaron and Troy, and told them he loved them, and that Genie was the boss while he was upstairs, and they should obey her. "Promise you'll do exactly what she tells you to."

They promised.

She watched him walk up the stairs. He looked back at her and smiled, giving her a thumbs-up sign.

Aaron and Troy looked at her expectantly.

"We're going to play a game," she whispered. "It's a long game, and it's—it's not easy, but I think you can do it."

"Of course we can," said Aaron, confident without even knowing what he was so sure of.

She went to the coat closet and carefully opened the door. She took out their winter wear. She bent to whisper to them again. "The first part of the game is called 'Secret Agents Get Ready to Go on a Mission.'"

"Like Mission San Juan Capistrano?" Aaron asked. Mom and Dad had recently taken them there on a study trip.

"No—keep your voice down. A mission is an assignment that spies and secret agents have. You have to be sneaky. We pretend we are staying inside, talking quietly, but the whole time you have to get dressed to go outside. But no one can know you are getting ready. Understand?"

They nodded.

Above them, they could hear Cleo pacing, speaking angrily, although they couldn't make out what she was saying.

"So no talking about going outside," Genie went on. "No clomping boots. Remember—be sneaky. Troy, you tell Aaron about dinosaurs while you're getting your jackets, hats, boots, and mittens on, okay?"

"Okay."

"Don't shout, just talk in quiet voices. I'm going upstairs, and I'll be right back down."

She quickly made her way to her bedroom, grabbed paper, a pen, and the flashlight.

In the hallway, she paused briefly to listen. Cleo was now talking to Dad in a low voice, so Genie still couldn't hear what was being said. Below, Troy was telling Aaron that pterosaurs were not true dinosaurs. Troy could talk about dinosaurs for hours, with Aaron a rapt audience for every minute of it.

She hurried quickly and quietly downstairs, saw that Aaron was too rapt an audience—Troy was pulling on his boots while Aaron sat staring at him.

She made a little growl of exasperation and helped Aaron dress, then put on her own warm clothing, all except the mittens. Troy nobly kept talking about dinosaurs, even starting to look a little happier as he lectured. Now he was on to one of his favorite arguments, saying that dinosaurs were not extinct because birds were dinosaurs. "Technically," he kept adding.

They followed her into the kitchen, where she gave each of them a small bottle of water to place in their jacket pockets.

She wrote out a note. She couldn't keep her handwriting from being shaky, but it was readable. She asked whoever was reading the note to call the police and to contact Irene Kelly of the *Las Piernas News Express,* who knew where the boys' sister Carrie was. She quickly wrote about who was here, about the booby trap and how to disarm it, about Cleo being dangerous. She carefully checked the part about the booby trap to make sure it was right.

Once in a while as she wrote, she entered the conversation with Troy and Aaron, so that if Cleo was listening, the big bully would hear her voice. Genie wondered how she was going to give the boys instructions, then it occurred to her that she could sign to them. They weren't as quick at reading sign language as Carrie was, so she didn't sign with them as often, but they understood finger spelling and the basics. It was easy to tell them that she was going to open the door and let them outside. Harder to say aloud something other than what she was signing, or to keep herself from signing what she was saying—it took more concentration than she thought it would.

While she signed the instructions, aloud she said, "I could understand it if you said that lizards were dinosaurs. That's what I always think." Then she changed the subject when she saw that Troy was ready to argue with her about dinosaurs rather than paying attention to the signs.

Run as fast as you can up the driveway, to the first set of big rocks.

"I suppose I should figure out what to make for dinner. We could have spaghetti. . . ."

Wait there for me. If I don't come outside in five minutes, keep going down the drive to the road, turn left . . . She gave them the instructions Dad had given her. Troy's face lost the happy look.

She handed the note to Troy. *If I'm not with you, give this piece of paper to the police. Or to—* She pointed to Irene Kelly's name in the note.

Troy started to read it aloud, but she stopped him. So he signed, *Who is Irene Kelly?*

Conscious of the amount of time that was passing, she simply signed, *Friend of Carrie's. Now let's go.*

They looked so scared, she almost changed her mind about her own plans.

She heard water running upstairs. The shower in the master bedroom. Dad or Cleo?

She let them out, hurried into the kitchen, and looked through the knives in the wooden block on the kitchen counter. They were all very sharp. She thought about taking the longest one, but was afraid she wouldn't be able to carry it hidden without cutting herself. She considered a boning knife, but worried it would be too short. She chose a filleting knife instead.

Time was passing. Any minute now Cleo might come downstairs. The boys were scared, and she could not rely on them to follow instructions and set out on their own. She quickly moved over to the desk and took out an entire roll of stamps and a Priority Mail envelope.

One of the green perimeter lights began to flash red. The boys were obeying her after all. But would Cleo notice the light, too? She prayed Cleo was the one in the shower.

She hurriedly left the cabin, saw the boys up just ahead. She didn't miss their look of relief. She ran with them toward the road, carefully holding the knife in her jacket pocket so that it wouldn't stab her if she fell.

When they reached the end of the long drive, she paused to catch her breath, then said, "Now we have to play the next part of the game. This part is called 'Secret Message.'" She quickly took a photo of the mailbox with Carrie's camera, with the boys in front of it. She stuffed the camera into the Priority Mail Flat-Rate envelope, sealed it, and gave the roll of stamps to the boys. "Put about twenty stamps on it while I write the address."

She addressed it to Irene Kelly. This was her Plan B, as Grandfather would call it. The boys watched and asked questions about Ms. Kelly while Genie wrote. "She's our friend. Carrie is with her," she said. "She'll help you. You can give her the note." She put the envelope into the mailbox.

"You need to put up the flag," Troy said.

"How do you know?" she asked.

He frowned. "I think we used to have a mailbox like this, and Dad let me put the flag up when I was little."

She didn't tell him that he was still little. They let Aaron put it up—Genie had to lift him so that he could do it.

Remembering the telescope on the deck, she said, "See that curve? When you get to it, sneak down this road—walk down to the side of it and hide behind trees until the road straightens out again. Then just keep walking toward the lake. If you see a car, you know what to do—but not if it's Uncle Dex or Uncle Nelson. They're friends of Cleo."

"Aren't you coming with us?" Troy asked.

"Are you scared?"

Troy shook his head no, Aaron nodded yes.

"If you get too scared, just hide until I come down the road. But you can help me and Dad the most if you get someone to call the police."

"What are you going to do?"

"I'm going to try to help Dad get away. This is another very important thing: Stay together. Okay?"

They nodded.

"If I can't help Dad, I'll catch up to you." She hugged them and gave them kisses, which they wiped off their cheeks. She felt her resolve waver—the boys needed her. Dad needed her.

"Be brave," she said, as much to them as to herself, and ran back toward the cabin.

CHAPTER 55

Wednesday, May 3
3:10 P.M.
SAN BERNARDINO MOUNTAINS

BETWEEN his forensic anthropology work and the number of searches he had worked on in the mountains, Ben and his dogs were known to most of the deputies at the Big Bear Station. The station's personnel was stretched thin—deputies had their hands full with their usual work and the searches going on in the other areas of the mountains, but they thanked us for stopping by to let them know we were in the area and didn't see any problem in our looking around. They were clearly unconvinced that we'd find anything, but we assured them we'd call if we came across any sign of the Fletchers.

We drove to the place where Mason's car had been found. I soon realized my search for the place where he might have been held—a nearby hideaway—wasn't going to be as easy to carry out as I had hoped. But we used a map and gut feeling and spent the first hour in Big Bear driving up roads, looking for relatively isolated cabins with garages (which eliminated a good number of homes), and windows or decks facing toward the place where Tadeo Garcia had found Mason.

We let the dogs out every so often, just to see if they reacted to anything. Ben had been teaching Caleb to work with Bool, so Ben alternated between Bingle and Altair while Caleb teamed with Bool. Bingle and Altair could work off lead; Bool worked in a harness and on a lead. Each dog had his idiosyncrasies, his way of doing the job, signaling his handler, being rewarded. Not for the first time, I marveled at Ben's ability to keep it all straight.

Caleb had one of his sister's shoes. A tiny girl's shoe—a doll's shoe, it seemed to me. He wore gloves as he handled it and made sure Bool could get the scent of the interior. So far, Bool hadn't hit on anything like it, although Ben was concerned that the scent might have degraded over time, or that it had been contaminated by others who might have handled the shoe less carefully. He groused about this and about the problems of having a family member working the dog, until I asked Caleb if he was okay, given all that he was having to cope with today. Ben can be a prickly son of a bitch, but he's not stupid or uncaring, so he stopped making complaints after that.

We had the windows down as I slowly drove the Jeep up Cold Creek Road, looking for driveways or private roads. Suddenly, Bingle and Altair came to their feet. A moment later they started going nuts.

"Stop the car!" Ben yelled.

I did, and he let them out. They bounded toward a clump of boulders, barked sharply, then came back to Ben. He told them how good they were as they led him toward the boulders, both of the big shepherds doggie-grinning and cavorting as if there could be no happier creatures on earth.

"Jenny!" Caleb called as he got out of the Jeep, then, remembering, said, "Genie? Aaron? Troy?"

Two small heads peered from one side of the boulders.

"Do those dogs bite?"

"No, they don't bite," Ben said. "They barked to tell me how happy they are to have found you." He signaled to the dogs and sent them running after the floppy Frisbees he had brought as their play reward.

Apparently it wasn't the dogs that scared the boys, though. They eyed us warily. Caleb was anxiously looking around for some sign of his sister, but to his credit, did his best to stay calm otherwise.

"You're Troy, aren't you?" I said to the boy who had spoken.

He nodded. "And this is my brother, Aaron. Would you please call the police? We aren't allowed to let you take us with you. We have to tell you we need the police."

Caleb pulled his cell phone out. "That's smart. We don't want to scare you. I'm Caleb, and I'm calling the police right now. That's Ben. And this is Irene."

"Irene?" they said in unison, staring at me.

"What's your last name?" Troy asked.

"Kelly."

"Do you live at the *Las Piernas News Express* at Six Hundred Broadway in Las Piernas, California?"

I couldn't hide my surprise. "Yes, I work there."

"Genie said you're our friend," Aaron said. They came out from behind the rocks. "What are the dogs' names?"

Caleb introduced them, then said, "Ben, is your phone working up here? I'm not getting a signal."

Ben came back with the dogs and took his phone out. "Not much of one, and I don't have much battery left."

I checked mine—like Caleb, I didn't have a signal.

Ben made the call. They answered. He said, "This is Ben Sheridan—," moved slightly, and the phone made a beeping sound as it disconnected.

Troy was studying me. "Genie said you know where our sister Carrie is. Do you?"

"Yes, and after the police know that everyone is okay, I'll make sure she gets a chance to talk to you."

"Our mom is on vacation," Aaron volunteered.

"Really?" I said, a little faintly. "You mentioned Genie. Where is she?"

Troy said, "She went back to save Daddy from Cousin Cleo."

Caleb went pale. "Oh, no . . ."

"Troy," Aaron said, "give her the note, remember?"

Troy fished in his jacket pocket, then handed me a piece of notebook paper. Caleb read over my shoulder.

Ben tried to call the San Bernardino Sheriff's Department again. He connected, but before he could give more than his name, he was transferred.

"What?" Ben shouted into the phone a moment later. "She's not part of any authorized search team. . . . No dogs? Arrest her. . . . I don't know what charges, but she's up to something.

She's connected to the"—he glanced at the boys—"the family. No, we broke up. But I'm not calling about Anna."

I extended the note toward him, and he reached for it, causing him to lose the connection again. He made a hissing sound of exasperation and, as he hit redial, told me, "Anna's up here. One of the guys in the SBSD saw her picking up a map from a real-estate office while he was on patrol."

He got through and gave the SBSD his attention again. "Listen," he said, "forget Anna. This is far more important, and my phone's not going to last. I'm on Cold Creek, and we've found the boys. Yes, Troy and Aaron. They seem to be okay, but their sister and Roy Fletcher—" A series of ominous beeps sounded from the phone. Only the presence of small children kept us from saying what ran through our minds.

Ben took a calming breath. "They heard me say we found the boys, I named this road, and they'll have my number on caller ID. The cell phone company may be able to tell them exactly where."

I asked the boys if anyone else was at the house.

"Just Dad, Genie, and Cleo," Troy said. "Cleo is really mean. And weird."

"You have mail there," Aaron told me. "I raised the flag on the mailbox."

"Mail?"

"A camera with pictures of us in it," Troy said. "And our snowman."

"But not our snowboy," Aaron added.

"I'm going up there," Caleb said.

"I'll go with you. Ben?"

"I'll stay here with Aaron and Troy and the dogs. I suppose it's useless to tell you not to approach until the sheriff's department arrives?"

"Useless," Caleb agreed. "We'll be careful."

"Better be," Troy warned us. "Cleo hurts people."

"Take the dogs to protect you," Aaron advised.

"They don't bite," Troy reminded him. "So they aren't guard dogs."

"The dogs will stay here with us, waiting for the sheriff's department," Ben said. He added sternly, "Irene and Caleb are not going to do anything but make sure that Cleo doesn't take Genie and your dad away from the cabin. Right?"

"Right," I agreed, although Caleb was already back in the Jeep and didn't hear him.

"Oh!" Troy said. "Don't drive up the road, because Cleo can see your car on the curve. You have to hide in the trees or she might catch you."

I tossed my keys to Ben. "We'd better approach on foot."

I motioned to Caleb. A minute later we were running up the road.

CHAPTER 56

GENIE got back to the cabin after seeing the boys on their way and let herself back in as quietly as possible. Upstairs, she could hear Cleo pacing around, yelling at Dad. As usual, Dad was just letting her yell.

Genie took off her gloves and hat. She took the knife out of her jacket pocket.

Now what?

She decided that she would hide in the linen closet near the top of the stairs. When Cleo came by, she would stab her and push her down the stairs so she would die, just like Mom died.

She made it to the closet under the cover of Cleo's shouting. It was dark inside the closet, but she kept the door open the barest crack to watch for Cleo, and after a little while, her eyes adjusted to the low light. Cleo's yelling took more breaks now. Once in a while Genie could hear the creaking of the bed. It wasn't hard to figure out what had made her mad. She was calling Dad a liar, saying he had tricked her. She used a whole lot of bad words. She said that no one had the right to mess with her. She knew the kids were gone. She was saying she was going to be gone, too, and leave him here to explain everything. She laughed at that, but soon she was yelling again. She said she had loved him and saved him and his miserable kids, and this was how he repaid her.

Genie tuned out most of what she was saying, but kept thinking that maybe she wouldn't have to stab Cleo. She was angry with her, but if Cleo left, then maybe they could all be safe. She would just wait for Cleo to go out of the house, then let Dad know she was here.

She heard the bedroom door open, then Cleo slammed it shut. She came marching by the closet, carrying two large duffel bags. She paused, doubled back to stand in front of the closet door. Genie held her breath. Cleo shouldered the door all the way shut with a bang, saying, "Damned kids made a mess of this place."

She went down the stairs.

Genie waited until she heard the front door open, eased the closet door open again, and peered around it, half-expecting Cleo to be waiting for her.

She heard the garage door open, heard the sound the SUV's alarm made when you pressed the remote on the keychain to disarm it and unlock all the doors. She put the knife back in her pocket, then hurried down the hall and opened the bedroom door.

She suddenly understood why Dad hadn't argued back. He was tied to the bed with duct tape, and there were strips of duct tape across his eyes and mouth. There was a sheet on top of his stomach and legs, but he didn't have any clothes on.

She hurried up to him, whispering, "Daddy, it's me, Genie. Don't worry, I'll help you. I'm going to take the tape off your mouth, but please don't say anything, even if it hurts."

Below, she heard the sound of the SUV starting up, backing out of the garage.

Wincing, she reached for the edge of the tape. His skin was cool to her touch. She pulled quickly, saying, "Sorry!" as it came free.

His jaw dropped, but he didn't say anything, just lay there open-mouthed. She bent closer but could feel no warm breath, no sound. In rising panic, she pressed her ear to his bare chest. It was cold and still—no heartbeat.

As she backed away in horror, she saw the swelling at his temple, the Beretta NEO on the floor.

Genie screamed, a sound from somewhere down inside her chest that came out loud and long and terrified.

"He wasn't expecting it, of course," Cleo said from the doorway.

Seeing Genie's shock, she laughed. "Go ahead, scream again."

Genie closed her mouth, her lips trembling, and locked her knees to prevent her legs from giving way beneath her. She looked at the Beretta and kicked it beneath the bed. As she did so, she tucked her hands in the deep pockets of her jacket and found the handle of the knife.

"Oh, that's interesting," Cleo said, leaning against the door frame. "You didn't try to pick it up and shoot me with it. Could it be that you're the one who emptied the gun? See, Roy— I know you call him your dad, but did you know he had your real father killed?"

"Shut up, you liar!" Genie screamed.

"I'm probably the first person to tell you the truth in five years, and you call me a liar?"

She walked into the room. Genie backed away from her.

"But I digress," Cleo said. She smiled at Genie, then reached back and ran a finger along Dad's face. "He looks surprised, doesn't he?"

Genie edged toward the door.

"I wouldn't try it, if I were you," Cleo said. "Even if I gave you a head start, I could outrun you and do just what I did to dear Roy. Your best bet is to keep me happy. I like you better than the boys, you know. I think you have promise. I do think you might have what it takes. Maybe I'll keep you for my own little girl, teach you, the way I was taught."

Genie felt sick to her stomach.

Cleo was watching her now. She reached into her pocket and pulled out tattered pieces of paper and scattered them over Dad's body, like flower petals. "Take, for example, writing this letter. I hate that bitch Irene Kelly, but not every girl would have thought of this."

Genie's eye caught the changing colors of the lights in the panel near the bed. She prayed to God that the boys weren't coming back. She had to distract Cleo.

"How do you know Dad—uh, Roy—killed my father?"

Cleo laughed. "Killed your father? Oh no. *I* killed your father." She stared at the body on the bed. "Both of them. Took them by surprise. Roy wasn't expecting me to hit him with an empty gun. Stunned him. That's what gave me the opportunity to break his neck. So I guess I should thank you for helping me do the unexpected. Now, be good, and tell me where my ammunition is, and after we get away from here, I'll teach you how to shoot better than the boys."

Genie took a chance. "So you know we found the other two guns, too?"

Cleo's smile grew sly. "The one in the desk and the one in the closet, yes. I suppose you found the one in the closet when you put your coats away. The other when you were looking for stamps?"

Genie nodded.

"What else have you found?"

"An envelope," she answered, as if she didn't know about the gun in the kitchen.

Cleo paused, listening. Genie still heard the sound of the engine of the SUV, idling outside.

Cleo looked at the alarm lights. "Goddammit!" she shouted, and rushed toward Genie.

Genie turned and ran for the stairs.

CHAPTER 57

Wednesday, May 3
3:28 P.M.

SAN BERNARDINO MOUNTAINS

W<small>E</small> worked our way down the drive quickly but carefully. We heard the SUV idling in front of the cabin before we caught a glimpse of it. We didn't want to risk getting shot by Cleo, but we also didn't want to helplessly watch as Genie was driven away by Roy and Cleo.

"Maybe she's in there, hurt," Caleb said anxiously.

"The sheriff's will be here in a few minutes."

"That could be a few minutes too long."

"We need to have some strategy," I said.

He looked over at me. "Like what?"

"I've been thinking about that booby trap. Maybe we could somehow get Genie out, keep Cleo and Roy in, and then somehow set the booby trap so that it turns the whole house into a kind of prison cell until the sheriff's department gets here."

"Sounds good," he said, and kept moving forward.

I wasn't so satisfied, because we hadn't worked out the whole "Genie gets out, they stay in" part, but I didn't have any solid suggestions to make.

We were still some distance from the cabin when we heard the scream—a child's high-pitched scream, a sound of utter terror. At that, we stopped being so cautious.

It wasn't until we were at the open door of the cabin that we heard voices—Cleo's and Genie's—and hesitated, just for a moment, aware that neither of us had any kind of weapon.

Then we heard Cleo yell, "Goddammit!" and heard running. We saw Genie reach the top of the stairs, saw Cleo grab her. That decided the matter—we ran for the stairs.

Caleb was ahead of me, charging toward the struggling pair. Genie had pulled a knife out of her jacket and made a stab at Cleo, who blocked with her forearm and got cut into the bargain. Although Cleo screeched, she didn't seem to be hurt much, and took hold of Genie's wrist in a hard grip. Genie dropped the knife, but by that time we had made it up the stairs, and Caleb kicked it out of range—it fell over the edge of the small landing and down into the living room. Caleb kept coming, and Cleo shoved Genie toward his feet. That sent both Genie and Caleb sprawling—and nearly caused me to fall on top of them. Caleb landed awkwardly, trying to avoid hurting Genie, and in the next instant Cleo delivered a vicious kick to Caleb's ribs.

That bit of meanness left her open to my own entry into the fight, and I used that opportunity to launch an unscientific but effective tackle. The three of us made a kind of dog pile, with an ever-changing top dog.

We didn't fall down the stairs so much as slowly and painfully roll and scrabble over one another until we reached the bottom, followed by Genie, who was the only one of us to get back on two feet at the same time. All of us were shouting, scratching, and swearing. Cleo caught hold of the banister, and while I pried her fingers loose, Caleb tried to keep her from kicking me.

She bucked and twisted and we rolled a little farther, changing positions. Now I tried grabbing the banister to keep myself from being squashed—this time Cleo pried my fingers loose, and she tried bending them backward until Caleb got hold of her neck and her attention went to him.

No rules applied—we all pulled on arms, legs, hair, and clothing. A sharp jab to the cut Genie had made on Cleo's right arm could be counted on to cause her to lose her grip and scream at us, but all the blood made her arm slippery. She landed a hard jab of her elbow in my face. I saw stars and felt blood stream over my mouth and chin, briefly went dizzy enough to wonder if I was going to be sick all over her, but I didn't loosen my grip on her.

Genie contributed furious kicking whenever she got a clear

shot at Cleo, which wasn't often, and some biting, but she quit that after she got me by mistake once.

We rolled off the stairs and onto the living-room floor. Nobody had the breath to do more than grunt or moan. We bashed into furniture and walls, backing up, going at it again. Cleo fought halfway free and pulled us toward the kitchen. She fell beneath our combined efforts to tackle her. She kicked and clawed at me, I kicked and clawed back. I could feel her tiring, although she still struggled. Caleb and I managed to get up to her shoulders at the same time, and we flattened her beneath our combined weight.

The place smelled like bleach, and I glanced up and saw an open bottle of it on the counter. The sharp scent cleared my head as effectively as smelling salts.

"Caleb, get your sister and get the hell out of here!" I shouted. "Take the SUV and go, now!"

"I'm not going to leave you here to get killed by this asshole," he said, pressing Cleo's face into the floor as he said it. She tried to kick him, but we had her legs pinned too well.

"Much more of this, and she'll kill both of us. Then who'll make sure your sister gets far enough away from her to be safe?"

He got the message, and I shifted over Cleo, covering her like a rug with my greater height and weight.

He staggered to his feet, grabbed Genie, and stumbled out the door. My last view of Genie was a worried look cast over her shoulder.

Cleo quickly proved that she was only giving herself a little breather. We began to fight again, never getting to our feet, knocking over kitchen chairs. My biggest challenge was keeping her hands out of drawers and cabinets. Kitchens are full of things that grate, stab, and puncture, and pots and pans can be lethal weapons, too. Twice I used a saucepan to smash the hell out of her fingers as she reached for the block of knives on the counter. She took some hits to the injured forearm blocking blows I aimed at her head, and a solid hit to the elbow of the other arm—the elbow she had used on my nose—caused her to howl in pain and rage.

I was almost on my feet, she was on her back, and I was thinking I might have half a chance if I just made a run for it myself, when all the rock and roll came to a halt. She pulled a gun from beneath one of the drawers and aimed it at me.

I tried very hard not to think about Sheila Dolson's hollow left eye as I backed up toward the sink, shielding myself with a nonstick three-quart saucepan.

She frowned at the gun for a brief moment, and I was wondering if by luck I had broken her trigger finger, but then she smiled that cold smile of hers.

I felt behind me, but the only thing that came into my hand was the bleach bottle.

Gunshots can be survivable, I told myself. *Ethan survived. Distract her aim.*

"Looks like you lose," she said. "Now we'll do things my way."

So I threw the pan to one side and tossed bleach into her face. The gun made a dull click, but I was only dimly aware of that, because she quickly dropped it and began screaming in pain, groping blindly toward me.

I ran without any grace or real speed toward the door, shut it behind me, and kept going. I came out of the cabin just as three sheriff's department cruisers came roaring up, screeching to a halt a few feet from me. The Jeep pulled up just behind them.

I live with a cop, so I knew to stand still and hold my hands away from my sides. I didn't match Cleo's description, and most of the deputies ran right past me, weapons ready. Others gently guided me to a seat in a cruiser. I sat there shaking and trying to catch my breath.

"What took you so long?" I asked Ben when he stepped out of the Jeep. Bingle, Bool, and Altair were greeting me with barks of gladness. It cheered me up.

Ben was frowning, though, and came quickly to my side.

"Call an ambulance," he said to the deputy.

"I don't need one, but Cleo might."

"You can't see yourself," he said.

"My luck holds," I muttered. I felt damned tired. "What took you so long?" I asked again.

"Anna told the deputies that she knew where her cousin's cabin was. They believed her. She's still claiming it was an innocent mistake—that, they don't believe."

"Caleb and Genie?"

"On the way to the hospital to get checked out. Which is what should be happening to you. The boys are fine, too—they went with Genie and Caleb. They wanted to wait for you, but I'm glad they aren't seeing you like this. They were worried enough about Caleb and Genie."

I watched the sheriff's deputies taking Cleo away in handcuffs. They had helped her rinse out her eyes and were going to take her to the hospital.

"I hope they know who they've got there," I said. "And that they keep her away from the kids."

"Don't worry," Ben said. "They've been warned about her."

"You told them about the booby trap?"

"Oh yes. Bomb squad is on the way."

"Ms. Kelly?" the deputy nearest to me said. "I've got a call from your husband, Detective Harriman, patched through." He handed me his phone.

"Irene?" Oh, how I love that voice.

"Please come here to me," I said before he could yell at me. "I need you."

He said he was on the way. That was a good way to end the call.

A MINUTE later someone asked me if I could explain about the dead man in the bed upstairs.

CHAPTER 58

HE didn't hang up this time.

The story made CNN, which his satellite dish picked up. The news was rather shocking.

Cleo—who might lose the sight in one eye—was under arrest, as was Anna.

Roy was dead.

Giles was dead.

Dexter was missing, being sought in Europe.

His own photo was displayed. The story, being told in a one-sided, brutal fashion, would probably soon make even this haven unsafe.

And on the screen, two people had made pleas directly to him.

Graydon Fletcher, telling him that he loved him, and hoped he would honor the family name by returning to those who cared for him. He would do all he could to help his son, and knew that Nelson would want to do what was right.

And Elisa. She looked directly into the camera and said, "Nelson, please come home to me. I need you."

She wouldn't answer the questions of the reporter who wanted to ask her how in heaven's name she could want to ever see the man who was responsible for so much evil.

Evil.

Did anyone ask the children if their lives had been miserable?

What would have happened to Troy if his drug-abusing parents had raised him? Would his life have been half as happy as it was in Roy's household? Not a chance. The boy might have been blown up in a meth-lab explosion by now.

And Aaron. A pot-smoking musician for a father and a whining loser for a mother—a woman who handled stress with a booze bottle. That boy had been worse off with Roy? No way.

Carrie, raised by a short-tempered man who hated her mother? That could only cause problems down the road.

Genie. Jenny. Well . . . she wasn't unhappy in her new family. Nelson had made sure of that.

BEING happy in your family was important. He had loved being a Fletcher, and now he couldn't even use the name.

He considered the people he had met here. Men who had bilked their business partners and fled the country. Men avoiding alimony and child support. Retired drug lords. Oh, there were many fine people, too, and the country was beautiful, but . . . he wouldn't be mixing with the fine people. Why complain about the others, and their pasts, though? There was no real crime here.

No real family.

No Elisa. He could hide in Antarctica, and she would still have a hold on him.

He was not meant to live like this.

He hadn't killed anyone. He didn't think anyone could prove he conspired to do so. Cleo might say so, but what was her word against his? He could always say that he didn't see Jenny until she was older, and that he didn't recognize her. And look how hard he had worked to free Mason!

If the worst happened and he went to prison, Elisa might still visit him. Might wait for him!

She needed him. Those words decided it.

He made the call.

CHAPTER 59

Tuesday, May 16
10:00 P.M.
THE SOUTH OF FRANCE

DEXTER FLETCHER got out of the used Renault he had purchased under a phony name and made his way up the stone walkway to the cottage. This would be the perfect place to wait for all the excitement to die down.

A soft breeze brought the fragrance of a nearby meadow to him. No other structures stood within miles of the cottage and its outbuildings. Solitude and quiet. He craved both.

He had come here with Cleo, some years ago, and knew it to be one of her favorite safe houses. The cottage held pleasant memories for him.

Cleo had installed a special doorknob that read fingerprints rather than codes, far more secure than a keypad entry system, and eliminating the need to carry a key. His only fear was that she had deleted him from the user list programmed into it.

He took hold of the doorknob and pressed his right thumb, then his left index finger, onto the reader. He heard a satisfying click and turned the knob.

His last thought, as he smiled and stepped onto the pressure-sensitive plate on the other side of the threshold, was, *Good old Cleo, always looking out for Uncle Dex.*

His DNA was in debris found half a kilometer away.

CHAPTER 60

Friday, June 16
10:00 P.M.
LAS PIERNAS

MASON FLETCHER might have spent another year or so in prison while a notoriously slow system worked on a review of his case, but the Fletcher family clout was still worth something, and the *Express* and other media outlets kept the pressure on, so the district attorney got on the bandwagon and agreed that he should be released, and before the end of May, a judge agreed. The full exoneration process was still in the works, but no one doubted Mason would be completely cleared.

NELSON FLETCHER was in custody. Elisa apologized to me—she told me that Ben had mentioned what I said to Frank on the phone that day in the mountains, and it occurred to her that she could use the same words to lure Nelson back to the U.S. "The difference being," she said, "that when I said them, I was utterly insincere. I owed him a little insincerity."

They were a changed family, she said, but a happy one. "Thank God for that therapist you and Ben recommended." They were in good hands, but I knew from personal experience that therapy isn't a breeze. Mason was still in the throes of readjusting, but helping him do that was Jenny—as she now insisted on being called. The help was mutual. Mason helped her to cope with the aftermath of her experience in the mountains. He was also teaching her to paint.

Caleb had moved back home. The bond between him and his brother was stronger than ever, and he was reestablishing his relationship with both his sister and a new foster brother—Troy had not been parted from his sister. They saw a lot of Carrie and Aaron—now known again as Carla and Luke—whose surviving parents saw the benefit of letting all of the children spend time together and keep connections, and be known by whatever names they chose. Set free from the confines of their previously hidden life, the four children were already showing an eagerness to explore the world around them.

"So," Elisa said to me, "I've gone from walking around by myself in a big empty house to waking up with four—sometimes six—children beneath my roof. Only if Richard were here could I be any happier. He would have loved this family."

It was an easy family to love, full of bright, bold beings. Having heard of his courage, I believed Richard Fletcher would have been proud of it on that count, too.

Caleb and Jenny were over their scrapes and bruises a little sooner than I was, but we all recovered nicely. I was especially glad that the bite mark she had given me healed, not because it hurt, but because the guilt I saw on Jenny's face—whenever she happened to notice that little crescent of bruising—was too hard to take.

ANNA STOVER claimed that she had merely been disoriented up in the mountains, but wasn't believed. It was hard to convince anyone that a woman who worked with Las Piernas's search-and-rescue team and had spent many hours training others in orienteering and searching those same mountains for lost hikers had become disoriented on paved and marked roads, but her lawyer was saying it had been a very stressful situation and could have happened to anyone. She was facing a number of charges, the district attorney arguing that she could have saved lives and prevented injuries if she hadn't impeded their investigation.

Ben said perhaps it was a case of misguided family loyalty, but he said it without conviction. The Las Piernas SAR group, suffering major public-relations problems, asked Ben to come back and take over. He declined. I suspect he's going to start his own team.

CLEO'S lawyers have a difficult client. They did talk her out of trying to claim that Caleb and I were a home-invasion team that killed Roy and tried to beat and blind her. She was able to prove that she was out of the country when Gerald Serre—Aaron/Luke's father—was killed. She claimed that had been Sheila's work. That would explain how Sheila knew where to be the day the remains were recovered, and her interest in the investigation, as well as the presence of her DNA on the cigarette butts at the scene, but no one was calling that case closed just yet.

One reason for that hesitation was that Sheila was being accused by her own killer. Cleo's DNA matched the DNA found in the shoe she left in Sheila's backyard. Striations on the bullet that killed Sheila were matched up to one of Cleo's many weapons. The ATF was interested in the design and material used on the booby trap at the cabin. They said they had a call from Interpol about a similar trap that had killed a man in France, at a place owned by someone matching Cleo's description.

IT took me a while to begin to trust Graydon Fletcher. He weathered a sudden drop-off in attendance at the private school, multiple investigations, arrests of several family members, and plenty of suspicion other than my own. Frank told me that he was fully cooperative with the police, and as more became known, the more I began to doubt that he had been part of Giles Fletcher's conspiracy.

I suppose it was his daughter Edith who paved the way for my ending up liking the old man. She was actively getting the rest of the family to reexamine certain attitudes toward insularity, and Graydon backed her up on all of it.

N O ONE had heard from Dexter. The largest donation toward the reward for his capture came from his wife.

O N E other thing made me decide I liked Graydon. When it was discovered that he was the sole beneficiary of Sheila Dolson's will, he made a gift of Altair to Ethan Shire.

A LTHOUGH he suffered a few permanent effects from his gunshot injuries, Ethan recovered and went back to work. Shortly after that, he moved in with Ben, who was teaching him how to work with Altair.

L ATE one evening, two days after Ethan moved out, Frank and I were sitting up in bed, finishing off bowls of chocolate ice cream in the nude. I got up and put the spoons and dishes in the kitchen sink without bothering to put on a robe. When I came back to bed, Frank had a look on his face that I couldn't quite read.

"What?"

"Awfully quiet around here," he said, reaching for me.

I felt my face break into a grin. "Ain't it great?"

"Damn straight," he said, and proceeded to try—successfully—to make me holler.

ABOUT THE AUTHOR

NATIONALLY BEST-SELLING author Jan Burke is the author of eleven novels and a collection of short stories. Among the awards her work has garnered are Mystery Writers of America's Edgar® for Best Novel, Malice Domestic's Agatha Award, Mystery Readers International's Macavity, and the RT Book Club's Best Contemporary Mystery.

She is the founder of the Crime Lab Project (www.crime labproject.com) and is a member of the board of the California Forensic Science Institute. She lives in Southern California with her husband and two dogs. Learn more about her at www.jan burke.com.